A Rude Awakening

It was a place, no doubt about that. In fact it was a recognizable room with a floor, walls, and a ceiling that shed gentle light. Also, he was not alone.

Someone said, "You were Lodovico Zaras. You were a professor of experimental psychology. You fell victim to a form of cancer which disseminated rapidly. Is this what you recall?"

He replied, not quite understanding how he was able to speak at all. "Yes, but how can I remember anything? I killed myself!"

"You are a ghost."

By John Brunner
Published by Ballantine Books:

Bedlam Planet
The Best of John Brunner
Catch a Falling Star
The Crucible of Time
Double, Double
The Dramaturges of Yan
The Infinitive of Go
The Long Result
Players at the Game of People
The Sheep Look Up
The Shockwave Rider
Stand on Zanzibar
The Tides of Time
Times Without Number
The Webs of Everywhere
The Whole Man

THE BEST OF JOHN BRUNNER

Introduction by
JOE HALDEMAN

A Del Rey Book

BALLANTINE BOOKS ● NEW YORK

Contents

half of the work in this collection comes from the period 1955–65.

In the early sixties, Brunner was ready to start writing something more challenging. As he says in a 1972 interview, "the depressing shallowness of much SF became apparent to me. The time of sheer wonderment at the infinite possibilities of applied technology was, in my view, over; the substantial theme that remained, and was primarily the prerogative of SF although being increasingly used in the so-called 'main stream,' consisted in the examination of the impact of technological change on the human personality."

The first complex, challenging science fiction book Brunner wrote was *The Squares of the City*, a novel whose plot derived from the moves of a famous chess match. But five years passed before an American house picked it up (for a 'derisory' advance payment, according to Brunner), and despite a considerable success in America, the novel went unpublished in Britain until almost a decade after it had been completed.

In reaction to this equivocal situation, Brunner said (again, writing in 1972), "I have found it necessary to regard my writing as being divided into two categories: 'ambitious' and 'fun-type.' There is in fact no discontinuity between the two in my own mind; I can often get as much enjoyment out of something light and amusing . . . as out of something substantial and demanding."

Some readers (if they are like my own) become uneasy or even indignant about this dichotomy. To put it in the present context, they might ask Brunner, "How could you write a serious, moving story like 'The Totally Rich,' and then turn around and knock off a light-hearted bit of fluff like 'What Friends Are For'?" Of course no one, writers included, is unremittingly serious or frivolous all of the time, but that's not the real answer. One part of it is that the satisfactions of your craft, in writing at least, are independent of its subject: a light-hearted story that you think was written well is undoubtedly more satisfying than a Deeply Important one that just won't come together. The other part of the answer is that stories are not always, or only, what they first seem. Are you sure that the bit of fluff doesn't have something quite serious at its core? That the serious one doesn't have an element of deadpan leg-pulling? Especially with Brunner.

So what follows here is a smorgasbord, about equally divided between heavy fare and light. To stretch that metaphor, though, recall that many a dessert would be characterless without a dash of salt, a drop of bitters; a meat course may be prepared with a barely detectable sprinkle of sugar, to bring out its flavor. At least in the hands of a master.

THE BEST OF
JOHN BRUNNER

The Totally Rich

John Cheever capped his writing career with the book The Stories of John Cheever, *which confounded the publishing world by perversely becoming a bestseller. (Story collections "don't sell," except presumably to people like you and me.) I saw an impudent and silly television interviewer ask Cheever just exactly what his new book was about.*

"Love and death," Cheever said, with a sweet smile.

Love and death and work and family are what most fictions are about, the first two being different because they are transcendental. Science fiction should be a wonderful tool for investigating the transcendental, since we have all of time and space at our beck and call; since we can take metaphor and twist it into a kind of temporary literal reality: love is two people made one, death is a waystation. Love is a mirror. Death is a wall, with a door.

But most science-fiction writers seem nervous around love and death; we're more comfortable with their workaday cousins, sex and violence. Brunner does well with quiet things, though, with undercurrents and grace notes, as in this tale of love and death intertwined.

━━ ━━ ━━ ━━ ━━ ━━ ━━ ━━

They are the totally rich. You've never heard of them because they are the only people in the world rich enough to buy what they want: a completely private life. The lightning can strike into your life and mine—you win a big prize or find yourself neighbor to an ax-murderer or buy a parrot suffering from psittacosis —and you are in the searchlight, blinking shyly and wishing to God you were dead.

They won their prizes by being born. They do not have neighbors, and if they require a murder they do not use so clumsy a means as an ax. They do not keep parrots. And if by some other million-to-one chance the searchlight does tend toward them, they buy it and instruct the man behind it to switch it off.

How many of them there are I don't know. I have tried to estimate the total by adding together the gross national product of every country on earth and dividing by the amount necessary to buy a government of a major industrial power. It goes without saying that you cannot maintain privacy unless you can buy any two governments.

I think there may be one hundred of these people. I have met one, and very nearly another.

By and large they are night people. The purchase of light from darkness was the first economic advance. But you will not find them by going and looking at two o'clock in the morning, any more than at two in the afternoon. Not at the approved clubs; not at the Polo Grounds; not in the Royal Enclosure at Ascot nor on the White House lawn.

They are not on maps. Do you understand that? Literally, where they choose to live becomes a blank space in the atlases. They are not in census lists, *Who's Who*, or Burke's *Peerage*. They do not figure in tax collectors' files, and the post office has no record of their addresses. Think of all the places where your name appears—the yellowing school registers, the hospital case records, the duplicate receipt form in the store, the signature on letters. In *no single* such place is there one of their names.

How it is done . . . no, I don't know. I can only hazard a guess that to almost all human beings the promise of having more than everything they have ever conceived as desirable acts like a traumatic shock. It is instantaneous brainwashing; in the moment the promise is believed, the pattern of obedience is imprinted, as the psychologists say. But they take no chances. They are not absolute rulers—indeed, they are not rulers of anything except what directly belongs to them—but they have much in common with that caliph of Baghdad to whom a sculptor came, commissioned to make a fountain. This fountain was the most beautiful in the world, and the caliph approved it. Then he demanded of the sculptor whether anyone else could have made so lovely a fountain, and the sculptor proudly said no one but he in the whole world could have achieved it.

Pay him what was promised, said the caliph. And also—put out his eyes.

I wanted champagne that evening, dancing girls, bright lights, music. All I had was a can of beer, but at least it was cold. I went to fetch it, and when I came back stood in the kitchen doorway looking at my . . . living room, workshop, lab, whatever. It was a bit of all these.

All right, I didn't believe it. It was August 23rd, and I had been here one year and one month, and the job was done. I didn't believe it, and I wouldn't be able to until I'd told people—called in my friends and handed the beer around and made them drink a toast.

I raised the can. I said, "To the end of the job!" I drank. That hadn't turned the trick. I said, "To the Cooper Effect!" That was a little more like it, but it still wasn't quite complete.

So I frowned for a moment, thought I'd got it, and said triumphantly, "To Santadora—the most wonderful place on earth, without which such concentration would never have been possible: may God bless her and all who sail from her."

I was drinking this third toast with a sense of satisfaction when Naomi spoke from the shadows of the open porch.

"Drink to me, Derek," she said. "You're coming closer, but you aren't quite there."

I slammed the beer can down on a handy table, strode across the room, and gave her a hug. She didn't respond; she was like a beautiful doll displaying Paris creations in a store window. I had never seen her wearing anything but black, and tonight it was a black blouse of hand-spun raw silk and tight black pants tapering down to black espadrilles. Her hair, corn-pale, her eyes, sapphire blue, her skin, luminous under a glowing tan, had always been so perfect they seemed unreal. I had never touched her before. Sometimes, lying awake at night, I had wondered why; she had no man. I had rationalized to myself that I prized this haven of peace, and the concentration I found possible here, too much to want to involve myself with a woman who never demanded anything but who—one knew it—would take nothing less than everything.

"It's done," I said, whirling and throwing out my arm. "The millennium has arrived! Success at last!" I ran to the haywire machine which I had never thought to see in real existence. "This calls for a celebration—I'm going out to collect everyone I can find and . . ."

I heard my voice trail away. She had walked a pace forward and lifted a hand that had been hanging by her side, weighed down by something. Now it caught the light. A bottle of champagne.

"How—?" I said. And thought of something else, too. I had never been alone with Naomi before, in the thirteen months since coming to Santadora.

"Sit down, Derek," she said. She put the champagne bottle on the same table as the beer can. "It's no good going out to collect anyone. There isn't anybody here except you and me."

I didn't say anything.

She cocked a quizzical eyebrow. "You don't believe me? You will."

Turning, she went to the kitchen. I waited for her to return with a pair of the glasses I kept for company; I was leaning forward with my hands on the back of a chair, and it suddenly seemed to me that I had subconsciously intended to put the chair between myself and this improbable stranger.

Dexterously she untwisted the wire of the champagne bottle, caught the froth which followed the cork in the first glass, poured the second and held it out to me. I came—moving like a stupid, stolid animal—to take hold of it.

"Sit down," she said again.

"But—where is everybody else? Where's Tim? Where are Conrad and Ella? Where—?"

"They've gone," she said. She came, carrying her glass, to sit facing me in the only other chair not cluttered with broken bits of my equipment. "They went about an hour ago."

"But—Pedro! And—!"

"They put out to sea. They are going somewhere else." She made a casual gesture "I don't know where, but they are provided for."

Raising her champagne, she added, "To you, Derek—and my compliments. I was never sure that you would do it, but it had to be tried."

I ran to the window which overlooked the sea, threw it open, and stared out into the gathering dark. I could see four or five fishing boats, their riding lights like shifting stars, moving out of the harbor. On the quay was a collection of abandoned furniture and some fishermen's gear. It *did* look as though they were making a permanent departure.

"Derek, *sit down*," Naomi said for the third time. "We're wasting time, and besides, your wine is getting flat."

"But how can they bring themselves to—?"

"Abandon their ancestral homes, dig up their roots, leave for fresh woods and pastures new?" Her tone was light and mocking. "They are doing nothing of the kind. They have no special attachment to Santadora. Santadora does not exist. Santadora was built eighteen months ago and will be torn down next month."

I said after an eternal silence, "Naomi, are you—are you feeling quite well?"

"I feel wonderful." She smiled, and the light glistened on her white teeth. "Moreover, the fishermen were not fishermen and Father Francisco is not a priest and Conrad and Ella are not artists except in a very small way of business, as a hobby. Also my name is not Naomi, but since you're used to it—and so am I—it'll serve."

Now, I had to drink the champagne. It was superb. It was the most perfect wine I had ever tasted. I was sorry not to be in the mood to appreciate the fact.

"Are you making out that this entire village is a sham?" I demanded. "A sort of colossal—what—movie set?"

"In a way. A stage setting would be a more accurate term. Go out on the porch and reach up to the fretted decoration overhanging the step. Pull it hard. It will come away. Look at what you find on the exposed surface. Do the same to any other house in the village which has a similar porch—there are five of them. Then come back and we can talk seriously."

She crossed her exquisite legs and sipped her champagne. She knew beyond doubt that I was going to do precisely as she said.

Determinedly, though more to prevent myself feeling foolish than for any better reason, I went on to the porch. I put on the light—a swinging yellow bulb, on a flex tacked amateurishly into place—and looked up at the fretted decoration on the edge of the overhang. The summer insects came buzzing in toward the attractive lamp.

I tugged at the piece of wood, and it came away. Holding it to the light, I read on the exposed surface, stamped in pale blue ink: *"Número 14.006—José Barcos, Barcelona."*

I had no ready-made reaction. Accordingly, holding the piece of wood like a talisman in front of me, I went back indoors and stood over Naomi in her chair. I was preparing to phrase some angry comment, but I never knew what it was to be, for at that moment my eye was caught by the label on the bottle. It was not champagne. The name of the firm was unknown to me.

"It is the best sparkling wine in the world," Naomi said. She had followed my gaze. "There is enough for about—oh—one dozen bottles a year."

My palate told me there was some truth at least in what she said. I made my way dizzily to my chair and sank into it at last. "I don't pretend to understand this. I—I haven't spent the last year in a place that doesn't exist!"

"But you have." Quite cool, she cradled her glass between her beautiful slim hands and set her elbows on the sides of the dirty chair. "By the way, have you noticed that there are never any mosquitoes among the insects that come to your lights? It was barely likely that you would have caught malaria, but the chance had to be guarded against."

I started. More than once I'd jokingly commented to Tim Hannigan that one of Santadora's greatest advantages was its freedom from mosquitoes . . .

"Good. The facts are beginning to make an impression on you. Cast your mind back now to the winter before last. Do you recall making the acquaintance of a man going under the name of Roger Gurney, whom you subsequently met one other time?"

I nodded. Of course I remembered Roger Gurney. Often, since coming to Santadora, I'd thought that that first meeting with him had been one of the two crucial events that changed my life.

"You gave Gurney a lift one rather unpleasant November night—his car had broken down and there was no hope of getting a necessary spare part before the morning, and he had to be in London for an urgent appointment at ten next day. You found him very congenial and charming. You put him up in your flat; you had dinner together and talked until 4 A.M. about what has now taken concrete form here in this room. You talked about the Cooper Effect."

I felt incredibly cold, as though a finger of that bleak November night had reached through the window and traced a cold smear down my spine. I said, "Then, that very night, I mentioned to him that I only saw one way of doing the necessary experiments. I said I'd have to find a village somewhere, without outside distractions, with no telephone or newspapers, without even a radio. A place where living was so cheap that I could devote myself for two or three years to my work and not have to worry about earning my living."

My God! I put my hand to my forehead. It was as if memory was re-emerging like invisible ink exposed to a fire.

"That's right." Naomi nodded with an air of satisfaction. "And the second and only other time you met this delightful Roger Gurney was the weekend you were celebrating your small win on the football pools. Two thousand one hundred and four pounds, seventeen shillings, and a penny. And he told you of a certain small Spanish village, named Santadora, where the conditions for your research were perfectly fulfilled. He said he had visited some friends here, named Conrad and Ella Williams. The possibility of turning your dreams into facts had barely occurred to you, but by the time you'd had a few drinks with Gurney, it seemed strange that you hadn't already laid your plans."

I slammed my glass down so hard it might have broken. I said harshly, "Who are you? What game are you playing with me?"

"No game, Derek." She was leaning forward now, her blue jewel-hard eyes fixed on my face. "A very serious business. And one in which you also have a stake. Can you honestly say that but for meeting Roger Gurney, but for winning this modest sum of money, you would be here—or anywhere—with the Cooper Effect translated into reality?"

I said after a long moment in which I reviewed one whole year of my life, "No. No, I must be honest. I can't."

"Then there's your answer to the question you put a few moments ago." She laid her glass on the table and took out a small cigarette case from the pocket of her tight pants. "I am the only person in the world who wanted to have and *use* the Cooper Effect. Nobody else was eager enough to bring it about—not even Derek Cooper. Take one of these cigarettes."

She held out the case; the mere opening of it had filled the air with a fragrance I found startling. There was no name on the cigarette I took, the only clue to its origin being a faint striping of the paper, but when I drew the first smoke I knew that this, like the wine, was the best in the world.

She watched my reaction with amusement. I relaxed fractionally—smiling made her seem familiar. How many times had I seen her smile like that, here or much more often at Tim's or at Conrad's?

"I wanted the Cooper Effect," she repeated. "And now I've got it."

I said, "Just a moment! I—"

"Then I want to rent it." She shrugged as though the matter was basically a trifling one. "After I've rented it, it is and will be forever yours. You have conceded yourself that but for—certain key interventions, let's call them—but for *me*, it would be a mere theory. An intellectual toy. I will not, even so, ask you to consider that a fair rental for it. For the use of your machine for one very specific purpose, I will pay you so much that for the rest of your life you may have anything *at all* your fancy turns to. Here!"

She tossed something—I didn't know where she had been hiding it—and I caught it reflexively. It was a long narrow wallet of soft, supple leather, zipped round the edge.

"Open it."

I obeyed. Inside I discovered one—two—three credit cards made out in my name, and a check book with my name printed ready on the checks. On each of the cards there was something I had never seen before: a single word overprinted in red. The word was UNLIMITED.

I put them back in the wallet. It had occurred to me to doubt that what she said was true, but the doubt had faded at once. Yes, Santadora had been created in order to permit me to work under ideal conditions. Yes, she had done it. After what she had said about Roger Gurney, I didn't have room to disbelieve.

Consequently I could go to Madrid, walk into a salesroom, and come out driving a Rolls-Royce; in it, I could drive to a bank and write the sum of one million pesetas on the first of those cheques and receive it—if the bank had that much in cash.

Still looking at the wallet, zipping and unzipping it mechanically, I said, "All right. You're the person who wanted the Effect. Who are you?"

"The person who could get it." She gave a little dry laugh and shook her head. Her hair waved around her face like wings.

"Don't trouble me with more inquiries, Derek. I won't answer them because the answers would mean nothing."

I was silent for a little while. Then, finally, because I had no other comment to make, I said, "At least you must say why you wanted what I could give you. After all, I'm still the only person in the world who understands it."

"Yes." She studied me. "Yes, that is true. Pour more wine for us; I think you like it."

While I was doing so, and while I was feeling my body grow calm after the shock and storm of the past ten minutes, she said, looking at the air, "You *are* unique, you know. A genius without equal in your single field. That's why you're here, why I went to a little trouble for you. I can get everything I want, but for certain things I'm inevitably dependent on the *one* person who can provide them."

Her eyes roved to my new, ramshackle—but functioning— machine.

"I wanted that machine to get me back a man," she said. "He has been dead for three years."

The world seemed to stop in its tracks. I had been blind ever since the vision of unlimited money dazzled me. I had accepted that because Naomi could get everything she knew what it was she was getting. And, of course, she didn't.

A little imaginary pageant played itself out in my mind, in which faceless dolls moved in a world of shifting, rosy clouds. A doll clothed in black, with long pale hair, said, "He's dead. I want him back. Don't argue. Find me a way."

The other dolls bowed and went away. Eventually one doll came back and said, "There is a man called Derek Cooper who has some unorthodox ideas. Nobody else in all the world is thinking about this problem."

"See that he gets what he needs," said the doll with pale hair.

I put down the bottle of wine. I hesitated—yes, I still did, I was still dazzled. But then I took up the soft leather wallet and tossed it into Naomi's lap. I said, "You've cheated yourself."

"What?" She didn't believe it. The wallet which had fallen in her lap was an apparition; she did not move to pick it up, as though touching it would turn it from a bad dream to a harsh fact.

I said, very thoughtfully because I was working out in my mind how it must be, "You talked about wanting my machine for a particular job. I was too dazed to wonder what the job might be—there *are* jobs which can be done with it, so I let it slide by. You are very rich, Naomi. You have been so rich all your life that you don't know about the one other thing that stands between the formulation of a problem and its solution. That's *time*, Naomi!"

I tapped the top of the machine. I was still proud of it. I had every right to be.

"You are like—like an empress of ancient China. Maybe she existed, I don't know. Imagine that one day she said, 'It has been revealed to me that my ancestors dwell in the moon. I wish to go there and pay the respects of a dutiful daughter. Find me a way.' So they hunted through the length and breadth of the empire, and one day a courtier came in with a poor and ragged man, and said to the empress, 'This man has invented a rocket.'"

"'Good,' said the empress. 'Perfect it so that I may go to the moon.'"

I had intended to tell the fable in a bantering tone—to laugh at the end of it. But I turned to glance at Naomi, and my laughter died.

Her face was as pale and still as a marble statue's, her lips a little parted, her eyes wide. On one cheek, like a diamond, glittered a tear.

All my levity evaporated. I had the sudden horrible impression that I had kicked at what seemed a stone and shattered a priceless bowl.

"No, Derek," she said after a while. "You don't have to tell me about time." She stirred, half turned in her chair, and looked at the table beside her. "Is this glass mine?" she added in a lighter tone, putting out her slim and beautiful hand to point. She did not wipe the tear; it remained on her cheek for some time, until the hot dry air of the night kissed it away.

Taking the glass at my nod, she stood up and came across to look at my machine. She regarded it without comment, then said,

"I hadn't meant to tell you what I wanted. Time drove me to it."

She drank deeply. "Now," she went on, "I want to know exactly what your pilot model *can* do."

I hesitated. So much of it was not yet in words; I had kept my word-thinking separate from my work-thinking all during the past year, and lately I had talked of nothing except commonplaces when I relaxed in the company of my friends. The closer I came to success, the more superstitious I had grown about mentioning the purpose of this project.

And—height of absurdity—now that I knew what she wanted, I was faintly ashamed that my triumph was reduced on close examination to such a little thing.

Sensing my mood, she glanced at me and gave a faint smile. "'Yes, Mr. Faraday'—or was it Humphry Davy?—'but what is it *good* for?' I'm sorry."

A newborn baby. Well enough. Somehow the phrase hit me—reached me emotionally—and I was suddenly not ashamed at all of anything; I was as proud as any father and much more so.

I pushed aside a stack of rough schematics on the corner of the table nearest the machine and perched where it had been. I held my glass between my palms, and it was so quiet I fancied I could hear the bubbles bursting as they surfaced in the wine.

I said, "It wasn't putting money in my way, or anything like that, which I owe you a debt of gratitude for. It was sending that persuasive and charming Roger Gurney after me. I had never met anyone else who was prepared to take my ideas except as an amusing talking point. I'd kicked the concept around with some of the finest intellects I know—people I knew at university, for instance, who've left me a long way behind since then." I hadn't thought of this before. I hadn't thought of a lot of things, apparently.

"But he could talk them real. What I said to him was much the same as what I'd said to others before then. I'd talked about the—the space a living organism defines around itself, by behaving as it does. A mobile does it. That's why I have one over there." I pointed, raising my arm, and as though by command a breeze came through the open window and stirred hanging metal

panels in the half-shadowed far corner of the room. They
squeaked a little as they turned; I'd been too busy to drop oil on
the bearings lately.

I was frowning, and the frown was knotting my forehead
muscles, and it was going to make my head ache, but I couldn't
prevent myself.

"There must be a total interrelationship between the organism
and its environment, including and especially its fellow organisms. Self-recognition was one of the first things they stumbled
across in building mechanical simulacra of living creatures. They
didn't plan for it—they built mechanical tortoises with little
lights on top and a simple light-seeking urge, and if you showed
this beast to a mirror, it would seem to recognize itself. . . . This
is the path, not the deliberate step-by-step piecing together of a
man, but the attempt to define the same shape as that which man
himself defines in reacting with other people.

"Plain enough, that. But are you to process a trillion bits of
information, store them, label them in time, translate them back
for reproduction as—well, as what? I can't think of anything.
What you want is . . ."

I shrugged, emptied my glass, and stood up. "You want the
Cooper Effect," I finished. "Here—take this."

From the little rack on top of my machine I took a flat translu-
cent disk about the size of a penny but thicker. To handle it I used
a key which plugged into a hole in the center so accurately that it
held the weight by simple friction. I held it out to Naomi.

My voice shook, because this was the first random test I had
ever made.

"Take hold of this. Then handle it—rub your fingers over it,
squeeze it gently on the flat sides, close your hand on it."

She obeyed. While it was in her hand, she looked at me.

"What is it?"

"It's an artificial piezoelectric crystal. All right, that should be
enough. Put it back on the key—I don't want to confuse the
readings by touching it myself."

It wasn't easy to slip the disk back on the key, and she made
two false attempts before catching my hand to steady it. I felt a

vibration coming through her fingers, as though her whole body were singing like a musical instrument.

"There," she said neutrally.

I carried the disk back to the machine. Gingerly I transferred it from the key to the little post on the top of the reader. It slid down like a record dropping to a turntable. A moment or two during which I didn't breathe. Then there was the reaction.

I studied the readings on the dials carefully. Not perfect. I was a little disappointed—I'd hoped for a perfect run this first time. Nonetheless, it was extraordinarily close, considering she had handled the disk for a bare ten seconds.

I said, "The machine tells me that you are female, slim, fair-haired and probably blue-eyed, potentially artistic, unaccustomed to manual labor, IQ in the range 120–140, under intense emotional stress—"

Her voice cut across mine like the slash of a whip. "How? How do I know the machine tells you this, not your own eyes?"

I didn't look up. I said, "The machine is telling me what changes were brought about in that little crystal disk when you touched it. I'm reading it as a kind of graph, if you like—looking across the pattern of the dials and interpreting them into words."

"Does it tell you anything else?"

"Yes—but it must be in error somewhere, I'm afraid. The calibration has been rather makeshift, and would have to be completed with a proper statistical sample of say a thousand people from all walks of life." I forced a laugh as I turned away from the machine. "You see, it says that you're forty-eight to fifty years old, and this is ridiculous on the face of it."

She sat very still. I had moved all the way to the table beside her, intending to refill my glass, before I realized how still. My hand on the bottle's neck, I stared at her.

"Is something wrong?"

She shook herself and came back to life instantly. She said lightly, "No. No, nothing at all. Derek, you are the most amazing man in the world. I shall be fifty years old next week."

"You're joking." I licked my lips. I'd have said . . . oh, thirty-five and childless and extremely careful of her looks. But not more. Not a day more."

A trace of bitterness crossed her face as she nodded.

"It's true. I wanted to be beautiful—I don't think I have to explain why. I wanted to go on being beautiful because it was the only gift I could give to someone who had, as I have, everything he could conceivably want. So I—I saw to it."

"What happened to him?"

"I would prefer you not to know." The answer was cool and final. She relaxed deliberately, stretching her legs out before her, and gave a lazy smile. Her foot touched something on the floor as she moved, and she glanced down.

"What—? Oh, that!" She reached for the soft leather wallet, which had fallen from her lap when she stood up after I had tossed it back at her. Holding it out, she said, "Take it, Derek. I know you've already earned it. By accident—by mistake—whatever you call it, you've proved that you can do what I was hoping for."

I did take it. But I didn't pocket it at first; I kept it in my hands, absently turning it over.

I said, "I'm not so sure, Naomi. Listen." I picked up my newly filled glass and returned to the chair facing her. "What I ultimately envisage is being able to deduce the individual from the traces he makes. You know that; that was the dream I told to Roger Gurney. But between now and then, between the simple superficial analysis of a specially prepared material and going over piece by piece, ten thousand objects affected not merely by the individual in question but by many others, some of whom probably cannot be found in order to identify and rule out their extraneous influence—and *then* processing the results to make a coherent whole—there may be years, decades, of work and study, a thousand false trails, a thousand preliminary experiments with animals. . . . Whole new techniques will have to be invented in order to employ the data produced! Assuming you have your —your analogue of a man: what are you going to do with it? Are you going to try and *make* a man, artificially, that fits the specifications?"

"Yes."

The simple word left me literally gasping; it was like a blow to the stomach, driving my breath away. She bent her brilliant gaze on me and once more smiled faintly.

"Don't worry, Derek. That's not your job. Work has been going on in many places for a long time—they tell me—on that problem. What nobody except yourself was doing was struggling with the problem of the total person."

I couldn't reply. She filled her own glass again before continuing, in a tenser voice.

"There's a question I've got to put to you, Derek. It's so crucial I'm afraid to hear the answer. But I can't endure to wait any longer, either. I want to know how long you think it will be before I can have what I want. Assume—remember that you've *got* to assume—the best men in the world can be set to work on the subsidiary problems; they'll probably make their reputations, they'll certainly make their fortunes. I want to hear what you think."

I said thickly, "Well, I find that pretty difficult! I've already mentioned the problem of isolating the traces from—"

"This man lived a different kind of existence from you, Derek. If you'd stop and think for a second, you'd guess that. I can take you to a place that was uniquely *his,* where his personality formed and molded and affected every grain of dust. Not a city where a million people have walked, not a house where a dozen families have lived."

It had to be true, incredible though I would have thought it a scant hour ago. I nodded.

"That's good. Well, I shall also have to work out ways of handling unprepared materials—calibrate the properties of every single substance. And there's the risk that the passage of time will have overlaid the traces with molecular noise and random movement. Moreover, the testing itself, before the actual readings, might disturb the traces."

"You are to assume"—she forced patience on the repetition— "that the best men in the world are going to tackle the side issues."

"It isn't a side issue, Naomi." I wished I didn't have to be honest. She was hurt by my insistence, and I was beginning to think that, for all the things one might envy her, she had been hurt very badly already. "It's simply a fact one has to face."

She drank down her wine and replaced the glass on the table. Musingly she said, "I guess it would be true to say that the—the object which a person affects most, and most directly, is his or her own body. If just handling your little disk reveals so much, how much more must be revealed by the hands themselves, the lips, the eyes!"

I said uncomfortably, "Yes, of course. But it's hardly practicable to process a human body."

She said, "I have his body."

This silence was a dreadful one. A stupid beetle, fat as a bullet, was battering its head on the shade of the lamp in the porch, and other insects were droning, too, and there was the sea distantly heard. The silence, nonetheless, was graveyard-deep.

But she went on at last. "Everything that could possibly be preserved is preserved, by every means that could be found. I had—" Her voice broke for a second. "I had it prepared. Only the thing which is *he*, the web in the brain, the little currents died. Curious, that a person is so fragile." Briskening, she launched her question anew.

"Derek, how long?"

I bit my lip and stared down at the floor by my feet. My mind churned as it considered, discarded relevant factors, envisaged problems, assumed them to be soluble, fined down everything to the simple irreducible of *time*. I might have said ten years and felt that I was being stupidly optimistic.

But in the end, I said nothing at all.

She waited. Then, quite unexpectedly, she gave a bright laugh and jumped to her feet. "Derek, it isn't fair!" she said. "You've achieved something fantastic, you want and deserve to relax and celebrate, and here I am plaguing you with questions and wanting answers out of the air. I know perfectly well that you're too honest to give me an estimate without time to think, maybe do a few calculations. And I'm keeping you shut up in your crowded room when probably what you most want is to get out of it for a while. Am I right?"

She put her hand out, her arm quite straight, as if to pull me from my chair. Her face was alight with what seemed pure pleasure, and to see it was to experience again the shock of hearing her say she was fifty years old. She looked—I can only say transformed. She looked like a girl at her first party.

But it lasted only a moment, this transformation. Her expression became grave and calm. She said, "I am sorry, Derek. I—I hate one thing about love. Have you ever thought how selfish it can make you?"

We wandered out of the house hand in hand, into the summer dark. There was a narrow slice of moon and the stars were like fierce hard lanterns. For the more than hundredth time I walked down the narrow ill-paved street leading from my temporary home toward the harbor; there was Conrad's house, and there was the grocery and wine shop; there was the church, its roof silvered by the moon; there were the little cottages all in a row facing the sea, where the families of fisherfolk lived. And here, abandoned, was the detritus of two hundred and seventy lives which had never actually existed—conjured up to order.

I said, when we had walked all the way to the quay, "Naomi, it's beyond belief, even though I know it's true. This village wasn't a sham, a showplace. It was real. I *know* it."

She looked around her. "Yes. It was intended to be real. But all it takes is thought and patience."

"What did you say? Did you tell—whoever it was—'Go and build a real village'?"

"I didn't have to. They knew. Does it interest you, how it was done?" She turned a curious face to me, which I could barely see in the thin light.

"Of course," I said. "My God! To create real people and a real place—when I'm ordered to re-create a real person—should I not be interested?"

"If it were as easy to re-create as it is to create," she said emptily, "I would not be . . . lonely."

We stopped, close by the low stone wall which ran from the quay to the sharp rocks of the little headland sheltering the beach, and leaned on it. At our backs, the row of little houses; before us, nothing but the sea. She was resting on both her elbows, staring over the water. At less than arm's reach, I leaned on one elbow, my hands clasped before me, studying her as though I had never seen her before tonight. Of course, I hadn't.

I said, "Are you afraid of not being beautiful? Something is troubling you."

She shrugged. "There is no such word as 'forever'—is there?"

"You make it seem as though there were."

"No, no." She chuckled. "Thank you for saying it, Derek. Even if I know—even if I can see in the mirror—that I am still so, it's delightful to be reassured."

How had she achieved it, anyway? I wanted, and yet didn't want, to ask. Perhaps she didn't know; she had just said she wanted it so, and it was. So I asked a different question.

"Because it's—the thing that is most *yours*?"

Her eyes came back from the sea, rested on me, returned. "Yes. The *only* thing that is mine. You're a rare person; you have compassion. Thank you."

"How do you live?" I said. I fumbled out cigarettes from my pocket, rather crumpled; she refused with a headshake, but I lit one for myself.

"How do I live?" she echoed. "Oh—many ways. As various people, of course, with various names. You see, I haven't even a name to call my own. Two women who look exactly like me exist for me, so that when I wish I can take their places in Switzerland or in Sweden or in South America. I borrow their lives, use them a while, give them back. I have seen them grow old, changed them for replacements—made into duplicates of me. But those are not persons; they are masks. I live behind masks. I suppose that's what you'd say."

"You can't do anything else," I said.

"No. No, of course I can't. And until this overtook me, I'd never conceived that I might want to."

I felt that I understood that. I tapped the first ash off my cigarette down toward the sea. Glancing around, I said irrelevantly, "You know, it seems like a shame to dismantle Santadora. It could be a charming little village. A real one, not a stage set."

"No," she said. And then, as she straightened and whirled around: "No! Look!" She ran wildly into the middle of the narrow street and pointed at the cobbles. "Don't you see? Already stones which weren't cracked are cracked! And the houses!" She flung up her arm and ran forward to the door of the nearest house. "The wood is warping! And that shutter—hanging loose on the hinges! And the step!" She dropped to her knees, felt along the low stone step giving directly on the street.

I was coming after her now, startled by her passion.

"Feel!" she commanded. "Feel it! It's been worn by people walking on it. And even the wall—don't you see the crack from the corner of the window is getting wider?" Again she was on her feet, running her hand over the rough wall. "Time is gnawing at it, like a dog at a bone. God, no, Derek! Am I to leave it and know that time is breaking it, breaking it, *breaking* it?"

I couldn't find words.

"Listen!" she said. "Oh God! Listen!" She had tensed like a frightened deer, head cocked.

"I don't hear anything," I said. I had to swallow hard.

"Like nails being driven into a coffin," she said. She was at the house door, battering on it, pushing at it. "You *must* hear it!"

Now, I did. From within the house there was a ticking noise —a huge, majestic, slow rhythm, so faint I had not noticed it until she commanded me to strain my ears. A clock. Just a clock.

Alarmed at her frenzy, I caught her by the shoulder. She turned and clung to me like a tearful child, burying her head against my chest. "I can't stand it," she said, her teeth set. I could feel her trembling.

"Come away," I murmured. "If it hurts you so much, come away."

"No, that isn't what I want. I'd go on hearing it—don't you

understand?" She drew back a little and looked up at me. "I'd go on hearing it!" Her eyes grew veiled, her whole attention focusing toward the clock inside the house. "Tick-tick-tick—God, it's like being buried alive!"

I hesitated a moment. Then I said, "All right, I'll fix it. Stand back."

She obeyed. I raised my foot and stamped it, sole and heel together, on the door. Something cracked; my leg stung all the way to the thigh with the impact. I did it again, and the jamb split. The door flew open. At once the ticking was loud and clear.

And visible in a shaft of moonlight opposite the door was the clock itself: a tall old grandfather, bigger than me, its pendulum glinting on every ponderous swing.

A snatch of an ancient and macabre Negro spiritual came to my mind:

The hammer keeps ringing on somebody's coffin . . .

Abruptly it was as doom-laden for me as Naomi. I strode across the room, tugged open the glass door of the clock, and stopped the pendulum with a quick finger. The silence was a relief like cold water after long thirst.

She came warily into the room after me, staring at the face of the clock as though hypnotized. It struck me that she was not wearing a watch, and I had never seen her wear one.

"Get rid of it," she said. She was still trembling. "Please, Derek—get rid of it."

I whistled, taking another look at the old monster. I said, "That's not going to be so easy! These clocks are heavy!"

"Please, Derek!" The urgency in her voice was frightening. She turned her back, staring into a corner of the room. Like all these cramped, imitation-antique houses, this one had a mere three rooms, and the room we were in was crowded with furniture—a big bed, a table, chairs, a chest. But for that, I felt she would have run to the corner to hide.

Well, I could try.

I studied the problem and came to the conclusion that it would be best to take it in parts.

"Is there a lamp?" I said. "I'd work better if I could see."

She murmured something inaudible; then there was the sound of a lighter, and a yellow flicker grew to a steady glow which illumined the room. The smell of kerosene reached my nostrils. She put the lamp on a table where its light fell past me on to the clock.

I unhitched the weights and pocketed them; then I unclipped a screwdriver from my breast pocket and attacked the screws at the corners of the face. As I had hoped, with those gone, it was possible to lift out the whole works, the chains following like umbilical cords, making little scraping sounds as they were dragged over the wooden ledge the movement had rested on.

"Here!" Naomi whispered, and snatched it from me. It was a surprisingly small proportion of the weight of the whole clock. She dashed out of the house and across the street. A moment, and there was a splash.

I felt a spasm of regret. And then was angry with myself. Quite likely this was no rare specimen of antique craftsmanship, but a fake. Like the whole village. I hugged the case to me and began to walk it on its front corners toward the door. I had been working with my cigarette in my mouth; now the smoke began to tease my eyes, and I spat it to the floor and ground it out.

Somehow I got the case out of the house, across the road, up on the seawall. I rested there for a second, wiping the sweat from my face, then got behind the thing and gave it the most violent push I could manage. It went over the wall, twisting once in the air, and splashed.

I looked down, and instantly wished that I hadn't. It looked exactly like a dark coffin floating off on the sea.

But I stayed there for a minute or so, unable to withdraw my gaze, because of an overwhelming impression that I had done some symbolic act, possessed of a meaning which could not be defined in logical terms, yet heavy, solid—real as that mass of wood drifting away.

I came back slowly, shaking my head, and found myself in the door of the house before I paid attention again to what was before my eyes. Then I stopped dead, one foot on the step which Naomi had cursed for being worn by passing feet. The flame of the yellow lamp was wavering a little in the wind, and it was too high—the smell of its smoke was strong, and the chimney was darkening.

Slowly, as though relishing each single movement, Naomi was unbuttoning the black shirt she wore, looking toward the lamp. She tugged it out of the waist of her pants and slipped it off. The brassiere she wore under it was black, too. I saw she had kicked away her espadrilles.

"Call it an act of defiance," she said in a musing tone— speaking more to herself, I thought, than to me. "I shall put off my mourning clothes." She unzipped her pants and let them fall. Her briefs were also black.

"Now I'm through with mourning. I believe it will be done. It will be done soon enough. Oh yes! Soon enough." Her slim golden arms reached up behind her back. She dropped the brassiere to the floor, but the last garment she caught up in her hand and hurled at the wall. For a moment she stood still; then seemed to become aware of my presence for the first time and turned slowly toward me.

"Am I beautiful?" she said.

My throat was very dry. I said, "God, yes. You're one of the most beautiful women I've ever seen."

She leaned over the lamp and blew it out. In the instant of falling darkness she said, "Show me."

And, a little later on the rough blanket of the bed, when I had said twice or three times, "Naomi—Naomi!" she spoke again. Her voice was cold and far away.

"I didn't mean to call myself Naomi. What I had in mind was Niobe, but I couldn't remember it."

And very much later, when she had drawn herself so close to me that it seemed she was clinging to comfort, to existence itself, with her arms around me and her legs locked with mine, under the blanket now because the night was chill, I felt her lips move against my ear.

"How long, Derek?"

I was almost lost; I had never before been so drained of myself, as though I had been cork-tossed on a stormy ocean and battered limp by rocks, I could barely open my eyes. I said in a blurred voice, "What?"

"How long?"

I fought a last statement from my weary mind, neither knowing nor caring what it was. "With luck," I muttered, "it might not take ten years. Naomi, I don't know—" And in a burst of absolute effort, finished, "My God, you do this to me and expect me to be able to think afterward?"

But that was the extraordinary thing. I had imagined myself about to go down into blackness, into coma, to sleep like a corpse. Instead, while my body rested, my mind rose to the pitch beyond consciousness—to a vantage point where it could survey the future. I was aware of the thing I had done. From my crude experimental machine, I knew, would come a second and a third, and the third would be sufficient for the task. I saw and recognized the associated problems, and knew them to be soluble. I conceived names of men I wanted to work on those problems— some who were known to me and who, given the chance I had been given, could create, in their various fields, such new techniques as I had created. Meshing like hand-matched cogs, the parts blended into the whole.

A calendar and a clock were in my mind all this while.

Not all of this was a dream; much of it was of the nature of inspiration, with the sole difference that I could feel it happening and that it was right. But toward the very end, I did have a dream—not in visual images but in a kind of emotional aura. I had a completely satisfying sensation, which derived from the fact that I was about to meet for the first time a man who was already my closest friend, whom I knew as minutely as any human being had ever known another.

I was waking. For a little while longer I wanted to bask in that fantastic warmth of emotion; I struggled not to wake while feeling that I was smiling and had been smiling for so long that my cheek muscles were cramped.

Also I had been crying, so that the pillow was damp.

I turned on my side and reached out gently for Naomi, already phrasing the wonderful gift-words I had for her. "Naomi! I know how long it will take now. It needn't take more than three years, perhaps as little as two and a half."

My hand, meeting nothing but the rough cloth, sought further. Then I opened my eyes and sat up with a start.

I was alone. Full daylight was pouring into the room: it was bright and sunny and very warm. Where was she? I must go in search of her and tell her the wonderful news.

My clothes were on the floor by the bed; I pulled them on, thrust my feet in my sandals, and padded to the door, pausing with one hand on the split jamb to accustom my eyes to the glare.

Just across the narrow street, leaning his elbows on the stone wall, was a man with his back to me. He gave not the slightest hint that he was aware of being watched. It was a man I knew at once, even though I'd met him no more than twice in my life. He called himself Roger Gurney.

I spoke his name, and he didn't turn around. He lifted one arm and made a kind of beckoning motion. I was sure then what had happened, but I walked forward to stand beside him, waiting for him to tell me.

Still he didn't look at me. He merely gestured toward the sharp rocks with which the end of the wall united. He said, "She came out at dawn and went up there. To the top. She was carrying her clothes in her hand. She threw them one by one into the sea. And then—" He turned his hand over, palm down, as though pouring away a little pile of sand.

I tried to say something, but my throat was choked.

"She couldn't swim," Gurney added after a moment. "Of course."

Now I could speak. I said, "But my God! Did you see it happen?"

He nodded.

"Didn't you go after her? Didn't you rescue her?"

"We recovered her body."

"Then—artificial respiration! You must have been able to do something!"

"She lost her race against time," Gurney said after a pause. "She had admitted it."

"I—" I checked myself. It was becoming so clear that I cursed myself for a fool. Slowly I went on, "How much longer would she have been beautiful?"

"Yes." He expressed the word with form. "That was the thing she was running from. She wanted *him* to return and find her still lovely, and no one in the world would promise her more than another three years. After that, the doctors say she would have" —he made an empty gesture—"crumbled."

"She would always have been beautiful," I said. "My God! Even looking her real age, she'd have been beautiful!"

"We think so," Gurney said.

"And so stupid, so futile!" I slammed my fist into my palm. "You too, Gurney—do you realize what you've *done*, you fool?" My voice shook with anger, and for the first time he faced me.

"Why in hell didn't you revive her and send for me? It needn't have taken more than three years! Last night she demanded an answer and I told her ten, but it came clear to me during the night how it could be done in less than three!"

"I thought that was how it must have been." His face was white, but the tips of his ears were—absurdly—brilliant pink. "If you hadn't said that, Cooper; if you hadn't said that."

And then (I was still that wave-tossed cork, up one moment, down the next, up again the next) it came to me what my inspiration of the night really implied. I clapped my hand to my forehead.

"Idiot!" I said. "I don't know what I'm doing yet! Look, you have her body! Get it to—to wherever it is, with the other one, *quick*. What the hell else have I been doing but working to re-create a human being? And now I've seen how it can be done, I can do it—I can re-create her as well as him!" I was in a fever of excitement, having darted forward in my mind to that strange future I had visited in my sleep, and my barely visualized theories were solid fact.

He was regarding me strangely. I thought he hadn't understood, and went on, "What are you standing there for? I can do it, I tell you—I've seen how it can be done. It's going to take men and money, but those can be got."

"No," Gurney said.

"What?" I let my arms fall to my sides, blinking in the sunlight.

"No," he repeated. He stood up, stretching arms cramped by long resting on the rough top of the wall. "You see, it isn't hers any longer. Now she's dead, it belongs to somebody else."

Dazed, I drew back a pace. I said, "Who?"

"How can I tell you? And what would it mean to you if I did? You ought to know by now what kind of people you're dealing with."

I put my hand in my pocket, feeling for my cigarettes. I was trying to make it come clear to myself: now Naomi was dead she no longer controlled the resources which could bring her back. So my dream was—a dream. Oh, God!

I was staring stupidly at the thing which had met my hand; it wasn't my pack of cigarettes, but the leather wallet she had given me.

"You can keep that," Gurney said. "I was told you could keep it."

I looked at him. And I *knew*.

Very slowly, I unzipped the wallet. I took out the three cards. They were sealed in plastic. I folded them in half, and the plastic cracked. I tore them across and let them fall to the ground. Then, one by one, I ripped the checks out of the book and let them drift confetti-wise over the wall, down to the sea.

He watched me, the color coming to his face until at last he was flushing red—with guilt, shame, I don't know. When I had finished, he said in a voice that was still level, "You're a fool, Cooper. You could still have bought your dreams with those."

I threw the wallet in his face and turned away. I had gone ten steps, blind with anger and sorrow, when I heard him speak my name and looked back. He was holding the wallet in both hands, and his mouth was working.

He said, "Damn you, Cooper. Oh, damn you to hell! I—I told myself I loved her, and I couldn't have done that. Why do you want to make me feel so *dirty*?"

"Because you are," I said. "And now you know it."

Three men I hadn't seen before came into my house as I was crating the machine. Silent as ghosts, impersonal as robots, they helped me to put my belongings in my car. I welcomed their aid simply because I wanted to get to hell out of this mock village as fast as possible. I told them to throw the things I wanted to take with me in the passenger seats and the luggage compartment, without bothering to pack cases. While I was at it, I saw Gurney come to the side of the house and stand by the car as though trying to pluck up courage to speak to me again, but I ignored him, and when I went out he had gone. I didn't find the wallet until I was in Barcelona sorting through the jumbled belongings. It held, this time, thirty-five thousand pesetas in new notes. He had just thrown it on the back seat under a pile of clothes.

Listen. It wasn't a *long* span of time which defeated Naomi. It wasn't three years, or ten years or any number of years. I worked it out later—too late. (So time defeated me, too, as it always defeats us.)

I don't know how her man died. But I'm sure I know why she wanted him back. Not because she loved him, as she herself believed. But because he loved her. And without him, she was afraid. It didn't need three years to re-create her. It didn't even need three hours. It needed *three words*.

And Gurney, the bastard, could have spoken them, long before I could—so long before that there was still time. He could have said, "I love you."

These are the totally rich. They inhabit the same planet, breathe the same air. But they are becoming, little by little, a different species, because what was most human in them is— well, this is my opinion—dead.

They keep apart, as I mentioned. And God! God! Aren't you grateful?

The Last Lonely Man

Immortality comes in a myriad of flavors in science fiction, from childish wishful thinking to positive high-tech speculation to its service as extended metaphor for maturity, or middle age, or existential cafard. It's a handy device for stories that are about conventional religious notions; about human limits or the possibility of limitlessness—but it's not often used for humor.

One of Brunner's particular strengths is the characterization of thoroughly unpleasant people. He outdoes himself here.

━━━ ━━━ ━━━ ━━━ ━━━ ━━━

"Don't see you in here much any more, Mr. Hale," Geraghty said as he set my glass in front of me.

"Must be eighteen months," I said. "But my wife's out of town and I thought I'd drop by for old times' sake." I looked down the long bar and round at the booths against the opposite wall, and added, "It looks as though you don't see anybody much any more. I never saw the place so empty at this time of evening. Will you have one?"

"Sparkling soda, if you please, Mr. Hale, and thank you very much." Geraghty got down a bottle and poured for himself. I never knew him to drink anything stronger than a beer, and that rarely.

"Things have changed," he went on after a pause. "You know what caused it, of course."

I shook my head.

"Contact, naturally. Like it's changed everything else."

I stared at him for a moment, and then I had to chuckle. I said, "Well, I knew it had hit a lot of things—like the churches in particular. But I wouldn't have thought it would affect you."

"Oh, yes." He hoisted himself on a stool behind the bar; that was new since I used to come here regularly. Eighteen months ago he wouldn't have the chance to sit down all evening long; he'd be dead on his feet when the bar closed. "I figure it this way. Contact has made people more careful in some ways, and less in others. But it's cut out a lot of reasons for going to bars and for drinking. You know how it used to be. A bartender was a sort of professional open ear, the guy to spill your troubles to. That didn't last long after Contact came in. I knew a tenderhearted bartender who went on being like that for a while after Contact. He got himself loaded to *here* with lonely guys—and gals too." Geraghty laid his palm on the top of his head.

"Occupational risk!" I said.

"Not for long, though. It hit him one day what it would be like if they all came home to roost, so he went and had them all expunged and started over with people he chose himself, the way anyone else does. And round about then it all dried up. People don't come and spill their troubles any /more. The need has mostly gone. And the other big reason for going to bars—chance company—that's faded out too. Now that people know they don't have to be scared of the biggest loneliness of all, it makes them calm and mainly self-reliant. Me, I'm looking round for another trade. Bars are closing down all over."

"You'd make a good Contact consultant," I suggested, not more than half-joking. He didn't take it as a joke, either.

"I've considered it," he said seriously. "I might just do that. I might just."

I looked around again. Now Geraghty had spelled it out for me, I could see how it must have happened. My own case, even if I hadn't realized it till now, was an illustration. I'd spilled troubles to bartenders in my time, gone to bars to escape loneliness. Contact had come in about three years ago, about two years ago it took fire and everyone but everyone lined up for the treatment, and a few months after that I quit coming here, where I'd formerly been as much of a fixture as the furniture. I'd thought nothing of it—put it down to being married and planning a family and spending money other ways.

But it wasn't for that. It was that the need had gone.

In the old style, there was a mirror mounted on the wall behind the bar, and in that mirror I could see some of the booths reflected. All were empty except one, and in that one was a couple. The man was nothing out of the ordinary, but the girl—no, woman—took my eye. She wasn't so young; she could be forty or so, but she had a certain something. A good figure helped, but most of it was in the face. She was thin, with a lively mouth and laughter wrinkles round the eyes, and she was clearly enjoying whatever she was talking about. It was pleasant to watch her enjoying it. I kept my eyes on her while Geraghty held forth.

"Like I say, it makes people more careful, and less careful. More careful about the way they treat others, because if they don't behave, their own Contacts are liable to expunge them, and then where will they be? Less careful about the way they treat themselves, because they aren't scared much of dying any more. They know that if it happens quick, without pain, it'll just be a blur and then confusion and then picking up again and then melting into someone else. No sharp break, no stopping. Have you picked anyone up, Mr. Hale?"

"Matter of fact, I have," I said. "I picked up my father just about a year ago."

"And was it okay?"

"Oh, smooth as oil. Disconcerting for a while—like having an itch I couldn't scratch—but that passed in about two or three months and then he just blended in and there it was."

I thought about it for a moment. In particular, I thought about the peculiar sensation of being able to remember from outside how I looked in my cradle, and things like that. But it was comforting as well as peculiar, and anyway there was never any doubt about whose memory it was. All the memories that came over when a contact was completed had indefinable auras that labeled them and helped keep the receiver's mind straight.

"And you?" I said.

Geraghty nodded. "Guy I knew in the Army. Just a few weeks back he had a car smash. Poor guy lived for ten days with a busted back, going through hell. He was in bad shape when he came over. Pain—it was terrible!"

"Ought to write your congressman," I said. "Get this new bill through. Hear about it?"

"Which one?"

"Legalize mercy killing provided the guy has a valid Contact. Everyone does nowadays, so why not?"

Geraghty looked thoughtful. "Yes, I did hear about it. I wasn't happy about it. But since I picked up my buddy and got his memory of what happened—well, I guess I'm changing my mind. I'll do like you say."

We were quiet for a bit then, thinking about what Contact had done for the world. Geraghty had said he wasn't happy at first about this euthanasia bill—well, I and a lot of other people weren't sure about Contact at first, either. Then we saw what it could do, and had a chance to think the matter out, and now I felt I didn't understand how I'd gone through so much of my life without it. I just couldn't think myself back to a world where when you died you had to stop. It was horrible!

With Contact, that problem was solved. Dying became like a change of vehicle. You blurred, maybe blacked out, knowing you would come to, as it were, looking out of somebody's eyes that you had Contact with. You wouldn't be in control any more, but he or she would have your memories, and for two or three months you'd ease around, fitting yourself to your new partner and then bit by bit there'd be a shift of viewpoint, and finally a melting together, and *click*. No interruption; just a smooth painless process taking you on into another installment of life as someone who was neither you nor someone else, but a product of the two.

For the receiver, as I knew from experience, it was at worst uncomfortable, but for someone you were fond of you could take far more than discomfort.

Thinking of what life had been like before Contact, I found myself shuddering. I ordered another drink—a double this time. I hadn't been out drinking for a long while.

I'd been telling Geraghty the news for maybe an hour, and I was on my third or fourth drink, when the door of the bar opened and a guy came in. He was medium-sized, rather ordinary, fairly well-dressed, and I wouldn't have looked at him twice except for the expression on his face. He looked so angry and miserable I couldn't believe my eyes.

He went up to his booth where the couple were sitting—the one where the woman was that I'd been watching—and planted his feet on the ground facing them. All the attractive light went out of the woman's face, and the man with her got half to his feet as if in alarm.

"You know," Geraghty said softly, "that looks like trouble. I haven't had a row in this bar for more than a year, but I remember what one looks like when it's brewing."

He got up off his stool watchfully, and moved down the bar so he could go through the gap in the counter if he had to.

I swiveled on my stool and caught some of the conversation. As far as I could hear, it was going like this.

"You expunged me, Mary!" the guy with the miserable face was saying. "*Did* you?"

"Now look here!" the other man cut in. "It's up to her whether she does or doesn't."

"You shut up," the newcomer said. "Well, Mary? *Did* you?"

"Yes, Mack, I did," she said. "Sam had nothing to do with it. It was entirely my idea—and your fault."

I couldn't see Mack's face, but his body sort of tightened up, shaking, and he put his ams out as though he was going to haul Mary out of her seat. Sam—I presumed Sam was the man in the booth—seized his arm, yelling at him.

That was where Geraghty came in, ordering them to quit where they were. They didn't like it, but they did, and Mary and Sam finished their drinks and went out of the bar, and Mack, after glaring after them, came up and took a stool next but one to mine.

"Rye," he said. "Gimme the bottle—I'll need it."

His voice was rasping and bitter, a tone I realized I hadn't heard in maybe months. I suppose I looked curious; anyway, he glanced at me and saw I was looking at him, and spoke to me.

"Know what that was all about?"

I shrugged. "Lost your girl?" I suggested.

"Much worse than that—and she isn't so much a lost girl as a heartless she-devil." He tossed down the first of the rye that Geraghty had brought for him. I noticed that Geraghty had moved to the other end of the counter and was washing glasses. If he was out of the habit of listening to people's troubles, I wouldn't blame him, I thought.

"She didn't look that way," I said at random.

"No, she doesn't." He took another drink and then sat for a while with the empty glass between his hands, staring at it.

"I suppose you have Contacts?" he said at last. It was a pretty odd question, and I answered it automatically out of sheer surprise.

"Well—yes, of course I have!"

"I haven't," he said. "Not now. Not any more. *Damn* that woman!"

I felt the nape of my neck prickle. If he was telling the truth —well, he was a kind of living ghost! Everyone I knew had at least one Contact; I had three. My wife and I had a mutual, of course, like all married couples, and as insurance against our being killed together in a car wreck or by some similar accident I had an extra one with my kid brother Joe and a third with a guy I'd known in college. At least, I was fairly sure I did; I hadn't heard from him in some months and he might perhaps have expunged me. I made a mental note to look him up and keep the friendship moving.

I studied this lonely guy. His name was Mack—I'd heard him called that. He was probably ten years older than I was, which made him in his middle forties—plenty old enough to have dozens of potential Contacts. There was nothing visibly wrong with him except this look of unspeakable misery he wore—and if he really had no Contacts at all, then I was surprised the look was of mere misery, not of terror.

"Did—uh—did Mary know that she was your only Contact?" I said.

"Oh, she knew. Of course. That's why she did it without telling me." Mack refilled his glass and held the bottle toward me. I was going to refuse, but if someone didn't keep the poor devil company, he'd probably empty the bottle himself, and then maybe walk out staggering drunk and fall under a car and be done for. I really felt sorry for him. Anyone would have.

"How did you find out?"

"She—well, she went out tonight and I called at her place and someone said she'd gone out with Sam, and Sam generally brings her here. And there she was, and when I put it to her she confessed. I guess it was as well the bartender stepped in, or I'd have lost control and maybe done something really serious to her."

I said, "Well—how come she's the only one? Have you no friends or anything?"

That opened the floodgates.

The poor guy—his full name was Mack Wilson—was an orphan brought up in a foundling home which he hated; he ran away in his teens and was committed to reform school for some petty theft or other, and hated that too, and by the time he got old enough to earn his living, he was sour on the world, but he'd done his best to set himself straight, only to find that he'd missed learning how. Somewhere along the line he'd failed to get the knack of making friends.

When he'd told me the whole story, I felt he was truly pitiable. When I contrasted his loneliness with my comfortable condition, I felt almost ashamed. Maybe the rye had a lot to do with it, but it didn't feel that way. I wanted to cry, and I hardly even felt foolish for wanting.

Round about ten or ten-thirty, when most of the bottle had gone, he slapped the counter and started to get down from his stool. He wobbled frighteningly. I caught hold of him, but he brushed me aside.

"Home, I guess," he said hopelessly. "If I can make it. If I don't get run down by some lucky so-and-so who's careless what he hits because he's all right, he has Contacts aplenty."

He was darned right—that was the trouble. I said, "Look, don't you think you should sober up first?"

"How in hell do you think I'll get to sleep if I'm not pickled?" he retorted. And he was probably right there, too. He went on, "You wouldn't know, I guess: what it's like to lie in bed, staring into the dark, without a Contact anywhere. It makes the whole world seem hateful and dark and hostile . . ."

"Jesus!" I said, because that really hit me.

A sudden glimmer of hope came into his eyes. He said, "I don't suppose—no, it's not fair. You're a total stranger. Forget it."

I pressed him, because it was good to see any trace of hope on *that* face. After a bit of hesitation, he came out with it.

"You wouldn't make a Contact with me, would you? Just to tide me over till I talk one of my friends round? I know guys at work I could maybe persuade. Just a few days, that's all."

"At this time of night?" I said. I wasn't sure I liked the idea; still, I'd have him on my conscience if I didn't fall in.

"They have all-night Contact service at LaGuardia Airport," he said. "For people who want to make an extra one as insurance before going on a long flight. We could go there."

"It'll have to be a one-way, not a mutual," I said. "I don't have twenty-five bucks to spare."

"You'll do it?" He looked as though he couldn't believe his ears. Then he grabbed my hand and pumped it up and down, and settled his check and hustled me to the door and found a cab and we were on the way to the airport before I really knew what was happening.

The consultant at the airport tried to talk me into having a mutual; Mack had offered to pay for it. But I stood firm on that. I don't believe in people adding Contacts to their list when the others are real friends. If something were to happen to me, I felt, and somebody other than my wife, or my brother, or my long-time friend from college, were to pick me up, I was certain they'd all three be very much hurt by it. So since there were quite a few customers waiting to make an extra Contact before flying to Europe, the consultant didn't try too hard.

It had always been a source of wonder to me that Contact was such a simple process. Three minutes' fiddling with the equipment; a minute or two to put the helmets properly on our heads; mere seconds for the scan to go to completion during which the brain buzzed with fragments of memory dredged up from nowhere and presented like single movie frames to consciousness . . . and finished.

The consultant gave us the standard certificates and the warranty form—valid five years, recommended reinforcement owing to personality development, temporal-geographical factor, in the event of death instantaneous transfer, adjustment lapse, in the event of more than one Contact being extant some possibility of choice, and so on. And there it was.

I never had been able to make sense of the principle on which Contact worked. I knew it wasn't possible before the advent of printed-molecule electronics, which pushed the information capacity of computers up to the level of the human brain and beyond. I knew vaguely that in the first place they had been trying to achieve mechanical telepathy, and that they succeeded in finding means to scan the entire content of a brain and transfer it to an electronic store. I knew also that telepathy didn't come, but immortality did.

What it amounted to, in lay terms, was this: only the advent of death was enough of a shock to the personality to make it want to get up and go. Then it wanted but *desperately*. If at some recent time the personality had been, as it were, shown to someone else's mind, there was a place ready for it to go to.

At that point I lost touch with the explanations. So did practically everybody. Resonance came into it, and maybe the receiver's mind vibrated in sympathy with the mind of the person about to die; that was a fair picture, and the process worked, so what more could anyone ask?

I was later in coming out from under than he was; this was a one-way, and he was being scanned which is quick, while I was being printed which is slightly slower. When I came out he was trying to get something straight with the consultant, who wasn't interested, but he wouldn't be just pushed aside—he had to have his answer. He got it as I was emerging from under the helmet.

"No, there's no known effect. Sober or drunk, the process goes through!"

The point had never occurred to me before—whether liquor would foul up the accuracy of the Contact.

Thinking of the liquor reminded me that I'd drunk a great deal of rye and it was the first time I'd had more than a couple of beers in many months. For a little while I had a warm glow, partly from the alcohol and partly from the knowledge that, thanks to me, this last lonely man wasn't lonely any more.

Then I began to lose touch. I think it was because Mack had brought the last of the bottle along and insisted on our toasting our new friendship—or words like that. Anyway, I remembered that he got the cab and told the hackie my address and then it was the next morning and he was sleeping on the couch in the rumpus room and the doorbell was going like an electric alarm.

I pieced these facts together a little afterward. When I opened the door, it was Mary standing there, the woman who had expunged Mack the day before.

She came in quite politely, but with a determined expression which I couldn't resist in my morning-after state, and told me to sit down and took a chair herself.

She said, "Was it true what Mack told me on the phone?"

I looked vacant. I *felt* vacant.

Impatiently, she said, "About him making a Contact with you. He called me up at two A.M. and told me the whole story. I wanted to throw the phone out the window, but I hung on and got your name out of him, and some of your address, and the rest from the phone book. Because I wouldn't want anybody to have Mack wished on him. Not anybody."

By this time I was starting to connect. But I didn't have much to say. I let her get on with it.

"I once read a story," she said. "I don't remember who by. Perhaps you've read it too. About a man who saved another man from drowning. And the guy was grateful, gave him presents, tried to do him favors, said he was his only friend in the world, dogged his footsteps, moved into his home—and finally the guy who'd saved him couldn't stand it any longer and took him and pushed him back in the river. That's Mack Wilson. That's why Mack Wilson has been expunged by everybody's he's conned into making Contact with him in the past two mortal years. I stood it for going on three months, and that's about the record, as I understand it."

There was a click, a door opening, and there was Mack in shirt and pants, roused from his sleep in the rumpus room by the sound of Mary's voice. She got in first. She said, "You see? He's started already."

"You!" Mack said. "Haven't you done enough?" And he turned to me. "She isn't satisfied with expunging me and leaving me without a Contact in the world. She has to come here and try to talk you into doing the same! Can you imagine anybody hating me like that?"

On the last word his voice broke, and I saw that there were real tears in his eyes.

I put my muddled mind together and found something to say.

"Look," I said. "All I did this for was just that I don't think anyone should have to go without a Contact nowadays. All I did it for was to tide Mack over." I was mainly talking to Mary. "I drank too much last night and he brought me home and that was why he's here this morning. I don't care who he is or what he's done—I have Contacts myself, I don't know what I'd do if I didn't, and until Mack fixes up something, maybe with some-body where he works, I'll go bail for him. That's all."

"That's the way it started with me," Mary said. "Then he moved into my apartment. Then he started following me on the street to make sure nothing happened to me. He said."

"Where would I have been if something had?" Mack pro-tested.

Just then I caught sight of the clock on the wall, and saw it was noon. I jumped up.

"Jesus!" I said. "My wife and kids get back at four, and I promised to clean the apartment while they were away."

"I'll give you a hand," Mack said. "I owe you that, at least."

Mary got to her feet. She was looking at me with a hopeless expression. "Don't say you weren't warned," she said.

So she was right. So Mack was very helpful. He was better around the house than a lot of women I've known, and, though it took right up until my wife got home with the children, the job was perfect. Even my wife was impressed. So since it was get-ting on toward the evening, she insisted on Mack staying for supper with us, and he went and got some beer, and over it he told my wife the spot that he'd been put in, and then, at around nine or half past, he said he wanted an early night because of work tomorrow, and went home.

Which seemed great under the circumstances. I dismissed what Mary had said as the bitterness of a disappointed woman, and felt sorry for her. She hadn't looked the type to be so bitter when I first saw her the evening before.

It was about three or four days later that I began to catch on. There was this new craze for going to see pre-Contact movies, and though I didn't feel that I would get a bang out of watching soldiers and gunmen kill each other without Contact to look for-ward to, my wife had been told by all her friends that she oughtn't to miss out on this eerie thrill.

Only there was the problem of the kids. We couldn't take eleven-month twins along, very well. And we'd lost our regular sitter, and when we checked up there just didn't seem to be any-one on hand.

I tried to talk her into going alone, but she didn't like the idea. I'd noticed that she'd given up watching pre-Contact programs on TV, so that was of a piece.

So we'd decided to scrap the idea, though I knew she was disappointed, until Mack called, heard the problem, and at once offered to sit in.

Great, we thought. He seemed willing, competent, and even eager to do us the favor, and we had no worries about going out. The kids were fast asleep before we left.

We parked the car and started to walk around to the movie house. It was getting dark, and it was chilly, so we hurried along although we had plenty of time before the start of the second feature.

Suddenly my wife glanced back and stopped dead in her tracks. A man and a boy following close behind bumped into her, and I had to apologize and when they'd gone on asked what on earth was the trouble.

"I thought I saw Mack following us," she said. "Funny..."

"Very funny," I agreed. "Where?" I looked along the sidewalk, but there were a lot of people, including several who were dressed and built similarly to Mack. I pointed this out, and she'd agreed that she'd probably been mistaken. I couldn't get her to go beyond *probably*.

The rest of our walk to the movie was a kind of sidelong hobble, because she kept staring behind her. It got embarrassing after a while, and suddenly I thought I understood why she was doing it.

I said, "You're not really looking forward to this, are you?"

"What do you mean?" she said, injured. "I've been looking forward to it all week."

"You can't really be," I argued. "Your subconscious is playing tricks on you—making you think you see Mack, so that you'll have an excuse to go back home instead of seeing the movies. If you're only here because of your *kaffeeklatsch* friends who've talked you into the idea, and you don't actually think you'll enjoy it, let's go."

I saw from her expression I was at least half right. But she shook her head. "Don't be silly," she said. "Mack would think it was awfully funny, wouldn't he, if we came right home? He might think we didn't trust him, or something."

So we went in, and we sat through the second feature and were duly reminded of what life was like—and worse, what death was like—in those distant days a few years ago when Contact didn't exist. When the lights went up briefly between the two pictures, I turned to my wife.

"I must say—" I began and broke off short, staring.

He *was* there, right across the aisle from us. I knew it was Mack, not just someone who looked like Mack, because of the way he was trying to duck down into his collar and prevent me from recognizing him. I pointed, and my wife's face went absolutely chalk-white.

We started to get to our feet. He saw us, and ran.

I caught him halfway down the block, grabbing his arm and spinning him round, and I said, "What in hell is this all about? This is just about the dirtiest trick that anyone ever played on me!"

If anything happened to those kids, of course, that was the end. You couldn't make a Contact for a child till past the age of reading, at the earliest.

And he had the gall to try and argue with me. To make excuses for himself. He said something like, "I'm sorry, but I got so worried I couldn't stand it any longer. I made sure everything was all right, and I only meant to be out for a little while, and—"

My wife had caught up by now, and she turned it on. I never suspected before that she knew so many dirty words, but she did, and she used them, and she finished up by slapping him across the face with her purse before leading me into a dash for the car. All the way home she was telling me what an idiot I'd been to get tangled up with Mack, and I was saying what was perfectly true —that I did the guy a favor because I didn't think anyone should have to be lonely and without a Contact anymore—but true or not it sounded hollow.

The most terrifying sound I ever heard was the noise of those two kids squalling as we came in. But nothing was wrong with either of them except they were lonely and miserable, and we comforted them and made a fuss of them till they quietened down.

The outside door opened while we were breathing sighs of relief and there he was again. Of course, we'd left him a key to the door while we were out, in case he had to step round the corner or anything. Well, a few minutes is one thing—but tracking us to the movie house and then sitting through the show was another altogether.

I was practically speechless when I saw who it was. I let him get the first few words in because of that. He said, "Please, you must understand! All I wanted was to make sure nothing happened to you! Suppose you'd had a crash on the way to the movie, and I didn't know—where would I be then? I sat there and worried about it till I just couldn't stand any more, and all I meant to do was make sure you were safe, but when I got down to the movie house I got worried about your coming home safe and—"

I still hadn't found any words because I was so blind angry. So, since I couldn't take any more, I wound up and let him have it on the chin. He went halfway backward through the open door behind him, catching at the jamb to stop himself falling, and his face screwed up like a mommy's darling who's got in a game too rough for him and he started to snivel.

"Don't drive me away!" he moaned. "You're the only friend I have in the world! Don't drive me away!"

"Friend!" I said. "After what you did this evening I wouldn't call you my friend if you were the last guy on Earth! I did you a favor and you've paid it back exactly the way Mary said you would. Get the hell *out* of here and don't try to come back, and first thing in the morning I'm going to stop by at a Contact agency and have you expunged!"

"No!" he shrieked. I never thought a man could scream like that—as though red-hot irons had been put against his face. "No! You can't do that! It's inhuman! It's—"

I grabbed hold of him and twisted the key out of his fingers, and for all he tried to cling to me and went on blubbering I pushed him out of the door and slammed it in his face.

That night I couldn't sleep. I lay tossing and turning, staring up into the darkness. After half an hour of this, I heard my wife sit up in the other bed.

"What's the trouble, honey?" she said.

"I don't know," I said. "I guess maybe I feel ashamed of myself for kicking Mack out the way I did."

"Nonsense!" she said sharply. "You're too soft-hearted. You couldn't have done anything else. Lonely, or not lonely, he played a disgusting, wicked trick on us—leaving the twins alone like that after he'd promised! You didn't promise him anything. You said you were doing him a favor. You couldn't know what sort of a person he'd turn out to be. Now you relax and go to sleep. I'm going to wake you early and make sure of getting you to a Contact agency before you go in to work."

At that precise moment, as though he'd been listening, I picked him up.

I could never describe—not if I tried for twenty lifetimes—the slimy, underhand, snivelly triumph that was in his mind when it happened. I couldn't convey the sensation of "Yah, tricked you again!" Or the undertone of "You treated me badly, see how badly I can treat you."

I think I screamed a few times when I realized what had happened. Of course. He'd conned me into making a Contact with him, just as he'd done to a lot of other people before—only they'd seen through him in good time and expunged without telling him, so that when he found out, it was too late to cheat on the deal the way he'd cheated me.

I'd told him I was going to expunge him in the morning—that's a unilateral decision, as they call it, and there wasn't a thing he could do to stop me. Something in my voice must have shown that I really meant it. Because, though he couldn't stop me, he could forestall me, and he'd done exactly that.

He'd shot himself in the heart.

I went on hoping for a little while. I fought the nastiness that had come into my mind—sent my wife and kids off to her parents again over the weekend—and tried to sweat it out by myself. I didn't make it. I was preoccupied for a while finding out exactly how many lies Mack had told me—about his reform school, his time in jail, his undiscovered thefts and shabby tricks played on people he called friends like the one he'd played on me—but then it snapped, and I had to go and call up my father-in-law and find out if my wife had arrived yet, and she hadn't, and I chewed my nails to the knuckle and called up my old friend Hank, who said hello, yes of course I still have your Contact you old so-and-so and how are you and say I may be flying up to New York next weekend—

I was *horrified*. I couldn't help it. I guess he thought I was crazy or at any rate idiotically rude, when I tried to talk him out of flying up, and we had a first-rate argument which practically finished with him saying he'd expunge the Contact if that was the way I was going to talk to an old pal.

Then I panicked and had to call my kid brother Joe, and he wasn't home—gone somewhere for the weekend, *my* part of my mind told me, and nothing to worry about. But Mack's part of my mind said he was probably dead and my old friend was going to desert me and pretty soon I wouldn't have a Contact left and then I'd be permanently dead and how about that movie last night with people being killed and having no Contacts at all?

So I called my father-in-law again and yes my wife and the twins were there now and they were going on the lake in a boat belonging to a friend and I was appalled and tried to say that it was too dangerous and don't let them and I'd come up myself and hold them back if I had to and—

It hasn't stopped. It's been quite a time blending Mack in with the rest of me; I hoped and hoped that when the *click* came things would be better. But they're worse.

Worse?

Well—I can't be sure about that. I mean, it's true that until now I was taking the most appalling risks. Like going out to work all day and leaving my wife at home alone—why, anything might have happened to her! And not seeing Hank for months on end. And not checking with Joe every chance I got, so that if he was killed I could have time to fix up another Contact to take his place.

It's safer now, though. Now I have this gun, and I don't go out to work, and I don't let my wife out of my sight at all, and we're going to drive very carefully down to Joe's place, and stop him doing foolish things too, and when I've got him lined up, we'll go to Hank's and prevent him from making that insanely risky flight to New York and then maybe things will be okay.

The thing that worries me, though, is that I'll have to go to sleep some time, and—what if something happens to them all when I'm asleep?

Galactic Consumer Report No. 1

This is the first of four tidbits that Brunner offers as a service to us readers so firmly ensconced in science-fictional reality that we need a buying guide to its appurtenances.

Is your only time machine problem that it ticks too loudly, or runs down if you don't wind it? Then the following may be solely of academic interest:

INEXPENSIVE TIME MACHINES

(Extract from Good Buy, *published by the Consolidated Galactic Federation of Consumers' Associations, issue dated January 2329 ESY)*

Introduction

Experiments with time travel on the Asimov-Notsodusti principle were made on Logaia as long ago as 2107, but a series of spectacular accidents, too notorious to be described in detail here, led to legislation confining its use to rare and extremely costly government-authorized research trips.

About a century ago, however (recent feedback has made the actual date so fluid as to be insusceptible of definition), a posthumous discussion with Einstein enabled Dr. Ajax Yak of the University of Spica to formulate the fundamental equations of petrified-field theory. The light shed on the subject by his celebrated postulate that yaktion and re-yaktion are equally apposite so simplified time travel that the legislation was subsequently repealed and a market opened for the sale of time machines to the public. (An operator's license is required on most planets; punch the yellow keyboard of your computer for details.)

Acceptable standards for the safety and performance of these machines have been laid down on Earth, Osiris, Confucius, and a number of other worlds, and a Galactic Standard is reportedly in draft. Unfortunately these do not have the force of law except insofar as their exclusion lists are concerned (see below). We think they should. As our members will have noticed, cut-price time machines are now being widely advertised and time travel is bidding fair to rival space travel as a popular vacation pastime. We cannot too strongly caution our members against blind acceptance of the advertisers' claims.

Brands Tested

Most major home-appliance manufacturers offer time machines in their current catalogues, and we hope in due course to make a thorough survey of the field. However, those priced at ten thousand credits or less are most likely to sell in large numbers to inexperienced purchasers, so we decided to conduct tests on all the models we found available below that limit. As always, we purchased our samples anonymously through regular retail outlets.

We bought two samples of each of two models whose full list price was above our ceiling but which can be had for less through a discount agency (*Worldline Wanderer* and *Chronokinetor*); one each at regular and discount prices of two models whose list price is under Cr. 10,000 (*Super Shifter* and *Tempora Mutantur*); and two each of two models apparently sold exclusively in the discount market (*Anytime Hopper* and *Eternity Twister*—the latter, incidentally, being described as "imported").

In order to complete a full range of tests on all models, we bought replacements for samples that failed during the course of our survey except when it was clear that doing so would waste our time and your money.

Appearance and Finish

In general, all machines are of acceptable standard, although one of the diamond instrument lights in the *Worldline Wanderer* had a flaw, while the gold and platinum inlay used for the floor of the *Super Shifter* was rated "cheap and garish" by all but one of our test panel. The inside door handles of the *Anytime Hopper* came off the first time we used them and had to be replaced. A fifteen-centimeter length of size 9 waveguide tube fits the socket, and we recommend this be substituted prior to making any trips in the machine, as waveguide tube of this caliber is not easily available in many popular historical periods, and since—as a sensible safety precaution—the machine is invisible and intangible so long as the doors are shut, there can be no question of asking a helpful native to let you out. (Or anyone else, for that matter.)

The emergency kits of tools and spares are adequate on all but the *Eternity Twister*, whose ratiocinator proved to be broken; the service manual was printed back to front in classical Arabic (presumably a computer error at the factory), and the forty-seven spare transistors were found to be lumps of contaminated polystyrene.

Guarantees

None of the guarantees is wholly satisfactory. That for the *Worldline Wanderer* is almost acceptable, in that it guarantees replacement of any part developing a fault during the first hundred hours of subjective occupation, but the owner is obliged to make his own arrangements for the return of the faulty parts to the factory—not easy on a trip of any length.

We recommend taking out a policy for retemporation insurance; several companies offer these at reasonable rates.

The guarantee supplied with the *Eternity Twister* runs to forty-eight pages of small print and required a computer evaluation to make it comprehensible. It proved to render the purchaser liable to distraint of his entire property by the importers of the machine if he makes any claim against them for any reason whatever. We feel that this should *not* be signed and returned to the company as they request.

Power Source, Drive and Controls

The *Worldline Wanderer* has a built-in fusion plant, of high output and fair reliability, although the cork of the magnetic bottle kept coming loose on both our samples and was difficult to replace with the Möbius wrench supplied, as the handle is too short.

All the others, bar one, have conventional fission piles. Only the *Chronokinetor* offers automatic dumping of exhausted fuel rods; the others have to be cleared manually. The makers of the *Tempora Mutantur* operate an exchange service for their rods, a good idea, but as yet imperfect from the consumer's standpoint. One of our testers was instructed to dispatch a consignment of rods while visiting the standard target area of 1779 and had to wait until 1812 for the replacements owing to mislabeling of the package at the factory.

The exception mentioned above is the *Eternity Twister,* powered by NiFe batteries supplemented by a pedal-driven generator. The importers claim that this furnishes ideal exercise to toughen up users on the way to barbaric time zones. Our testers followed the directions supplied, but all except one (silver medalist for weight lifting in the last Jovian Olympics) found it necessary to rest up for a week or so on arrival. This would not perhaps be the ideal start to a family vacation.

In five of the six machines the drive mechanism is a recognizable variant of the original Yak design, and any qualified service mechanic ought to be able to cure minor faults. (NB: Mechanics are not available earlier than 2304 except to users of the *Super Shifter*, whose makers have launched a training scheme for native labor in a few popular vacation zones farther back. A list of these comes with the machine.)

We are unable to make a positive statement as to the drive mechanism of the *Eternity Twister*, as the petrified field is generated in a black box labeled "Not To Be Opened." Attempts to inspect the interior resulted in messy, though not fatal, explosions. We consider this a serious design fault.

The controls on the cheaper machines, though stark, are adequate with fair accessibility. We faulted the *Chronokinetor* because its three-vee display is reflected by the master time-range dial and makes the pointer difficult to read; the *Tempora Mutantur* because the dashboard is devoted to three-vee, piped music, sensishow outputs and perfumolator orifices, while the controls are on the arms of the operator's chair and can easily be activated by a careless elbow; and the *Worldline Wanderer* because the forward- and reverse-lever had been mislabeled on one of our samples: the first trial filled the testing lab with a horde of noisy and ill-dressed savages, later identified as Mongols, who defied our best efforts to return them to the machine and eventually had to be deported under a government regulation forbidding unauthorized entry to the present.

The *Eternity Twister* has a good range of controls and instruments. Inspection revealed, however, that four out of a total of eighteen of them are not connected to anything. One of the range-finding dials on the *Anytime Hopper* had to be read in a mirror, but its pointer has not been made to rotate counterclockwise to compensate. The makers claim that it can be read directly, but if this was the intention, we think they should have included with their standard equipment a jar of liniment suitable for stiff necks.

Performance

As already mentioned, the Galactic Standard has not yet been published. We took the Confucian Standard CS as the basis for our tests, modifying it to the more stringent requirements of the Terrestrial Standard TS in respect of excluded zones.

First we measured the radius of the petrified field (CS and TS: five meters). All passed except two.

On one sample of the *Anytime Hopper* the field collapsed to half size during a test jump to 1898, leaving the tester's head in that year and his feet in the present. Repairs were speedily put in hand, but unfortunately an enterprising carnival operator discovered the tester's isolated upper portion and for some eight hours before rescue was effected employed it as a novel target in his sideshow. (This was of the type known as an "Aunt Sally," in which contestants received prizes for their accuracy in hurling wooden balls.)

The importers of the *Eternity Twister* state in their advertisements that the radius of their machine's field is "in accordance with the relevant Standards." One of our samples managed 4.1 meters, but the other never did better than 3.7. *The Worldline Wanderer* and the *Super Shifter* expanded to 10 meters without difficulty, and we are lobbying for this to be made the minimum for the Galactic Standard.

Next, we carried out tests to determine range and accuracy. The CS lays down 5,000 Confucian years (about 4,762 Earthside Standard Years) as the shortest qualifying range, with an accuracy of plus or minus one month over ten repetitions at any lesser distance.

All sustained this over ranges below about 1,000 ESY. However, none was satisfactory on longer trips. In particular, one sample of the *Chronokinetor* landed twice in the Upper Pleistocene and the other in the Triassic owing to power surges. Both performed satisfactorily after we replaced the pile-moderators. The *Worldline Wanderer* has a repeatable extreme of 11,421 ESY, well in excess of the Standard, but at this high power level the cork kept coming out of the bottle.

The *Eternity Twister* recorded one maximum of 2,389 years, but this was not repeatable on either sample, and the average for both was one year seventeen days. One sample refused to go anywhere until the fuses had been replaced with five-centimeter busbars, while on the other the insulation burned out. Inspection revealed that it consists of badly tanned animal hide. We substituted a modern synthetic, but it proved impossible to get rid of the smell.

Finally we turned to the question of excluded time zones, and here applied the TS rather than the CS because the TS stipulates a greater conformity with people's prejudices.

Some confusion exists as to the reason for having exclusions, so a word of explanation may be in order. It is often thought that excluded zones are those highly susceptible to paradox feedback, in which casual tourists might upset the sequence of cause and effect. It is true that such zones are excluded, but not by us. They are patrolled by armed Temporal Police generally believed to be based around 10,600 ESY, and there is no question of tourists being able to get at them.

What we are now referring to are the zones surrounding events in the traditional version of which certain pressure groups have a vested interest: for example, the wanderings of the Children of Israel, the meditation of Buddha under the bo tree, the Sanctification of Emily Dong, the Aspiration of Bert Tuddle, and so forth.

On virtually all planets the only legislation governing the use of time machines (apart from operator's license regulations) concerns the automatic cutouts with which any machine offered for sale on that world must be fitted. To some extent, these can be varied at the wish of the purchaser, so that on Earth one can choose from at least a dozen rival Christian lists, but the chance of obtaining a Koranic list on New Jerusalem is effectively nil (and the attempt is punishable with a heavy fine). And so forth.

No machine can be held to have passed the Standard unless it operates according to at least one of these lists, of which there are some two hundred. To secure as large a share of the market as possible, manufacturers generally offer a basic range of about twenty, with others optional at additional cost.

It would have been a prohibitively long job to try all the lists on all the machines, so we chose ten of the most popular, ten in average demand, and ten favored by minority groups. Our report follows:

Worldline Wanderer: Excellent for all Euro-American lists, including Judaic and Catholic, but poor on Asiatic and only fair on the remainder.

Super Shifter: Good in all areas except Moslem (the Hegira cutout failed on both samples).

Tempora Mutantur: Good, but unlikely to be favored by Neo-Pagans, as the list of available extras does not include the period of Julian the Apostate.

Chronokinetor: Excellent for Hellenic Revivalists (it is made by a Greek firm), fair in other areas.

Anytime Hopper: Fair to good in all areas except that the Wesleyan list is faulty; it proved possible to witness the composition of at least seven hymns.

Eternity Twister: Not rated. There are cutouts, and on the surviving sample of the two tested they operate well, all things considered. However, their operation is either absolutely arbitrary or geared to some exclusion list not available to the testing staff. Our testers meticulously visited every area supposed to be inaccessible. An indication of the seriousness of the fault: the unfortunate tester assigned to check on the zone of the Aspiration of Bert Tuddle returned to the present suffering from uncontrollable hysteria, and his report was delayed for three hours while we tried to make him stop laughing.

Value for Credits

Apart from the episode of the invading Mongols, the *Worldline Wanderer* performs well and meets the various standards we applied to it. We therefore name it our Best Buy. Those prepared to sacrifice performance to greater comfort may prefer the *Super Shifter*, which is less expensive, and those who bore very easily indeed may like the *Tempora Mutantur*'s wide range of entertainment facilities. We do not, though, feel that any of these machines should be bought without a good retemporation policy.

And we do NOT under any circumstances recommend the purchase of an *Eternity Twister*. After the episode of the burning insulation, we sent samples of the animal hide to be analyzed. When it turned out to be Logaian lizard skin, we became suspicious and carried out further inquiries.

It turns out that these machines are being imported from 2107. They were built to the design of a self-taught "scientist" named Brong, who was left with about thirty million of them on his hands when time travel was restricted by law. Taking advantage of the recent repeal of these regulations, the importers now marketing them bought his entire surplus at a price alleged to be Cr. 18 apiece for resale at Cr. 3,500. We have reported this blatant profiteering to the Galactic Chamber of Commerce. Our advice is that even the purchase price of eighteen credits is too high. We disposed of ours to a scrap dealer: the best we could get was Cr. 11.

Fair

It's hard to believe that this story originally saw print more than thirty years ago. One of Brunner's first stories, it presages the British New Wave movement by more than a decade, at least on its surface—flamboyant and experimental in language and structure.

The plot itself is based on a traditional science fiction theme which is central to the latest North American science-fiction movement, or style: "cyberpunk."

———————

"Roll up! Roll up!"

The words were English, and therefore human, but the vocal cords behind it were electrons strung out on a wire, the resonating chambers which gave it volume the vacuum in radio tubes, the throats which sent it blasting its message into the night multiple and gigantic.

"YOU'LL FIND IT HERE! WHATEVER IT IS!"

...Wrapped in a gaudy package three miles across and tied with a blood-red bow. The package is more important than the merchandise; wrap it right and the one-every-minute men (and women) will buy. And buy. And buy.

"DO YOU WANT ROMANCE?"

Maybe he was a genius, the man who got that shuddering, suggestive, leering note into that sterile mechanical uncomprehending roar. He was certainly a success.

"DO YOU WANT THRILLS?"

Add sub- and supersonics to taste; result, a rising of the hair on the back of the neck, a fearful but somehow pleasant tonic dose of adrenaline through the system. Knowing how it's done makes no difference. It reminds the maiden lady of the night she was *sure* there was a man following her—but she doesn't come here, does she? We can forget about her. It reminded Jevons of the sensation of hanging in space produced by turning over on top of a loop—fifty, a hundred thousand feet above the earth, at a thousand, fifteen hundred miles an hour.

"DO YOU WANT AMUSEMENT?"

Some people are amused by odd things, the monstrous tone seemed to imply, faking a conniving, understanding innuendo which it could never have possessed, a tolerance of human foibles which it did not know except as figures in an accounting bank. There was a hint of a belly laugh; Jevons thought wildly of Moloch, and his brazen stomach filled with fire.

"WELL? COME AND GET IT!"

But there was one thing they didn't offer, something you weren't supposed to want because there wasn't any of it to speak of. Peace and quiet.

"SEE THE COLOSSAL—WATCH THE TREMENDOUS—COME TO THE GIGANTIC—"

Have you nothing but superlatives in your vocabulary? Jevons found the mechanical voice setting up a conversation in his mind;

he was talking to the overtones, verbally duelling with an intelligence that wasn't there. And, in a way, he was answered.

"THIS IS THE BIGGEST! THIS IS THE BEST!"

Lights! Sound! (No camera—this is *here* and *now* and *real*.) ACTION! Okay, boys, roll 'em! Where? Why the hell should I care? In the hay, maybe. After all, it's up to you. Who are *you*? Why the hell should I care? I'm a machine. But for the sake of argument with yourself, you might be Alec Jevons, ex-test pilot, ex-serviceman, ex-child and ex-husband, ex-this and ex-that, ex-practically everything. Even approaching the ultimate—almost an ex-*man*. But I started out with an advantage. I was *never* human. I don't know what I'm missing.

"—shillings please. That will be five shillings please. That will be five shil—"

This is *here* and *now*—remember that. It isn't at home and it isn't five thousand miles away, and home is where the heart is except that hearts haven't got anything to do with it and you know what people are like five thousand miles away—*don't you*? You're supposed to; after all, you've been told often enough. Be a good boy and say *ugh*.

The turnstile clicked, and as if it had been the cradle switch of a phone sounding, the undercurrent dialogue in Jevon's head went with it. The brass-lunged giant had served its purpose; he was inside. Once he was in, the giant became aware of him as a symbol in a computer memory bank, a member statistic in a profit and loss account. But he no longer heard its voice.

Overhead, the rolling way; he could hear it rumble a basso ostinato to the twiddling discordant flashy runs in the right hand which the soprano, alto and tenor cries of the concession-holders flung at random into the night. They offered to scare him out of his wits, to shock him and/or delight him; they offered to let him prove himself—various things. Kind of them, thought Jevons sourly. To let you pay for admission, pay them as well, and then get you to do the work.

He walked forward blindly into the swirl and whirl of the Fair, down one of the mile-long arteries which bore the lifeblood of the machines toward its multiple hearts. The lifeblood was money;

the people were incidental, ornery, hard to cope with. Money obeyed the rules of statistical distribution, and what you gained upon the roundabouts you lost upon the swings, in general, except when man—the wild factor—decided to be cussed and awkward. Then you changed the rules.

The crowd broke around him like polychrome waves against a granite rock, and that wasn't too bad as a metaphor except that the rock too was moving. It *was* gray as granite, compared to the humming-bird gaudiness of the flush-faced girls, the black-and-white starkness of the boys (implication: efficiency, masculinity, no nonsense). He walked straight ahead, which would have been impossible for most people; he attracted stares. For one thing, he was—not young. The other fairgoers were, for the most part. Youth is the hectic time. The remainder were recapturers of youth, busy failing to recreate more than an awareness that they could not stand the pace so well any more, never realizing that if the young people they envied could have their elders' self-knowledge and so little false pride they too would have admitted that the pace was less than ecstatically bearable.

They stared for a moment. Then—somehow—they forgot to notice the wrinkles on his face, the gray hairs at his temples. Instead, they noticed his shoulders, and read purpose—incomprehensible, hence to be shunned, to be feared, to be hated—behind the watery blue eyes. He looked dangerous. Therefore he managed to walk a straight path through the Fair, which would have been to most men impossible and to all women unthinkable, what with the youths lounging at corners waiting for a woman to impress, snatch at, crush casually—if their ennui had reached extreme—and toss back as if she were an undersized fish into the running rolling stream carrying the lifeblood of money to the organs of the Fair—the steam organs, electronic organs, pseudo-human organs like the throats of the shouting giant who roared out across the countryside to come and be merry, even if you didn't eat anything but salted nuts and popcorn and even if you drank nothing but a milk-shake (correction: soya-milk-shake; everything at the Fair was expensive, but not prohibitive, for that slowed down the lifeblood's trickle) for tomorrow we die, or if not tomorrow then the next day or the next.

I shouldn't be *here*, thought Jevons suddenly. This is a place for people who can't think and must do. I'm a person who can do but must think. Why did I come here, anyway? Looking for an answer? And if so, what's my question?

"Lonely, honey?"

Lord above, is she really so bad she has to solicit right here in the Fair? Guess she must be.

"Go to hell!"

And that's liable to be my answer, thought Jevons. If I ever find a question that makes even as much sense as hers.

He reached the base of a spiraling escalator, channeling a flow into the upper level of the Fair—the level of the rolling way which was an entertainment in itself, worth the entrance money alone, if one was young and agile and with fast reflexes. The outer strip girdled the Fair at five miles an hour, but the inmost one was doing fifty. Escalators laid out flat—mostly. But you could be bumped if you stayed on more than once around the Fair; the spot on which you stood remembered your weight and incited you to patronize a concession instead of a service. The game was to stay on your feet at a fifty-mile lick after completing the circle.

Or so he'd heard. The Fair had been less elaborate in his young days. Watch it, Jevons! You're starting to admit your age. (And why not? Because if you remember that you've been around so long, you admit that you were responsible—this was your doing, this mechanical time-destroying hurlyburly, this feverish seeking after temporary nirvana. *This was your fault!*)

All right, admit your age in terms of time, but not in terms of senility. The spiral escalator wound its challenge at him, and he thrust aside a youth in black whose shoulder bulged with the shape of a gun. It had to be one of the modern plastic models, or the scanners at the gate would have taken it away. Almost too late Jevons flung an acid and unmeant apology toward the muzzle of the weapon where it had suddenly appeared in the boy's hand; the spiral had taken him out of sight and range before the whitening finger could close on the trigger, but he heard the scream from the disappointed girl, the gunman's companion: "Whyncha do it, huh? Whyncha? Ya think I wanna be alla time with a bassard who can be shoved aroun' like he was—"

The escalator's inverted peristalsis pushed him out like vomit from its yellow-lipped mouth, on to the upper level, and the Fair was all around him, swirling and breathing like angry water. The noise was redoubled. Across the way from him the crowd parted and the source of screaming, frenetic music was plain: a band of girls in minuscule costumes blasting through shiny brass horns, and one thundering out incessant rhythm on a kit of amplified drums. She was fat; she shook. In an ecstasy of concupiscence by proxy a fat old man on the next concession stared and shook between howling the attractions of his show.

The way scampered past him, a hundred feet broad, in sections. He had had reflexes good enough to put ten or twenty tons of airplane through impossible maneuvers fifty feet from the ground—not long ago. As if in a dream he stepped forward, adjusting to the roll and flow of the way like a dancer allowing for a clumsy partner. Ahead, a girl was being bumped for completing her circuit; she rode the writhing spot on the way for ten seconds before it flung her rolling and screaming among the feet of a party of men on the forty-mile section. One of the men gave her a sharp kick, and they were past.

Staggering, the girl made for the edge, and an Uncle in the jester's uniform which made the patrolmen of the Fair a grim joke caught her arm.

"Whatcha mean tryin' ta ride the way when ya know it's for goin' someplace else not comin' backa where ya were?"

The girl was crying, rivers of tears spreading and splotching her heavy make-up. The Uncle turned to throw her off the way, and by that time Jevons had been carried out of sight.

And what's it to you anyway? he asked himself savagely, and immediately knew that the answer was in the thrill of the beat of the rollers beneath his feet, in the shudder and grind of the occasional worn, unoiled bearing which punctuated the smooth rhythm of the ride, taking him and sliding its suppleness into the bones of his body, saying do this and do this—

—and he was sidling across the way toward the fifty-mile strip as if he had been riding it since he was a child, taking up and absorbing ten miles an hour more at every transition without a tremor or a stumble.

This is the spot, he thought, as he finally steadied on the central strip. Okay; now do your damnedest.

Around him the Fair whirled into a multi-colored pool of sounds and smells. There weren't many people running the way tonight. A party of kids around ten or twelve fought on to the middle strip not too far from him, but soon caught sight of an attraction ahead and tumbled away again. Watching them, Jevons was immediately back at their age, remembering how he had come out to watch the construction of this first and greatest of the Fairs, which had been only an amusement park. The roller coaster had been bigger and better than any other; that had been the start of it. Now there were others—so many others. A million people a night in this Fair alone, the slogans claimed. A million people on the run from the uncomfortable reality of silence and thought, from the danger of tomorrow, from the waiting death poised above them in the sky—which, mercifully, you couldn't see inside the Fair because it was roofed against rain . . .

And now admit the blame, will you? His relaxing body let him get at the idea and worry it like a dog with a beloved bone, shooting agony through ancient and rotting teeth in the consciousness which was the only justification for the human race, and which these people were doing their level best to lose for the space of a hectic pleasure-filled night . . .

Where did it all start? You should know; you were there at the time. Prophesy after the event—go on! It *began* when the first mother comforted her frightened child with some distraction; it went on when men forgot to grow up, when the bogeyman of childhood became the real men over the sea, the bogeyman who waited all the time to drop H-bombs and nerve-gas on the silent, comfortable homes—from which, naturally, they fled.

Oh, war was coming. It had been coming for years and years,

it had always been coming and always would be until it came and no one questioned the fact any longer. As sure as you're born to a heritage of fear, he told a child ahead of him silently, it's going to come. Because people have been told it will for so long they feel it's sort of—expected of them.

And then the end of the Fairs and the beginning of hell—and yet wasn't this already hell in some people's books, this eternity of disappointment, of seeking for something forever out of reach?

Escapism. Escape. Get away. *Run*—run the way at the Fair because you might get your fool self killed, and is life worth living anyway?

All over the country, a million people a night here, those who aren't lying awake and worrying into the darkness of their rooms, those without a future—they're diving into one everlasting present, they think, only it doesn't last, for dawn comes again and again, and the sun reminds you of the hydrogen bomb and rain reminds you of a nerve-gas spray (shout it! "Gas! Gas!" And would they bother, though they've been trained in passive defense and anti-gas and anti-radiation exercises, the boys and girls in the two years they sacrifice on the altar of hate—would they take the trouble to run further and faster than they've run already, which is all the way from reality?)

Five and a half miles at fifty miles an hour and WHOOMP the floor began to shift under his feet. The bumps started small; they would grow if he did not heed their warning. He was too far away in time—the way had not even been built then—and he shifted automatically with the ease of a surfrider taking a wave.

Well, it began—his mind ran on—and that was all right for a while. It can't hurt to flee to imagination from an imaginary menace; it's losing the battle with something real that makes it so bad.

Shift; turn. No good. Try twisting. But the data reveal to the memory bank that the same weight, plus or minus alterations caused by different distribution of it, remains. A quarter-mile too far. Half a mile.

But they had lost that battle. And it was his fault—his and all the others who should have seen it coming. Who could have taken their lives in their hands and refused to allow the slow growth of the hatred and the fear which now dominated (no, not his children—ex-husband, likewise ex-father) these youths and their girls, tarts before they were twenty, but lost and empty and without a future since they were ten.

Three-quarters of a mile too far, and the surface of the way tossing like the Atlantic in a gale, and the man riding it without more than a twitch, an exquisitely controlled adjustment of position.

"Hey, cobbers! Here's an old cabbage who can really do it! Come eye! Say, *lookit* that 'tique-o go, babe!"

A mile too far, and the unheard-of, the improbable, but not the impossible: the relays stretched farther than the designers had allowed for, the switches closed, the circuits cooled, the floor relaxing into levelness, and the way swirling onward and onward, round and round, until it caught up with itself—but it was not a snake, it had no threat of total disappearance hanging over it. Not that way.

"Hey, fatha! Where'd ya learn ta ride the way like that? Man, I sure wish I coulda done that! Mister how come who the hell are say fatha could you use a girl lord above antique you gave me the screamin' WHAT'S THE BIG IDEA BUSTER?"

Out of the chattering acclamation of the boys and girls, the shout of an Uncle, his face thunderous with rage and as incongruous with his gaudy jester's dress as the automatic he wore at his hip instead of a fool's bauble. Jevons was suddenly back from railing at himself and his generation, and there was noise and tinsel reality about him again. One of the youths rounded on the Uncle.

"Go cart yourself, ya lousy interferin' crot," he said in a voice as sweet as honey. The Uncle wasn't looking at or listening to him: he was seeing the expression in Jevons's eyes—the look of a ghost compelled forever to haunt the scene of the murder for which he was damned. It was that, that only which suddenly closed his mouth, damped his jauntiness, lost him again across the flowing writhing track amid the yowls of the concessionaires.

But the girl who hung on the speaker's arm looked up with

adoring eyes and told him how clever he was to have driven the Uncle away, and the boy, sharp to collect his advantage, was gone with her to seek the darkness of a corner where the only intruders would be other couples bent on the same errand. The remainder of the group clamored at Jevons, praising him, making his mind squirm with the effusiveness of their hero-worship.

"Guess you old-timers can still show us a thing or two," said one of the girls—the one he had half-heard offering to ditch her boy for him—with reluctant affected candidness: begging, pleading to be shown a thing or two her boy was too young to have learned to do properly, and Jevons felt suddenly sick.

So he had beaten the machine, the brain of glass and germanium and copper which poured out the endless river of the way. *So what?* Take your praise and stick it—well, anyway. Show you a thing or two, sister? (Daughter, more like.) You wouldn't understand what I'd like to show you; you wouldn't want to. He rebuked himself for accepting their hollow plaudits even for a fraction of a second, and their cries rang like curses behind his head as he swam blindly back across the river of mankind towards the bank, the solidity, the beach of the concessions.

"COME AND—" they blasted at him. "DO YOU WANT TO—" they screamed at him.

All right. So we began by running away from the enemy who never showed his hand. That was twenty-thirty years ago. We hated him: first because of the things we were told he was going to do, then because of the things he hadn't done after all. What heroism is there—what medals are there to be won—what glamour is there in a war which has never been fought, in a war which when it is fought will be a hell with all the appurtenances—roasting flesh and slow torment for everyone?

Goddamned lousy stinking miserable son of a—foreigner . . .

"Sorry, Jevons. We can't use you any longer."

"*What?* Why?"

"Well, your mother—"

Okay, so she was naturalized. Laughing boy is half-foreign; would those kids have smothered him with praise if they had known? If he had addressed them in the tongue he had spoken fluently before he could mumble a word of English? Would the Uncle have retreated? Would his gun have stayed in its holster? Not on your sweet life.

"I'm sorry, Alec. But you can't expect me to go on. You haven't got a job and no prospect of finding another. I'm leaving you—that's flat!" ("And I'm going to sue for divorce because of non-support"—only she hadn't said that; then it was just in her mind.)

Would that longing-eyed girl have offered herself body and—well, whatever she kept under that thatch of dyed hair? Never. There would have been the horror waiting a few years ahead: "Sorry, Miss—"

What the hell would her name be, anyway? A good Anglo-Saxon one, probably. Say Smith. "No, Miss Smith. We find that five years ago you—uh—associated with a man whose anteced-ents were open to suspicion."

Clang! went the iron gate in his mind. Now, as yet, it was only the gateway to most jobs, all government posts, all privi-leges; perhaps by that time it would be the entrance to a prison.

Begin by hating the man across the sea. There's no reason for it—there doesn't have to be. If you don't need a reason for hating somebody, why stop there? Why not hate the man next door? It's just as valid.

There was a concession down there on his right which had a less garish, less noisy display than most, but it was big and the posters were subtle. He was drawn toward it, aimlessly, unthink-ingly.

It was popular, as he came up, the doors opened and the crowd moved out, seeming replete, seeming subdued by what they had been through: no screaming, laughing, giggling... What did they have done to them in there? Have the guts scared out of them? That was the sort of thing they might call fun—to run, masochistically, from a world of fear to a world of fear.

He raised his head and read slowly down the wording of the nearest poster, and at the end of it he said to himself: well, this is it. This is the ultimate betrayal. This is THE END, and you, you brass-lunged giants, can shout it for the world to hear.

The poster said—and quite quietly, in restrained lettering (which was wrong: the end of the world should be announced in bold-face type and for preference on paper edged with mourning black)— it said: BE SOMEONE ELSE! WHO DO YOU WANT TO BE? A TEST PILOT/MOVIE STAR/BIG GAME HUNTER/DEEPSEA DIVER/ GREAT LOVER!!!!!!

The picture showed a dozen unlikely dancing girls performing for a handsome, grinning youth.

There was a man in a dark suit on a platform before the ticket-booth. He was an odd barker. He used no pitch (touch a barker's pitch and be defiled, put in Jevons's mind irrelevantly). He didn't have to. The posters were enough to keep the flow going.

This was what had been going to eliminate movies and TV, Jevons remembered, before the Fairs took away their trade by offering more and better entertainment wrapped in a giant economy-size package. He had heard about it. Total sensory identification was what they called it. They used it for training intelligence agents, to find out who would break fastest under what kind of interrogation, to dress a man in another personality. Totsensid for short. *Tot* was German for "dead," so that meant the sense of your id was dead. Joke. Ha ha.

And here it was, fouling the comparatively clean air of the Fair. Here is the last word: we save you *all* the trouble. Get out of your body as well as your worries. Don't be yourself—you're a slob anyway. Be someone bigger and better and more successful, and when it's all over everybody will be one person, and we'll change his name to Adam and this is where we came in.

"Next house just starting, sir," said the barker who was less like a barker than any other concessionaire at the Fair. "Why don't you come in? I can assure you it's very popular, our show."

It would be, thought Jevons sourly. How to "get away from it all" without even taking the trouble to *go*. Yes, and why shouldn't he take a basinful? You've come to expiate your sin, haven't you? Your sin of omission? You're here to take part in the hell you've bequeathed to the younger generation; how can you stop now?

He nodded wearily. "Yes, I'm coming in."

The room held about a hundred couches, singles, and quiet ushers divided the customers, men on the right, women on the left. Jevons saw a man (?) begging an usher to let him (?) go where he (?) wanted, and red-painted fingernails flashed as he (?) tried to press money into the usher's hand. The usher looked sick, and Jevons felt sick; he dropped himself uncaring on a vacant couch and looked at the brain-box he was supposed to slide his head into. All done without mirrors; equally, without screens or cathode-ray tubes—with only the senses of the people taking part.

Then the lights went out and a voice from nowhere cried to the audience to press their heads into position and he did so and he was no longer Alec Jevons—

But he was back in the cockpit of a plane and it was a sweet piece of machinery at that. It had a surge of power when he opened the fuel feed which flattened him against his seat; he felt the familiar swell of the g-suit, pressing the blood away from his limbs as he hurled the plane into a tight turn.

The illusion was perfect, and it struck a chord deeper than he had known existed in him. Oh, to be back where I came from! he cried out, realizing with a small part of his mind that he wasn't *really* here but content to lose that knowledge—

And yet that was running away, too. What had he liked about the high and lonely reaches of the air, up there with the daytime stars? Nobody else, no more milling yelling seething humanity.

And it was over, and he was sweating. So that was why he wanted to get back into a plane which no one would ever use in the war which was supposed to be coming, instead of being down here on solid ground trying to put right the effects of those same sins of omission he was running from.

The next one was equally perfect, and he was married. He was just married. But married according to some ceremony which was foreign (and the word came with a bang up to his consciousness) and he didn't care because it was the happiest day of his life and there was a splendidly pretty girl waiting for him when night fell, and she reached out to him in the doorway of their hut (*hut?*) with her teeth standing out brilliantly in her black face (BLACK???) and he looked down in growing astonishment and found that his skin too was black and he didn't give a damn because the sensory effects were going all the way. All—the—way. All . . . the . . . way . . .

And the lights were on, and people rose slowly, satedly and worriedly from their couches, as if there was something wrong they couldn't quite place, and yet with quiet satisfaction, and there was a sudden tenderness in the way the youths went to meet their girls, girls they had quite probably never seen before they picked them up on the edge of the way tonight. He sat for a long time on his couch with his head in his hands, until an usher tapped his shoulder.

"Do you want to stay for the next house, sir? It's a complete change of program, you know—but we have to insist on a separate payment for each performance—"

"Yes," said Jevons with sudden decision. "Yes, I'm staying." The money he paid out represented his supper for tonight, now that he was unemployed, but hell, he had put his finger on something and he wanted to make sure what it was.

Few other people had stayed. Few others who had been a test pilot—this evening—and an African bride or bridegroom, dived with him into the eerie green-blue wastes of a Pacific pearl-fishery and became a Malay dying slowly of an overtaxed heart and overtaxed lungs and ruptured eardrums and near-starvation. It was not pleasant, but it was *real*.

Afterward he had just been married by a ritual he did not recognize but which he guessed might well be Jewish, and the girl he had married called him dearest in the flat-sounding syllables of Russian, which he understood in a peculiar double way: half through the brain-box, half because he knew quite well what she was saying anyway.

It was that which made him gasp, and which cleared his mind and brought him up fiercely from the couch with complete disregard for the fate of the brain-box he tore off and sent him to the nearest usher to demand who was in charge.

"In charge, sir? The man you'll find on the stand in front of the concession—he's the manager."

Jevons had gone before the usher had finished speaking, was clawing at the sleeve of the man on the stand—the barker who was not like a barker. "How did you think of this?" he demanded almost savagely, in fear lest this hope should be denied him.

The barker gave him a long slow thoughtful searching look and said, "You are a very intelligent man, Mr.—?"

"Jevons, Alec Jevons."

"How do you see it, then?"

"You're teaching these people about the men and women they hate because they think they're different. They come out realizing that an African and a Russian—"

"And a German and a Chinese and a Malay—that's about as far as our range goes at the moment—"

"—have exactly the same feelings and emotions, pleasures and troubles as ourselves!" Jevons finished the sentence in a flushed rush, color boiling to his face with excitement, pouring over his words.

"Very clever of you, Mr. Jevons," said the barker. "You are our first customer who has realized."

"But—the Russian sequence in particular—how did you get it past the censors set? And the sex, too?"

"This is a government-sponsored concern, of course. Surely you didn't think Totsensid was a process a private firm could market? The sex, I admit, is a bait—but you noticed it is *not* the cheap kind you pick up at a Fair."

Jevon's heart was singing a silent paean of rejoicing; he chuckled, and the sound threatened to soar into hysterical laughter.

"We don't often get people here as—old—as you," the barker said. "It's tomorrow we're interested in, not today. We've spent too long making a mess of the world to put it right in a hurry, but we've made a beginning. The brotherhood of man is on the way, as we usually say. Yes, *both* sides of the Iron Curtain." He eyed Jevons's untidy clothes. "You could be one of those who helped it along, if you want. Need a job?"

Jevons had started to say yes, when he remembered. "A government concern? They wouldn't have me. My mother was naturalized—that's why I was thrown out of my last job."

"Don't be a fool," said the barker flatly. "What do you think we're trying to get rid of? Report tomorrow evening at seven, will you? I'll have it fixed by then. So long."

Back across the way, back down the spiral, back through the turnstile, back to a world in which there was a sort of hope after all, back to the reality in which there would *not* be hell, there would *not* be war, and the Fairs would vanish because life would be worth living instead of foreboding.

The turnstile clicked; the conversation began again, only this time Jevons was echoing instead of arguing with the brass-lunged giant.

"THIS IS THE BIGGEST!" shouted the giant. "THIS IS THE BEST!"

And in Jevons's heart a small voice loaned the machine the humanity it did not possess. "This *is* the biggest!" Jevons shouted happily to the world. "This *is* the best!"

Such Stuff

This story reminds me of the best of Sturgeon, not only for its superior and deliberately florid language, but also the way it grabs you in some deep and creepy place, from the first paragraph on. It combines the looking-over-your-shoulder apprehensiveness of a good horror story with the scientific "reasonableness" of good science fiction, a rare combination.

With the leads of the electroencephalograph stringing out from his skull like webs spun by a drunken spider, the soft adhesive pads laid on his eyes like pennies, Starling resembled a corpse which time had festooned with its musty garlands. But a vampire-corpse, plump and rosy in its state of not-quite-death. The room was as still as any mausoleum, but it smelt of floor polish, not dust; his coffin was a hospital bed and his shroud a fluffless cotton blanket.

Except for the little yellow pilot lights in the electronic equipment beside the bed, which could just be seen through the ventilation holes in the casing, the room was in darkness. But when Wills opened the door from the corridor, the shaft of light which came over his shoulder enabled him to see Starling clearly.

He would rather not have seen him at all—laid out thus, lacking candles only because he was not dead. That could be remedied, given the proper tools: a sharpened stake, a silver bullet, crossroads at which to conduct the burial—

Wills checked himself, his face prickly with new sweat. It had hit him again! The insane idea kept recurring, like reflex, like pupils expanding under belladonna, for all he could do to drive it down. Starling lay like a corpse because he had grown used to not pulling loose the leads taped to his head—*that's all! That's all! That's all!*

He used the words like a club to beat his mind into submission. Starling had slept like this for months. He lay on one side, in a typical sleeper's attitude, but because of the leads he barely moved enough in the course of a night to disturb the bedclothes. He breathed naturally. Everything was normal.

Except that he had done it for months, which was incredible and impossible and not in the least natural.

Shaking from head to foot, Wills began to step back through the door. As he did so, it happened again—now it was happening dozens of times a night. A dream began.

The electroencephalograph recorded a change in brain activity. The pads on Starling's eyes sensed eye movements and signaled them. A relay closed. A faint but shrill buzzer sounded.

Starling grunted, stirred, moved economically as though to dislodge a fly that had settled on him. The buzzer stopped. Starling had been woken; the thread of his dream was snapped.

And he was asleep again.

Wills visualized him waking fully and realizing he was not alone in the room. Cat-silent, he crept back into the corridor and closed the door, his heart thundering as though he had had a narrow escape from disaster.

Why? In daytime he could talk normally with Starling, run

tests on him as impersonally as on anyone else. Yet at night—

He slapped down visions of Starling by day, Starling corpse-like in his bed at night, and moved down the long corridor with his teeth set to save them from chattering. He paused at other doors, pressing his ear to them or glancing inside for a moment. Some of those doors led to private infernos which ought to have jarred on his own normality with shocking violence, as they always used to. But none affected him like Starling's passiveness —not even the moaning prayers of the woman in Room 11, who was being hounded to death by imaginary demons.

Conclusion: his normality had gone.

That thought also recurred in spite of attempts to blank it out. In the long corridor which framed his aching mind like a micro-wave guide tube, Wills faced it. And found no grounds for re-jecting it. They were in the wards; he in the corridor. So what? Starling was in a ward, and he was not a patient. He was sane, free to leave whenever he wished. In remaining here he was simply being co-operative.

And telling him to go away would solve nothing at all.

His rounds were over. He went back toward the office like a man resolutely marching toward inevitable doom. Lambert—the duty nurse—was snoring on the couch in the corner; it was against regulations for the duty nurse to sleep, but Wills had had more than he could bear of the man's conversation about drink and women and what he was missing tonight on television and had told him to lie down.

He prodded Lambert to make him close his mouth and sat down at the desk, drawing the night report toward him. On the printed lines of the form his hand crawled with its shadow limp-ing behind, leaving a trail of words contorted like the path of a crazy snail.

5 a.m. All quiet except Room 11. Patient there normal.

Then he saw what he had written. Angrily, he slashed a line through the last word, another and another till it was illegible, and substituted "much as usual." Normal!

I am in the asylum of myself.

He tilted the lamp on the desk so it shone on his face and

turned to look at himself in the wall mirror provided for the use of female duty nurses. He was a little haggard after the night without sleep, but nothing else was visibly wrong with him. Much as usual, like the patient in Room 11.

And yet Starling was sleeping the night away without dreams, undead.

Wills started, fancying that something black and threadlike had brushed his shoulder. A picture came to him of Starling reaching out from his bed with the tentacle leads of the EEG, as if he were emitting them from spinnerets, and weaving the hospital together into a net of his own, trapping Wills in the middle like a fly.

He pictured himself being drained of his juices, like a fly.

Suddenly Lambert was sitting up on the couch, his eyes flicking open like the shutters of a house being aired for a new day. He said, "What's the matter, doc? You're as white as a flaming sheet!"

There was no black threadlike thing on his shoulder. Wills said with an effort, "Nothing. Just tired, I think."

He thought of sleeping, and wondered what he would dream.

The morning was bright and warm. He was never good at sleeping in the daytime; when he woke for the fourth or fifth time, unrested, he gave up. It was Daventry's day for coming here, he remembered. Maybe he should go and talk to him.

He dressed and went out of doors, his eyes dark-ringed. In the garden a number of the less ill patients were working listlessly. Daventry and the matron moved among them, complimenting them on their flowers, their thorough weeding, the lack of aphis and blackfly. Daventry had no interest in gardening except insofar as it was useful for therapy. The patients, no matter how twisted their minds were, recognized this, but Daventry apparently didn't know they knew. Wills might have laughed, but he felt laughter was receding from him. Unused faculties, like unused limbs, atrophy.

Daventry saw him approach. The bird eyes behind his glasses flicked poultry-wise over him, and a word passed from the thin-lipped mouth to the matron, who nodded and moved away. The sharp face was lit by a smile; brisk legs began to carry him over the tiny lawn, which was not mown by the patients because mowers were too dangerous.

"Ah, Harry!" in Daventry's optimistic voice. "I want a word with you. Shall we go to the office?" He took Wills's arm as he turned, companionably; Wills, who found the habit intolerable, broke the grip before it closed.

He said, "As it happens, I want a word with you, too."

The edginess of his tone sawed into Daventry's composure. The bird eyes scanned his face, the head tipped a little on one side. The list of Daventry's mannerisms was a long one, but he knew the reasons for all of them and often explained them.

"Hah!" he said. "I can guess what this will be about!"

They passed into the building and walked side by side with their footsteps beating irregularly like two palpitating hearts. In the passageway Daventry spoke again.

"I presume there's been no change in Starling, or you'd have left a note for me—you were on night duty last night, weren't you? I didn't see him today, unfortunately; I was at a conference and didn't get here till lunchtime."

Wills looked straight ahead, to the looming door of Daventry's office. He said, "No—no change. But that's what I wanted to talk about. I don't think we should go on."

"Ah!" said Daventry. It was automatic. It meant something altogether different, like "I'm astonished"—but professionally Daventry disavowed astonishment. The office accepted them, and they sat down to the idiot noise of a bluebottle hammering its head on the window.

"Why not?" Daventry said abruptly.

Wills had not yet composed his answer. He could hardly speak of the undead Starling with pads on his eyes like pennies, of the black tentacles reaching out through the hospital night, of the formulated but suppressed notion that he must be treated with sharp stakes and silver bullets, and soon. He was forced to throw up improvisation like an emergency earthwork, knowing it could be breached at a dozen points.

"Well—all our other cases suggest that serious mental disturbance results from interference with the dreaming process. Even the most resistant of our other volunteers broke down after less than two weeks. We've prevented Starling from dreaming every night for five months now, and even if there are no signs of harm yet it's probable that we *are* harming him."

Daventry had lit a cigarette while Wills talked. Now he waved it in front of him, as though to ward off Wills's arguments with an adequate barrier—a wisp of smoke.

"Good gracious, Harry!" he said affably. "What damage are we doing? Did you detect any signs of it last time you ran Starling through the tests?"

"No—that was last week and he's due for another run tomorrow—no, what I'm saying is that everything points to dreaming being essential. We may not have a test in the battery which shows the effect of depriving Starling of his dreams, but the effect must be there."

Daventry gave a neutral nod. He said, "Have you asked Starling's own opinion on this?"

Again, concede defeat from honesty: "Yes. He said he's perfectly happy to go on. He said he feels fine."

"Where is he at the moment?"

"Today's Tuesday. He goes to see his sister in the town on Tuesday afternoons. I could check if you like, but—"

Daventry shrugged. "Don't bother. I have good news for you, you see. In my view, six months is quite long enough to establish Starling's tolerance of dream deprivation. What's next of interest is the nature of his dreams when he's allowed to resume. So three weeks from now I propose to end the experiment and find out."

"He'll probably wake himself up reflexively," Wills said.

Daventry was prepared to take the words with utmost seriousness. He said, "What makes you think that?"

Wills had meant it as a bitter joke; when he reconsidered, he found reason after all. He said, "The way he's stood the treatment when no one else could. Like everyone else we tested, his dreaming frequency went up in the first few days; then it peaked at about thirty-four times a night, and dropped back to its current level of about twenty-six, which has remained constant for about four months now. Why? His mind seems to be malleable, and I can't believe that. People need dreams; a man who can manage without them is as unlikely as one who can do without food or water."

"So we thought," Daventry said briskly. Wills could see the conference papers being compiled in his mind, the reports for the *Journal of Psychology* and the four pages in *Scientific American*, with photographs. And so on. "So we thought. Until we happened across Starling, and he just proved we were wrong."

"I—" began Wills. Daventry took no notice and went on.

"Dement's work at Mount Sinai wasn't utterly definitive, you know. Clinging to first findings is a false attitude. We're now compelled to drop the idea that dreaming is indispensable, because Starling has gone without dreams for months and so far as we can tell—oh, I grant that: so far and no further—he hasn't suffered under the experience."

He knocked ash into a bowl on his desk. "Well, that was my news for you, Harry: that we finish the Starling series at the six-month mark. Then we'll see if he goes back to normal dreaming. There was nothing unusual about his dreaming before he volunteered; it will be most interesting . . ."

It was cold comfort, but it did give him a sort of deadline to work to. It also rid him of part of the horror he had suffered from having to face the presence in his mind of the vampire-corpse like a threat looming down the whole length of his future life-path. It actually heartened him till the time came to retest Starling.

He sat waiting in his office for half an hour beforehand, because everything was otherwise quiet and because before he came up for psychological examination Starling always underwent a physical examination by another member of the staff. Not that the physicals ever turned anything up. But the psychologicals hadn't either. It was all in Wills's mind. Or in Starling's. But if it was in Starling's, he himself didn't know.

He knew the Starling file almost by heart now—thick, much thumbed, annotated by himself and by Daventry. Nonetheless, he turned back to the beginning of it, to the time five months and a week ago when Starling was just one volunteer among six men and six women engaged in a follow-up to check on Dement's findings of 1960 with superior equipment.

There were transcripts of dreams with Freudian commentary, in their limited way extraordinarily revealing, but not giving a hint of the most astonishing secret—that Starling could get by without them.

I am in a railway station. People are going to work and coming home at the same time. A tall man approaches and asks for my ticket. I try to explain that I haven't bought one yet. He grows angry and calls a policeman, but the policeman is my grandfather. I cannot understand what he says.

I am talking to one of my schoolteachers, Mr. Bullen. I am very rich and I have come to visit my old school. I am very happy. I invite Mr. Bullen to ride in my car, which is big and new. When he gets in the door handle comes off in his hand. The door won't lock. I cannot start the engine. The car is old and covered with rust. Mr. Bullen is very angry but I do not care very much.

I am in a restaurant. The menu is in French and I order something I don't know. When it comes I can't eat it. I call the manager to make a complaint and he arrives in a sailor's uniform. The restaurant is on a boat and rocks so that I feel ill. The manager says he will put me in irons. People in the restaurant laugh at me. I break the plates on which the food is served, but they make no noise and no one notices. So I eat the food after all.

That last one was exactly what you would expect from Starling, Wills thought. He ate the food after all, and liked it.

These were records extracted from the control period—the week during which his dreams and those of the other volunteers were being noted for comparison with later ones, after the experiment had terminated. In all the other eleven cases that was from three days to thirteen days later. But in Starling's—!

The dreams fitted Starling admirably. Miserable, small-minded, he had gone through life being frustrated, and hence the dreams went wrong for him, sometimes through the intervention of figures of authority from childhood, such as his hated grandfather and the schoolteacher. It seemed that he never fought back; he—ate the food after all.

No wonder he was content to go on co-operating in Daventry's experiment, Wills thought bleakly. With free board and lodging, no outside problems involved, he was probably in paradise.

Or a kind of gratifying hell.

He turned up the dreams of the other volunteers—the ones who had been driven to quit after a few nights. The records of their control week showed without exception indications of sexual tension, dramatized resolutions of problems, positive attacks on personal difficulties. Only Starling provided continual evidence of total surrender.

Not that he was outwardly inadequate. Considering the frustration he had endured first from his parents, then from his tyrannical grandfather and his teachers, he had adjusted well. He was mild-mannered and rather shy, and he lived with his sister and her husband, but he held down a fairly good job, and he had a small, constant circle of acquaintances mainly met through his sister's husband, on whom he made no great impression but who all "quite liked" him.

Quite was a word central to Starling's life. Hardly any absolutes. Yet—his dreams to the contrary—he could never have surrendered altogether. He'd made the best of things.

The volunteers were a mixed bag: seven students, a teacher on sabbatical leave, an out-of-work actor, a struggling writer, a beatnik who didn't care, and Starling. They were subjected to the process developed by Dement at New York's Mount Sinai Hospital, as improved and automatized by Daventry—the process still being applied to Starling even now, which woke him with a buzzer whenever the signs indicating dreaming occurred. In the eleven other cases, the effect found was the same as what Dement established: interrupting the subjects' dreaming made them nervous, irritable, victims of uncontrolled nervous tension. The toughest quit after thirteen days

Except for Starling, that was to say.

It wasn't having their sleep disturbed that upset them; that could be proved by waking them between, instead of during, dreams. It was not being *allowed* to dream that caused trouble.

In general, people seemed to spend about an hour a night dreaming, in four or five "installments." That indicated that dreaming served a purpose: what? Dissipation of antisocial tensions? A grooming of the ego as repressed desires were satisfied? That was too glib an answer. But without Starling to cock a snook in their faces, the experimenters would have accepted a similar generalization and left the matter there till the distant day when the science of mind was better equipped to weigh and measure the impalpable stuff of dreams.

Only Starling *had* cropped up. At first he reacted predictably. The frequency of his dreaming shot up from five times a night to twenty, thirty and beyond, as the buzzer aborted each embryo dream, whirling into nothing his abominable grandfather, his tyrannical teachers—

Was there a clue there? Wills had wondered that before. Was it possible that, whereas other people *needed* to dream, Starling hated it? Were his dreams so miserable that to go without them was a liberation to him?

The idea was attractive because straightforward, but it didn't hold water. In the light of previous experiments, it was about equivalent to saying that a man could be liberated from the need to excrete by denying him food and water.

But there was no detectable effect on Starling! He had not lost weight, nor grown more irritable; he talked lucidly, he responded within predictable limits to IQ tests and Rorschach tests and every other test Wills could find.

It was purely unnatural.

Wills checked himself. Facing his own reaction squarely, he saw it for what it must be—an instinctive but irrational fear, like the fear of the stranger who comes over the hill with a different accent and different table manners. Starling was human; *ergo*, his reactions were natural; *ergo*, either the other experiments had agreed by coincidence and dreaming wasn't indispensable, or Starling's reactions were the same as everyone's and were just being held down until they blew like a boiler straining past its tested pressure.

There were only three more weeks to go, of course.

The habitual shy knock came to the door. Wills grunted for Starling to enter, and wondered as he looked at him how the sight of him passive in bed could inspire thoughts of garlic, sharpened stakes and burial at crossroads.

The fault must be in his own mind, not in Starling's.

The tests were exactly as usual. That wrecked Wills's tentative idea about Starling welcoming the absence of his dreams. If indeed he was liberated from a burden, that should show up in a trend toward a stronger, more assured personality. The microscopic trend he actually detected could be assigned to the fact that for several months Starling had been in this totally undemanding and restful environment.

No help there.

He shoved aside the pile of test papers. "Mr. Starling," he said, "what made you volunteer for these experiments in the first place? I must have asked you before, but I've forgotten."

It was all on the file, but he wanted to check.

"Why, I don't really know, doctor," Starling's mild voice said. Starling's cowlike eyes rested on his face. "I think my sister knew someone who had volunteered, and my brother-in-law is a blood donor and kept saying that everyone should do something to benefit society, and while I didn't like the idea of being bled, because I've never liked injections and things like that, this idea seemed all right, so I said I'd do it. Then, of course, when Dr. Daventry said I was unusual and would I go on with it, I said I hadn't suffered by it and I didn't see why I shouldn't, if it was in the cause of science—"

The voice droned on, adding nothing new. Starling was very little interested in new things. He had never asked Wills the purpose of any test he submitted to; probably he had never asked his own doctor what was on a prescription form filled out for him, being content to regard the medical abbreviations as a kind of talisman. Perhaps he was so used to being snubbed or choked off if he showed too much interest that he felt he was incapable of understanding the pattern of which Wills and the hospital formed part.

He *was* malleable. It was the galling voice of his brother-in-law, sounding off about his uselessness, which pushed him into this. Watching him, Wills realized that the decision to offer himself for the experiment was probably the biggest he had ever taken, comparable in the life of anyone else with a decision to marry, or to go into a monastery. And yet that was wrong, too. Starling didn't take decisions on such a level. Things like that would merely happen to him.

Impulsively, Wills said, "And how about when the experiment is over, Mr. Starling? I suppose it can't go on forever."

Placid, the voice shaped inevitable words. "Well, you know, doctor, I hadn't given that very much thought."

No, it wasn't a liberation to him to be freed of his dreaming. It was nothing to him. Nothing was anything to him. Starling was undead. Starling was neuter in a human scale of values. Starling was the malleable thing that filled the hole available for it, the thing without will of its own which made the best of what there was and did nothing more.

Wills wished he could punish the mind that gave him such thoughts, and asked their source to go from him. But though his physical presence went, his nonexistent existence stayed, and burned and loomed and was impassive and cocked snooks in every hole and corner of Wills's chaotic brain.

Those last three weeks were the worst of all. The silver bullet and the sharpened stake, the crossroads for the burial—Wills chained the images down in his mind, but he ached from the strain of hanging on to the chains. *Horror, horror, horror,* sang an eldritch voice somewhere deep and dark within him. *Not natural,* said another in a professionally judicious tone. He fought the voices and thought of other things.

Daventry said—and was correct according to the principles of the experiment, of course—that so as to have a true control for comparison they must simply disconnect the buzzer attached to the EEG when the time came, and not tell Starling what they had done, and see what happened. He would be free to finish his dreams again. Perhaps they would be more vivid, and he would remember more clearly after such a long interruption. He would—

But Wills listened with only half an ear. They hadn't predicted Starling's reaction when they deprived him of dreams; why should they be able to predict what would happen when he received them back? A chill premonition iced solid in his mind, but he did not mention it to Daventry. What it amounted to was this: whatever Starling's response was, it would be the wrong one.

He told Daventry of his partial breaking of the news that the experiment was to end, and his chief frowned.

"That's a pity, Harry," he said. "Even Starling might put two and two together when he realizes six months have gone by. Never mind. We'll let it run for another few days, shall we? Let him think that he was wrong about the deadline."

He looked at the calendar. "Give him three extra days," he said. "Cut it on the fourth. How's that?"

By coincidence—or not?—Wills's turn for night duty came up again on that day; it came up once in eight days, and the last few times had been absolutely unbearable. He wondered if Daventry had selected the date deliberately. Maybe. What difference did it make?

He said, "Will you be there to see what happens?"

Daventry's face set in a reflex mask of regret. "Unfortunately, no—I'm attending a congress in Italy that week. But I have absolute confidence in you, Harry, you know that. By the way, I'm doing up a paper on Starling for *Journ. Psych.*"—mannerisms, as always: he made it into the single word "jurnsike"—"and I think you should appear as co-author."

Cerberus duly sopped, Daventry went on his way.

That night the duty nurse was Green, a small clever man who knew judo. In a way that was a relief; Wills usually didn't mind Green's company, and had even learned some judo holds from him, useful for restraining but not harming violent patients. Tonight, though . . .

They spoke desultorily together for the first half-hour of the shift, but Wills sometimes lost track of the conversation because

is mind's eye was distracted by a picture of what was going on
a that room along the corridor where Starling held embalmed
ourt among shadows and pilot lights. No one breached his pri-
acy now as he went to bed; he did everything for himself, at-
ached the leads, planted the penny-pads on his eyes, switched on
ae equipment. There was some risk of his discovering that the
uzzer was disconnected, but it had always been set to sound
nly after thirty minutes or more of typical simple sleep-readings.

Starling, though he never did anything to tire himself out,
lways went to sleep quickly. Another proof of his malleable
nind, Wills thought sourly. To get into bed suggested going to
leep, and he slept.

Usually it was three-quarters of an hour before the first at-
empted dream would burgeon in his round skull. For six months
nd a couple of days the buzzer had smashed the first and all that
ollowed; the sleeper had adjusted his position without much dis-
urbing the bedding, and—

But not tonight.

After forty minutes Wills got up, dry-lipped. "I'll be in Staring's room if you want me," he said. "We've turned off his
uzzer, and he's due to start dreaming again—normally." The
vord sounded unconvincing.

Green nodded, picking up a magazine from the table. "On to
omething pretty unusual there, aren't we, doc?" he said.

"God only knows," Wills said, and went out.

His heart was pumping so loudly he felt it might waken the
leepers around him; his footsteps sounded like colossal hammer
lows and his blood roared in his ears. He had to fight a dizzy,
umbling sensation which made the still lines of the corridor—
loor-with-wall a pair of lines, wall-with-ceiling another pair—
wist like a four-strand plait, like the bit of a hand drill or a stick
of candy turned mysteriously and topologically outside-in. Sway-
ng as though drunk, he came to Starling's door and watched his
and go to the handle.

*I refuse the responsibility. I'll refuse to co-author the paper on
him. It's Daventry's fault.*

Nevertheless he acquiesced in opening the door, as he ha
acquiesced all along in the experiment.

He was intellectually aware that he entered soundlessly, but h
imagined himself going like an elephant on broken glass. Every
thing was as usual, except, of course, the buzzer.

He drew a rubber-shod chair to a position from which h
could watch the paper tapes being paid out by the EEG, and sa
down. As yet there were only typical early sleep rhythms—Star
ling had not yet started his first dream of the night. If he waite
till that dream arrived, and saw that all was going well, perhaps i
would lay the phantoms in his mind.

He put his hand in the pocket of his jacket and closed i
around a clove of garlic.

Startled, he drew the garlic out and stared at it. He had n
memory of putting it there. But the last time he was on night dut
and haunted by the undead appearance of Starling as he slept, h
had spent most of the silent hours drawing batwing figures, stab
bing their hearts with the point of his pencil, sketching crossroad
around them, throwing the paper away with the hole pierced i
the center of the sheet.

Oh, God! It was going to be such a relief to be free of thi
obsession!

But at least providing himself with a clove of garlic was a
harmless symptom. He dropped it back in his pocket. He notice
two things at the same time directly afterward. The first was th
alteration in the line on the EEG tapes which indicated the begin
ning of a dream. The second was that he had a very sharp penci
in his pocket, as well as the clove of garlic—

No, not a pencil. He took it out and saw that it was a piece o
rough wood, about eight inches long, pointed at one end. Tha
was all he needed. That, and something to drive it home with. H
fumbled in all his pockets. He was carrying a rubber hammer fo
testing reflexes. Of course, that wouldn't do, but anyway. . .

Chance had opened a gap in Starling's pajama jacket. He
poised the stake carefully over his heart and swung the hammer.

As though the flesh were soft as cheese, the stake sank home
Blood welled up around it like a spring in mud, trickled ove

tarling's chest, began to stain the bed. Starling himself did not waken, but simply went more limp—naturally, for he was un- ead and not asleep. Sweating, Wills let the rubber hammer fall nd wondered at what he had done. Relief filled him as the un- easing stream of blood filled the bed.

The door behind him was ajar. Through it he heard the cat- ight footfalls of Green, and his voice saying urgently, "It's Room 1, doc! I think she's—"

And then Green saw what had been done to Starling.

His eyes wide with amazement, he turned to stare at Wills. Iis mouth worked, but for a while his expression conveyed more han the unshaped words he uttered.

"Doc!" Green said finally, and that was all.

Wills ignored him. He looked down at the undead, seeing the lood as though it were luminous paint in the dim-lit room—on is hands, his coat, the floor, the bed, flooding out now in a iver, pouring from the pens that waggled the traces of a dream n the paper tapes, making his feet squelch stickily in his wet hoes.

"You've wrecked the experiment," Daventry said coldly as he ame in. "After I'd been generous enough to offer you co-author- hip of my paper in *Journ. Psych.*, too! How could you?"

Hot shame flooded into Wills's mind. He would never be able o face Daventry again.

"We must call a policeman," Daventry said with authority. 'Fortunately, he always said he thought he ought to be a blood lonor."

He took up from the floor a gigantic syringe, like a hypoder- nic for a titan, and after dipping the needle into the river of blood auled on the plunger. The red level rose inside the glass.

And *click*.

Through a crack in Wills's benighted skull a fact dropped. Daventry was in Italy. Therefore he couldn't be here. Therefore e wasn't. Therefore—

Wills felt his eyes creak open like old heavy doors on hinges tiff with rust, and found that he was looking down at Starling in he bed. The pens tracing the activity of his brain had reverted to a typical sleep-rhythm. There was no stake. There was no blood

Weak with relief, Wills shuddered at remembered horror. H leaned back in his chair, struggling to understand.

He had told himself that whatever Starling's reaction to bein given back his dreams might be, it would be the wrong one Well, here it was. He couldn't have predicted it. But he coul explain it now—more or less. Though the mechanics of it woul have to wait a while.

If he was right about Starling, a lifetime of frustration an making the best of things had sapped his power of action to th point at which he never even considered tackling an obstacle. H would just meekly try and find a way around it. If there wasn' one—well, there wasn't, and he left it at that.

Having his dreams stopped was an obstacle. The eleven othe volunteers, more aggressive, had developed symptoms which ex pressed their resentment in manifold ways: irritability, rage, in sulting behavior. But not Starling. To Starling it was unthinkabl to express resentment.

Patiently, accustomed to disappointment because that was th constant feature of his life, he had sought a way around the ob stacle. And he had found it. He had learned how to dream wit someone else's mind instead of his own.

Of course, until tonight the buzzer had broken off every drean he attempted, and he had endured that like everything else. Bu tonight there was no buzzer, and he had dreamed *in* and *wit* Wills. The driving of the stake, the blood, the intrusion of Green the appearance of Daventry, were part of a dream to which Will contributed some images and Starling contributed the rest, sucl as the policeman who didn't have time to arrive, and the gian hypodermic. He feared injections.

Wills made up his mind. Daventry wouldn't believe him—no unless he experienced the phenomenon himself—but that was problem for tomorrow. Right now he had had enough, and mor than enough. He was going to reconnect the buzzer and get th hell out of here.

He tried to lift his arm toward the boxes of equipment on th bedside table, and was puzzled to find it heavy and sluggish.

Invisible weights seemed to hang on his wrist. Even when, sweating, he managed to force his hand toward the buzzer, his fingers felt like sausages and would not grip the delicate wire he had to attach to the terminal.

He had fought for what seemed like an eternity, and was crying with frustration, when he finally understood.

The typical pattern of all Starling's dreams centered on failure to achieve what he attempted; he expected his greatest efforts to be disappointed. Hence Wills, his mind somehow linked to Starling's and his consciousness seeming to Starling to be a dream, would never be able to reconnect that buzzer.

Wills let his hands fall limp on his dangling arms. He looked at Starling, naked fear rising in his throat. How much dreaming could a man do in a single night when he had been deprived for six mortal months?

In his pocket were a sharp wooden stake and a hammer. He was going to put an end to Starling's dreaming once for all.

He was still in the chair, weeping without tears, tied by invisible chains, when Starling awoke puzzled in the morning and found him.

Galactic Consumer Report No. 2

I once made a typing error that was so intriguing I had to write a whole story about it. One wonders . . .

AUTOMATIC TWIN-TUBE WISHING MACHINES

(Extract from Good Buy, published by
ConGalFedConAss, issue dated July 2329 ESY)

Introduction

We have received many letters asking what we think of twin-tube wishing machines. Typical is the following:

> I'm overworked and underpaid. Sometimes it seems there are only two choices left to me—the third, suicide, wouldn't help because I can't keep up the payments on suicide insurance.

Either I'll have to have myself twinned so I can moonlight a second job—and I don't know what I could do that would cover the cost of the twinning—or else I'll have to go ten percent deeper into hock and buy a wishing machine. At twenty-five thousand credits or so they aren't cheap, but on the other hand the idea of making everything for ourselves seems wonderful. My wife says yes, get one, because it would be living like our ancestors used to, completely self-sufficient (we have strong pioneer traditions here on New Frontier), but I said no, I guess there may be a catch, let's wait till *Good Buy* covers them.

Not everyone, alas, has that much good sense. Over the past decade scores of news stories have testified to the fate of hasty purchasers who succumbed to wild advertising claims.

Swamped by debt, Ebenezer J. Younghusband of Venables' World boasted to his friends that he'd seen a way out of his difficulties. He mortgaged his grandchildren's earning capacity to buy a wishing machine. He envisaged making and selling uranium-235 on a rising market to recoup his expenditure. Three thousand casualties occurred, mostly fatal, when he allowed ten kilograms to accumulate in the hopper.

Likewise, rendered desperate by the problem of supporting her eleven children, widowed Mrs. Honoria Quonsett of Hysteria sold six of her offspring to an illegal service agency and invested in a wishing machine, thinking she could redeem them when it had stabilized her affairs. The machine she was able to afford was inadequately insulated against feedback from the user's subconscious, and—since she was naturally concerned with her children's fate above all—began to manufacture duplicates of them. The more frantic she grew, the more the machine churned out. As even the finest machine is unable to create a fully functioning human, ninety-five imbeciles are now a charge on the Hysterian government, and Mrs. Quonsett is permanently hospitalized.

So, if you're considering buying a wishing machine, bear three points in mind: the advertisers' claims are exaggerated; extreme care is always necessary in use; and—most important of all—these machines are *machines*, not magic wands!

Background

Immediately Charlie Voluminous MacDiomnaid, a century or so ago, turned "transmutation without radiation" from a vote-catching slogan into a practical reality, all technically advanced planets began to dream of short-circuiting the conventional manufacturing processes and creating articles at need from crude matter and raw energy.

In 2276 the first notable step toward this goal was accomplished accidentally on Cacohymnia, when Abdul Fidler gave up trying to describe the instruments he wanted to play his famous *Catastrophe Suite* and had himself spliced directly into the computer-operated controls of a woodwind factory. Further development led to one of the two essential elements of a modern manufacturing complex: the visualizer tube, which extracts from the mind of the person in charge the characteristics of the desired product.

The necessity for a second controlling element emerged when Fidler discovered that human musicians couldn't play the instruments he had devised. For his *Variations on the Theme of Planetary Collision* he attempted to surpass his earlier achievement and create a superior musician, too. The life form resulting had an enormous brain, incredibly acute hearing, twenty-eight pairs of hands and sufficient mouths to play eleven wind instruments at once.

On seeing it, Fidler let out a cry of joy approximately a sixth of a tone below G flat *in altissimo*, and the creature—so sensitive it could not endure this deviation from perfect pitch—manipulated him until he was screaming exactly on the note. The loss of his talent was a severe blow to galactic music, but his death established the need for the moderator tube, charged with powers of judgment regarding the feasibility and permissibility of the product. Not unexpectedly, the immense range of the human imagination meant that the early installations had to be huge— the pilot version covered about a hectare of ground.

However, though such size confined the process to commercial undertakings, partial success was better than none, and soon factories working on these principles were a common sight on prosperous planets.

The ultimate target—providing private consumers with home appliances that they need only switch on and think into—appeared as remote as ever until the genius of Gordian Bludgeon, a factory hand on Odin, broke the deadlock.

One day, during a five-minute period of random thinking intended to clear his mind for a changeover from family spaceboats to sanitary appliances, he snapped his fingers and started to concentrate on the idea of an automatic twin-tube wishing machine no larger than a robochef.

It is pointless to deny that, like so many unsung geniuses, Bludgeon enjoyed imperfect mental stability; however, it is indisputable that without his brilliant inspiration wishing machines for home use would not yet be available. Though refinements have subsequently been incorporated, every machine we found on sale was a modification of his original version.

(Chief among the refinements, incidentally, is the elimination of a circuit he included because his former girlfriend had just married the factory manager. It is now illegal to describe in print what this was intended to do, but by reading between the lines of the distorted account in Harold Knockermaker's *Bludgeon the Man*, any averagely aggressive male should be able to figure it out.)

Brands Tested

We found a total of seven wishing machines that fitted the strict definition of "twin-tube" (i.e., having both a visualizer and a moderator) and "automatic" (i.e., not requiring the preliminary insertion of ready-made parts). All of them cost in the region of twenty-five thousand credits.

Cheaper models are on offer, but they lack the moderator tube. *They should not be bought under any circumstances*. The fact that Eblis is currently quarantined from the rest of the galaxy and languishing under the most savage dictatorship in history is directly attributable to the purchase by a Mrs. Phobia Luncheon of such a machine. Her five-year-old son, Elgin, in a tantrum over the refusal of an ice-cream soda, started the machine and set it to making nuclear-armed robot soldiers two meters tall, with whose aid he overran the planet and set up a drugstore with a soda fountain a kilometer long. (He is expected to die of malnutrition in about 2335, but it is impossible to estimate how many of Eblis's population will survive him.)

These are the models we tested, and the chief slogans used to advertise them:

Cornucopia: "A Horn of Plenty in the Home"
Midas: "Better than the Golden Touch"
Croesus: "Everything money can or can't buy"
Inexhaustible: "Everyone is on the make!"
Zillionaire: "Beyond the dreams of avarice"
Wizard: "Magical manufacturing"
Domesticated Djinn: "There is no God but Allah; however, the profit is entirely yours"

On inspection, the *Midas* and *Croesus* proved to be identical except for the nameplate affixed to the front of the cabinet. The former costs two hundred credits more than the latter. The makers refused to comment on this.

Appearance and Finish

With the following qualifications the finish of the products was rated "acceptable" by our test panel.

The *Cornucopia* is nearly twice as big as the largest of the others, and the makers recommend that the first use it be put to after purchase is the construction of an extra room to hold it.

The output hopper supplied with the *Midas* and *Croesus* imposes an arbitrary limit on the size of the articles manufactured. Anything larger than approximately two by three meters comes out concertinaed. In the end we sent for one of the range of nonstandard oversize hoppers available at extra charge. (We tried making our own with the machine, but the tolerances were of the

order of two micrometers and the controls were insufficiently
precise.)

The *Domesticated Djinn* is inscribed all over with excerpts
from the Koran and is time-switched to prevent its use when the
owner is supposed to be facing Mecca for prayer. Five periods of
nonavailability per day, each lasting fifteen minutes, may constitute a drawback in the view of non-Moslems.

The *Zillionaire* is smaller than the others in every respect,
including its visualizer cap, which fitted only one of our test
panel (an eight-year-old boy chosen for the vividness of his imagination). We had to substitute the cap from the basically similar
Wizard. The user's chair was rated "very uncomfortable" by the
entire panel, and we had to pack it with foam padding before
anyone could sit through a production cycle.

The *Inexhaustible* posed us several problems. Our attention
had already been caught by the curious advertising copy an-
nouncing it. (Sample: "MOST SPLENDIFEROUS THE NOT
COSTLY WISHING MACHINE. YOU WANT, IT MAKE, NO
MATTER WHATEVER THE DESIRE WITHIN REASONS OF
COARSE!")

The attractive gray cabinet is finished in a manner we had not
previously encountered. When touched, it humps and rubs
against the hand, at the same time secreting a gummy fluid with a
strong smell resembling banana oil. The output (no hopper is
fitted) is on top of the casing and can only be reached by steplad-
der. The controls are on two boards at opposite ends of the housing, which means that unless the user's reach exceeds 3.2 meters
and he has had the foresight to install wall mirrors to reflect the
dials, he has to walk back and forth all the time. This is rendered
difficult by the hard, flat bench, tilted at thirty-five degrees, fitted
in place of a user's chair. Also there is no visualizer cap; twenty-
one separate leads have to be attached to the head with suction
cups, and the handbook advises shaving before use.

Instruction Manuals, etc.

Handbooks are supplied with five of the machines. That for
the *Cornucopia* promises: "No adjustment will be required for at

least one Earth Standard Year." (But see below, *Performance*.
The cheaper *Croesus* has a handbook; the *Midas* does not, which
seems odd. We used the same for both. That for the *Domesticated
Djinn* opens with an invocation: "In the name of Allah, the Merciful, let no harm befall users of this machine!" (Again, see
below.)

The *Zillionaire* has no instructions except a swing-ticket attached to the on-off switch, which reads: "Any fault that develops
in this machine can easily be rectified by having it produce a
replacement part." We should like to repeat the comment of our
eight-year-old, but this publication has to go through the Galactic
mails.

The instructions for the *Wizard* are in 174 languages, an admirable idea. Unfortunately the text in 173 of them (the exception
being High Canal Martian) refers to an earlier model discontinued four years ago.

The manual for the *Inexhaustible* had apparently been produced on the machine by an inexperienced operator. It is a handsome volume of about a hundred pages, of which all but the first
sixteen are blank.

Guarantees

The guarantee for the *Cornucopia* is acceptable, subject to the
deletion (don't forget to thumbprint it in the margin) of the clause
which runs: "The manufacturers will not be held liable for (a) the
products of a diseased imagination; (b) operation of the machine
by a minor; (c) death, disablement, or disfigurement of any user
by his/her productions."

None of the other guarantees is worth the permafilm they are
printed in. The *Domesticated Djinn*'s states, *inter alia*, "Omission of five-times-daily prayer voids this warranty." The *Zillionaire*'s says: "We reserve the right to cancel this or any other
ostensible warranty at our entire discretion." The *Inexhaustible*'s
has at least the virtue of honesty (we think); it runs simply: "We
decline responsibilities, all shapes, all sizes, all colors."

Power Source and Mode of Operation

As stated above, all wishing machines on sale are similar to Bludgeon's original concept. The user sits in a chair (*Inexhaustible*: scrambles back and forth over a sloping bench) and puts on a cap connected to the visualizer (*Inexhaustible*: shaves scalp and attaches twenty-one leads), adjusts manual controls to broad categories of mass, switches on the power and concentrates on visualizing the appearance and performance of a known end product, or the performance of something desired but not hitherto invented. This eventually appears in the output hopper, or not, as the case may be.

The *Midas*, *Croesus* and *Wizard* are fitted with a useful extra: a warning bell on the moderator to indicate if production of the article has been vetoed. With the slower machines, especially the *Zillionaire*, it is sometimes possible to hang around hopefully for an hour or more before realizing that nothing is going to emerge.

The *Cornucopia*, *Midas/Croesus* and *Wizard* draw domestic current on planets where a piped-plasma grid exists; otherwise they require a portable fusion plant. The *Domesticated Djinn* and *Zillionaire* can also be run off solar or other energy sources, but performance on anything but plasma is unsatisfactory. The *Zillionaire*, using solar energy, required six and a half hours of steady concentration to produce a meal for two people, which the hungry tester then immediately devoured.

The *Inexhaustible* is unique in having to be primed with twelve kilograms of technetium (this is apparently what the advertisements mean by "SELF-CONTAINING SAUCE OF POWER–OUTSIDE POWER IS NEEDLESS!!!"). The cost of furnishing this initial load is about seventeen thousand credits; however, an efficient auxiliary circuit keeps the level of fuel constant, using thermal energy from the air of the room, providing sufficient downtime is allowed.

Performance

Theoretically a wishing machine will make almost anything, subject to the veto of the moderating tube. In practice, the latter is by no means consistent, and what you get out depends anyhow on how good you are at concentrating. (It also depends on how good the visualizer tube is at sifting conscious from subconscious mental images.)

It was clearly impossible to attempt a cross section of users' desires. We settled for three groups of tests.

First, we had to establish that everyday requirements could be met. We instructed the testers to make (a) a meal for two people which they personally enjoyed; (b) clothing for themselves, from hat to shoes; (c) an item of household equipment, preferably furniture.

All passed, with the following qualifications:

Food produced on the initial runs of the *Cornucopia* resisted knives, forks and teeth, and its piece of furniture (a table) proved to be of collapsed steel. We had to send for a crane to remove it from the output hopper. Investigation showed that the durability control needed adjustment; it was set to "101 percent." A setting of one produced edible food and twenty-five produced usable furniture in later runs.

Clothing manufactured on the *Midas* was adequately warm and waterproof, but when we sent out a female tester in the garments she had made, to see how well they wore, the next we heard of her she was in jail on a charge of indecent exposure. Hers, and all other female clothing produced by this machine, turned perfectly transparent one hour after putting on. A complaint to the makers produced an apology and a statement to the effect that the factory hand in charge of this batch has been sent for psychotherapy to eliminate his Peeping-Tom syndrome.

All the testers who ate meals prepared by the *Domesticated Djinn* were hospitalized with acute food poisoning.

The *Inexhaustible* needed enormous extra effort before it would produce food uncontaminated with bromine and arsenic and of any other color than purple (though some of our testers found purple steak and potatoes attractive visually, they tasted bad), or clothing less than four centimeters in thickness, devoid of fiberglass scales and with sleeves less than 1.8 meters long.

* * *

Second, we had to establish that it was economical to produce household durables available through more conventional channels. We tried for a threevee set and an air conditioner.

In all cases it was cheaper (sometimes one hundred percent cheaper) to buy commercially. However, the following points should be noted:

The *Cornucopia*, in response to a tester who claimed not to have the faintest notion of how a threevee set works, produced one in working order, superior to any we had ever seen and based on what proved to be a radically new means of receiving broadcast signals. We are working on this and hope shortly to market a commercial version, which may go some way toward making up the anticipated deficit in next year's balance sheet. (See "Message from your Chairman," this issue.)

Sets made by the *Zillionaire* would not receive anything, but merely repeated what the tester was visualizing at the time. We had to fire one tester whose set depicted a positively obscene episode from *Peyton Planet*. And those from the *Domesticated Djinn* would receive only Mecca, Medina, and New Cairo.

The air conditioners mostly worked okay, except for the *Inexhaustible*'s. After a few minutes' operation, the room was full of the reek of chlorine, and inspection showed that a miniature transmuter had been set into the housing, which was busy getting rid of the oxygen in favor of chlorine, bromine, iodine, and inert gases.

Finally we had to determine how safe the machines are. There is no Galactic Standard yet, but an Earthside law lays down that the moderator must prevent the creation of "any noxious or vicious article, object, or creature whatsoever." Cutouts built into the moderator are supposed to enforce this.

In practice, it's clear that definitions vary. Even on the best of the machines, the *Cornucopia*, all testers were able to make infectious bacteria (see *Obituary*, inside back cover). And our eight-year-old, using the *Zillionaire*, was able to make a spanking machine (from which his parents were rescued in a state of extreme exhaustion), a suit of battle armor, his own size, in which to make good his escape, and enough sleepy-gas to blank out the ConGalFedConAss Building while he was leaving.

We will not go into detail on the tests we conducted for adult fantasy, except to point out that on all planets with stringent blue laws importation of the *Domesticated Djinn* is forbidden. It is specifically designed to make mindless but beautiful houris, and two divorces are pending among our panel of testers.

Our performance tests of the *Inexhaustible* were inconclusive. We were tempted to abandon them when we discovered that, although insulation against subconscious feedback leaves something to be desired on all the machines, the insulation on this one tends to filter out conscious images and let subconscious ones go through. (The events which led us to this impression need not be gone into, as the tests were abortive.)

However, we felt we owed it to our members to determine whether the extravagant claim implied in the trade name *Inexhaustible* is true or false. Our change of address, noted on the inside cover, stems largely from our persistence.

We decided to make up a cyclic tape for some article of which any family is likely to consume large quantities, and run it until the machine stopped working. Our first choice was paper handkerchiefs, but the machine's vulnerability to subconscious associations compelled the Greater Greater New York Public Health Authority to step in. (We were glad to learn, just before press time, that the influenza epidemic is officially "under control.")

It was then suggested that the item which a family consumes most is *money*.

This choice had the secondary advantage that the use of a wishing machine to make galactic currency is counterfeiting, and if the machine's moderator permitted an illegal act, we would be compelled to inform our members that it was an offense to buy one.

We regret to announce that on this test the machine performed flawlessly. Our calculations show that the technetium will run out when the pile of bills now covering the site of our former headquarters is about three hundred twenty meters high, unless a strong wind gets up, so the machine is not in fact "inexhaustible," but this is a slim consolation. (Anyone finding wind-blown bills, incidentally, is requested to forward them to the office of our Attorney for the Defense before the first of next month, when the case is due for hearing.)

Value for Credits

The *Cornucopia* performs reasonably well, and its guarantee can be rendered acceptable by one deletion. Although it is capable of considerable improvement, we are bound to name it as our Best Buy.

Not Recommended

We learn from the Superdistrict Attorney's staff that an investigation has been made into the origins of the *Inexhaustible*. It emanates from a space-going factory parked about a thousand parsecs outside the galaxy in the direction of Andromeda. The authorities are proceeding on the assumption that it represents an economic assault by the dominant civilization of M-31. The design of it accords with the known characteristics of that race: they would be very comfortable on the sloping bench provided for the user, they have arms and eyes at both ends of their bodies and are extremely tall, so would be able to operate the divided controls as well as to fish the end product out of the top, and they prefer an atmosphere of chlorine, iodine, neon, and argon.

Do not—repeat, *do not*—buy this machine! Apart from its being capable of an illegal act (counterfeiting), our advice is that it can only be properly controlled by an Andromedan. If you meet anyone who claims to have had no trouble with an *Inexhaustible*, report him at once to the nearest office of the Galactic Bureau of Investigation. He's probably an Andromedan spy.

Tracking With Close-ups
(21) and (23)

*Of all the stories in this book, this may be least like a "story,"
with beginning, middle, end, and characters bumping into each
other. It's also my personal favorite, and perhaps the one that
best demonstrates Brunner's individual brand of intelligence and
originality.*

Excerpted from Stand on Zanzibar.

━━━ ━━━ ━━━ ━━━ ━━━ ━━━ ━━━ ━━━

THE DRY CHILD

Linguistic evaluation suggests the earliest form of the name
"Begi" is transliterable rather as "Mpengi" and in consequence it
is generally rendered "winter-born". The more close rendering
would be "child of dry season". December and January in north-
ern Beninia (where he was supposedly born) are both least humid
months of every year.

It has been suggested the name was originally "Kpegi" (i.e. "foreigner") but this would not give rise to the "Mpengi" form mentioned above. In any case Shinka superstition has it that a child conceived at the breaking of the maximum summer rains (hence born in midwinter) is likely to be livelier than average. Attempts to show that Begi was in fact a solar myth originating in latitudes where seasons are marked enough to foster concepts of death and rebirth of the sun are tantalizing, but fruitless in the absence of any other than oral evidence, though it is highly possible that prehistoric cross-cultural interaction provided some elements of the Begi myth which has descended to us. On the other hand . . .[1]

BEGI AND HIS GREEDY SISTER

One day Begi was lying on the floor near a basket of fried chicken his mother had made for a festival. His sister thought Begi was asleep and took the largest chicken-leg and hid it under the roof.

When the family gathered to eat Begi refused what he was offered from the basket. He said, "There is a bigger bird roosting under the roof."

"You're silly," said his mother, but his sister knew what he meant.

He climbed up and got the chicken-leg and ate it.

"You stole it and put it there," his sister accused. "You wanted to have the biggest piece."

"No," Begi said, "I dreamed that wanting to have the biggest piece was the best way to get the smallest."

And he gave her the gnawed bone.[2]

[1]Preamble to doctorate thesis submitted by Mrs. Kitty Gbe of Port Mey, Beninia: Univ. of Ghana, Legon, Accra, 1989 (xii + 91 pp., 3 illus., map).
[2]*Op. cit.* p.4.

BEGI AND THE FOREIGN MERCHANT

Once Begi went to the big market in Lalendi. There he saw a merchant from another tribe. The man was selling pots he claimed were made of gold, but Begi went behind him and took a knife and tried to cut the metal. It would not cut like soft gold although it was shiny and yellow.

So Begi picked up the biggest pot and pissed on the ground underneath and put it back.

Then he went around to the front and there were many people wanting to buy those gold pots which Begi knew were only made of brass.

Begi said, "That is a fine big pot there. I need a pot like that to piss in at night."

And everybody laughed, thinking he was a fool to put that liquid in a pot fit to hold the chief's finest palm-wine.

"Piss in it and show me if it leaks," Begi said. The merchant laughed with everyone else and did so, saying what a shame it was to defile such a valuable pot with urine.

Begi lifted it up when the merchant had finished and the ground underneath was wet with piss. He said, "I will not buy a pot no matter how fine it looks if it leaks when you piss in it."

So all the people beat the merchant and made him give their money back.[3]

BEGI AND THE SEA-MONSTER

After he had left the house of the fat old woman, Begi walked along the trail through the forest whistling the tune he had learned from her and plucking the five wooden tongues of the *kethalazi*

[3]*Ibid.* p. 18.

—what the British nicknamed the "pocket piano" when they came much later to Begi's part of the world.

A little bird heard him and fluttered down to the side of the trail, eager to listen to this fine new tune but a little afraid because Begi was a man.

Seeing how timid the bird was, Begi stopped on the path and sat down. He said, "Do not be afraid, little cousin. Do you want to learn my song? I will teach it to you if you will teach me one of yours."

"That's a good bargain," said the bird. "But I can't help being afraid of you. You're as much bigger than I am as the monster from the sea is bigger than man-people."

"Certainly you're smaller than I am," Begi said. "But your voice is far sweeter than mine. I have heard you make the whole forest echo with your melody. By the bye, though," he added, "what is this monster you just mentioned?"

The bird told him that at a village near the sea, a day's walk distant, a huge monster had come out of the water and caught two children and eaten them, and everyone had run away to hide in the bush.

"I am bigger than you are," Begi said. "But I can't sing better than you. Perhaps the monster is bigger than I am. It remains to be seen if he can think better than I do. I shall go there and find out."

The bird said, "If you are not afraid of the monster I will try not to be afraid of you." He perched on Begi's head and dug his toes into the woolly hair there.

So Begi walked all day carrying the bird and teaching him to sing the old woman's song. After many hours' journey he came to the village where everyone had run away from the monster.

"Little cousin!" he said. "What is that I see on the horizon, where the dark blue water meets the light blue sky?"

The bird flew out over the sea to find out. When he came back, he said, "There is a storm coming. There are clouds and lightning."

"Very good," said Begi, and went to look for the monster.

There he was lying in the market square, as much bigger than

Begi as Begi was bigger than the little bird, and the bird had all he could do not to fly off in terror. But he clung to Begi's hair with all his might.

The monster roared at Begi, "Hey there, weakling! You come at the right time! I have finished digesting the children I had for breakfast and I'll have you for my supper!"

"I'm hungry too," said Begi. "I haven't eaten today."

"There's something to eat sitting on your head," the monster exclaimed. "You'd better make the most of it before I gobble you up!"

Privately to the bird, Begi whispered, "There's no need to be afraid. I would rather hear you sing than make a meal of you. But I don't believe this monster cares about music."

Addressing the monster more loudly, he went on, "No! I'm saving this bird for the time when I'm so weak I cannot go and hunt for food."

The monster laughed. "If I eat you, when will the day come which finds you so hungry you must eat your pet?"

"I don't know," answered Begi. "Any more than you know when the day will come when the giant whose back you ride on will need to eat you."

"I don't ride on anybody's back," declared the monster.

"In that case," said Begi, "whose are the jaws I see closing on you? Whose is the voice I hear making the welkin ring?" He raised his blunt spear and pointed.

The monster looked out to sea and saw the black clouds looming down on the village and the waves rippling like the tongue of a hungry beast licking its chops and heard the sound of thunder like the grumbling of hunger.

"There is the giant whose back you have been riding on," said Begi. "It's called the sea. We men are like fleas compared to it, so we are usually safe—we would not even make a mouthful for such a colossus. Even so, sometimes it hurts us when we annoy it and it scratches. But you are as much bigger than I am as I am bigger than this bird on my head. And by the sound of it the sea is *very* hungry."

The monster saw the flash of lightning like the gleam of white fangs in the mouth of the ocean, and he jumped up howling and ran away. He was never heard of again.

When the people came back to the village from where they had been hiding in the bush, they asked Begi, "Are you not a mighty warrior, to have driven away that horrible monster?"

So Begi showed them his blunt spear and the shield with a hole in it which he always carried, and they said, "What does this mean?"

"It means," he explained, "that you cannot use a spear to kill a flea which is biting you, and a shield is no use against a monster that could gobble you up shield and all. There is only one way to win against both a flea and a monster: you must think better than either of them."[4]

BEGI AND THE GHOST

Once the people were much troubled by a *tlele-ki* (ancestral spirit) which terrified the women going to fetch water and made the children have bad dreams.

Begi's father the chief called together the *kotlanga* (council of adults), and Ethlezi (lit. "sorcerer, medicine-man") told him, "It is the spirit of your father, Begi's grandfather."

The chief was very upset. He asked Begi, "What can grandfather want with us?"

Begi said, "There is only one way to find out what a ghost wants. We will go and ask him. Or if you won't, I will by myself."

So he learned from Ethlezi the right way to speak politely to a ghost and went out at night to the dark lonely place where it had been seen. He said, "Grandfather, I have brought you palm-wine and goat's blood. Eat if you will but talk to me."

[4]From "Tales of Our African Brethren: Folklore of Beninia and the Gold Coast" by The Rev. Jerome Coulter, DD: London 1911 (vi + 347 pp., col. frontis., 112 line drgs. in text).

The ghost came and drank the wine and took the blood to make itself strong. It said, "Begi, here I am."

"What do you want with us?" Begi asked.

"I keep watch on the village. I see that everything is going badly. The lawsuits are not judged as I would have judged them. Young people are disrespectful to their elders. The girls go with boys they do not intend to marry. There is too much food so that people grow fat and lazy and there is so much palm-wine that they get drunk and sleep when they should be hunting."

"My father the new chief judges lawsuits differently because he is dealing with different people," Begi said. "The young people learned how to talk to their elders from their parents, who were taught by you. The girls choose their own husbands now and when they marry they are happier than their mothers. As for being lazy and sleeping, why not, when we know that spirits like you keep watch over the village?"

The ghost had no answer to that and it went away.[5]

BEGI AND THE WICKED SORCERER

Begi came to a village where everybody was afraid of a sorcerer called Tgu. He could make cows and women miscarry, he could set huts on fire without going near, he could make witch-dolls and if he stabbed with his special knife the footprint someone left in a muddy path the person would fall sick or die.

Begi said to Tgu, "I want you to help me kill a man whose name I cannot tell you."

The sorcerer said, "Pay me. But you must bring something of his—a hair or a scrap of nail or some of the clothes he has worn."

"I will bring you something of his," said Begi. He went away

[5]From "Begi, an African 'Jack the Giant Killer'" by Roger F. Woodsman in *Anthropological Communications*, vol. XII, no. 3.

and came back with some excrement. Also he gave the sorcerer a mirror and some valuable herbs he had gathered.

The sorcerer made a witch-doll and roasted it at the fire singing powerful magical chants. When it was dawn the people of the village came to see because they were afraid to come at night, the magic was so strong.

"The man will die," said the sorcerer.

"Now I can tell you his name," said Begi. "It is Tgu."

The sorcerer fell on the ground in a fit, shrieking that he had been tricked. He said he was sure to die at once.

Begi took the chief of the village apart and said, "Wait one more hour. Then you can tell him the excrement belonged to a friend of mine called Tgu in another village. I am going away to laugh with my friend at the foolishness of the sorcerer."[6]

BEGI AND THE STEAMSHIP

(Author's note: this must be a very late accretal to the mythos.)

Begi went to the seaside and there he saw a big ship with smoke coming out. A white man from the ship met him on the shore and talked with him.

Begi said, "Welcome. Be my guest while you are here."

The white man said, "That is a foolish offer. I am coming to live here."

Begi said, "Then I will help you build your hut."

The white man said, "I will not live in a hut. I will live in a house of iron with smoke coming out of the top and be very rich."

Begi said, "Why do you wish to come here?"

The white man said, "I am going to rule over you."

[6]Gbe, *op. cit.* p. 80.

Begi said, "Is it better living here than where you come from?"

The white man said, "It is too hot, it rains, it is muddy, I do not like the food and there are none of my own women."

Begi said, "But if you want to come and live here it must be better in some respect. If you don't like the weather, the food or the women, then you must think it is better governed than your own country, and my father the chief rules us."

The white man said, "I am going to rule you."

Begi said, "If you have left your own home you must have been sent away. How can a man who has been sent from home into exile rule better than my father the chief?"

The white man said, "I have a big steamship with many strong guns."

Begi said, "Let me see you make another."

The white man said, "I cannot."

Begi said, "I see the way of it. You are good at using what other people have made and nothing else." (*Author's note: it is an insult in Shinka to say that a man cannot make anything, as a self-respecting adult is expected to build his own house and carve his own furniture.*)

But the white man was too stupid to see Begi's point and he came and lived here anyway.

However, after a hundred years he learned better and went home.[7]

BEGI AND THE ORACLE

Begi came to a village where the people believed in omens, signs and portents. He asked them, "What is this about?"

They said, "We pay that old wise woman and she tells us what

---

[7]Woodsman, *loc. cit.*

day is best to hunt, or court a wife, or build a new house, or bury the dead so that ghosts will not walk."

Begi said, "How does she do that?"

They said, "She is very old and very wise and she must be right because she has become very rich."

So Begi went to the house of the wise woman and said, "I shall go hunting tomorrow. Tell me if it will be a good day."

The woman said, "Promise to pay me half of anything you bring home." Begi promised, and she took bones and threw them to the ground. Also she made a little fire with feathers and herbs.

"Tomorrow will be a good day for hunting," she said.

So next day Begi went into the bush taking his spear and shield and also some meat and a gourd of palm-wine and rice boiled and folded in a leaf and wearing his best leopard-skin around him. At night he came back naked without anything at all and went into the wise woman's house.

He broke a spear on the wall and with the head he cut in half a shield that was there and gave away half the meat she had and half the rice she had to the other people and poured out on the ground half her pot of palm-wine.

The old woman said, "That is mine! What are you doing?"

"I am giving you half of what I brought back from my hunting," said Begi.

Then he tore off half the old woman's cloak and put it on and went away.

After that the people made up their own minds and did not have to pay the old woman anything.

X-HERO

This little gem is a literary rarity: a science-fiction "short-short" story that really works. Some sad examples are written in ignorance of the fact that the short-short is not just a short story with something left out; it's a completely different form. Most of the ones you read are silly jokes or thin vignettes. This one is completely satisfying in a literary way and also supplies the pleasant shock of sense of wonder.

━━ ━━ ━━ ━━ ━━ ━━ ━━

By September I had had all I could stand of the *touristiké* atmosphere in Athens and Glyphada. My head was ringing like a phone bell with the trite stridencies of commercial bouzouki music. I was sick of Fix beer from American iceboxes and Chevrolet taxis with frilled curtains and plastic flowers in the back windows. In the bare-bone heat of the summer, with the smell of dust driving down the scent of the sea, I wanted something plain. No frills. No plastic flowers.

Armed with enough of the language to buy a meal and to book a room, I headed south into the Peloponnese, keeping off the good roads patronized by the German campers, looking for something that was neither pre-packaged modern nor jacked up on a classical pedestal. I found rugged paths between gray-green fields in which white stones, sun-bleached, were piled into cairns. Tired sheep and goats harried by dogs whose coats were full of botflies looked at me incuriously, and sometimes the shepherd had energy to spare for a gruff *"Kaliméra!"*

On the tenth night I came to the village of Sophkada. Those same stones piled cairnwise in the sparse fields had been piled to form the village. One rubble-paved street ran steeply down its spine. One graveled square was fronted by the village's only taverna and the homes of those who passed for rich in the community. The chapel-like church was recently painted white, and so were the wayside shrines I passed on the road. A bent old woman in black—all the women wear black after a certain age—was tending the oil lamp in one of the shrines, but she would not answer when I spoke to her. I also saw the *papa*, the village priest, from a distance, his full beard blending into his robe, but he ignored me.

The first to greet me was the proprietor of the taverna, where I requested a room and food. As soon as I sat down, he served me sticky loukoumi and a glass of good water—a sure sign that there were few visitors in Sophkada, for good water is served to house-guests, not tourists. Then he sent a small boy scurrying off through the village. He later explained to me he had gone in search of the woman who owned the single store so that a loan might be arranged and some food brought to me. Eventually I had raw garlic, good bread, and a can of Fray Bentos corned beef for my meal. And ouzo beforehand, and considerable retsina during, and more after, which I was to regret.

The Greeks, civilized people, generally consider drinking without eating a barbarian custom; so when you order ouzo, you receive at least a token snack, even if, as in Sophkada, it is nothing but chunks of feta (goat cheese—hard, white, and pungent). But, as I might have predicted, there were men who came down to see and talk to me who broke the habit because it was not mine and because I was the guest.

Wherever you go in that country and let slip a few words of English, sooner or later a man will come and say, "I speak English." Often it is a portly man, as full of dignity as a statue in the Acropolis museum, dark-suited and heavy-hatted even in the blaze of August, who ran a tailoring business in the Bronx or a restaurant in Chicago—thinking, thinking all the time, for forty or sixty years, of a village like Sophkada: dry-white stone, dry-fawn dust, dry-gray grass. The pile made, the years spent, he came home to die in the same house where he was born, or in another across the street, as if the entire world beyond were a dream and he had reawakened to the unique reality: one small village missing from the maps.

Sometimes it is another reason that bestows knowledge of English—war. In Sophkada there were bullet scars on the sides of the church, and an olive tree not far from the taverna leaned as if it were resting against a wall, its roots shifted by a mortar shell. War shifted the men of the village, too. They were sailors, paratroopers, guerrillas—and they thought of Sophkada while they were away. When it was over, they came home to their own real world.

Oh, this is not uncommon. Other small towns of the world are like this: in midwestern America, Yorkshire coalfields, peasant Greece, the reality of the town's remoteness grips men and pulls them back. Only the alien language seems to revive the dream. You see it in the drinking, when they forget to temper the retsina with food because that custom is local and their minds are elsewhere.

In any one village there are seldom two men who served side by side in World War II. There have been other wars since then —civil wars—but one prefers not to talk about them. The scarred church or the tilted olive tree says as much as anyone cares to hear. In a sense, the men do not even discuss the big war, its causes or its purpose. In a village like Sophkada it is a natural phenomenon, to be accepted like a drought, its origin inconceivable to the mind, its effects definably evil but endurable.

No, the talk is of the larger world, of the dream, because a visitor is a reminder.

In Sophkada that night there were no fewer than three who spoke fair to excellent English, constituting themselves a *syndicat d'initiative* and taking me in charge under an oil lamp amid cricket-loud darkness. Spiro came first—squat, mahogany tanned, graying at fifty-plus. He had served with the Royal Navy in the Mediterranean, performing some kind of commando duty.

Next was Gheorghios—exceptionally tall, with a dark and sullen face, who spoke better English than either Spiro or the third one, Nico. I realized this when Gheorghios shook hands and uttered a soft greeting, but later he said almost nothing during the three hours we spent around the table. He only sat, nodding occasionally and studying me with a frown.

This disturbed me. I paid as little attention to him as I politely could.

Fortunately, Nico helped by nearly monopolizing the conversation. He had learned English on Cyprus, where he had been one of Gheorghios Grivas's key EOKA saboteurs. By my guess, he was the only one of these three travelers who still boasted about his exploits to his friends. At any rate, though I found his excited relation of anecdotes amusing, all of them turning on the stupidity of the British and the native genius of the Greek spirit, I noticed Spiro was bored and presumed that the silent Gheorghios was, as well.

We talked anyway. We drank, and I managed to pay for a fresh carafe about three times. The rest of the time they insisted on buying, which was absurd, but it was no use arguing. Gheorghios drank the least of the four of us and sat a little apart, his long legs vanishing into shadow, and he hardly took his eyes off me.

Later, Nico and Spiro left and the proprietor of the taverna went into his bar to sit behind its counter and moodily contemplate a bulbous girl in lurid colors on an old calendar. I was very full by then. I didn't know it until I tried to get up and go to bed; then the retsina and the day's trudge combined, knocking me back into my chair as if a heavy hand had been laid on my shoulder.

That was when Gheorghios spoke. He sounded relieved.

"Got it," he said.

I looked at him.

"Got it," he repeated. "Who you remind me of. Tiger Bear Molgun." He pulled himself up on his chair, from which he had been about to slide completely, and leaned a tanned elbow on the table between us. His English was as fluent and well accented as my own.

"I made you pretty uncomfortable," he added with a chuckle. "Staring at you all evening the way I did. Sorry! I just could *not* place the likeness."

He closed his long-fingered hand around his glass of wine, drained the glass, and sighed as he set it down.

"Who is this character I remind you of?" I asked. My mind wasn't really on the question. I was wondering whether I could make it to the primitive outside toilet of the taverna before the load I'd taken on, together with my tiredness and the sun, finished me off.

"Is?" Gheorghios stretched and yawned. "Was, I'm afraid. He was the fourth officer—drive maintenance—on the *Betelgeuse*. Got his from the same hellbomb that pushed me over the gamma limit and put me out of service. So I never did square accounts with the Veenies." Another yawn ended the sentence, and he grinned a little shyly, like a nice boy not knowing quite how to phrase an apology for gaping that way.

"Well, it's late," he concluded, standing up. "Nice to have met you, pal." He offered his hand.

I did not move to take it. I said, as carefully as my state would allow, "What . . . did you say?"

"Oh, you've had your ear bent enough for tonight," he answered, "what with Nico flying the same orbit all the time. It gets to be too much."

Not even trying to conceal his eagerness to close up, the proprietor came out to collect the glasses and carafes from the table.

Gheorghios bade him good-night and lingered only because he had just realized how drunk I was. I had forgotten.

"What were you, then?" I demanded, wishing to God the world wouldn't rock and twist around me.

"Me? Oh, just a missile hand. I never even put up a stripe before I got radiated. Funny, you know!" He laughed abruptly. "We had a man on our deck just like Nico, always playing back the same message. We fixed him good in the end, shut him in an empty lock by accident done on purpose, and fed a looped tape of himself running at the mouth nonstop into his helmet phones. He was awfully quiet after that. Don't want to risk it happening to me."

He grinned again and strode off into the night. I turned frantically to the proprietor, trying to make him understand that I wanted to talk to Gheorghios some more or at least to know where I could find him in the morning. But my Greek would not stretch that far, and the proprietor knew no English at all.

I traced him the next day. People pointed him out to me, a lean and distant figure outlined against the unbearable blue sky who was scrambling over a rocky hill in pursuit of a limping goat. He was singing at the top of his voice—a magnificent, wailing tenor with long, controlled, Balkan shaking on the held notes.

I thought I was going to wait for him to come down. I thought I was going to pester him with questions, but I didn't. I found myself on the road leading from Sophkada, not even looking to see whether he was still in sight.

Last night he had thought back to a dream, like Spiro and Nico and a score of others I had met in this time-forgotten country. He had spoken the language of a dream. Now he had wakened to reality again.

I was not sure that I had. But I wasn't going to stay to find out.

No Future In It

This is a lark of a story, a tongue-in-cheek medieval period piece with a "Connecticut Yankee" kind of twist. And a horrible joke at the end.

———————————

Nothing.

Alfieri waited optimistically for quite fifteen seconds, his hopes dwindling away. Then he took his second-best wand (the ivory and ebony one) and beat his apprentice. Not that the failure could by any stretch of the imagination be attributed to young Monasticus, but he needed *some* means of working off his annoyance.

At intervals between blows and the cries of the youngster he looked around at the pentacle in case there should be a residual effect, but the space between the smoking lamps remained obstinately empty. At last he let the apprentice wriggle free.

"Impurities in the bats' blood, I'll be bound," he growled. He noticed that Monasticus was not snivelling as wholeheartedly as he should have been, and the cloud of gloom which had been hovering over him suddenly turned the purple color of a thunderstorm. He did not suspect the boy of fiddling with his ingredients —frankly, he had too low an opinion of his intelligence, though it would have been balm to his wounded ego if he had been able to accept that as an explanation. It was sorely distressing that a man with the best reputation for wizardry in half a country should not be able to conjure up so much as a small fire-demon.

And if this run of failures continued, he would have to answer to Monasticus Senior himself. At the very best, he could expect ducking and running out of town. At the worst—

Alfieri's blood ran cold and he hastily changed his mental subject. If he could get the boy away somehow, he could experiment without anyone knowing he was only trying . . .

The obvious solution presented itself. It had a double advantage: he could palm off some of the blame on to old Gargreen at the same time. He stormed across the room in a first-class rage (this to cow young Monasticus, who was not only coming to place a most un-apprentice-like lack of faith in his mentor, but whom Alfieri shrewdly suspected of reporting all these failures to his father) and seized a quill from the rack. As an afterthought, he charged it with owls' blood. That'd show he meant business! The more window-dressing and atmosphere, the better; he would be completely ruined if anyone should suspect he was perfectly aware no blame resided in the ingredients he was using—only in himself.

"To Master Gargreen, self-named purveyor of magical necessaries," (he began).

". . . I am forced to indicate to thee after the above fashion, sin' it be by thine own styling of such a purveyor that men miscall thee. Be it known, natheless, that never have I, Alfieri, sometime student of the University of Alcala, found so much fault with any man's wares.

"As thou hadst the temerity to say, were I not pleased with thy provisions, thou wouldst reimburse to me the sum I thereon expended, do thou therefore return to me the silver groat I gave thee for thy vial of bats' blood. Fail me in this, and I shall make of thee a horned and warty toad."

"ALFIERI"

"Monasticus!" he added aloud, folding the parchment into four and sealing it with black wax stamped with his Seal of Suleiman. "Get thee to Master Gargreen and convey him my epistle with no compliments. Wait there until he doth refund to thee my silver groat. And get thee back hither with all speed, else shall I beat thee again. Out!"

Monasticus took the letter and departed hastily. As soon as the door slammed, Alfieri dropped into the nearest chair and drew a deep breath. How did he come to get himself into a fix like this? Now he was going to have to be hard on old Gargreen, which was the last thing he wanted—he was a nice fellow, really, as nice as anyone could be expected to be whose life's work consisted of being out at unlikely hours of the night gathering fennel or snaring bats in the dark of the moon, or sneaking into the church to obtain dust from a corpse.

His mind went back to the day when he had first come to this town. Then, he had been no more than a happy, healthy cow doctor. In fact, his bundles of cow-herbs were still in the old leather knapsack on the wall yonder. He regarded it with fond eyes. The herbs, at least, worked, as he had found by trial and error.

Yet, in a sense, they had brought about his downfall. Belphegor take the day that he had come hither and cured Mistress Walker's only heifer of the croup! If it hadn't been for that interfering old bag, he might never have been forced into wizardry.

How clear it all was, now that he looked back on it! And how foolish it had all appeared at the time. First of all, Mistress Walker had gone around the town telling anyone who cared to listen that he had lifted a spell from the sick beast, and since the town already had its standard complement of one witch—old Mistress Comfrey—it had been taken by everybody except Alfieri as a challenge to combat.

What a fight! He hadn't done a single blessed—or for that matter a single damned—thing. Mistress Comfrey had heard the rumors and vowed her intention of destroying the intruder. Since no one had thought to tell Alfieri he was being spelled, none of her maledictions had the slightest effect. And on top of that, the old hag had caught the whooping cough and died of it.

His reputation was made after that, naturally. It wasn't every town that had a killing-power wizard for a resident, though the countryside was stiff with second-rate witches capable of turning milk sour or drying up a stream come summertime. Of course, the local churchmen had at once thundered against him, and if he had known what was in store, he would cheerfully have let himself be run out of town—public opinion was against having him burnt at the stake. Too many people had had a grudge against Mistress Comfrey.

A thought struck him. If only he had happened to chance on the witch standing out naked on the crossroads at midnight working her spells, he could have carried her off to her warm bed and spared her her last illness.

But then, of course, old Monasticus had taken him under his wing, and that was his undoing. It had seemed like a very sound policy at the time when the vicar was after him. Not only was Monasticus the richest merchant in ten counties: it was whispered that he had got his name from being the illegitimate son of a priest, and it was also said that he himself was a dabbler in black arts. You don't go around offending a man like that. Alfieri had spun the tale that he was a successful practitioner of magic, and Monasticus, knowing when he was on to a good thing, had set him up in business—had even gone so far as to make his own son his apprentice. Alfieri had a shrewd suspicion that the object of this was to keep the business in the family, so to speak, and that the pupil was to displace the master when he was proficient enough.

Alfieri cursed his lying tongue roundly, calling on names which, if the books were to be trusted, ought to have made the entire town vanish in a clap of thunder. They did nothing of the kind. Books! He had no faith in them any more. He had managed to talk the old man into buying him a complete library of thaumaturgy, giving the excuse that he had formerly had a false apprentice who conjured up a fire-demon when he was out and let it get out of hand. But the books, though they gave plenty of recipes, didn't provide any that worked!

He glanced along the shelf. Simon Magus—ugh! Michael Psellus—phooey! Hermes Trismegistus—nuts!

Liars, the lot of them.

And yet—well, maybe he'd been living up to his own imaginary qualifications for so long that he was even coming to believe them himself, but damn it, there must be *some* truth in the matter! Hadn't there been that character over in Wuerttemberg—Foster? Faustus—that was it. He'd been pretty successful to all accounts. Wine out of tables, and that sort of thing. But on the other hand he'd been a genuine wizard; he'd probably been in the business a long time before he got results. He wasn't just an itinerant cowhealer, with no assets but a sharp tongue and a lot of luck, most of it bad.

Well, might as well go through it again for practice, he supposed. He certainly needed plenty of that! After all, even if Gargreen had tried to swindle him on the bats' blood—which was entirely possible, what with him having supplied so many genuine wizards—he had made rather a boss shot at that name Eleusthis in the last spell.

Eleusthis. *Eleusthis.* He thought he had it right. Maybe if he articulated carefully he would get it out this time.

He took down his best wand (the gold one with silver ends) and positioned himself carefully at the side of the pentagram. With frequent glances at a book open beside him, he recharged the lamps, burnt another red cock-feather, scattered some more dried herbs on his brazier, and began:

"In nomine Belphegoris, conjuro te—"

There was a sudden spurt of light in the middle of the pentacle, and a figure appeared and looked around with astonishment.

Weakly, Alfieri reached out for support, found a table near to hand and leaned heavily against it. This was all wrong! He hadn't even reached the part about Eleusthis yet. But nonetheless—he peered with narrowed eyes through the murk—he had got something. And if it wasn't what he had been expecting, it was at any rate a genuine, twenty-four carat, unmistakable demon. It couldn't be anything else!

He said challengingly, feigning more confidence than he felt, "Aroint thee, demon! I charge thee to do my will!"

The flow of words which this called forth from the demon was completely unintelligible, and Alfieri's heart sank. If he had the bad luck to call up one of those Arabian things Al-Hazred mentioned—a djinnee—he would get no change out of this. His Latin was bad, but his Arabic was appalling.

He tried again, tentatively. "Who art thou?" he demanded. "Make thyself known."

The fitful light of the lamps made it hard for him to see exactly what this demon looked like, but by dint of concentration he made out that it was roughly the size of a man—a little on the tall side, perhaps—and had no tail, no horns, not even flames coming out of its mouth. This was a strictly second-rate manifestation. His first success seemed momently more and more like a failure. And the worst thing about it was, he was alone, with no witnesses to his triumph.

But nonetheless there was something definitely inhuman about this apparition. He spoke for a third time, with determination. "In nomine Belphegoris, Adonis, Osiris, Lamachthani—"

His voice tailed away, and he was suddenly filled with a mixture of delight and terror. The demon had reached out his hand, produced fire from his fingertips, applied it to something he held in his mouth, and was breathing smoke! Alfieri let out a strangled gasp and clung more tightly to the edge of the table.

Abruptly, after gazing slowly around the room, the demon seemed to come to a decision. He spoke aloud, in a rolling voice that echoed from all four walls. His accent was odd, but maybe he came from a department of the nether regions not concerned with modern English-speaking people. He said, "What an amazing thing to happen! He's got the set-up almost perfectly. Five sources of infra-red—I suppose the molar vibrations are supplied by intoning a spell. Maybe this is the origin of the legends of ghosts and devils. Hey, you!"

Alfieri nearly jumped through the roof. "Y-yes?" he quavered.

"Are you a wizard, or a warlock, or something?"

"I'm a wizard," said Alfieri, grabbing tight hold of the remnants of his courage. In the hope of making the demon a little more impressed, he added, "I'm a former student of the University of Alcala, and I command thee to serve me."

The demon disregarded the last part of his remarks, and went on surveying the room. "What an absolutely perfect set-up," he repeated musingly. "I wonder if I've had the luck to meet one of the real big-timers. Are you Faustus, by any chance?" he demanded.

"Nay," admitted Alfieri. He gave his name.

"Never heard of you," said the demon, with a gesture of dismissal. "My name's Al Sneed, by the way."

Alfieri felt the situation getting more and more out of control. He seized on the one comprehensible admission the other had yet made. He ventured, "Art from Araby, Al-Snid?"

"Too low a culture level to accept the idea of time-travel," diagnosed Sneed. "No, I'm from London. Look, we aren't going to get anywhere talking like this. I'd love to stay and have a chat, but I have a date to watch Julius Caesar land in Britain in 55 B.C., and elapsed time is catching up on me. Excuse me." He did something to a gadget hung at his waist, and Alfieri, who had been having some difficulty in following Sneed's remarks, but who had gathered that he was on the point of losing his first incontrovertible demon, grabbed his book of spells and began again with, "Conjuro te—"

The demon looked up. "All right," he said disgustedly. "I might have known it. Coincidence or not, you've got an absolutely unbreakable temporal barrier here. I can't go forward or backward until you blow out the lamps. Do that, will you?"

"Never!" said Alfieri triumphantly. "Thou'rt the first honest demon I've yet conjured, and before I let thee go, needs must I display thee to my patron in earnest of my ability—else will he have me dismembered and burnt."

Sneed caught the note of desperation in his voice. He said, "Well, I guess someone else can check up on old Julius. He's waited twenty-one hundred years for me, if you look at it that way. You sound as if you're in a spot of trouble yourself."

"In very sooth," admitted Alfieri. And then, before he realized, he was telling the whole story of how he became a wizard in spite of himself.

Sneed heard him out with a sympathetic expression. He cluck-clucked at the end of the story. "Now let me see if I've got this right," he said. "You've managed to lie yourself into a spot where everyone thinks you're a wizard and can conjure up demons and make gold and like that. You—"

"Verily can I conjure demons," asserted Alfieri, remembering. "Has thou not been ensnared by me?"

Sneed looked at his elapsed time meter again with a frown. "Yes, you have caught me, haven't you?" he admitted. "Still— even though I'm not a demon, I don't want to live out my life trying to explain the fourth dimension and temporal mass-exchange. Might cause ructions in the time-line even if I did manage to get it across, at that. All I'm interested in is getting out of here. Can we do a deal?"

"Huh?" Alfieri was becoming more and more convinced that one success doesn't make a thaumaturge.

"I mean," said Sneed with great patience, "is there anything you want which I can give you to let me go?"

Alfieri caught on slowly, but when he had the idea he didn't let it go. He said, "Thou hast powers? Thou canst fulfill my wishes?"

"Mmm." Sneed considered. "Let's say yes, within limits. I can grant one or two minor wishes. I can't change history too much, but I can get by with a minor alteration. As I see it, old Monasticus—the bod who got you up your tree in the first place —is in this strictly on a cash basis. He wants a quick return. Profit!"

"Thou speakest sooth," sighed Alfieri.

Sneed took out a notebook and pencil, and trod his cigarette underfoot. "Have you a table I can do some figuring on?" he asked.

"Leave not thy pentacle!" said Alfieri, suddenly remembering stories of the sad fate of wizards who had made that mistake.

"I'm insulated," said Sneed cheerfully. "The temporal static can't go away to ground." He walked over the chalk lines and set his notepad down on the table beside Alfieri, who shut his eyes and waited for the house to disappear. When he had decided this would not happen, he opened them again by stages. They did not stop at their usual size—they kept on getting rounder and rounder till it seemed they would leave their sockets. Sneed was working out a complicated equation with the aid of a slide-rule and a pocket map of three thousand years of history.

Eventually he turned in triumph. "Would three and a quarter kilograms of gold be any use to you?" he asked. "I can give you that much without causing more than a Stage Sub-Three disturbance in the time-line."

Alfieri seized on the operative word. "Thou canst give me gold?" he said. "Fain would Monasticus see good red gold."

"Fine," nodded Sneed. "Got anything you don't much value? Preferably something fairly massive—long-range transmutation is a bit beyond the power of portable equipment. Ah, the very thing!" He indicated a small iron cauldron. "Do you need this very much?"

Alfieri shook his head dumbly.

Sneed unhooked a small object from his belt and pressed its end. It immediately glowed with a pure white light. "Stand back," he said over his shoulder. "You might get burnt." He pulled a pair of shaded goggles over his eyes and began to play the light over the cauldron.

Alfieri needed no injunction to stand back. At that moment he wanted nothing so wholeheartedly as to be well clear of the house.

Sneed worked on, humming as he did so. The beam of light bathed the dull black metal of the pot, and slowly it began to reflect yellow. After ten minutes he turned to Alfieri.

"Chemically pure and perfectly genuine," he said cheerfully. "There isn't better gold this side of El Dorado. That's a bit more than three and a quarter kilos really, but I think it's still on the safe side."

Fearfully, Alfieri reached out and touched the pot. His eyes were glazed with awe.

"Now," said Sneed sternly, "do you blow out those lamps or do I turn you into a warthog?" The threat was quite empty, but Alfieri had just seen the impossible done and had no wish to feel it happen to him. Convulsively, he reached for a snuffer. It was a pity that no one could witness his success, but still, there was the gold.

Smack! went the snuffer, and there was a sudden blast of air rushing into the vacant space left by the instant departure of the demon.

Alfieri dropped back into his chair and breathed a heartfelt sigh of relief. *That* was over! And he had got off amazingly lightly. The demon hadn't even asked for his soul.

A sobering thought struck him. Maybe, next time, he wouldn't be so lucky. Next time—

He came to a sudden decision. He could keep a suitable amount of the gold for his personal needs. With the rest he could prove to Monasticus Senior that he was no fake. If he took advantage of the old man's first surprise, he could be three counties away in a day or two. There wasn't going to be a *next time*.

He got up and moved purposefully toward his library.

There was a slamming noise and the door jarred back on its hinges. Monasticus Junior entered the room, talking loudly.

"Master Gargreen said his bats' blood was good enough for Mistress Comfrey, and he will not return the groat. Prithee, shall I be about gathering herbs to turn him into a toa-o-*oh*!"

His final word turned into a gasp of amazement as he saw the solid gold pot on the floor.

"Master, what dost thou?" he demanded.

"No more thy master," said Alfieri proudly. "I have fulfilled my contract with thy father. I have made him gold. That done, I shall return to my erstwhile task of curing cows of sickness."

He dropped an armful of parchments into the still smoldering brazier, and whirled on Monasticus. "Harken, boy!" he said. "Let not this gold beguile thee. Avoid magic—'tis a perilous calling, and there's no future in it."

Galactic Consumer Report No. 3

This "Consumer Report" is a tour de force of imagination, squandering a story idea in almost every paragraph. It would be a good thing to show people—and there are a lot of them—who say they would like to write sf but don't know how you come up with all those ideas. Hand them this story with a pitying look.

━━ ━━ ━━ ━━ ━━ ━━ ━━ ━━

A SURVEY OF THE MEMBERSHIP

(Extract from Good Buy, *the journal of the Consolidated Galactic Federation of Consumers Associations, February 2330 ESY)*

Elsewhere in this issue you will find the complete results of our questionnaire intended to discover exactly who (or what) are our current members, why they joined, whether they are satisfied with our service, and what products you whom we are here to serve want us to test in the immediate future. Owing to circumstances beyond our control, some of which are set out below in the most temperate language of which we are at present capable, most of the data are primarily of academic or historical interest now, but we can at least pride ourselves on the fact that no similar undertaking has ever before been attempted, even though we could not in honesty advise anyone else to try it again.

When we first circulated the questionnaire, eight years ago, we promised that its findings would appear in one of the regular issues of this journal. We have managed to keep that promise. The information is condensed in microdot form as the last full stop on the last page of the comparative study of high-precision microdot decipherers, and both the items nominated as Best Buys will enable you to read it, the magnification required being only of the order of x 1,000,000.

Subscribers to the deluxe edition (apart from the two members on Alpheratz IX who withheld seventeen credits from their dues on the grounds that they are anyway capable of distinguishing individual molecules with the naked eye) will eventually be sent the book version of the report. However, we must warn them that, since it runs to twenty-three fat volumes occupying a meter and a half of shelf space, under current galactic mailing regulations it can only be shipped by uncrewed ion-rocket; consequently only members belonging to species of exceptional longevity can expect to receive their copies personally. The rest will have to be satisfied with bequeathing them to their grandchildren.

Doubtless by now you're asking: "How did this delay arise?" Well, to start with, the level of response exceeded not only our wildest expectations but also those of the computer we hired to assess the likely return. It advised us that not more than one per million of the membership would be bothered to fill out such a complex form.

What we *in fact* got back was more like a sixty-seven percent

sponse. As, relying on the computer's assessment, we had
one no more by way of preparation than rent a small room in
owntown Buenos Aires and hire an elderly female clerk with
a hand-operated punch-card analyzer, the sudden arrival of
,619,312,003 questionnaires caused a minor technical hitch.

By the way, in a future issue we prepose to conduct a survey
f commercial computer-advice services. Meantime, we must
aution you against employing the Buckingham and Ketshwayo
ervice for Honest Oracular Pronouncements, which our staff is
ow accustomed to refer to as the Bucket Shop. They are not, on
resent evidence, a "Good Buy."

We are also, incidentally, anxious to recruit volunteers to help
s in a survey of planetside postal services. We feel it is high time
establish a Galactic Postal Convention to assure the private
orrespondence of any intelligent organism whatever proper pro-
ction in transit and reasonable speed of delivery. The treatment
ve have been accorded by the Earthside authorities beggars be-
ief, and it is highly probable that some of the questionnaires
vhich members on outlying planets went to a lot of trouble to
omplete and forward have never reached us.

For example, we regard it as inexcusable that merely because
he only type of stationery available to a citizen of Shalimar hap-
ens to be fresh water-lily leaves and pale green bog slime in-
tead of paper and ink, some jumped-up jack-in-office at the
Galactic Mail Center in Lhasa should be allowed to class his
nvelope as "perishable foodstuffs improperly packaged" and de-
line responsibility for its delivery.

Furthermore, it's mere common civility on Toothanclaw to
vrap any missive to a person one wishes to flatter or defer to in
he hide of one's latest kill. The more ambitious the kill (and
here are creatures on that planet none of our staff would care to
andle without battle armor and a lase gun!), the greater the re-
pect which the writer expresses toward the recipient.

One of our members there, obviously extremely appreciative
f the services of ConGalFedConAss, chose to employ the hide
f a mugglebuck in which to return his questionnaire. That this
ide continues to secrete pure hydrofluoric acid for nine years

after being flayed, we submit, is as nothing beside the basic requirement that it be delivered to the address inscribed on the outside. The fact that mugglebuck skin remains dangerous to handle after the animal is killed is essentially a symbolic equivalent of the customary salutation, "Your humble and obedient servant," but no postal authority would decline to accept mail because it included that phrase!

It was only by chance that we received the questionnaire sent us by a member on Caligula, moreover. She had gone to enormous trouble to address her package, because the yoggoth worms there customarily employed for the purpose have been selectively bred to adopt the forms of the Devanagari alphabet rather than the Terrestrial Roman system; it must have required several months of patient labor to train them to display an Earthside address code.

All this nearly went for nothing when the Health Department sterilized the worms with insecticide—whereupon, of course, they reverted to the post-mortem straight position. Had it not been for an observant staff member who was visiting the post office on another errand altogether, that questionnaire would doubtless have gone into the dead-letter file.

But the last straw was the authorities' refusal to allow one of our members on Hydatia to answer our questionnaire at all—a flagrant example of bureaucratic censorship at its worst. Much as we dislike expending our funds on litigation, we feel that in this case there is an important point of principle at stake, and have instituted proceedings in the cause of interplanetary tolerance.

Hydatians do possess a written language, but they reserve it entirely for public inscriptions, advertising puffs and other works of fiction. The only form of private communication expressed in writing is an invitation to a duel to the death, so great an insult is it not to convey your messages in person.

Wishing to reply to our questionnaire, our member there adopted the normal course and put himself into suspended animation after attaching address labels and sufficient postage to his left ear. On arrival at our office, he would have delivered the infor-

mation he had imprinted on his mind, and relapsed into his co-
matose state until restored to his home swamp.

However, despite being properly stamped for both the outward
and return journeys, our member was forbidden admission to
Earth—first by the Customs and Excise, which proposed to clas-
sify him as a museum exhibit subject to arbitrary valuation and
five-hundred percent duty; then, when we'd sorted that out, by
the Immigration Service, which argued that he lacked a visa.

Without being delivered, of course, the poor fellow will never
wake up from his trance, so merely shipping him home doesn't
solve the problem. A test case is now in progress before the
Appellate Tribunal of the Pan-Galactic Court, and we will keep
you apprised of developments.

Meantime, if anyone can offer us storage space for one inert
male Hydatian approximately thirty-seven meters by eleven by
four, capable of being maintained at a pressure of 325 kg./sq.
cm. at 120° C., we would be obliged. At present we are having to
pay rent on a bonded warehouse at a rate which promises that we
shall go bankrupt around the second week of August.

We had hoped that one of the things this questionnaire would
enable us to do is to revolutionize our method of selecting products to be tested by insuring that the items we choose are all
goods that the members are eager to know about.

We have no wish to appear unappreciative of all the trouble
you went to, but the sad truth is that after processing, catalog-
uing, and analyzing the various products suggested by a substantial number of our members (arbitrarily, one million or more), we
have decided to keep right on the way we have been going already.

You see, the largest single batch of requests for tests on a
single type of product which we received came from Triskelion.
We had 8,623,517 of them. (Curiously enough, this was exactly
the book strength of the Hawk party in the Archduchy of Axen-
heim at the time our questionnaires arrived there.)

But we simply haven't got the facilities to evaluate the comparative merits of the various brands of planet-busting bombs at

present on the market! We feel that if the Hawk party wish to substantiate their election slogan ("More Crash for a Credit!") they should institute their own testing program, preferably well away from Galactic trade routes.

We moreover feel very strongly that the two million-odd inquirers from Phagia who asked us to test them for edibility ought to set up their own planetary chapter of ConGalFedConAss. We cannot possibly hope to determine which of them will prove tastiest at his or her funeral feast—a matter of fierce rivalry among that species, in case you didn't know. Our entire permanent staff is human, and sampling creatures who live in an atmosphere of hydrogen sulfide at the boiling point of water would give us acute food poisoning, thus hopelessly biasing the results.

By the way, we have exercised our discretionary right to terminate membership in the case of the young lady from Hippodamia who asked us to test the thirty-seven men who are suing for her hand in marriage. Frivolity of this kind is not in keeping with the high ideals of our organization. And we would have done the same to the member on Gyges who complained that his voyeur suit had gone wrong, and because it was stuck at the invisible setting, he couldn't read the brand name on the label—would we test all the makes on the market and tell him which kind has the switch under the left arm? But during his enforced imperceptibility he was run down by a rocket sled. *De mortuis* . . .

Having had this rather gloomy picture of the outcome of our survey painted for you, you may now be asking, "Was there any point in mounting it anyway?"

We are delighted to say that the answer is a resounding "yes!"

If it did nothing else, the survey showed us that we have been unforgivably neglectful of the true requirements of a very large proportion of our subscribers. We can only apologize for this and plead that one of the lessons we hoped to derive from the survey was to discover the nature of our median member.

Obviously, our *average* subscriber would be a nonsensical compound creature—to be exact, one and two-thirds of a married female with an annual income of 2,800 credits, a batch of hoopoe eggs and seven-eighths of a hectare of reed matting, chiefly interested in the Zagnabovian question, potlatch, and the superior merits of strychnine over prussic acid as a seasoning for beef Bourguignon.

Our statisticians did, however, advise us that we could hope to determine a typical person who corresponded to the largest possible number of the membership. Somewhat to our surprise, when we punched the computer for this information, we discovered that our median is a citizen of Luxor, Lonestar or Eldorado, with an income of 27,000,000 credits, taking the deluxe calf-bound vellum edition of this journal with hand-tooled gilt lettering on the spine and built-in pentasensory commentator—in quintuplicate or sextuplicate so that there would be a copy of each month's issue for every member of the family, often including the dog! Very nearly one in ten of the entire membership, reported the computer, fits this general description.

Frankly, we were astounded. The level of affluence on those planets is so high that palladium-plated spaceboats are marketed by Neiman-Marcus-Harrods-Wojcecenski not in pairs but in groups of three labeled "His," "Hers" and "Its", so that the odd one can be thrown in the garbage on delivery.

Why, we asked ourselves, should *Good Buy*— dedicated to helping people secure maximum return for minimum outlay—be so popular on worlds where it doesn't make any difference at all whether what people buy is fit for use or not? (Except insofar as there is a risk of overloading garbage-clearance facilities—but even that doesn't seem especially significant. Most people there own robotic disposers that automatically shunt refuse into the local sun.)

And then we received a note, along with a copy of our questionnaire, picked out in individual diamonds on lead plates and expressed to us by Class Triple A* galactic mail (which costs three thousand credits per gram), from which we discovered the explanation.

We have had to edit the letter slightly, but the gist of it was as follows:

Why the [deleted] don't you [deleted] Earthside [deleted] get your heads out of that heap of [deleted] and catch on to what [deleted] like us really want? If my three-year-old daughter hadn't started to try and eat her copy of your last issue, it would have gone straight in the chute as it usually does and I wouldn't have seen your questionnaire!

I don't want to be told how to economize! I subscribe to your publication purely because I can always do with having expensive things shipped to me from distant worlds like Earth. (By the way, do you know where I could order a live blue whale not less than twenty meters long? Or a pair of Indian elephants would do, in a pinch.)

Sorry. I'm being too hard on you. At least you take the trouble to quote nice exorbitant terms.

Look, the problem here is this. According to our tax laws, every Midsummer Day the government takes away all the money you haven't managed to spend since last time. It's a great way of minimizing bureaucratic interference with the daily lives of our citizens, not having sales taxes and income taxes and all that other [deleted]. But think what happens if we don't spend enough!

Lord, it's hard to find things one can buy as it is. If the government, armed with all the surplus revenue it collects from the citizens as I explained before, were to start bidding against private individuals, there wouldn't be anything left for us at all!

Sure, charity donations are tax deductible—in theory. But the last planetary census showed that the lowest income anyone had filed was four and a half million credits, and that wasn't even for a human being, but a canary! How the blazes do you operate a charity under those conditions?

And gifts are tax deductible, too. You find me someone who's willing to take a present from me, though! If anybody offered to give me a few million credits, I'd *run*. I don't think I'd even stop to get in a rocket, in spite of having a fleet of thirty of them. (Or possibly forty—I think I ordered some more the other day.)

I'm going out of my skull, believe me! Right now I have the builders in—they're doing over the east wing in neo-rococo. But it's the third time I've had to rebuild the house this financial year, and I kind of liked the Moorish style we had before the pseudobrutalist installed last month. Only I couldn't afford to keep on with it! As a result, here I am with rain streaming in through the cracked marble ceiling, trying to stop my daughter from breaking her neck on the floor of the sub-basement (sixty meters deep and due to be enlarged tomorrow) while they stick up all kinds of hideous gold and red fretwork in place of the black and white bricks they're scrapping. I have to do a lot of traveling—it's a good way of getting rid of extra credits —but once in a while I'd like to recognize my home when I come back to it!

To cap the lot, I see on the morning news where the unions are threatening to strike for lower pay, and this blasted socialist government of ours always assesses tax deductions at the current union scale. If they stay on strike until the tax year ends, moreover, I can't legally pay them anything!

Help! HELP!!!

Yours faithfully [signed]:
Getty C. Midas XXXIII

In face of a heartfelt cry like that, what decent being could refrain from coming to the rescue? As an interim measure, we have quadrupled the subscription rates for the deluxe edition, and expressions of gratitude are already coming in. But we don't propose to stop there. Plans are afoot to produce an ultra-deluxe edition on hygroscopic paper with soluble ink, guaranteed to become illegible within fifteen minutes of leaving the presses, so that indefinite repeat orders can be filed with no prospect of ever actually receiving a legible copy. And as of next month we shall start to issue a special supplement to *Good Buy*, entitled *Extravaganza*, printed in thirty-six-point type on platinum sheets, and dedicated to the ringing, clarion call of our new slogan: "The more you spend, the less you get."

Getty C. Midas, do not despair! The Consolidated Galactic Federation of Consumers' Associations is on your side!

What Friends Are For

Robots are made for comedy, whether the R2-D2 kind of slap-stick or the more sophisticated ironies of the Tin Woodman "what is man?" variety: If this creature is not a man, what is it?

I've never seen one used quite like this, though, as a nurse-maid prodigy attending to one of the most revolting children in all of literature. The story is funny in a peculiarly universal way. If Disney had made a cartoon of it, it would be equally amusing to Lapland farmer, Australian bushman, Soviet bureaucrat, and us. A classic.

▬▬▬▬▬▬▬▬

After Tim killed and buried the neighbors' prize terrier the Pattersons took him to the best-reputed—and most expensive—counselor in the state: Dr. Hend.

They spent forty of the fifty minutes they had purchased snapping at each other in the waiting room outside his office, breaking off now and then when a scream or a smashing noise eluded the soundproofing, only to resume more fiercely a moment later.

Eventually Tim was borne out, howling, by a strong male nurse who seemed impervious to being kicked in the belly with all the force an eight-year-old can muster, and the Pattersons were bidden to take his place in Dr. Hend's presence. There was no sign of the chaos the boy had caused. The counselor was a specialist in such cases, and there were smooth procedures for eliminating incidental mess.

"Well, doctor?" Jack Patterson demanded.

Dr. Hend studied him thoughtfully for a long moment, then glanced at his wife, Lorna, reconfirming the assessment he had made when they arrived. On the male side: expensive clothing, bluff good looks, a carefully constructed image of success. On the female: the most being made of what had to begin with been a somewhat shallow prettiness, even more expensive clothes, plus ultrafashionable hair style, cosmetics, and perfume.

He said at last, "That son of yours is going to be in court very shortly. Even if he is only eight, chronologically."

"What?" Jack Patterson erupted. "But we came here to—"

"You came here," the doctor cut in, "to be told the truth. It was your privilege to opt for a condensed-development child. You did it after being informed of the implications. Now you must face up to your responsibilities."

"No, we came here for help!" Lorna burst out. Her husband favored her with a scowl: *Shut up!*

"You have seven minutes of my time left," Dr. Hend said wearily. "You can spend it wrangling or listening to me. Shall I proceed?"

The Pattersons exchanged sour looks, then both nodded.

"*Thank* you. I can see precisely one alternative to having your child placed in a public institution. You'll have to get him a Friend."

"What? And show the world we can't cope?" Jack Patterson rasped. "You must be out of your mind!"

Dr. Hend just gazed at him.

"They're—they're terribly expensive, aren't they?" Lorna whispered.

The counselor leaned back and set his fingertips together.

"As to being out of my mind . . . Well, I'm in good company. It's customary on every inhabited planet we know of to entrust the raising of the young to Friends programed by a consensus of opinion among other intelligent races. There was an ancient proverb about not seeing the forest for the trees; it is well established that the best possible advice regarding optimum exploitation of juvenile talent comes from those who can analyze the local society in absolute, rather than committed, terms. And the habit is growing commoner here. Many families, if they can afford to, acquire a Friend from choice, not necessity.

"As to expense—yes, Mrs. Patterson, you're right. Anything which has had to be shipped over interstellar distances can hardly be cheap. But consider: this dog belonging to your neighbors was a show champion with at least one best-of-breed certificate, quite apart from being the boon companion of their small daughter. I imagine the courts will award a substantial sum by way of damages . . . Incidentally, did Tim previously advance the excuse that he couldn't stand the noise it made when it barked?"

"Uh . . ." Jack Patterson licked his lips. "Yes, he did."

"I suspected it might have been rehearsed. It had that kind of flavor. As did his excuse for breaking the arm of the little boy who was the best batter in your local junior ball team, and the excuse for setting fire to the school's free-fall gymnasium, and so forth. You have to accept the fact, I'm afraid, that thanks to his condensed-development therapy your son is a total egocentric. The universe has never yet proved sufficiently intractable to progress him out of the emotional stage most infants leave behind about the time they learn to walk. Physically he is ahead of the average for his age. Emotionally, he is concerned about nothing but his own gratification. He's incapable of empathy, sympathy, worrying about the opinions of others. He is a classic case of arrested personal development."

"But we've done everything we can to—"

"Yes, indeed you have. And it is not enough." Dr. Hend allowed the comment to rankle for a few seconds, then resumed.

"We were talking about expense. Well, let me remind you that it costs a lot of money to maintain Tim in the special school you've been compelled to send him to because he made life hell for his classmates at a regular school. The companionship of a Friend is legally equivalent to a formal course of schooling. Maybe you weren't aware of that."

"Sure!" Jack snapped. "But—oh, hell! I simply don't fancy the idea of turning my son over to some ambulating alien arti-fact!"

"I grant it may seem to you to be a radical step, but juvenile maladjustment is one area where the old saw remains true, about desperate diseases requiring desperate measures. And have you considered the outcome if you don't adopt a radical solution?"

It was clear from their glum faces that they had, but he spelled it out for them nonetheless.

"By opting for a modified child, you rendered yourselves liable for his maintenance and good behavior for a minimum period of twenty years, regardless of divorce or other legal interventions. If Tim is adjudged socially incorrigible, you will find yourselves obliged to support him indefinitely in a state institution. At present the annual cost of keeping one patient in such an establishment is thirty thousand dollars. Inflation at the current rate will double that by the twenty-year mark, and in view of the extensive alterations you insisted on having made in Tim's heredity I think it unlikely that any court would agree to discontinue your liability as early as twelve years from now. I put it to you that the acquisition of a Friend is your only sensible course of action—whatever you may think of the way alien intelligences have evaluated our society. Besides, you don't have to buy one. You can always rent."

He glanced at his desk clock. "I see your time is up. Good morning. My bill will be faxed to you this afternoon."

That night there was shouting from the living area of the Patterson house. Tim heard it, lying in bed with the door ajar, and grinned from ear to shell-like ear. He was an extremely beautiful child, with curly fair hair, perfectly proportioned features, ideally regular teeth, eyes blue and deep as mountain pools, a sprinkling of freckles as per specification to make him a trifle less angelic, a fraction more boylike, and—naturally—he was big for his age. That had been in the specification, too.

Moreover, his vocabulary was enormous compared to an unmodified kid's—as was his IQ, theoretically, though he had never cooperated on a test which might have proved the fact—and he fully understood what was being said.

"You and your goddamn vanity! Insisting on all those special features like wavy golden hair and baby-blue eyes and—and, my God, *freckles*! And now the little devil is apt to drive us into bankruptcy! Have you *seen* what it costs to rent a Friend, even a cheap one from Procyon?"

"Oh, stop trying to lay all the blame on me, will you? They warned you that your demand for tallness and extra strength might be incompatible with the rest, and you took not a blind bit of notice—"

"But he's a boy, dammit, a *boy*, and if you hadn't wanted him to look more like a girl—"

"I did not, I did not! I wanted him to be *handsome* and you wanted to make him into some kind of crazy beefcake type, loaded down with useless muscles! Just because you never made the college gladiator squad he was condemned before birth to—"

"One more word about what I *didn't* do, and I'll smash your teeth down your ugly throat! How about talking about what I *have* done for a change? Youngest area manager in the corporation, tipped to be the youngest-ever vice-president . . . Small thanks to you, of course. When I think where I might have gotten to by now if you hadn't been tied around my neck—"

Tim's grin grew so wide it was almost painful. He was becoming drowsy because that outburst in the counselor's office had expended a lot of energy, but there was one more thing he could do before he dropped off to sleep. He crept from his bed, went to the door on tiptoe, and carefully urinated through the gap onto the landing carpet outside. Then, chuckling, he scrambled

back under the coverlet and a few minutes later was lost in color-
ful dreams.

The doorbell rang when his mother was in the bathroom and
his father was calling on the lawyers to see whether the matter of
the dog could be kept out of court after all.

At once Lorna yelled, "Tim, stay right where you are—I'll
get it!"

But he was already heading for the door at a dead run. He
liked being the first to greet a visitor. It was such fun to show
himself stark naked and shock puritanical callers, or scream and
yell about how Dad had beaten him mercilessly, showing off
bruises collected by banging into furniture and blood trickling
from cuts and scratches. But today an even more inspired idea
came to him, and he made a rapid detour through the kitchen and
raided the garbage pail as he passed.

He opened the door with his left hand and delivered a soggy
mass of rotten fruit, vegetable peelings and coffee grounds with
his right, as hard as he could and at about face height for a
grownup.

Approximately half a second later the whole loathsome mass
splattered over him, part on his face so that his open mouth tasted
the foulness of it, part on his chest so that it dropped inside his
open shirt. And a reproachful voice said, "Tim! I'm your Friend!
And that's no way to treat a friend, is it?"

Reflex had brought him to the point of screaming. His lungs
were filling, his muscles were tensing, when he saw what had
arrived on the threshold and his embryo yell turned into a simple
gape of astonishment.

The Friend was humanoid, a few inches taller than himself
and a great deal broader, possessed of two legs and two arms and
a head with eyes and a mouth and a pair of ears . . . but it was
covered all over in shaggy fur of a brilliant emerald green. Its
sole decoration—apart from a trace of the multicolored garbage
it had caught and heaved back at him, which still adhered to the
palm of its left hand—was a belt around its waist bearing a label
stamped in bright red letters AUTHORIZED AUTONOMIC ARTI-

FACT (SELF-DELIVERING), followed by the Patterson family's address.

"Invite me in," said the apparition. "You don't keep a friend standing on the doorstep, you know, and I am your Friend, as I just explained."

"Tim! *Tim!*" At a stumbling run, belting a robe around her, his mother appeared from the direction of the bathroom, a towel clumsily knotted over her newly washed hair. On seeing the nature of the visitor, she stopped dead.

"But the rental agency said not to expect you until—" She broke off. It was the first time in her life she had spoken to an alien biofact, although she had seen many both live and on tri-vee.

"We were able to include more than the anticipated quantity in the last shipment from Procyon," the Friend said. "There has been an advance in packaging methods. Permit me to identify myself." It marched past Tim and removed its belt, complete with label, and handed it to Lorna. "I trust you will find that I conform to your requirements."

"You stinking bastard! I won't have you fucking around in my home!" Tim shrieked. He had small conception of what the words he was using meant, except in a very abstract way, but he was sure of one thing: they always made his parents good and mad.

The Friend, not sparing him a glance said, "Tim, you should have introduced me to your mother. Since you did not I am having to introduce myself. Do not compound your impoliteness by interrupting, because that makes an even worse impression."

"Get out!" Tim bellowed, and launched himself at the Friend in a flurry of kicking feet and clenched fists. At once he found himself suspended a foot off the floor with the waistband of his pants tight in a grip like a crane's.

To Lorna the Friend said, "All you're requested to do is thumbprint the acceptance box and fax the datum back to the rental company. That is, if you do agree to accept me."

She looked at it, and her son, for a long moment, and then firmly planted her thumb on the reverse of the label.

"Thank you. Now, Tim!" The Friend swiveled him around so

hat it could look directly at him. "I'm sorry to see how dirty you
re. It's not the way one would wish to find a friend. I shall give
ou a bath and a change of clothes."

"I had a bath!" Tim howled, flailing arms and legs impotently.

Ignoring him, the Friend continued, "Mrs. Patterson, if you'll
indly show me where Tim's clothes are kept, I'll attend to the
matter right away."

A slow smile spread over Lorna's face. "You know some-
hing?" she said to the air. "I guess that counselor was on the
ight track after all. Come this way—uh . . . Say! What do we
all you?"

"It's customary to have the young person I'm assigned to se-
ect a name for me."

"If I know Tim," Lorna said, "he'll pick on something so
ilthy it can't be used in company!"

Tim stopped screaming for a moment. That was an idea which
adn't occurred to him.

"But," Lorna declared, "we'll avoid that, and just call you
Buddy right from the start. Is that okay?"

"I shall memorize the datum at once. Come along, Tim!"

"Well, I guess it's good to find such prompt service these
days," Jack Patterson muttered, looking at the green form of
Buddy curled up by the door of Tim's bedroom. Howls, yells and
moans were pouring from the room, but during the past half-hour
hey had grown less loud, and sometimes intervals of two or three
minutes interrupted the racket, as though exhaustion were over-
coming the boy. "I still hate to think what the neighbors are going
o say, though. It's about the most public admission of defeat that
parents can make, to let their kid be seen with one of those things
at his heels!"

"Stop thinking about what the neighbors will say and think
about how I feel for once!" rapped his wife. "You had an easy
day today—"

"The hell I did! Those damned lawyers—"

"You were sitting in a nice quiet office! If it hadn't been for
Buddy, I'd have had more than even my usual kind of hell! I

think Dr. Hend had a terrific idea. I'm impressed."

"Typical!" Jack grunted. "You can't cope with this, buy a
machine; you can't cope with that, buy another machine . . . Now
it turns out you can't even cope with your own son. I'm no
impressed!"

"Why, you goddamn—"

"Look, I paid good money to make sure of having a kid who'd
be bright and talented and a regular all-around guy, and I got one
But who's been looking after him? You have! You've screwed
him up with your laziness and bad temper!"

"How much time do you waste on helping to raise him?" She
confronted him, hands on hips and eyes aflame. "Every evening
it's the same story, every weekend it's the same—'Get this kid
off my neck because I'm worn out!'"

"Oh, shut up. It sounds as though he's finally dropped off
Want to wake him again and make things worse? I'm going to fix
a drink. I need one."

He spun on his heel and headed downstairs. Fuming, Lorna
followed him.

By the door of Tim's room, Buddy remained immobile except
that one of his large green ears swiveled slightly and curled over
at the tip.

At breakfast next day Lorna served hot cereal—to Buddy as
well as Tim, because among the advantages of this model of
Friend was the fact that it could eat anything its assigned family
was eating.

Tim picked up his dish as soon as it was set before him and
threw it with all his might at Buddy. The Friend caught it with
such dexterity that hardly a drop splashed on the table.

"Thank you, Tim," it said, and ate the lot in a single slurping
mouthful. "According to my instructions you like this kind of
cereal, so giving it to me is a very generous act. Though you
might have delivered the dish somewhat more gently."

Tim's semiangelic face crumpled like a mask made of wet
paper. He drew a deep breath, and then flung himself forward
across the table, aiming to knock everything off it onto the floor.

Nothing could break—long and bitter experience had taught the Pattersons to buy only resilient plastic utensils—but spilling the milk, sugar, juice, and other items could have made a magnificent mess.

A hair's breadth away from the nearest object, the milk bottle, Tim found himself pinioned in a gentle but inflexible clutch.

"It appears that it is time to begin lessons for the day," Buddy said. "Excuse me, Mrs. Patterson. I shall take Tim into the backyard, where there is more space."

"To begin lessons?" Lorna echoed. "Well—uh . . . But he hasn't had any breakfast yet!"

"If you'll forgive my saying so, he has. He chose not to eat it. He is somewhat overweight, and one presumes that lunch will be served at the customary time. Between now and noon it is unlikely that malnutrition will claim him. Besides, this offers an admirable opportunity for a practical demonstration of the nature of mass, inertia, and friction."

With no further comment Buddy rose and, carrying Tim in effortless fashion, marched over to the door giving access to the yard.

"So how has that hideous green beast behaved today?" Jack demanded.

"Oh, it's fantastic! I'm starting to get the hang of what it's designed to do." Lorna leaned back in her easy chair with a smug expression.

"Yes?" Jack's face by contrast was sour. "Such as what?"

"Well, it puts up with everything Tim can do—and that's a tough job because he's pulling out all the stops he can think of—and interprets it in the most favorable way it can. It keeps insisting that it's Tim's Friend, so he's doing what a friend ought to do."

Jack blinked at her. "What the hell are you talking about?" he rasped.

"If you'd listen, you might find out!" she snapped back. "He threw his breakfast at Buddy, so Buddy ate it and said thank you. Then because he got hungry he climbed up and got at the candy jar, and Buddy took that and ate the lot and said thank you again, and . . . Oh, it's all part of a pattern, and very clever."

"Are you crazy? You let this monstrosity eat not only Tim's breakfast but all his candy, and you didn't try and stop it?"

"I don't think you read the instructions," Lorna said.

"Quit needling me, will you? Of course I read the instructions!"

"Then you know that if you interfere with what a Friend does, your contract is automatically void and you have to pay the balance of the rental in a lump sum!"

"And how is it interfering to give your own son some more breakfast in place of what the horrible thing took?"

"But Tim threw his dish at—"

"If you gave him a decent diet he'd—"

It continued. Above, on the landing outside Tim's door, Buddy kept his furry green ears cocked, soaking up every word.

"Tim!"

"Shut up, you fucking awful nuisance!"

"Tim, if you climb that tree past the first fork, you will be on a branch that's not strong enough to bear your weight. You will fall about nine feet to the ground, and the ground is hard because the weather this summer has been so dry."

"*Shut up!* All I want is to get away from you!"

Crack!

"What you are suffering from is a bruise, technically called a subcutaneous hemorrhage. That means a leak of blood under the skin. You also appear to have a slight rupture of the left Achilles tendon. That's this sinew here, which . . ."

"In view of your limited skill in swimming, it's not advisable to go more than five feet from the edge of this pool. Beyond that point the bottom dips very sharply."

"*Shut up!* I'm trying to get away from you, so—*glug!*"

"Insufficient oxygen is dissolved in water to support an air-breathing creature like a human. Fish, on the other hand, can utilize the oxygen dissolved in water, because they have gills and not lungs. Your ancestors . . ."

"Why, there's that little bastard Tim Patterson! And look at what he's got trailing behind him! Hey, Tim! Who said you had to live with this funny green teddy bear? Did you have to go have your head shrunk?"

Crowding around him, a dozen neighborhood kids, both sexes, various ages from nine to fourteen.

"Tim's head, as you can doubtless see, is of normal proportions. I am assigned to him as his Friend."

"Hah! Don't give us that shit! Who'd want to be a friend of Tim's? He busted my brother's arm and laughed about it!"

"He set fire to the gym at my school!"

"He killed my dog—he killed my Towser!"

"So I understand. Tim, you have the opportunity to say you were sorry, don't you?"

"Ah, he made that stinking row all the time, barking his silly head off—"

"You bastard! *You killed my dog!*"

"Buddy, help! *Help!*"

"As I said, Tim, you have an excellent opportunity to say how sorry you are . . . No, little girl: please put down that rock. It's extremely uncivil, and also dangerous, to throw things like that at people."

"*Shut up!*"

"Let's beat the hell out of him! Let him go whining back home and tell how all those terrible kids attacked him, and see how he likes his own medicine!"

"Kindly refrain from attempting to inflict injuries on my assigned charge."

"I told you to shut up, greenie!"

"I did caution you, as you'll recall. I did say that it was both uncivil and dangerous to throw rocks at people. I believe what I should do is inform your parents. Come, Tim."

"*No!*"

"Very well, as you wish. I shall release this juvenile to continue the aggression with rocks."

"No!"

"But, Tim, your two decisions are incompatible. Either you come with me to inform this child's parents of the fact that rocks were thrown at you, or I shall have to let go and a great many more rocks will probably be thrown—perhaps more than I can catch before they hit you."

"I—uh . . . I—I'm sorry that I hurt your dog. It just made me so mad that he kept on barking and barking all the time, and never shut up!"

"But he didn't bark all the time! He got hurt—he cut his paw and he wanted help!"

"He did so bark all the time!"

"He did not! You just got mad because he did it that one time!"

"I—uh . . . Well, I guess maybe . . ."

"To be precise, there had been three complaints recorded about your dog's excessive noise. On each occasion you had gone out and left him alone for several hours."

"Right! Thank you, Buddy! *See?*"

"But you didn't have to kill him!"

"Correct, Tim. You did not. You could have become acquainted with him, and then looked after him when it was necessary to leave him by himself."

"Ah, who'd want to care for a dog like that shaggy brute?"

"Perhaps someone who never was allowed his own dog?"

"Okay. *Okay!* Sure I wanted a dog, and they never let me have one! Kept saying I'd—I'd torture it or something! So I said fine, if that's how you think of me, let's go right ahead! You always like to be proven right!"

"Kind of quiet around here tonight," Jack Patterson said. "What's been going on?"

"You can thank Buddy," Lorna answered.

"Can I now? So what's he done that I can't do, this time?"

"Persuaded Tim to go to bed on time and without yelling his head off, that's what!"

"Don't feed me that line! 'Persuaded'! Cowed him, don't you mean?"

"All I can say is that tonight's the first time he's let Buddy sleep inside the room instead of on the landing by the door."

"You keep saying I didn't read the instructions—now it turns out you didn't read them! Friends don't sleep, not the way we do at any rate. They're supposed to be on watch twenty-four hours per day."

"Oh, stop it! The first peaceful evening we've had in heaven knows how long, and you're determined to ruin it!"

"I am not!"

"Then why the hell don't you keep quiet?"

Upstairs, beyond the door of Tim's room, which was as ever ajar, Buddy's ears remained alert with their tips curled over to make them acoustically ultrasensitive.

"Who—? Oh! I know *you*! You're Tim Patterson, aren't you? Well, what do you want?"

"I...I..."

"Tim wishes to know whether your son would care to play ball with him, madam."

"You have to be joking! I'm not going to let Teddy play with Tim after the way Tim broke his elbow with a baseball bat!"

"It did happen quite a long time ago, madam, and—"

"No! That's final! *No!*"

Slam!

"Well, thanks for trying, Buddy. It would have been kind of fun to...Ah, well!"

"That little girl is ill-advised to play so close to a road carrying fast traffic—Oh, dear. Tim, I shall need help in coping with this emergency. Kindly take off your belt and place it around her leg about *here*...That's correct. Now pull it tight. See how the flow of blood is reduced? You've put a tourniquet on the relevant pressure point, that's to say a spot where a large artery passes near the skin. If much blood were allowed to leak, it might be fatal. I note there is a pen in the pocket of her dress. Please write a letter T on her forehead, and add the exact time; you see, there's a clock over there. When she gets to the hospital the surgeon will know how long the blood supply to her leg has been cut off. It must not be restricted more than twenty minutes."

"Uh . . . Buddy, I can't write a T. And I can't tell the time either."

"How old did you say you were?"

"Well . . . Eight. And a half."

"Yes, Tim. I'm actually aware both of your age and of your incompetence. Give me the pen, please . . . There. Now go to the nearest house and ask someone to telephone for an ambulance. Unless the driver, who I see is backing up, has a phone right in his car."

"Yes, what do you want?" Jack Patterson stared at the couple who had arrived without warning on the doorstep.

"Mr. Patterson? I'm William Vickers, from up on the 1100 block, and this is my wife, Judy. We thought we ought to call around after what your boy Tim did today. Louise—that's our daughter—she's still in the hospital, of course, but . . . Well, they say she's going to make a quick recovery."

"What the hell is that about Tim?" From the living area Lorna emerged, glowering and reeking of gin. "Did you say Tim put your daughter in the hospital? Well, that finishes it! Jack Patterson, I'm damned if I'm going to waste any more of my life looking after your goddamn son! I am through with him and you both—d'you hear me? *Through!*"

"But you've got it all wrong," Vickers protested feebly. "Thanks to his quick thinking, and that Friend who goes with him everywhere, Louise got off amazingly lightly. Just some cuts, and a bit of blood lost—nothing serious. Nothing like as badly hurt as you'd expect a kid to be when a car had knocked her down."

Lorna's mouth stood half-open like that of a stranded fish.

There was a pause; then Judy Vickers plucked at her husband's sleeve.

"Darling, I—uh—think we came at a bad moment. We ought to get on home. But . . . Well, you do understand how grateful we are, don't you?"

She turned away, and so, after a bewildered glance at both Jack and Lorna, did her husband.

"You stupid bitch!" Jack roared. "Why the hell did you have to jump to such an idiotic conclusion? Two people come around to say thanks to Tim for—for whatever the hell he did, and *you* have to assume the worst! Don't you have any respect for your son at all . . . or any love?"

"Of course I love him! I'm his mother! I do care about him!" Lorna was returning to the living area, crabwise because her head was turned to shout at Jack over her shoulder. "For you, though, he's nothing but a possession, a status symbol, a—"

"A correction, Mrs. Patterson," a firm voice said. She gasped and whirled. In the middle of the living area's largest rug was Buddy, his green fur making a hideous clash with the royal blue of the oblong he was standing on.

"Hey! What are you doing down here?" Jack exploded. "You're supposed to be up with Tim!"

"Tim is fast asleep and will remain so for the time being," the Friend said calmly. "Though I would suggest that you keep your voices quiet."

"Now look here! I'm not going to take orders from—"

"Mr. Patterson, there is no question of orders involved. I simply wish to clarify a misconception on your wife's part. While she has accurately diagnosed your attitude toward your son—as she just stated, you have never regarded him as a person, but only as an attribute to bolster your own total image, which is that of the successful corporation executive—she is still under the misapprehension that she, quote unquote, 'loves' Tim. It would be more accurate to say that she welcomes his intractability because it offers her the chance to vent her jealousy against you. She resents—No, Mrs. Patterson, I would not recommend the employment of physical violence. I am engineered to a far more rapid level of nervous response than human beings enjoy."

One arm upraised, with a heavy cut-crystal glass poised ready to throw, Lorna hesitated, then sighed and repented.

"Yeah, okay. I've seen you catch everything Tim's thrown at you . . . But you shut up, hear me?" With a return of her former rage. "It's no damned business of yours to criticize me! Nor Jack either!"

"Right!" Jack said. "I've never been so insulted in my life!"

"Perhaps it would have been salutary for you to be told some unpleasant truths long ago," Buddy said. "My assignment is to help actualize the potential which—I must remind you—you arranged to build into Tim's genetic endowment. He did not ask to be born the way he is. He did not ask to come into the world as the son of parents who were so vain they could not be content with a natural child, but demanded the latest luxury model. You have systematically wasted his talents. No child of eight years and six months with an IQ in the range 160–175 should be incapable of reading, writing, telling the time, counting, and so forth. This is the predicament you've wished on Tim."

"If you don't shut up I'll—"

"Mr. Patterson, I repeat my advice to keep your voice down."

"I'm not going to take advice or any other kind of nonsense from you, you green horror!"

"Nor am I!" Lorna shouted. "To be told I don't love my own son, and just use him as a stick to beat Jack with—"

"Right, *right*! And I'm not going to put up with being told I treat him as some kind of ornament, a . . . What did you call it?"

Prompt, Buddy said, "An attribute to bolster your image."

"That's it—Now just a second!" Jack strode toward the Friend. "You're mocking me, aren't you?"

"And me!" Lorna cried.

"Well, I've had enough! First thing tomorrow morning I call the rental company and tell them to take you away. I'm sick of having you run our lives as though we were morons unfit to look after ourselves, and above all I'm sick of my son being put in charge of—Tim! What the hell are you doing out of bed?"

"I did advise you to speak more quietly," Buddy murmured.

"Get back to your room at once!" Lorna stormed at the small tousle-haired figure descending the stairs in blue pajamas. Tears were streaming across his cheeks, glistening in the light of the living area's lamps.

"Didn't you hear your mother?" Jack bellowed. "Get back to bed this minute!"

But Tim kept on coming down, with stolid determined paces, and reached the floor level and walked straight toward Buddy and linked his thin pink fingers with Buddy's green furry ones. Only then did he speak.

"You're not going to send Buddy away! This is my friend!"

"Don't use that tone to your father! I'll do what the hell I like with that thing!"

"No, you won't." Tim's words were full of finality. "You aren't allowed to. I read the contract. It says you can't."

"What do you mean, you 'read the contract'?" Lorna rasped. "You can't read anything, you little fool!"

"As a matter of fact, he can," Buddy said mildly. "I taught him to read this afternoon."

"You—you what?"

"I taught him to read this afternoon. The skill was present in his mind but had been rendered latent through neglect, a problem which I have now rectified. Apart from certain inconsistent sound-to-symbol relationships, Tim should be capable of reading literally anything in a couple of days."

"And I did so read the contract!" Tim declared. "So I know Buddy can be with me for ever and ever!"

"You exaggerate," Buddy murmured.

"Oh, sure I do! But ten full years is a long time." Tim tightened his grip on Buddy's hand. "So let's not have any more silly talk, hm? And no more shouting either, please. Buddy has explained why kids my age need plenty of sleep, and I guess I ought to go back to bed. Coming, Buddy?"

"Yes, of course. Good night, Mr. Patterson, Mrs. Patterson. Do please ponder my remarks. And Tim's too, because he knows you so much better than I do."

Turning toward the stairs, Buddy at his side, Tim glanced

back with a grave face on which the tears by now had dried.

"Don't worry," he said. "I'm not going to be such a handful any more. I realize now you can't help how you behave."

"He's so goddamn patronizing!" Jack Patterson exploded next time he and Lorna were in Dr. Hend's office. As part of the out-of-court settlement of the dead-dog affair they were obliged to bring Tim here once a month. It was marginally cheaper than hiring the kind of legal computer capacity which might save the kid from being institutionalized.

"Yes, I can well imagine that he must be," Dr. Hend sighed. "But, you see, a biofact like Buddy is designed to maximize the characteristics which leading anthropologists from Procyon, Regulus, Sigma Draconis, and elsewhere have diagnosed as being beneficial in human society but in dangerously short supply. Chief among these, of course, is empathy. Fellow-feeling, compassion, that kind of thing. And to encourage the development of it, one must start by inculcating patience. Which involves setting an example."

"Patience? There's nothing patient about Tim!" Lorna retorted. "Granted, he used to be self-willed and destructive and foul-mouthed, and that's over, but now he never gives us a moment's peace! All the time it's gimme this, gimme that, I want to make a boat, I want to build a model starship, I want glass so I can make a what's-it to watch ants breeding in . . . I want, I want! It's just as bad and maybe worse."

"Right!" Jack said morosely. "What Buddy's done is turn our son against us."

"On the contrary. It's turned him *for* you. However belatedly, he's now doing his best to live up to the ideals you envisaged in the first place. You wanted a child with a lively mind and a high IQ. You've got one." Dr. Hend's voice betrayed the fact that his temper was fraying. "He's back in a regular school, he's establishing a fine scholastic record, he's doing well at free-fall gymnastics and countless other subjects. Buddy has made him over into precisely the sort of son you originally ordered."

"No, I told you!" Jack barked. "He—he kind of looks down on us, and I can't stand it!"

"Mr. Patterson, if you stopped to think occasionally you might realize why that could not have been avoided."

"I say it could and should have been avoided!"

"It could not! To break Tim out of his isolation in the shortest possible time, to cure him of his inability to relate to other people's feelings, Buddy used the most practical means at hand. It taught Tim a sense of pity—a trick I often wish I could work, but I'm only human, myself. It wasn't Buddy's fault, any more than it was Tim's, that the first people the boy learned how to pity had to be you.

"So if you want him to switch over to respecting you, you'd better ask Buddy's advice. He'll explain how to go about it. After all, that's what Friends are for: to make us better at being human.

"Now you must excuse me, because I have other clients waiting. Good afternoon!"

The Taste of the Dish
and the Savor of the Day

Do yourself a favor and be near a source of good food when you read this next one—or far away, if you're on a diet. I was hideously trapped aboard an airplane, doomed to a "meal" of soggy sandwiches and the sort of wine they serve in cans. I guess it travels well.

I'm more gourmand than gourmet, but kept thinking, "Boy, if I were home, I could pile up some caviar on a cracker and unwrap a few interesting cheeses and pull the cork on something they would never serve in a tin can with wings. . . ."

Even the title is delicious.

━━ ━━ ━━ ━━ ━━ ━━ ━━ ━━

The Baron's circumstances had altered since our only previous encounter a year ago. This I was prepared for. His conversation at that time had made it abundantly clear that he had, as the charmingly archaic phrase goes, "expectations."

I was by no means sure they would materialize . . . Still, even though I half suspected him of being a confidence trickster, that hadn't stopped me from taking a considerable liking to him. After all, being a novelist makes me a professional liar myself, in a certain sense.

So, finding myself obliged to visit my publishers in Paris, I dropped a note to what turned out to be an address the Baron had left. He answered anyway, in somewhat flowery fashion, saying how extremely pleased he would be were I to dine with him *tête-à-tête* at home—home now being an apartment in an expensive block only a few minutes from what Parisians still impenitently call *l'Étoile*. I was as much delighted as surprised; for him to have moved to such a location implied that there had indeed been substance in his former claims.

Yet from the moment of my arrival I was haunted by a sense of incongruity.

I was admitted by a man-servant who ushered me into a *salon*, cleanly if plainly decorated, and furnished in a style neither fashionable nor *démodé*, but nonetheless entirely out of keeping, consisting mainly of the sort of chairs you see at a pavement café, with a couple of tables to match, and a pair of cane-and-wicker armchairs. The impression was of a collection put together in the thirties by a newly married couple down on their luck, who had hoped to replace everything by stages and found they couldn't afford to after having children.

I was still surveying the room when the Baron himself entered, and his appearance added to my feeling of unease. He greeted me with a restrained version of his old effusiveness; he settled me solicitously in one of the armchairs—it creaked abominably!—and turned to pour me an *apéritif*. I took the chance of observing him in detail. And noticed . . .

For example, that although it was clean and crisply pressed and was of excellent quality, the suit he had on this evening was one I remembered from a year ago—then trespassing on, now drifting over, the verge of shabbiness. His shoes were to match: brilliantly polished, yet discernibly wrinkled. In general, indeed, so far as his appearance was concerned, whatever he could attend to for himself—as his manicure, his shave, the set of his tie-knot—was without a flaw. But his haircut, it immediately struck me, was scarcely the masterpiece of France's finest barber.

Nor was his manner of a piece with what I would have predicted. I recalled him as voluble, concerned to create a memorable impact; in place of that warmth which, affected or not, had made him an agreeable companion, there was a stiltedness, a sense of going through formally prescribed routines.

He gave the impression of being . . . How shall I define it? Out of focus!

Furthermore, the *apéritif* he handed me was unworthy of his old aspirations: nothing but a commonplace vermouth with a chip off a tired lemon dropped into it as by afterthought. For himself he took only a little Vichy water.

Astonished that someone who, whatever his other attributes, was indisputably a *gourmet*, should thus deny himself, I was about to inquire why he was so abstemious. Then it occurred to me that he must have had bad news from his doctor. Or, on reflection (which took half a second), might wish me to believe so. I was much more prepared now than I had been a year ago to accept that he was a genuine hereditary baron. However, even if one is a scion of a family that lost its worldly goods apart from a miserly pittance in the Events of 1789, one can still be a con man. There is no incompatibility between those rôles any more than there is between being an author and being a sucker. So I forbore to comment, and was unable to decide whether or not a shadow of disappointment crossed his face.

By the time when I declined a second helping of that indifferent vermouth, I might well have been in the mood to regret my decision to re-contact the Baron, and have decided to limit my visit to the minimum consistent with politeness, but for an aroma which had gradually begun to permeate the air a few minutes after I sat down. It was inexpressibly delectable and savory, setting my tastebuds to tingle *à l'avance*. Perhaps everything was going to be for the best after all. A dinner which broadcast such olfactory harbingers was bound to be worthwhile!

Except that when we actually went to table, it wasn't.

At my own place I found a sort of symbolic gesture in the direction of an *hors d'oeuvre*: a limp leaf of lettuce, a lump of cucumber, a soft tomato, and some grated carrot that had seen better days before it met the *mandoline*, over which a bit of salt and oil had been sprinkled. To accompany this mini-feast I was given a dose of dry white *ordinaire* from a bottle without a label. Before the Baron, though, the servant set no food, only pouring for him more Vichy water which he sipped at in a distracted manner while his eyes followed my glass on its way to my lips and the discovery that such a wine would have shamed a *relais routier sans panonceau*. His face was pitiable. He looked envious!

Of rabbit-food and immature vinegar?

I was so confused, I could not comment. I made what inroads I could on the plate before me, trying to preserve at least a polite expression on my own face. And thinking about the servant. Had I not seen the fellow elsewhere?

As he answered the door to me, I'd scarcely glanced at him. Now, when he came to check whether I'd finished with my first course—I yielded it with relief—I was able to take a longer though still covert look. And concluded: yes, I had seen him.

Moreover I recalled when and where. During my last trip to France, in Guex-sur-Saône where they had held that year's French National Science Fiction Congress—and incidentally where I had met the Baron—and what is more, he had been in the same car as the Baron.

But a year ago my host could not possibly have afforded a manservant! He had not even been able to afford his bill at the Restaurant du Tertre to which he had recommended, and accompanied, me and my wife and the friends we were with; he still owed me an embarrassing trifle of seven francs eighty which I was not proposing to mention again if he did not, because the meal had been—as he'd promised—incredibly good value.

The incongruities here began at last to form a pattern in my mind. Had he received the benefit of his "expectations" and then let silly pride tempt him into an extravagance he now regretted? Was it because, thinking a servant appropriate to his new station in life, he had hired one, that he still wore the same suit and couldn't afford to have his hair properly barbered? Was it economy rather than health that drove him to refrain from even such poor refreshment as a guest was offered in this apartment which, though in a smart *quartier*, either was furnished out of a flea market or hadn't been refurnished since what one buys at flea markets was last in style?

Hmm . . . !

The interior of the head of a professional writer is a little like a mirror maze and a little like a haunted house. From the most trivial impetus, the mind inside can find countless unpredictable directions in which to jump. While I was waiting for the main course to be brought in, mine took off towards the past and reviewed key details of our meeting in Guex.

Of all the science fiction events I have attended—and in the course of twenty-five years there have been not a few—that was the most chaotic it has been my misfortune to participate in. The organizers chose a date already preempted by a reunion of *anciens combattants de la Résistance*, so that all the hotels in the center of town were full and we had been farmed out to somewhere miles away. It was, I suppose, entirely in keeping with the rest of the arrangements that on the last evening of the congress we should find ourselves, and the only other English people present—the guest of honor, his wife, and their baby—abandoned in front of the cinema where the congress was being held because the committee and anyone else who was *au fait* had piled into cars and gone into the country for dinner. So many people had turned up for the reunion of the Resistance, there wasn't a restaurant in walking distance with a vacant table.

Hungry and stranded, we made the acquaintance of the Baron: a youngish man—I'd have said thirty-two and prematurely world-weary—lean, with a certain old-fashioned elegance, and out of place. I'd exchanged a word or two with him earlier in the day, when he'd chanced on me standing about as usual waiting for one of the organizers to put in an appearance so I could find out what was happening, and asked me whether a member of the public might attend the movie then showing, since he had a few hours to kill. Seemingly he had enjoyed the picture, for he had stayed over or come back for another.

Emerging now, drawing on unseasonable gloves with an air of distraction as though he were vaguely put out by the absence of a coachman to convey him to his next destination, he spotted and remembered me, and approached with a flourish of his hat to thank me for the trivial service I'd performed.

My answer was doubtless a curt one. Sensing something amiss, he inquired whether he might in turn be of assistance. We explained . . . choosing, of course, terms less than libelous, though we were inclined to use strong language.

Ah! Well, if we would accept a suggestion from someone who was almost as much a stranger as ourselves . . . ? (We would.) And did we have transportation? (We did, although my car was at the hotel, twenty minutes' walk away.) In that case, we might be interested to know that he had been informed of a certain restaurant, not widely advertised, in a village a few kilometers distant, and had wondered whether during his brief stay in Guex he might sample its cuisine. He had precise directions for finding it. It was reputed to offer outstanding value. Were we . . . ?

We were. And somehow managed to cram into my car and not die of suffocation on the way; it's theoretically designed for four, but no more than three can be comfortable. Still, we got there.

The evening proved to be an education—on two distinct levels.

I found myself instantly compelled to admire the deftness with which our chance acquaintance inserted data about himself into a discussion about an entirely different subject. Even before I came back with the car the others had learned about his aristocratic background; I noticed he was already being addressed as *Monsieur le Baron*. His technique was superb! Always on the *qui-vive* for new tricks that might enable me to condense the detail a reader needs to know into a form which doesn't slow down the story, I paid fascinated attention. Almost without our noticing that he was monopolizing the conversation, we were told about his lineage, his ancestors' sufferings at the rude hands of the mob, the death of the elderly aunt for whose funeral he had come to Guex, a lady of remarkable age whose existence he had been ignorant of until a lawyer wrote and advised him he might benefit under her will... (The French are far less coy about discussing bequests than are we Anglophones.)

But on the other and much more impressive hand, within—I swear—five minutes of our being seated in the restaurant, the word had got around behind the scenes that someone of *grand standing* was present tonight. In turn the waiter—it was too small a restaurant to boast a head waiter—and the *sommelier* and the *chef* and finally the proprietor put in their successive appearances at our table as *M. le Baron* proceeded with the composition of our meal. He laid down that there should not be an excess of fennel with the trout, and that the Vouvray should be cellar-cool and served in chilled glasses but on no account iced, which would incarcerate its "nose" and prevent it from competing with the fennel (he was right); that with the subsequent *escalope de veau Marengo* one should not drink the Sancerre of which the *patron* was so proud but a Saint-Pourçain only two years old (he was right about that too), just so long as the *saucier* did not add more than a splash—what he actually said was *une goutte goutteuse*, a phrase that stuck in my mind because it literally means "a drop with the gout"—of wine vinegar to the salad dressing. And so on.

I was not the only one to be impressed. When we had finished our dessert, the owner sent us a complimentary glass apiece of a local liqueur scented with violets, wild strawberries, and something called *reine des bois* which I later discovered to be woodruff. It was so delicious, we asked where else it could be got, and were told regretfully that it was not generally available, being compounded to a secret recipe dating back two centuries or more. Well, one meets that kind of thing quite frequently in France...

Let me draw a veil over the arrival of the bill, except to mention that after my eyes and the Baron's had met and I'd summed up the situation I let an extra fifty-franc note rest for a moment on the table. The dexterity with which it became forty-two francs twenty reminded me of the skill of a cardsharp. I don't think even the waiter noticed.

Well, he was after all in Guex on the sort of business that doesn't conduce to commonsensical precautions; attending a funeral, I wouldn't think to line my billfold with a wad of spare cash against the chance of going out to dinner with a group of foreign strangers. I let the matter ride. The meal had been superb, and worth far more than we were being charged.

Whether for that reason, though, or because he had found out he was in the company of two writers, or simply because the wines and the liqueur had made him garrulous, he appended to the information he had earlier imparted a few more precise details. His elderly aunt had possessed a *château* nearby (not a castle—the word corresponds quite exactly to the English term "manor house" and need not necessarily have turrets and a moat), and although the lawyers were still wrangling it did seem he must be the closest of her surviving relatives. So he might just, with luck, look forward to inheriting a country seat in keeping with his patent—patent of nobility, that is, a term I'd previously run across only in history books.

By then we were all very mellow, so we toasted his chances in another round of that exquisite liqueur. After which we drove back to Guex.

Carefully.

Arriving at his hotel, we said goodbye in a flurry of alcoholic *bonhomie*, exchanging names and addresses although I don't think we honestly imagined we would meet again, for tomorrow was the last day of the congress, and the Baron had said that directly after the funeral—scheduled for the morning—he was obliged to return to Paris.

But we did in fact cross paths next day. As we were emerging from the cinema after the closing ceremony of the congress, a large black limousine passed which unmistakably belonged to a firm of undertakers. It stopped and backed up, and from its window the Baron called a greeting. With him were three other passengers, all men.

And, although I'd only seen him for as long as it took me and my wife to shake hands with the Baron and confirm our intention of getting in touch again one day, I was certain that one of them was the same who now was bringing in a trolley from the kitchen, on which reposed a dish whose lid when lifted freed into the air the concentrated version of the odor I had already detected in diluted form.

I was instantly detached from the here and now. I had to close my eyes. Never have my nostrils been assailed by so delectable a scent! My mouth watered until I might have drowned in saliva but that all my glands—the very cells of my body!—wanted to experience the aroma and declined to be insulated against it.

When I recovered, more at a loss than ever, I found that something brown and nondescript-looking had been dumped on my plate, which was chipped; that a half-full glass of red wine as sour as the white had been set alongside, while the Baron's water-glass had been topped up; and that he was eating busily.

Busily?

This was not the person I had met last year. That version of the Baron not only cared about but loved his food—paid deliberate and sensitive attention to every mouthful of any dish that warranted it. Now he was shoveling the stuff up, apparently determined to clear his plate in record time. And that was absurd. For, as I discovered when I sampled my unprepossessing dollop of what's-it, its flavor matched its aroma. I had taken only a small forkful; nonetheless, as I rolled it across my tongue, choirs sang and flowers burst into bloom and new stars shone in the heavens. I simply did not believe what I was eating.

In the upshot I was reluctant even to swallow that first morsel. I had never dreamed it was possible to create in the modern world a counterpart of ambrosia, the food of the gods. I was afraid to let it slide down my throat for fear the second taste might fall short of the first.

When I did finally get it down in a sort of belated convulsion, I found that the Baron had cleared his plate and was regarding me with a strange expression.

"Ah, you must be enjoying it," he said.

Even as I sought words to express my delight I could feel a tingling warmth moving down me—down not so much in the gravitational as in the evolutionary sense, to lower and lower levels of being, so that instead of just registering on palate and tastebuds and olfactory nerves this stuff, this stew, seemed to be transfusing energy direct into my entire system.

But I did not say so. For I could suddenly read on my host's face what I could also hear unmistakably in his tone of voice: such hopelessness as Mephistopheles might know, something which would be to despair as starvation is to appetite. He spoke as a man who, after long and bitter experience, now knew he would never again enjoy anything.

The tissues of my body were crying out for that miraculous incredible food. I fought and thought for half eternity except that in retrospect I judge it to have been seconds.

And pushed away my plate.

I doubt I shall match that act of will until my dying day. But it was my turn to rise to the occasion, as he had done for stranded foreigners at Guex, and trust to being helped over the consequences.

He stared at me. "Is it possible," he inquired, "that in fact you do not like it?"

"*Mais oui!*" I cried. "I do! But..." It came to me without warning what I ought to say. "But it's the only food I've tasted in my life which is so delicious that it frightens me."

In one of his books William Burroughs hypothesizes a drug to which a person would become addicted after a single dose. I had perhaps had that remark vaguely at the back of my mind. Without having read it, possibly I might not have—Ah, but I had, and I did.

There was a frozen pause. Then a smile spread over the

Baron's face so revolutionizing in its effect it was like the spring thaw overtaking an arctic landscape.

"I knew I was right," he said. "I knew! If anyone could understand it must be an artist of some kind—an author, a poet . . . We shall withdraw so that you may smoke a cigar and I shall instruct Grégoire to bring something to make good the deficiencies of this repast."

He clapped his hands. The servant entered promptly, and stopped dead on seeing my plate practically as full as when he had handed it to me.

"Your dish does not meet with the approval of my guest," the Baron said. "Remove it. Bring fruit and nuts to the *salon*."

Pushing back my chair, anxious to leave the room, I found the fellow glaring at me. And took stock of him properly for the first time. I cannot say he was ill-favored; he was of a type one might pass by the thousand on the streets of any city in France. But, as though he had been insulted to his very marrow by my unwillingness to eat what he had prepared, he was regarding me with indescribable malevolence. For a heartbeat or two I could have believed in the Evil Eye.

How had the Baron, a person of taste, hit on this clown for his "gentleman's gentleman"? Was this some hanger-on of his aunt's, tied to him as a condition of her will?

Well, doubtless I should be enlightened soon enough. The time for speculation was over.

As soon as he had recalled Grégoire to his duties, which were sullenly undertaken, the Baron escorted me into the *salon* and from a corner cupboard produced a bottle I thought I recognized. Noticing that I was staring at it, he turned it so that I could read the label. Yes, indeed; it did say *Le Digestif du Tertre*. When he drew the cork and poured me some, I acknowledged the aroma of violets and strawberries and woodruff like an old friend.

The bottle was full; in fact I doubt it had been previously opened. Yet the Baron poured none for himself. Now I could brace myself to ask why.

He answered with the greatest possible obliquity.

"Because," he said, "Grégoire is more than two hundred years
old."

I must have looked like a figure in a cartoon film. I had a
cigar in one hand and a burning match in the other, and my
mouth fell ajar in disbelief and stayed that way until the flame
scorched me back to life. Cursing, I disposed of the charred stick
and licked my finger.

And was at long last able to say, "*What*?"

"To be precise," the Baron amplified, "he was born in the year
the American Revolution broke out, and by the time the French
Revolution was launched in imitation of it he was already a turnspit and apprentice *saucier* in the kitchens of my late aunt's *château* near Guex . . . which did turn out to devolve on me as her
closest surviving relative, but which unfortunately was not accompanied by funds which would have permitted the repair of its
neglected fabric. A shame! I found it necessary to realize its
value in ready money, and the sum was dismayingly small after
the *sacré* lawyer took his share. I said, by the way, my aunt. This
is something of a misnomer. According to incontrovertible proofs
shown to me by Grégoire, she was my great-aunt at least eleven
times over."

I had just had time to visualize a sort of slantwise genealogical
tree in which aunts and uncles turned out to be much younger
than any of their nephews and nieces, when he corrected himself.

"By that I mean she was my eleven-times-great aunt. Sister of
an ancestor on my father's mother's side who was abridged by the
guillotine during the Terror, for no fouler crime than having managed his estates better than most of his neighbors and occasionally saved a bit of cash in consequence."

Having made those dogmatic statements, he fixed me with an
unwavering gaze and awaited my response.

Was I in two minds? No, I was in half-a-dozen. Out of all the
assumptions facing me, the simplest was that the Baron—whom
I'd suspected of setting me up for a confidence trick—had himself been brilliantly conned.

Only . . .

By whom? By Grégoire? But in that case he would have car
ried on with the act when I refused to finish my meal, no
scowled as though he wished me to drop dead.

And in addition there was the matter of the food itself. I wa
having to struggle, even after one brief taste, against the urge t
run back and take more, especially since its seductive aroma sti
permeated the air.

My uncertainty showed on my face. The Baron said, "I ca
tell that you are not convinced. But I will not weary you b
detailing the evidence which has persuaded me. I will not eve
ask you to credit the argument I put forward—I shall be conten
if you treat it as one of your fantastic fictions and merely judg
whether the plot can be resolved on a happy ending . . . for
swear I can't see such an outcome. But already you have proof
do you not? Consult the cells of your body. Are they not re
proaching you for eating so little of what was offered?"

Grégoire entered, favoring me with another savage glare, de
posited a bowl containing a couple of oranges and some walnut
more or less within reach of me, and went out again. This gav
me a chance to bring my chaotic mind under control.

As the door shut, I managed to say, "Who—who invented it?"

The Baron almost crowed with relief, but the sweat pearling
on his face indicated how afraid he had been that I would moc
him.

"Grégoire's father did," he answered. "A failed alchemist wh
was driven to accept a post in the kitchens of my family home
and there continued his experiments while becoming a renowned
chef. From Grégoire, though he is a person exceedingly difficul
to talk to, I have the impression that his employers believed hin
to be compounding the Philosophers' Stone and hoped, I imagine, that one day they might find themselves eating off plates o
gold that yesterday were pewter . . . But he was in fact obsessed
with the Elixir of Life, which I confess has always struck me a
being by far the most possible of the alchemical goals. Doubtless
the succession of delectable dishes which issued from his kitchen
and were in part answerable for the decline in my ancestors
fortunes, for such was their fame that the King himself, and

many of his relatives and courtiers, used to invite themselves for long stays at our *château*, despite the cramped accommodation it had to offer . . . I digress; forgive me.

"As I was about to say, those marvellous dishes were each a step along the path toward his supreme achievement. Ironically, for himself it was too late. Earlier he had been misled into believing that mercury was a sovereign cure for old age, and his frame was so ravaged by ill-judged experiments with it that when he did finally hit on the ideal combination he could only witness its effects on his son, not benefit in person.

"He left his collection of recipes to his son, having previously taught the boy to cook the perfected version by means of such repeated beatings that the child could, and I suspect sometimes did, mix the stuff while half asleep.

"But, possibly because of the mercury poisoning which had made him 'mad as a hatter,' to cite that very apt English phrase, Grégoire *père* overlooked a key point. He omitted to teach the boy how to read and write.

"Finding that his sole bequest from his father was a satchel full of papers, he consulted the only member of the family who had been kind to him: a spinster lady, sister of the then Baron. She did know how to read."

"This is supposed to be the lady you buried just under a year ago?" I demanded.

He gave me a cool look of reproach. "Permit me to lay all before you and reserve your comments . . . ?"

I sighed and nodded and leaned back in my uncomfortable, noisy chair.

"But you are, as it happens, correct," he admitted when he had retrieved the thread of his narrative.

"I cannot show you the satchel I alluded to. Grégoire is keenly aware of its value, though I often suspect he is aware of little else outside his daily cycle from one meal to another. Only because it must have dawned on his loutish brain that he would have to make some adjustment following the death of my—my *aunt*, did he force himself to part with it long enough for me and her lawyer to examine the contents.

"We found inside nearly eighty sheets of paper and five or parchment, all in the same crabbed hand, with what I later established to be a great use of alchemical jargon and an improbably archaic turn of phrase—seventeenth rather than eighteenth century, say the experts I've consulted. How did I get the documents into the hands of experts?

"Well, the lawyer—who is a fool—showed little or no interest in them. He disliked my aunt as you would expect a bigoted peasant to do, inasmuch as since time immemorial it had been known in the district that she lived alone except for a male companion and never put in an appearance at church. Moreover he was furious at having found that in the estate there was only a fraction of the profit he had looked forward to.

"However, he does possess a photocopier, and before Grégoire's terror overcame him to the point of insisting on being given back all his precious papers, I had contrived to feed six or seven of them through the machine. If you're equipped to judge them, I can show them to you. I warn you, though: the language is impenetrably ancient and technical. Have you wondered why my inheritance has not improved my *façon de vivre*? It is upon the attempt to resolve the dilemma posed by Grégoire's patrimony that I've expended what meager income my portion yields. New clothes, new furniture—such trivia can wait, for if what I believe to be true is true I shall later on have all the time imaginable to make good these transient deficiencies!"

He spoke in the unmistakable tone of someone trying to reassure himself. As much to provide a distraction which would help me not to think about that strange food as for any less selfish reason, I said, "How did Grégoire get his claws into you?"

He laid his finger across his lips with reflex speed. "Do not say such things! Grégoire is the sole repository of a secret which, had it been noised abroad, would have been the downfall of empires!"

Which told me one thing I wanted to know: among the half-dozen papers the Baron had contrived to copy there was *not* the recipe of the dish served to us tonight.

"But your aunt is dead," I countered.

"After more than two hundred years! And I'm convinced she expired thanks to industrial pollution—poisonous organic compounds, heavy metals, disgusting effluents ruining what would otherwise be wholesome foodstuffs . . ."

But his voice tailed away. While he was speaking I had reached for the nuts, cracked one against another in my palm, and was sampling the flesh. There was nothing memorable about this particular nut, but it was perfectly good, and I found I could savor it. Moreover I could enjoy the rich smoke of my cigar. I made it obvious I was doing so—cruelly, perhaps, from the Baron's point of view, for his eyes hung on my every movement and he kept biting his lower lip. Something, though, made me feel that my behavior was therapeutic for him. I rubbed salt in the wound by topping up my glass of liqueur without asking permission.

"And in what manner," I inquired, "did your aunt spend her two centuries of existence? Waiting out a daily cycle from one meal to the next, always of the same food, as you've said Grégoire does?"

The Baron slumped.

"I suppose so," he admitted. "At first, with that delirious sensation on one's palate, one thinks, 'Ah, this is the supreme food, which will never cloy!' After the hundredth day, after the two hundredth . . . Well, you have seen.

"You asked how Grégoire snared me. It was simple—simple enough for his dull wits to work out a method! How could I decline to share a conveyance, *en route* to and from the funeral, with my late aunt's sole loyal retainer? How could I decline to agree when, in the hearing of her lawyer and his *huissier*, he offered to cook me her favorite meal if I would provide him with the cost of the ingredients? The sum was—well, let me say substantial. Luckily the lawyer, upon whom may there be defecation, was willing to part with a few *sous* as an advance against my inheritance.

"And what he gave me was the dish you sampled tonight. With neither garnishing nor salad nor . . . Nothing! He has never learned to cook anything else, for his father's orders were explicit: eat this alone, and drink spring water. But he caught me at my most vulnerable moment. Overwhelmed by the subtlety of the dish, its richness, its fragrance, its ability to arouse appetite even in a person who, like myself at that time, is given over to the most melancholy reflections, I was netted like a pigeon."

In horrified disbelief I said, "For almost a year you have eaten this same dish over and over, without even a choice of wines to set it off? Without dessert? Without *anything*?"

"But it does work!" he cried. "The longevity of my aunt is evidence! Even though during the Nazi occupation it was hard to find certain important spices, she—Wait! Perhaps it wasn't modern pollution that hastened her end. Perhaps it was lack of those special ingredients while the *sales Boches* were overrunning our beloved country. Perhaps Grégoire kept them back from her, cheated the helpless old lady who had been the only one to help him when he was orphaned!"

"And kept her Elixir to herself, content to watch her brother die, and his wife, and their children and the rest of the family, in the hope of inheriting the lot, which she eventually did. And she then spent her fortune on the food because only Grégoire could tell her how much it was going to cost to buy the necessary ingredients."

The Baron gaped at me. "You talk as if this is all common knowledge," he whispered. I made a dismissive gesture.

"If the recipe works, what other reason can there be for the fact that the rest of her generation aren't still among us?"

"Under the Directory—" he parried.

"If they'd known they had a chance of immortality, it would have made sense for them to realize their assets and bribe their way to safety. You said just now that you will have unimaginable time before you if what you think is actually true. Why didn't the same thought occur to your forebears? Because this old bitch kept the news from them—correct?"

The corners of his mouth turned down. "Truly, life can do no more than imitate art. I invited you to treat this like a plot for a story, and thus far I cannot fault your logic."

"Despite which you plan to imitate someone who shamed not

only your family name but indeed her nation and her species?" I crushed my cigar into the nearest ashtray and gulped the rest of my liqueur. "I am appalled! I am revolted! The gastronomic masters of the ages have performed something approaching a miracle. They've transmuted what to savages is mere refuelling into a series of splendid compositions akin to works of art, akin to symphonies, to landscapes, to statues! To leaf through a book like *Larousse Gastronomique* is to find the civilized counterpart of Homer and Vergil—a paean to the heroes who instead of curtailing life amplified it!"

"I think the same—" he began. I cut him short.

"You used to think so, of which I'm well aware. Now you cannot! Now, by your own decision, you've been reduced to the plight of a prisoner who has to coax and wheedle his jailer before he gets even his daily ration of slop. If a single year has done this to you, what will ten years do, or fifty, or a hundred? What use are you going to make of your oversize lifespan? Do you have plans to reform the world? How appropriate will they be when for decades your mind has been clouded by one solitary obsession?"

I saw he was wavering, and rammed home my advantage.

"And think what you'll be giving up—what you have given up already, on the say-so of a half-moronic turnspit so dull-witted his father couldn't teach him to read! This liqueur, for a start!" I helped myself to more again, and in exaggerated pantomime relished another swig. "Oh, how it brings back that delectable *truite flambée au fenouil* which preceeded it, and the marvellous veal, and that salad which on your instructions was dressed as lightly as dewfall . . ."

I am not what they call in French *croyant*. But if there are such things as souls and hells, I think maybe that night I saved one of the former from the latter.

Given my lead, lent reassurance by the way I could see envy gathering in the Baron's face, I waxed lyrical about—making a random choice—oysters *Bercy* and *moules en brochette* and lobster *à l'armoricaine*, invoking some proper wines to correspond. I enthused over quail and partridge and grouse, and from the air I conjured vegetables to serve with them, artichokes and cardoons and salsify and other wonders that the soil affords. These I dressed with sauces so delightfully seasoned I could have sworn their perfume was in the room. I did not, of course, forget that supreme miracle the truffle, nor did I neglect the *cèpe* or the *faux mousseron* or the beefsteak mushroom which is nothing like a steak but gave me *entrée*, as it were, to the main course.

Whereupon I became ecstatic. Roasts and grills, and pies and casseroles and pasties, were succeeded by a roll-call of those cheeses which make walking through a French street-market like entering Aladdin's cave. Then I reviewed fruits of all sizes, shapes, colors, flavors: plums and pomegranates, quinces and medlars, pineapples and nectarines. Then I briefly touched on a few desserts, like *profiteroles* and *crêpes* and *tarte alsacienne* . . .

I was poised to start all over again at the beginning if I must; I had scarcely scraped the surface of even French *cuisine*, and beyond Europe lay China and the Indies and a whole wide world of fabulous fare. But I forbore. I saw suddenly that one shiny drop on the Baron's cheek was not perspiration after all. It was a tear.

Falling silent, I waited.

At length the Baron rose with the air of a man going to face the firing squad. Stiffly, he selected a glass for himself from the tray beside the liqueur bottle, poured himself a slug, and turned to face me, making a half-bow.

"*Mon ami*," he said with great formality, "I am forever in your debt. Or at any rate, for the duration of my—my *natural* life."

I was afraid he was going to take the drink like medicine, or poison. But instead he checked as he raised it to his lips, inhaled, gave an approving nod, closed his eyes and let a little of it roll around his tongue, smiling.

That was more like it!

He took a second and more generous swig, and resumed his chair.

"That is," he murmured, "a considerable relief. I can after all now appreciate this. I had wondered whether my sense of taste might prove to be negated—whether the food I have subsisted on might entail addiction . . . The latter possibility no doubt remains; however, when all else fails there is always the treatment called *le dindon froid.*"

Or, as they say in English, cold turkey . . . Whatever his other faults, I realized, one could not call the Baron a coward.

"*Ach!*" he went on. "In principle I knew all you have told me months ago. You are right in so many ways, I'm embarrassed by your perspicuity. Am I the person to reform the world? I, whom they have encouraged since childhood to believe that the world's primary function is to provide me with a living regardless of whether or not I have worked to earn it? Sometimes I've been amused to the point of laughing aloud by the silliness of my ambition. And yet—and yet . . ."

"*Figurez-vous, mon vieux,* what it is like always to have a voice saying in your head, 'Suppose this time the dish that sustained your aunt two hundred years can be developed into the vehicle of true immortality?' There's no denying that it's a wonderful hybrid between cuisine and medicine."

That I was obliged to grant.

"So, you see, I'm stuck with an appalling moral dilemma," the Baron said. He emptied his glass and set it aside. "It occurs to me," he interpolated, "that I may just have incurred a second one—perhaps infringing Grégoire's father's injunction about eating nothing except his food constitutes a form of suicide? But luckily I feel better for it, so the riddle can be postponed . . . Where was I? Oh, yes: my dilemma. If I break my compact with Grégoire, what's to become of him? If there is no employer to provide him with the funds he needs to buy his ingredients and the kitchen and the pans and stove to cook them, will he die? Or will he be driven like a junkie to robbery and possibly murder? *Mon brave, mon ami,* what the hell am I to do about Grégoire?"

It was as though my panegyric on gastronomy had drained my resources of both speech and enthusiasm. Perhaps more of the liqueur would restore them; I took some.

"By the way," the Baron said, copying me, "an amusing coincidence! While I was still in Guex-sur-Saône, I recalled . . . Are you all right?"

"I—I think so. Yes," I said.

For a moment I'd been overcome by an irresoluble though fortunately transient problem. I was thinking back on the discourse I'd improvised about cookery when it suddenly dawned on me that I'd praised to the skies things I'd never run across. I hadn't tasted half of what I'd talked about with such excitement, and as for the wines, why, only a millionaire could aspire to keep that lot in his cellar!

This *digestif du Tertre* must be powerful stuff on an empty belly!

Recovering, I said, "Please go on."

"I was about to say that while poring over the papers of Grégoire's that I'd managed to copy, I recalled what the *patron* of the Restaurant du Tertre had said about basing his *digestif* on an eighteenth-century recipe. Thinking that if he had such a recipe he might help me decipher some of those by Grégoire's father, I went back to the restaurant, ostensibly of course to buy a bottle of their speciality—I did in fact buy that very bottle yonder.

"And when, having chatted with the *patron* for a while, I produced the most apposite-seeming of the half-dozen recipes I'd acquired, he was appalled. After scarcely more than a glance, he declared that this was identical with the recipe used for his liqueur, and was on the verge of trying to bribe me and prevent it coming to the notice of a commercial manufacturer!"

Chuckling, he helped himself to half a glassful.

"I mention that not so much as an example of how small-minded people in commerce tend to be—though is it not better that something outstanding should be shared if there is a means of creating enough of it, rather than kept for the private profit of a few?—nor even as a demonstration that the influence of the kitchens at my family's *château* must have lingered long after the declaration of the Republic—no! I cite it as evidence that had he not been obsessed with his alchemical aspirations, Grégoire's father could have become a culinary pioneer to stand beside Carême and Brillat-Savarin, indeed take precedence of them! What a tragedy that his genius was diverted into other channels, and that his son—Well!"

"And yet . . ." I said.

"And yet . . ." he echoed, with a heavy sigh.

And that was when I had the only brilliant inspiration of my life.

Or possibly, as I wondered later, credit ought to go to the *digestif.*

At all events, we dined the following night at the Tour d'Argent. And, apart from drinking rather too much so that he wished a hangover on himself, the Baron made an excellent recovery—which removed his last objection to my scheme.

I have one faint regret about the whole affair, and that is that nowadays I have rather less time for my writing. On the other hand I no longer feel the intense financial pressure which so often compelled me to cobble together an unessential bit of make-work simply so that I could meet the bills that month. My routine outgoings are automatically taken care of by the admirable performance of my holdings in Eurobrita Health Food SA, a concern whose product we often patronize and can recommend.

What did we do about Grégoire?

Oh, that was my inspiration. What the Baron had overlooked, you see, was the fact that despite my having slandered him for effect Grégoire was not absolutely stupid. He couldn't be. I confirmed that the moment I put my head around the door of the kitchen he was working in and found it fitted with an electric stove and separate glass-fronted, high-level oven, a far cry from the kitchens at the family *château* with their open fires. A few minutes of questioning, and he opened up like a mussel in a hot pan, as though he had never before been asked about the one thing he really understood: cooking equipment. Which, given the character I'd deduced for his longest-term employer, was not I suppose very surprising.

It emerged that he had advanced by way of coal-fired, cast-iron ranges, and then gas, and had even had experience of bottled gas and kerosene stoves, and had gone back to wood during hard times. I think once he burned some furniture, but on that point he would not be pinned down.

Well, with his enormous experience of different sorts of kitchen, did he not think it time he was put in charge of a really large one, with staff under him? And what is more, I pressed, we can give you a title!

His sullenness evaporated on the instant. *That* was the ambition he had cherished all his two centuries of life: to be addressed with an honorific. Truly he was a child of the years before the Revolution! His is not quite the sort of title one used to have in those days, of course, but his experience with so many various means of cooking had borne it in on him that there had been certain changes in the world.

And now, in a room larger than the great hall of the *château*, full of vast stainless-steel vats and boilers, to which the necessary ingredients are delivered by the truckload—being much cheaper bought in bulk—Grégoire rejoices in the status of *Contrôleur du Service de Surveillance Qualitative*, and everybody, even the Baron, calls him *Maître*.

He learned almost before he could grow a beard that he must never discuss his longevity with anybody except his employer, so there has been no trouble on that score; his uncertainty in a big city was put down to the fact that he had been isolated near Guex in a small backward village. Inevitably, someone is sooner or later going to notice that on his unvarying diet he doesn't visibly age.

But that will be extremely good for sales.

Galactic Consumer Report No. 4

This last Consumer Report puts us in touch with the Galaxy's super-rich, the ultimate consumers, and finishes off a knot of paradoxes with a neat little bow.

————————

THING-OF-THE-MONTH CLUBS

From Extravaganza, *a quarterly supplement to the journal of the Consolidated Galactic Federation of Consumers' Associations, Spring issue 2333 ESY*

Foreword

For the benefit of our members on Luxor, Lonestar and Eldorado, with their average income of Cr. 27,000,000 and tax laws which annually take away all that they haven't managed to spend since last time, three years ago we conceived this supplementary publication and its resounding motto, "The more you spend, the less you get!"

Unfortunately there have been delays beyond our control in launching it. It was not until the proceeds from quadrupling the deluxe subscription rate to our regular journal GOOD BUY began to accumulate that we could even make down payments on adequately expensive articles to be tested. When at long last we had the funds at our disposal, we made the dismaying discovery that just about everything costly enough to be worth our attention had already been bought up by citizens of the three above-named planets. There is not, for example, a quunch machine to be had at present for love or money; they are all in private hands despite their original price-tag of Cr. 16,000,000; and until their builders, the Yog, cycle back into this part of the galaxy in about fifty thousand years presumably no more will come on the market.

For a while we considered opening a special branch on Luxor so that at least we could *borrow* a few articles to test. However, the operation of a nonprofit organization like ours is strictly forbidden there, so we had to drop the idea.

Now at last, though, we have come up with a category of services potentially useful to people hunting for ways of bleeding off their excess purchasing power. We have conducted a far more hasty survey of them than we usually do, we must admit, but for once we only had to apply a single criterion to determine their desirability: did they, or did they not, cost a hell of a lot for absolutely minimal return?

Several of the following undoubtedly do that, and we would refer you to the inside front cover for the increased subscription rates we have found it necessary to introduce as a result.

Background

Thing-of-the-Month Clubs have a long history, stretching (according to some authorities) clear back to the pre-Atomic dark ages. Allegedly the original intention was to offer exceptional value for money, but it did not take long for them to evolve into their modern form: that is to say, they provide a captive group of potential purchasers for just about anything you need to get rid of in quantity. In this century, for instance, we have seen the Bomb-of-the-Month Club, which enabled the Neo-Pacifist Party on Bellatrix not merely to fulfill its election pledges concerning general disarmament but also to show a healthy credit balance in its first budget after assuming power—although admittedly the consequences on other planets where subscribers suddenly found themselves in possession of the galaxy's most modern weaponry at a few hundred credits a throw were not quite so satisfactory, and the club had to cease operation rather suddenly.

We have also seen the Virus-of-the-Month Club, aimed at the specialized but enormous market of hypochondriacs who refused to believe their doctors when assured there was nothing wrong with them. This, however, suffered from excessive client wastage as they were compelled to seek ever more exotic diseases, and the management finally succumbed to a batch of Glotzman's Germ which was accidentally dropped in the packing department and which turned them all livid green with totally ankylosed joints. And so on.

Few of the myriad such ventures currently advertised meet our basic yardstick: outlay per annum of not less than a million credits with negligible value received. Our reports on those which do follow herewith.

Test Reports

We were naturally first attracted to one of the longest established of all TOTM Clubs: the JUNK-OF-THE-MONTH CLUB founded in 2176 by the solitary occupant of the garbage-dump world Gehenna, Lord Albert Grease-Throgmorton. Fired with ambition to create the galactic counterpart of the sort of stately home his ancestors had occupied on Earth in the old days, he advertised rubbish for sale (his own selection) at a rate of Cr. 100,000 a month, which puts the subscription well above our minimum level. Owing to the fact that ever since the club's inception all selections have been shipped in uncrewed sub-light-speed projectiles built from old plastic buckets and soda-water syphons, there is a good chance that subscribers as far distant as Luxor, Lonestar and Eldorado will not live to see the delivery of their monthly junk.

We must, however, warn you that the delay—sometimes amounting to centuries—between dispatch and receipt can lead to one major difficulty. What was garbage a hundred years ago can easily become today's valuable antique. One Croesian subscriber, for example, received the left hand of a statue by Harrison Grabthrush, which had been missing since the Great Moonquake of 2206. A museum on Grabthrush's birthworld of Moralia bid Cr. 10,000,000 for it; the Croesian government promptly taxed the offer at 500%, and the poor fellow was ruined.

Another package contained a copy of the Forbidden Book of Scritch which some very strongminded reader must have managed to throw away before becoming caught up in its insidious wheedling. The new owner was not so lucky and committed suicide at page 34 (held by students of the subject to be below average for the course; page 66 is generally regarded as the breaking point).

We can therefore only recommend the JUNK-OF-THE-MONTH CLUB with serious reservations.

The next to attract our attention was the PLANET-OF-THE-MONTH CLUB, operated from a point close to the galactic center by the only race yet known with control over the process of continuous creation, the Flooge. Since this was by a factor of several hundred the most expensive club we had encountered, our hopes ran high for several weeks until we began to wonder why we were unable to trace any customers, satisfied or otherwise. We were sure that the club would not advertise on the extensive scale it does had there not been significant response from human beings.

Perhaps we were obtuse, but it took an advanced computer to spot what the problem is if you join this club. It turned out to be such an acute one that we did not ourselves feel inclined to test any samples of the product.

The trouble is, simply, storage space. As is usual with these clubs, a premium or bonus offer is made to induce people to join, and in this case it consists of a small gas-giant in addition to the regular selection of Earth-type worlds. In the only case we have been able to document, Mrs. Hylla Handelstein, titular owner of the two largest continents on Freesia, decided she would like more elbow-room and duly filled out the application form. Her planets were, we must admit, dispatched very promptly indeed and we are not in any sense implying that the PLANET-OF-THE-MONTH CLUB is not a bona-fide organization. However, that is small comfort to Mrs. Handelstein and the few surviving inhabitants of Freesia—the gas-giant has already dragged away ninety per cent of its atmosphere, and tides and earthquakes are seriously hampering evacuation.

If you *must* join this club, we advise giving an address in an uninhabited system.

A somewhat more innocuous undertaking might appear to be the MASTERPIECE-OF-THE-MONTH CLUB, which operates on a round-robin basis and requires members to dispatch their monthly selection, after four weeks of enjoyment, to the next person on the list. This too, though, has certain drawbacks. Despite an enormous backlog of original masterpieces to draw on (the Club was instituted to make amends for the depredations of the trillionaire art thief Jeremiah Gung-ho Waterboy, who, as is well known, contrived during his century and a half of operation to transfer the entire contents of the British Museum, the Louvre, the Guggenheim and the Leningrad Hermitage to his private estate on Rafflesworld, replacing each item with a virtually perfect copy to escape detection) the membership has recently expanded to the point where non-human masterworks have been introduced to supplement the existing stocks.

Whatever the pleasure to be derived from a month's contemplation of the Mona Lisa or the Elgin Marbles, we do not feel that it adequately compensates for the experience of one of our test panel, who was sent as his very first selection a flaying-machine by the great Skrinnian artist Three-and-a-half Ug. Admittedly it was of exquisite craftsmanship and unparalleled precision; nonetheless, human beings do *not* count the removal of their epidermis according to predetermined symbolic patterns among the artforms they are capable of appreciating. (We are glad to report that our tester is expected to leave the hospital soon.)

Administrative oversights of a similar nature likewise prevent us from unreservedly recommending the MATE-OF-THE-MONTH CLUB. We would stress that racial prejudice has absolutely nothing to do with our opinion—no organization with chapters among as many different species as has ConGalFedCon-Ass could possibly be open to that charge. Nor are we square, or prissy; we fully recognize that people's tastes vary very widely, and they should be free to indulge them provided they neither interfere with others against their will nor disturb the galactic peace.

However, we do feel that the warning about the penalty for non-consummation which is included in the MATE-OF-THE-MONTH CLUB's advertisements should be supplemented by a clause concerning non-*consumption*. It was only with the greatest difficulty that the female members of our testing panel extricated themselves from the embrace of their respective selections for the first month of their trial membership, and in two or three cases quite extensive surgery was called for.

The selection for that month happened to be Voracian male, and Voracians—as we were *not* informed by the instruction leaflet—have habits which constitute a sort of mirror-image of those of the Black Widow spiders. In other words, the male achieves climax by ingesting his partner. Luckily, the average size of this species is only about half a meter, and their capacity is accordingly rather limited. Nonetheless, we exercised our option to discontinue membership after an initial trial and were glad of the chance to do so, as we had been threatened with mass resignations by all our testers.

* * *

A new venture, announced a few months ago by the PET-OF-THE-MONTH CLUB, brought them also into our range. They are now operating an ultra-deluxe category of membership for those wishing to own exceptionally large pets. The idea would seem an admirable one; regrettably, our own experience has not borne it out in practice.

The first selection we received was a Tyrcodon from Haglith's World, a rather beautiful creature standing some twelve meters tall and covered with glistening red and yellow scales. The dietary instructions furnished with it, however, proved to refer to the *previous* selection, a regular African elephant, and by the time we discovered that Tyrcodons subsist exclusively on fluorspar, the beast had felt the first pangs of hunger. This was fatal . . . or very nearly so. When they're hungry, Tyrcodons emit a howling noise in the low supersonic range at sufficient strength to bring down the average Earthside city-block. Fortunately, experience in the past had persuaded us to establish our testing-labs in a block reinforced against anything short of major meteorite impact, but the consequences might have been alarming.

And our second selection turned out to be a Gigas whale, whose natural environment is a deep ammonia-methane ocean with a pressure of about 100 kg./sq. cm. at -230° C. When opened inadvertently to Earth-normal pressure and temperature, the creature burst and showered long and *disgusting* strands of its internal organs all over everywhere. We have ceded the balance of our membership to an impecunious zoo on Pennywise and hope that the proceeds from later exhibitions of the selections will cover the suit being brought against us for creating a health hazard in Greater Greater New York.

A club which struck us as very promising but which is suspended at the time of writing for reasons detailed below is the PERSONALITY-OF-THE-MONTH CLUB, a venture launched on Schizophrenia but already so successful as to have attracted members on over twenty planets. Members receive a printed-molecule brain-program and an automatic imposer worn over the scalp (wigs are offered as an optional extra to conceal the device in use). So long as the imposer remains in position, the wearer's personality is altered toward a desired character chosen from a wide range indeed—currently more than three thousand choices.

As we said above, however, the club is temporarily suspended owing to a legal dispute. The population of a certain town on Puritania joined the club virtually *en masse*, and in a single month ninety-two per cent of the male residents chose the Casanova program, while eighty-six per cent of the female residents selected the corresponding Messalina program. Owing to this imbalance between male and female, fierce rivalry developed over the favors of the available ladies and so many duels were fought in the first week that the planetary government was compelled to step in. The survivors, deprived of their imposers, naturally reverted to the normal customs of their world and at the time of writing there are factorial-17,321 divorce suits pending, sufficient—according to our computers—to occupy the entire time of the Puritanian courts until well into the next universal cycle. Unofficial sources suggest that the government, faced with this problem, plans to change the name of its world to Saturnalia and give up, but we have been unable to confirm the rumor.

A club which has membership fees well below our minimum standard, but which involves incidental outlay bringing the total cost considerably above it, is the HATRED-OF-THE-MONTH CLUB. This operates on a principle related to that of the last-mentioned club, but instead of an imposer an injection of programmed RNA is employed to induce temporary detestation of items from an imaginatively chosen list. Among other things which our test-panel sampled, we would cite plate-glass windows, water-sculpture, plastic minijerkins, autojazz generators, and (perhaps most useful of all for our purposes) money.

As you will doubtless have realized, though, it's the legal costs which increase the expenditure of this club so substantially, and we can only recommend it to people who have time to spare for frequent appearances in court.

Best Buy

Having read the foregoing, you will by this time probably be wondering: did we not come across any Thing-of-the-Month Club which we can wholeheartedly recommend? We did indeed!

Astonishingly, it is a club with no membership dues, open to anyone on completion of a simple application form such as is enclosed with this issue of EXTRAVAGANZA. The only fee charged by the management is for incidental expenses.

We are, of course, referring to the absolutely brand-new THEFT-OF-THE-MONTH CLUB.

This is a club without strings, membership being subject to only one condition: that if the proceeds from your monthly burglary fall below Cr. 100,000, service will be automatically discontinued and is nonrenewable. It meets all requirements stated by ConGalFedConAss's members on all three of the galaxy's wealthiest worlds, and its impeccable reliability is attested by the fact that it is under the personal supervision of the retiring editor of this magazine, who wishes to take this opportunity of saying that having served the public for so long in one capacity he regards this move to a new job as no more than a logical extension of his previous activities and hopes that many of the subscribers who have so loyally supported ConGalFedConAss for so long will find everything they have been seeking in the THEFT-OF-THE-MONTH CLUB.

Fill out the application right away. The forms will be dealt with strictly in order of receipt.

The Man Who Saw the Thousand-Year Reich

All writers are also readers, at once producers and consumers, which sometimes creates in us a kind of double vision. We know that even the most enjoyable, light-hearted story may have cost its creator hours of floor-pacing and hair-pulling as the seemingly endless drafts piled up. (They used to pile up literally, in shoals of crumpled-up paper; now the old discarded words just sail off to some electronic Nirvana.) Sometimes it's sadly apparent that extraordinary effort went into making the story behave. The whip, the chair, the pistol full of blanks: Into the cage, Simba . . . whew! Thought she had me there.

But other times when you read a story, you know the writer enjoyed every minute of the writing. I do know a little something about Brunner's politics, specifically about his commitment to racial equality—and can imagine him chuckling audibly as he arranged the bizarre fate of Herr General Horst Wentschler.

If Mr. Secrett says to me one more time that there are some people destined for the *culs-de-sac* of history, that he's one, and he thinks I'm another, I shall scream.

Because I'm dreadfully afraid he must be right.

How else to account for the fact that no matter how weird or extraordinary my current problem may be, Mr. Secrett invariably turns up in connection with it? Worse still, he always produces—

I was about to say an explanation. Maybe hallucination would be more correct.

Yet to look at him one would never guess what wild yarns he's given to spinning. Especially when abroad, he's the perfect caricature of the old-style Englishman, given to Aertex shirts and Austin Reed chokers, and politely patronizing toward foreigners.

Except, of course, for the Swiss, whom the British have always looked on as psychological cousins: citizens of a landlocked island, as it were, blending German, French, Italian and Romansh language-groups as though they were the counterparts of English, Scottish, Welsh and Irish.

So really I suppose I should not have been surprised when the phone rang in my hotel room in Riehen, near Basel, which is in one of those odd little peninsulas where Switzerland juts into Germany for some long-forgotten historical reason, and through a hangover fog due to too much of a superb *Poire William* liqueur I heard his all-too-familiar voice saying, "Scrivener! What in the world possessed you to utter such a farrago of nonsense about General Wentschler?"

I reviewed a whole range of curses, decided that while they might be efficacious against anybody else I knew they would have absolutely no impact on Mr. Secrett, and in the end contented myself with saying bitterly, "I suppose you know the real story."

"Of course I do!" he boomed with the sort of cheerfulness which is particularly loathsome before breakfast . . . although, as I discovered when I checked my watch, it was now nine fifteen and he had doubtless been up and about since seven. Or even six.

"Then why," I said, "didn't you go on the telly last night instead of me?"

"Oh, they wouldn't have asked me, would they? The internationally celebrated Mr. Scrivener, on the other hand . . ."

"Stop it!" I told him crossly. "Where are you?"

"In the hotel lobby. I don't imagine you've had breakfast yet?"

"No, not yet," I agreed with heavy irony.

"I have, of course, but I could manage another cup of hot chocolate—they do it so well here, don't they? See you at the reception desk in ten minutes."

For a while after I put down the phone, I contemplated going back to sleep; the curtains were still drawn and the room was temptingly dark.

Then curiosity got the better of me, and I grumpily swung my legs to the floor. Besides, the old bastard was right: I was ashamed of the performance I'd put up last night, and the only excuse I could offer was that the fee they were paying was generous enough to make me—shall we say?—anxious to please . . .

But if only Mr. Secrett hadn't shown up, I could have salved my conscience by ascribing it all to necessary experience and gone happily home a week, or at any rate a few days, later than scheduled. I was on what I justified to myself by calling it a "working holiday," following up what had looked like a promising lead for a series of articles. Two days after getting here, I'd discovered that someone from *Der Spiegel* had beaten me to it, and his stuff was being syndicated.

Trying not to look too disappointed, and not wanting to head for home until I ran completely out of funds, I'd been swanning around the area hoping that sheer luck might lead me to some other project, when exactly that happened. A TV producer in Basel got hold of a very odd story indeed and went looking for people who might comment authoritatively on it, and learned that a foreign writer was in Riehen and, what was more, spoke enough German to answer a few questions on screen.

Fabelhaft! From my point of view as well as his, especially after I'd mentally converted his offer into sterling.

So they sent a limousine, wined and dined me, told me the story (three times, to make sure my creaky command of German didn't lead to an embarrassing misunderstanding) and sat back and waited for me to produce an explanation *à la* von Däniken or Laszlo Perkins.

Which—I confess it with blushes—was all I *had* been able to come up with. But I can at least plead in mitigation that I only heard the story two hours before I went on camera.

What they told me was this:

A month before, when the spring thaw set in across the Alps, a patrol setting off explosives to forestall avalanches in the vicinity of a winter-sports center had found a man's body frozen into a deeply crevassed glacier. Assuming it must be some unfortunate climber, they chopped it free . . . only to find it clad in full evening dress, patent leather pumps, and an overcoat which, even though it had a fur collar, was not exactly designed for mountaineering.

They were able to work out the rate of movement of the glacier and concluded the man must have been caught in a snowfall some thirty to fifty years previously. Searching the corpse for clues, the surgeon at the local mortuary found some tattoo marks under the left arm.

They were a blood-group—group O—and a series of figures which one of his assistants recognized. It was a Waffen-SS number.

Checking with the famous Nazi-hunter Simon Wiesenthal, they discovered that it belonged to General Horst Wentschler, who had been in overall charge of the "final solution to the Jewish problem" from September 1943 to April 1944 in the *Gau*, or administrative region, of Bohemia. And Bohemia, which is now once again in what had already briefly been Czechoslovakia, was a long way from Switzerland—particularly in wartime.

It was officially on record, for documents concerning the event had survived World War II, that General Wentschler had last been seen by his batman on 3rd April 1944 in high spirits. He had hinted that some kind of honor was to be bestowed on him; the batman gathered he had been summoned to receive yet another decoration from the Führer. A car collected him from the castle which was serving as headquarters. Its driver presented what appeared to be authentic papers, but must obviously have been forged, for he was never seen again alive.

Everybody jumped to the conclusion he had been kidnapped by a clever resistance group. Hostages were taken, and after a week they were publicly executed in the main square of the nearest town.

Now here he had turned up again, frozen to death, but apparently uninjured, with even a flower in his lapel. Yet without his identity documents—without his cherished Iron Cross—and across the frontier in a neutral country.

Opposite me on the TV show was a local journalist who got in first with all the suggestions I'd have liked to make: Wentschler had decided that the Germans were bound to lose the war, so he had bargained with some unknown intermediary to smuggle him to a noncombatant nation, but no one showed up at the rendezvous to take him further; in despair he set out on foot through the snow to look for help, got lost, died of exposure . . . Moderately neat; I wanted to find out why he was in evening dress and such unsuitable shoes and was even busy inventing some plausible reasons.

But then I decided I was perhaps the lucky one after all, for the presenter of the show came back with some devastating counterblows. Wentschler was a fanatical Nazi, who had been repeatedly commended for sparing no pains in the performance of his "duty"; he was one of the youngest men to be promoted general in all the SS corps; he left behind a personal fortune which, because he was single and childless, he willed to the furtherance of Nazi domination; and he had not been reported by any guard or sentry or policeman on his way from Bohemia to the Swiss frontier, at a time when the tide of war had begun to turn and the strictest possible controls were being kept on everybody's movements, even generals'.

That drove me back to the kidnapping idea. When the cameras

turned on me, I feebly suggested that he must indeed have been tricked by a resistance group, but not a local one—perhaps people with first-rate support from Allied special services. The presenter gave me a warning frown. That was not what he expected from me, with my wild writer's imagination. Besides, as he said aloud, surely such a group would have taken him alive to an Allied base for interrogation, not released him when over the Swiss border.

So maybe he managed to escape, I offered . . . but that sounded weak even to my ears, and by this stage I had cottoned on. In the nick of time I remembered H. Beam Piper's classic story *He Walked Around the Horses* and spent the next five minutes elaborating a time-space warp—not a very easy task in German, at least not to someone whose vocabulary is as limited as mine. But that was just what everyone was looking for. There were beaming faces all round the studio when the show came to its end, and the producer insisted on taking me to the hospitality room and plying me with that excellent liqueur. Around midnight they piled me into a car and took me back to Riehen.

I had guilty dreams.

"I thought that might have been the way of it," said Mr. Secrett, pouring me a third cup of coffee. "But I'm ashamed of you nonetheless. Space-time warps, forsooth! A moment's reflection should have shown you the only logical conclusion without needing me to spell it out."

"Spare me the sarcasm," I muttered. "I'm in such a state, I can't work out whether you're really here, or whether I'm still having nightmares."

He looked hurt. "Surely you know I take a walking tour in mountain country every spring . . . ? Ah, of course. I don't believe I've seen you since I decided to come to Switzerland this year instead of the Pyrenees or the Harz. You should keep in closer touch, old boy!" He prodded me playfully with his nearer elbow. I winced.

"Anyhow," he resumed, "I reached the hostelry where I'd reserved a room, and it was too early to turn in. So I watched television for a while to see how the other half lives, ha-ha! And there you were, large as life but not so natural, talking about Wentschler, of all people. So I thought I might do a favor to a fellow-countryman and get to you before the journalists. You've read the newspapers——? No, of course not. But I did see a rather sensational rag on the bus, and apparently the show you were on has a reputation for pandering to the viewers' baser impulses, in an attempt to hold the audience against competition from across the border."

"That figures," I sighed. "But do you honestly know what really happened to this bloody general?"

"For once," said Mr. Secrett, leaning back and staring into nowhere, "I will concur with your choice of adjective. Ordinarily I regard words like 'bloody' as an infuriating waste of breath. But in the case of Horst Albrecht Wentschler the term is peculiarly apt. Which is why I can't be sorry that he became the victim of the most ingenious practical joke in history. Picture, if you will . . ."

It was late evening. Weary, for he had spent today investigating, proving, and executing the guilty parties to a charge that Jews were successfully bribing concentration-camp guards to supply food in exchange for gold tooth-fillings, General Wentschler strode into his bedroom, where a bright fire burned.

And stopped dead, reaching for his pistol. Instead of his batman awaiting him, there was a stranger, sitting in his own favorite chair.

But the man was making no attempt to conceal himself. He was rising and giving a crisp "Heil Hitler!" Moreover he was clad in a uniform almost identical to Wentschler's own: black, with silver insignia. *Almost* identical. Where, if ever, had been seen before that device of a skull and crossed rockets?

"Herr General! Permit me to present myself! I am Leon Kalkhaver and I have the honor to be Oberkommandant of the Wissenschaft-SS. And"—like magic he had produced his own pistol while Wentschler was still letting his hand hover above the holster, and it looked like no pistol the general had seen before—"I must instruct you that if you so much as mention to any living soul without express permission from myself, Herr Himmler, or the Führer, that you know of my organization's existence, I shall be obliged to ensure your silence. Be seated. You will find what I have to say most interesting."

There was something in the eyes of this stranger which prevented Wentschler from shouting for his aides. Slowly he thought through what he had just heard, and a thrill pervaded him.

Wissenschaft-SS?

He had never before heard of a "scientific" branch of the Schutzstaffel. But it was entirely credible! One knew about the superweapons which would snatch victory for Germany from the very jaws of defeat—the rockets which would rain destruction not only on Britain but even on America, once they were deployed. Whenever the clouds of battle loomed darkest, something always appeared to lighten the prospect of tomorrow, even if it were only a faster poison gas to eliminate more Jews in a shorter time.

"How did you get in here?" he barked, retaining all he could of his customary air of command.

"Oh!"—with a shrug. "We of the Wissenschaft-SS come and go as we choose, subject only to the decisions of the Führer. And it is upon a mission from him personally that I visit you."

Holstering his pistol again, he waved at the room's other chair.

"Be seated, Herr General. I have instructed my orderly to bring wine."

"Your orderly—? What about mine?"

"Your staff are admirably trained. They have been taught to recognize superior authority by instinct, which is the hallmark of the true Aryan. Had it not been so"—with an access of fierceness—"I assure you I would have abandoned my mission and returned to Berlin!"

"What," said Wentschler, and with the question surrendered all intention of challenging this intruder's rights, "do you want of me?"

"To bestow on you a reward which, for the time being, the Führer in his wisdom has decreed must be confined to a handful of those most loyal to the ideal of the Thousand Year Reich—a reward far surpassing any medal or decoration or promotion. A reward which has already been granted to two people you know, but which they, in duty bound, have never mentioned to anybody, nor will they until the time is ripe. Nonetheless, it has happened, and it will also happen to you."

Conscious that his listener was hanging on every word, Kalkhaver removed his severe peaked cap, revealing a head of flawlessly blond hair cut not quite short enough to let the skin gleam through.

"There has been much talk of traveling through space, Herr General. It will indeed be through space that we launch our continental rockets to shatter the cities of Jew-dominated America. But a defense against that form of attack is at least conceivable.

"Have you, on the other hand, ever considered an attack through time?"

For a long moment Wentschler stood transfixed. To go back and eliminate an enemy commander before a crucial battle! To remove Churchill, Stalin or Roosevelt, leaving only second-rate substitutes to fill their shoes! What a vista of marvels opened up with those few words!

"Have we already—?" he husked. But Kalkhaver shook his head, sinking back into his chair; a moment, and Wentschler imitated him.

"Unfortunately we have many problems to resolve. I take it you instantly thought of altering the past?"

Dry-mouthed, Wentschler nodded.

"We are still working on that aspect of it. So far, what we have achieved is to move, not objects—oh, apart from garments and other insignificant items—but people into the future. It appears time-travel is easiest when dealing with the fluidity of the days to come. Well, that's not very surprising; it's easier to build a shell than to re-assemble it after it's gone off. But wait a moment." Kalkhaver drew back his sleeve and consulted a watch with improbably many dials. "The orderly will enter any moment and he is not cleared to hear such talk."

A few heartbeats ticked away, and there came a tap at the door. Kalkhaver's curt "*Herein!*" produced a thick-set man with a moon face and vacant grin, who bore on a silver tray a bottle of French champagne, two cut-crystal glasses, and a bowl of little crackers with dark-green inclusions.

"Japanese," Kalkhaver said casually as he dismissed the orderly and opened the wine himself, spilling not a drop. "One of our *pro-tem.* allies' few contributions to civilization . . . By the way," he added as the door closed, "that man is one of our pilot genetic products. Typical of what the Slavs will turn into when we need them to farm the rich lands of the Ukraine: a perfect serf who will never argue with his master. You realize, we *Wissenschaftskünstler* regard your way of going about the eugenic problem as somewhat wasteful—though," he hastily corrected himself, "so long as the Führer deems it necessary, we can only admire your thoroughness. Already you're showing a profit in terms of fabric, tooth-stoppings, and recyclable fats, though the cost at two marks per head for cremation of the remains . . . Excuse me! Do sample this wine. Even though the Führer is, as you're aware, a vegetarian and a teetotaler, he accords it a place in the cellar at Berchtesgaden."

Raising his glass with a mechanical "*Prosit!*", Wentschler sipped—and sipped again, and swigged the lot.

"And now," Kalkhaver said, giving him a refill, "to the meat of my errand."

"I have told you that certain persons have visited the future and that all of them were dedicated to the ideal of the Thousand Year Reich. You can easily guess the purpose of this undertaking."

"They are to report back on which of certain key decisions paid off?"

Kalkhaver beamed. "Congratulations, Herr General! Not even —but I must guard my tongue! Let me just say that you have broken all records among your predecessors for quickness on the uptake. You will readily see why total loyalty to the principles of National Socialism is the prime condition for the selection of our pioneers; how otherwise could we be certain of an honest report?"

"But surely," Wentschler ventured, "if you are already working on the problem of sending information back through time, they will have solved it by—by some future date?"

A cloud seemed to cross Kalkhaver's brow. He said, "It grieves me to admit it, but it might well be that the problem is intractable. Conflicts with a law of nature. Barring this one case which we had the good fortune to chance on almost as soon as our research paid off. That is, that information in a human brain is exempt. We can't send a message to the future and ask for a reply. We can send a living man and interrogate him on his return. It is not easy! We are prevented, for some strange reason, from choosing—oh—someone gifted with exceptional powers of memory and simply sending him ahead to a library and telling him to memorize a history book. All our successes, and I may admit to you that the process does not always succeed, have been with people who in themselves constituted some kind of turning point of history. You can guess at the identity of some of them by thinking of the military commanders who since the inception of the project—that's to say, from about this time last year—have brilliantly turned defeat into victory. There have been a number of disappointments, too... But I'm sure you won't be among them."

"You think I'm one of those—those crucial people?"

"If you were not so regarded, I would not be here," Kalkhaver declared with finality and, having drained his glass, threw it into the fireplace. "Read this, which I was given personally by Hitler yesterday, and decide whether you will accept the challenge!"

He drew from his pocket an envelope bearing Chancellery seals of heavy red wax. Opening it, Wentschler discovered that miracle of miracles, a letter in the Führer's own hand. Words danced before his eyes.

Very honored General! This comes to you by the hand of well-trusted Oberkommandant Kalkhaver who will explain to you why

*or once the Leader must be a follower. It makes me sadder than I
an say that reason persuades me to postpone that moment when
can myself witness the consequences of my actions. Bring me
those data I need to conclude the war swiftly, and I shall be
orever in your debt.*

Appended were the familiar signature and the seal showing an
agle surmounting a ring with a swastika inside.

"Well?" Kalkhaver said, permitting himself a smile. "Do you
ccept, or must we dismiss you as unworthy and arrange your
limination before you have a chance to reveal the existence of
his project to a third party?"

Handing back the letter, Wentschler sprang to attention. "Let
t never be said," he whispered, "that I failed my leader in his
our of need!"

"I was certain you would react this way," Kalkhaver said, also
ising as he took back the letter. "Be so good as to obey the rest
f my instructions, then! Change at once into civilian dress—
*v*ening clothes would be most suitable. Divest yourself of any-
hing to connect you with present time, all identity papers, all
*r*ders, medals, and so forth."

Wentschler felt a pang of dismay.

"Even my Iron Cross?"

"Everything," said Kalkhaver firmly. "Reflect a moment!
Whom do we wish to arrive first in the future wearing the full
*anoply of Nazism . . . ?"

"Oh!"

"Precisely! Were we to tackle the matter otherwise, we might
isk some sort of cult of personality, even of resurrection! A reli-
ion might well result!"

"That has not been stamped out?"

"Not so far as our techniques at this stage permit us to reach.
You are acquainted with the term 'feedback'?"

"Ah . . . yes, I believe so."

"At all costs we must avoid destabilizing the continuum. We
*must employ our methods to create the Nazi future before we can
isk exploring the alternatives. Not that it matters, naturally. All
lternatives are by definition inferior. Do as I say, please."

Wentschler was momentarily at a loss. He said after a pause, "You want me to change into plain evening dress?"

"I already said so!" Kalkhaver replied, glancing again at his strange watch. "Hurry! There is a deadline to meet!"

"But I'm afraid . . ." The confession cost Wentschler dear. "I'm afraid I don't know where my evening clothes are."

"But you possess some?"

"Of course! In the charge of my batman!"

Kalkhaver pondered a moment. At last he said with a sigh, "Very well, then. Call him, get changed, see me at the main door in ten minutes. And don't fail!"

"I swear by my honor as an officer, by the motto on my dagger, I shall not!"

Mollified, Kalkhaver turned to go.

"One thing!" Wentschler threw after him.

"Yes?"

"How far am I to be sent?"

"Ah! Like all our volunteers, you would like to go into the far future, yes? So would we—so would I! I can only say, with regret, it must be a matter of a very short journey: five, ten, at best fifteen years. We rely on you, on your return, to tell us exactly when you arrived. And, of course, to pay attention to absolutely everything, especially news reports, which you have witnessed. And one more thing, which I blame myself for having overlooked.

"Before actually putting you through the transmitter—which for obvious reasons you will not be allowed to see or even deduce the location of—we shall perform a minor surgical operation. An explosive charge will be implanted in your neck, adjacent to the spinal column. At the first hint you plan to betray your identity, it will explode. The incision will be imperceptible, apart from a slight soreness. I trust this does not incline you to change your mind?"

"But if I can't tell anybody who I am, then how—?"

"It's very simple. We send instructions by what we call 'the slow road'—in other words, we leave messages where our successors are bound to find them—explaining what we plan to do.

arrangements are made at the receiving end. Owing to the short
range we can presently achieve, our techniques are still being
researched in secret, but our successors *do* get the message and
to make the arrangements. In fact, most of our volunteers so far
have had rather a good time: a dinner party, for example, or a
ball, or the chance to witness a military parade and be entertained
afterward in an officers' mess . . . But you press me too far, Herr
General!"

The door slammed.

In a fever of excitement, Wentschler ordered his batman to
produce the garments called for by Kalkhaver while he washed
and shaved. It was beneath him, however, to admit that he was
leaving behind his prized decorations; he hid those where he was
sure they would not be chanced on before his return. It occurred
to him that perhaps that might not be long hence; with control
over time, the Wissenschaft-SS might be able to bring him back
almost before his absence was noticed . . . which obviously ac-
counted for Kalkhaver's failure to mention the need to explain his
departure to his superiors.

Humming contentedly, letting his batman draw what conclu-
sions he liked from his master's behavior, Wentschler dressed
precisely as instructed and went down to the main gate, where a
Horch staff-car awaited him.

Less than two kilometers from the castle, a needle slid up
from the cushions of the back seat where Kalkhaver was completing his briefing, and before Wentschler could complain about
the prick, he was washed away into unconsciousness.

The last thing he heard was his companion saying gently,
"Remember, Herr General, even you may not know where our
equipment is located . . ."

He woke in a normal physical state (bar a dull ache on the side
of his neck, which he had after all been warned about), to find
himself stretched out fully clad except for his hat, overcoat and
gloves on a silk-covered bed in a room where four wall-lamps

shed a peach-colored glow. It was night, as he realized the moment his eyes lit on the window, for the curtains were partly open. He had woken prepared to be angry at what Kalkhaver had done, and now reflex brought him to his feet, his mind full of blackout regulations.

But the instant he looked beyond the glass, he realized he was making a mistake. There were streetlamps shining to left and right, and other lighted windows.

This was no city in danger of air raids.

For the first time he began to believe the miracle Kalkhaver had described to him.

If only he could climb out and go exploring! But Kalkhaver had explained why he must not, and anyhow there were stout bars to prevent him.

As though alerted by his leaving the bed, a man appeared in the doorway of the room. He was a magnificent Aryan specimen: blue-eyed, blond-haired, almost two meters tall. He wore a black bowtie with a tailcoat . . . but perhaps fashions had changed.

He said, "I'm glad to see you awake, sir. Your host and hostess await you below as soon as you have performed your ablutions. Be so kind as to knock on the door when you are ready, and I shall be pleased to escort you downstairs."

He vanished again, and the door shut with a firm clunk.

Presumably, since he was the first contact the general had had since—well, since "arrival"—that man would be party to the time-travel secret . . . ?

But he must take nothing for granted. Kalkhaver had emphasized that as yet the scientists knew little of the strange and wonderful new world he was visiting. Above all, they had insisted on finding out nothing about their successors, for fear of creating the destabilizing feedback effect.

So he must simply do as he was told for the time being, even though he was sorry not to remember how he had been transmitted here. A shining archway, or a silver tunnel, or—

Never mind! He reprimanded himself. And, on noticing a washbasin beside the bed, remembered he was supposed to "perform ablutions." Welcome enough; he felt soiled by his trip.

Turning on the taps and reaching for the soap, which was brand-new, he caught sight of something in a wastebasket.

Out of curiosity he picked it up. It proved to be the wrapper from the soap . . . and that in itself was remarkable, for he had long been used to soap that came naked, four-square and functional. And on it he read:

JASMINE SOAP. Formula copyright 1950 by Imperial Chemical Industries for all countries of the world.

1950!

He had no time to reflect on the implications of the rest of the text, for here was the tall blond man again, waiting impassive in the doorway, saying, "Excuse me, sir, but the entire company is assembled for dinner except yourself, and it is long past sundown."

Hastily drying his hands and making use of a spotlessly clean comb which lay beside the basin, Wentschler turned to go.

"Are you the son of the house?" he inquired.

"No, sir!"—in a tone of vague puzzlement. "I'm the underbutler. Kindly follow me."

Out along a broad landing overlooking a handsomely tiled hall, down wide stairs thickly carpeted, toward a double-doored anteroom from which came music and lively chat. On the way Wentschler was casting about for useful information, but all he worked out was the obvious: his host was extremely well-to-do. On the walls there were carefully lighted paintings and, here and there, carvings in illuminated niches. It dismayed the general to notice that the pictures were of a type he regarded as thoroughly decadent—most of them abstracts—and the sculptures were a mixture of primitive African and modern nonrepresentational. However, it was known that even Reichsmarschall Göring had granted a place in his collection to a few such works, so . . .

The underbutler opened the door and stood aside. Within, another servant announced him by the name Kalkhaver had said all their time-travelers adopted: "Herr Hans Schmidt!"

And Wentschler advanced to meet his host and hostess, just in time repressing his automatic "Heil Hitler!", for the man who turned beaming to him was offering his hand to be shaken.

But the company of guests was an even worse shock than the pictures. Nine people were present: a coal-black African in tribal robes, an Indian woman in a sari, a man who could only be Chinese, one very blond girl with long hair in a gown that scarcely pretended to cover her bosom, a Eurasian woman, a swarthy man who looked like a gypsy, a boy of about sixteen with close-curling negroid hair and a complexion like milky coffee, and a woman with short red hair wearing something like backless beach-pajamas and a lot of rings, and finally the man proffering his hand, whose bald pate was surrounded by slicked-down black hair and whose nose was distinctly hooked.

Moreover, the music, which emanated from a radio-gramophone adjacent to a large televisor—the latter's screen at present dark—was nigger music of the kind called "swing" . . .

Pretending he was perfectly at ease, but shocked to his very soul, "Schmidt" briefly touched hands and could not help clicking his heels, which provoked some raised eyebrows.

"Welcome, welcome!" the host said hastily. "I'm Jakob Feuerstein! Let me present you to my wife. My dear, you'll remember my mentioning that Herr Schmidt has been abroad for a long while—yes?"

And this was getting worse by the moment. For his wife was the Eurasian woman, small and delicate, smiling up at him and elevating her hand in a way that made it clear she expected it to be kissed.

"And my son Paul, from my first marriage of course—"

The boy, whose grin was broad and handshake firm.

"And Herr and Frau Sikelole from South Africa—"

The tall black man and, incredibly, the splendidly Aryan blonde. "And Fräulein O'Keefe—" The redhead.

"And Fräulein Dass—"

The one in a sari, slim and elegant and very conscious of being the most beautiful woman in the room . . . but Wentschler was immune from such reactions.

"And Herr Ling and Herr Nagy! Now you know everybody, let me offer you a drink. Franz!"—with a snap of his fingers toward the butler. "Whisky, gin, port, sherry, or would you prefer champagne?"

"A glass of mineral water, if you please," Wentschler said through lips that had become as stiff as cardboard. This was terrible! What could have gone wrong? How could this be the future of the Reich? What were these mongrels, these simians, doing in this magnificent house and speaking fluent German, albeit with strange accents? Why were the servants so obviously members of the Herrenvolk? And why was the blonde girl smiling and clinging to the arm of her black husband like that? The sight nauseated him!

Had it not been for the ache in his neck, which reminded him of the doom that awaited any admission of his identity, he would have marched out and gone to explore the city. Of course, if he were to do that, when the unpredictable time came for his return —he had learned that much from Kalkhaver as they were leaving the castle—he might not be in range of the mysterious energy-field which governed his presence and his return to 1944 . . .

No, he dared not. He must keep up the act, if only to report that on this trip something had gone most dreadfully wrong.

"Cigarette?" suggested the boy Paul, offering a cardboard pack of the sliding-drawer type.

"Thank you, but I don't," the general answered stiffly, and the boy returned the pack to his pocket, but not before Wentschler, eyes keen for any hint or clue about this terrifying future, had seen that it bore the trademark of a bearded sailor within a life preserver and the legend *Players Export*. In English . . .

Which set his mind on another tack. Where was the picture of Hitler one would expect to see in such a room? No sign, no hint, of the Reich's glories! There was no newspaper to be seen—he would have clutched greedily at it—and only a select few books, mostly large, luxuriously bound volumes of art-reproductions and guides to the collection of antiques.

Affable, plainly eager to set his strange guest at ease, Feuerstein was chatting to him as his glass of water arrived on a silver tray. It was clear at once that he was a dealer in *objets d'art* and expected everyone else to share his passion for them. His dedication to the past was visible all around this room; there was nothing remotely "modern" in it except the televisor and radiogram, and even those were disguised in mock-antique cabinets.

Of all the filthy, horrible ill-luck! To wind up *here*, wasting a unique chance to gather information and report back to Kalkhaver and through him to the Führer!

But he must make the most of every slightest hint and clue, and here was one. Feuerstein was indicating what to Wentschler looked like a perfectly ordinary flower-vase on a low marble-topped table.

"That's one of my recent acquisitions," he was boasting. "Picked it up for a song! Stuff from the 1920's is due for a revival, mark my words. It isn't how old a piece is that turns it from a household commonplace into a valuable prize—it's how many are left, and things like this got smashed by the million, naturally."

Seizing his opening, Wentschler demanded, "And just how old is this particular item?"

His hopes of finding out what year this was, which he was forbidden to ask directly for fear of betraying his identity, were instantly dashed.

"It's marked 1928," Feuerstein said with a shrug, and at that moment the butler Franz caught his eye and he continued, "Ah, I see dinner is served. Herr Schmidt, will you take my wife in?"

Double doors on the far side of the anteroom were swung back. Revealed was a table set with fine silver and crystal, unlighted candles, loaves of bread of a curious braided design, and decanters of wine. A pretty girl in maid's uniform, again a blonde, was waiting in the far corner by a laden sideboard.

Numbly, Wentschler allowed Frau Feuerstein to take his arm and guide him to the right-hand seat at the bottom of the table. The rest of the company followed and stood behind their chairs. The maid handed the hostess a lighted taper, and she applied a flame to each candle in turn until all were lit. There were seven. The electric lights were then turned out.

Feuerstein poured some wine into the glass that stood at his place, the head of the table, and said heartily, "We don't keep up the full observances, of course, not nowadays! But—'Let melancholy and passion, born of spleen and bile, be banished from all hearts!'"

He sipped the wine, making it a toast to the company, and everybody sat down, chatting merrily at once—except Wentschler. Some sort of liver pâté was served, with celery and olives and little crisp biscuits. It was good, if rich, and he forced himself to comment on it to the hostess, who was conversing with the black man on her other side.

Smiling, they both waited for him to say more.

"Ah . . ." He improvised a safe ploy. "And how are things in your part of the world?"

"Very good at present," Sikelole answered. "They were tough for a while, until the Boers came round, but now the universal-education program is under way, everybody's rather pleased. I'm lecturing in moral philosophy at the University of Cape Town, by the way."

Moral philosophy was a subject the general knew nothing about. Nor did he understand much about architecture, the profession of the Irish woman sitting on his right, or abnormal psychology, specialty of Fräulein Dass, who sat on Sikelole's left—it seemed she was some kind of consultant at a mental hospital. To Wentschler, who believed that the insane should be liquidated if they could not be made to perform useful work, this was peculiarly anathematical.

Yet everyone else seemed ready and willing to discuss these and a hundred other subjects, arguing knowledgeably on all of them. Why in heaven's name would they not turn to something of real interest—recent history, above all?

Alert for the least snippet of data, Wentschler did pick up a few tantalizing clues: a summer holiday in New York last year, by a new high-speed trans-Atlantic plane; the comparative merits of Rolls-Royce and Packard cars; a miracle drug recently isolated from a South American plant, promising cures in previously intractable patients . . . and that was where Wentschler's heart leapt up, for Fräulein Dass leaned toward Frau Feuerstein and with a dazzling smile inquired if it would be ungracious to ask to watch the television news bulletin at ten o'clock, for there was to be a feature about this drug and the work of her hospital.

"Will you actually be appearing in it?" the hostess asked in high delight. "Yes? Then of course we must watch! I'll make sure we're through eating in good time."

A fish loaf with horseradish sauce succeeded the pâté, and the distraction served to cover Wentschler's excitement. A television news broadcast! Nothing could be better!

Relaxing for the first time, he decided he could after all risk at least one glass of wine without dulling his perception or judgment.

Also he rediscovered appetite and did justice to a soup with dumplings and a roast chicken with mixed vegetables and finally a dish of apples stewed with cinnamon and brown sugar. By now it was nearly ten, as reported by a grandfather clock in a corner of the dining room.

Frau Feuerstein signaled to her husband and rose.

"Let's take our coffee and brandy in the other room, so we can watch Anitra on television!"

Black coffee was poured out, and an excellent cognac, and cigars were offered to the men and cigarettes to the women. Wentschler paid no attention to this; his gaze was glued to the TV screen.

He was of course familiar with television; after all, it had only been last year that the Witzleben transmitter had been bombed out of service—

He caught himself. It had been in 1943. *Not* last year.

And that brought back all his misgivings, which had been temporarily masked by relief. Kalkhaver had mentioned inferior alternative futures; could this be one? If so, it implied that someone other than the Wissenschaft-SS had discovered time travel, and he had been deliberately diverted. That made chills run down his spine. The notion of a war being fought on the battlefields of time—

But there was nothing of a wartime atmosphere about this

house, or this city! One could hear normal traffic going by at intervals, though since his brief glimpse from the bedroom window he had had no chance to look outside. Anyhow, Feuerstein, consulting his watch, was turning on the TV.

"It won't be a very long item," Fräulein Dass was saying apologetically. "And it'll probably be well toward the end, so if you just want to leave the sound turned down—"

Wentschler's voice rasped across hers.

"If you will permit me, I should like to see the entire program! As you know, I've been abroad and—uh—I'm somewhat out of touch, so I try never to miss the news."

And returned to his chair as the screen lit, showing a clock face just coming up to ten P.M.—and, marvel of marvels, in color! White, on a blue ground!

Soon, as bells chimed from the loudspeaker, the clock was replaced by a polychrome array of flags, and a superimposed sign said *Weltnachrichten—World News*.

Infuriatingly, there was no date.

Then suddenly Wentschler's fingers closed so tight on his brandy glass it almost cracked. He could see the Stars and Stripes, the Union Jack, the Tricolor, and a hundred more.

Where was the Reich's black swastika on white and red?

While he was still trying to persuade himself that it must be masked by the title card, an announcer started to list tonight's topics: a pan-European conference on the abolition of visas for foreign travel; a trade agreement with Brazil, signed in Rio; a new air-speed record; a visit by a troupe of Cossack dancers; a breakthrough in psychiatric medicine ("That's us!" Fräulein Dass exclaimed excitedly); and sports news, including film of a baseball game between Canada and Belgium for the world covered-stadium championship.

Baseball???

Sweating, furious, but maintaining impassivity, the general endured the trivial nonsense that flowed across the screen: mostly shots of dignitaries uttering formal platitudes in a mixture of languages, with German commentary. Not one of them wore uniform; they were all civilians. Then a white speck flashed across the screen, an aircraft at high altitude, after which engineers were seen inspecting a plane with both pusher and tractor airscrews, so much like the still-secret Dornier Do335 of his own day, Wentschler had to bite back an exclamation of horror . . . but this was a Swedish design, the first to exceed the speed of sound.

Next came the dancers, and—horror of horrors!—they were performing agianst a red backdrop bearing a giant gold hammer and sickle!

"Herr Schmidt!" Feuerstein was whispering at his side. "Are you all right?"

"I'm fine!" the general forced out. It wasn't true. He was beginning to suffer abdominal cramps, and very shortly he was going to be driven from the room, but he dared not miss a moment of this shocking news bulletin.

"And now, from our scientific correspondent, an account of an astonishing new treatment for the mentally deranged. The following interview was filmed earlier today at the National Hospital for the Criminally Insane."

Views of a large modern building: staff escorting men and women in pajama-like uniforms; long wards with twenty beds a side; then three people sitting around a table, including Fräulein Dass, a little nervous man with the general appearance of an Armenian, and a black man who spoke with a strong American accent.

American???

Off-screen, the interviewer was asking about this new and wonderful drug, and the little nervous man, prompted now and then by his colleagues, was explaining how it could cure hitherto untreatable megalomania, paranoia and obsessive behavior.

"You've had one really spectacular success, I gather," the interviewer said eventually. The three smiled proudly. The scene cut away to a man Wentschler recognized. Older—much older, with gray hair—and a deal slimmer, but absolutely unmistakable, in a dark uniform with a peaked cap, against a background of archeological exhibits. Clearly he was a museum guide; equally definitely, he was Hermann Göring . . .

Bile rose in Wentschler's throat as the scene reverted to the trio around the table. The black man was saying, "Yes, he's been working at the State Museum for three months now, with no sign of a relapse. Naturally the therapy will have to continue for a while yet, but he's adjusted splendidly. We even have hopes for Goebbels, you know."

The interviewer said, "And the arch-criminal?"

Shrugs from all three. Fräulein Dass said, "Well, of course his delusions were so heavily reinforced for such a long time by everybody who obeyed his lunatic orders . . . but even in his case we haven't given up *all* hope."

"Thank you very much."

Back to the flags, and the commentator saying: "Now, sport—"

It was too much for Wentschler. His head was swimming and his bowels were griping. Rising to his feet, struggling to preserve a semblance of self-control, he looked a question at Feuerstein.

Divining his need, the host beckoned Franz.

With maddeningly deliberate strides the tall Aryan—servant, in God's name, *servant* to this brood of kikes and niggers and Lord knew what half-breeds!—showed Wentschler to a washroom on the far side of the hall. Such was his haste now, he could only slam, not bolt, the door before having to drag down his trousers and vent a gush of stinking liquid.

When were they going to haul him back to his own time? He could stand no more! This was torture beyond his worst nightmares!

Gradually the agony receded. Strains of lively music rang out again; doors were opened, and it sounded as though people were starting to dance on the tiled floor of the hall, more suitable than the carpet in the other rooms he had seen. He had sudden visions of one of them walking in, and reached hastily for the toilet roll, which was discreetly concealed inside a white plastic dispenser.

So that not until he drew down and tore off a couple of sheets did he realize that they, and all the rest, were stamped with the only swastikas he had seen since his arrival.

That was the breaking-point. That was when he screamed, and

the butler and underbutler entered and with brisk, impersonal efficiency strangled him into unconsciousness.

"Then," said Mr. Secrett, "he was given an injection to keep him under and driven in a car fitted with snow chains to the foot of a badly crevassed glacier. From there he was carried—Franz and his assistant were members of the Swiss mountain-rescue service, so his weight was no problem—about two hundred meters upward and dumped on a convenient ledge. It was over by dawn: the carefully constructed newsreel, incorporating footage from a science fiction film that nobody had seen because it had had to be abandoned at the outbreak of war, the soap wrapper, the toilet paper, all the little taunts and the final sledge-hammer blow, were destroyed, and the actors went back to their daily lives. Not, of course, that they were professionals. They were simply people who had nearly as much reason to hate the Nazis as the man who called himself Feuerstein, and not nearly as much money. The whole thing must have cost him at least a million pounds; think of the people he had to bribe, just to start with! But it was a very fair reprisal for what had been done, on Wentschler's orders, to his mother and father, and some of the touches I think were absolutely brilliant . . ."

We were now the only people in the breakfast room, and the staff were beginning to drop heavy hints. But even after Mr. Secrett had stopped talking, I sat in dazed immobility. He was the first to stir.

"Well, old chap," he said, glancing at his watch, "I see I only have a few minutes to catch my bus back to Basel. I'm flying home today, back to the old grindstone, y'know."

"Wait!" I said frantically. "Who was Feuerstein really?"

"You can't expect me to tell you that! Anyhow, he's dead."

"Oh, marvelous!" I exclaimed, my visions of tracing and interviewing him gone up in smoke. "Then what proof do you have that this is the true story of Wentschler's fate?"

"None whatever, old man! I told you: anything that might have given the game away was destroyed. Even though the forecast was for snow, there was a chance that Wentschler might be found alive, and kidnapping an officer of the German forces would have been no small offense, Switzerland being a nonbelligerent."

"It did happen in Switzerland, then?"

"Where else? As I said, he saw there was no blackout and heard normal civilian traffic passing the house. *That* couldn't have been faked."

"So how in heaven's name did you find out about it?"

Mr. Secrett was gathering various belongings, ready to rise. For a moment a strange, wistful look crossed his face.

"Later on," he said almost reluctantly, "I contracted a—shall we say?—close friendship with one of the participants. We talked more freely to one another, I suppose, than I've ever done with anybody else . . . but that too is history, and my bus is waiting. So long, old fellow—see you in London!"

And headed for the door.

A dozen questions were still fighting in my head for utterance, but I knew better than to try and delay him. Something in his attitude, though, hinted that he had still one more thing to say, as so often in the past.

I was right. He spun around and hurried back, his expression anxious.

"By the way, old man," he said in a low tone, "I didn't mean to imply that I don't feel at ease talking freely to *you*! I most certainly do, and there are damned few people I can say that about, I promise. Do come and see me when you can, or ask me to drop in. You know how much I'd appreciate it, don't you?"

I forced a nod and a smile, and he seized my hand and pressed it warmly, and was really gone. Until the next time.

What in the hell did I do to deserve Mr. Secrett?

An Elixir for the Emperor

This story has the fascinating texture of Robert Graves's two Claudius *books; absolute political power, ruthless scheming, and murder of the highest, played out against the background of the last true world empire. The science-fictional part involves an archetypal character who has never been done better. To say more would be to give away too much.*

▬▬▬▬▬▬▬▬▬

The roar of the crowd was very good to his ears, just as the warm Italian sunshine was good on his body after three years of durance in the chill of Eastern Gaul. Few things made the general Publius Cinnus Metellus smile, but now, for moments only, his hard face relaxed as he made his way to the seat of honor overlooking the circus. There was winding of buccinae by trumpeters f his own legions, but the sound was almost lost in the shout of welcome.

This was what the populace liked from their generals: a profit-ble campaign, a splendid triumph and a good day of games to inish with.

Slowly the cries faded into the ordinary hum of conversation s Metellus took his place and glanced around at his companions, cknowledging them with curt nods.

"It'll be good to see some decent games again, Marcus," he grunted to the plump elderly man next to him. "If you'd had to sit hrough the third-rate makeshifts one suffers in Gaul . . . You did s I asked you, by the way?"

"Of course," lisped Marcus Placidus. "Though why you were worried, I don't know. You brought enough livestock back with you to keep the arena awash for a week—some of those Ger-manic wolves, in particular . . . No, you're paying well. You'll get the best games Rome has seen in years."

"I hope so. I certainly hope so." Metellus let his eyes rove across the gaudy crowd. "But I'm not going to risk being cheated by some rascally lanista who wants to copper his bets! And . . . And things have changed here since I've been away. I feel out of touch."

He made the confession in a voice so low it reached no one but Marcus Placidus, and immediately looked as though he re-gretted uttering it at all. Marcus pursed his fleshy lips.

"Yes, there have been changes," he concurred.

After a brief pause, Metellus shifted on his chair. He said, "Well, now I'm here, where's the ringmaster? He ought to be on hand to open the show."

"We're waiting for the Emperor, of course," Marcus said with real or feigned surprise. "It would be an insult to begin without him."

"I didn't think he was coming!" Metellus exclaimed. His gaze fastened on the gorgeous purple-hung imperial box. "I thought the insult was going to pass in the opposite direction. After all, he's snubbed me before, hasn't he? You were there, Marcus! He said I bled my provinces white! A fine emperor, that wants no tribute for Rome! He doesn't even seem to realize that you have to keep your foot on the neck of those barbarians. If you don't, you wake up one morning with your throat slit. I've seen."

He started forward on his chair, staring about him for the missing ringmaster. "Nothing would please me better than to show the world what I think of his milk-and-water notions. I'm the editor of these games, and I say when they open!"

Marcus laid a restraining hand on the general's arm. He said apologetically, "The people wouldn't stand for it, you know."

"I know nothing of the sort! Since when would a Roman crowd prefer to sit broiling in the sun like chickens on a spit, rather than start the games?"

"Since you've been away, perhaps," Marcus murmured, and hauled his bulky body out of his chair. "Here he is now, anyway."

Scowling, Metellus also stood up. Shields clanged as the ranks of the guard completed the perfectly drilled movements of the salute, and the yell went up from the crowd. *The* yell—not just from the bottom of the lungs, but from the bottom of the heart. It went on. It lasted longer than the applause which had greeted Metellus, and seemed still to be gaining volume when the Emperor took his place.

As the roar echoed and re-echoed, the general clenched his fists. When, two years before, a courier had brought the news of Cinatus's accession, together with the warrant for the renewal of his proconsulship, Metellus had shrugged his shoulders. It was a wonder, of course, that they had ever allowed the old man to assume the imperial toga in succession to his childless nephew— whose short and bloody reign was memorable to Metellus for one thing: his chance to pick the plum of Eastern Gaul.

But with rival factions sprouting all over the Empire, it was probable the old man had been chosen because he wouldn't offend too many influential people. He certainly had not been expected to last so long. Or to handle his impossible task so well . . .

"Aren't they ever going to stop screaming?" Metellus snarled. "Who's editing these games, anyway?"

"You don't understand how they feel," was Marcus's only reply.

At that moment Cinatus, having made himself comfortable, caught Metellus's eye and shook his head in the Greek affirmative that was one of his few affectations. As though by magic the giant ringmaster popped into view in the arena.

"*At* last," grunted Metellus, and signalled for the games to be opened.

After the ritual procession, the ringmaster took his stand before the imperial box. All talking died away as the crowd waited eagerly to learn which of the many fabulous acts they'd just had a foretaste of would constitute the first spectacle.

"What did you decide to start with?" Marcus inquired behind his hand. "You were in two minds when I spoke to you yesterday."

"A perfect item, I think," Metellus answered. "It should put the crowd in a good humor straight away."

"A battle!" screamed the ringmaster. "Of the sunbaked South —against the frigid North! Six wild Germanic wolves from the forests of Eastern Gaul, brought hither by special command of the general—"

The next words were lost in a shout of excitement. Marcus gave a nod. "Ah, the wolves!" he commented. "I said they looked promising. But against what? Each other?"

"Not quite," Metellus said. "You'll see."

Once more the ringmaster bellowed. "And opposing them . . . !" He turned with a flourish, and all eyes followed the movement as a gate was thrown back to admit into the arena— head bowed to avoid a final blow from his jailer—an elderly dark-skinned man clad only in a ragged kilt and worn sandals after the Egyptian pattern, whose back was laced with the marks of the scourge. In one hand he clasped a sword, which he seemed not to know what to do with.

A gale of laughter went up from the crowd, in which Metellus joined rather rustily. "Excellent," he muttered to Marcus. "I told my procurator to find someone—some criminal—who would look really ridiculous. And there he is. Afterward, you see, there's a giant bull—"

"I warn you," said Marcus in a very flat voice, "the Emperor is not laughing."

The general swung around. Indeed, Cinatus's face was set in a stern frown. He whispered to one of his attendants, who called to the ringmaster over the front of the box.

"Caesar desires to know with what crime this old man is charged!"

At a gesture, the ringmaster's assistants caught hold of the dark man and dragged him across the sand to answer for himself. He seemed to have recovered his wits, for as he straightened and looked up he gave a passable salute with his sword.

"My name is Apodorius of Nubia, O Caesar! And the crime of which I am accused is one I freely confess. I hold that neither you nor any other man who has assumed the purple thereupon became a god."

A low *o-o-oh!* went around the circus. Metellus sat back, satisfied. Surely Cinatus would not take that lightly.

But a hint of a smile played on the Emperor's lips. He spoke again to his aide, who relayed the question: "Why say you so?"

"Gods are not made by the will of men, and not all the words in the world can create divinity!"

"By the same token, then," came the good-humored answer, "not all the talk in the world can unmake a god. Ringmaster, release this man, for it pleases Caesar to be merciful."

Aghast, Metellus turned to Marcus. "Can I believe my ears? Does he intend to ruin my games, as well as insulting me about the way I ran my province? Surely the people will not stand for this!"

"They are standing for it," said Marcus calmly. "Can you hear any objections?"

Indeed there were very few, quickly drowned out by a roar of cheers.

"But how is this possible?" Metellus demanded.

"You don't understand," said Marcus again. "They love their Emperor."

Though the rest of the show proceeded without interruption, Metellus hardly paid any attention. He sat with a scowl carved deep on his features, disturbed only when he growled—at frequent intervals—that it was a plot to make his accomplishments look small, that Cinatus was jealous of his popularity with the plebs. Marcus endured his complaints patiently, but it was a relief when the last item on the program ended and the sated crowd surged like a flood toward the exits. Rising with a curt word of farewell, and an even curter salute to Cinatus, Metellus ordered his retinue to clear a way to the street and stormed from the circus.

Following more slowly, looking thoughtful, Marcus Placidus listened to the comments of the departing audience. As he passed one young couple—an elegant and handsome youth accompanied by a pretty girl whom he had noticed in a front-row seat on the shadow side, naked as was the custom among the more expensive courtesans—he eavesdropped with the skill of long practice.

"Good games," the youth said.

"Was it not gracious of Caesar to pardon that old man?" the girl countered.

"It was so. We have seen many wear the purple who would rather have ordered that the wolves' teeth be specially sharpened because the meat on his old bones must be tough!"

"Would that such an emperor could be with us for ever!"

Marcus stopped dead in his tracks for the space of a heartbeat, and then continued forward. After a while he did something quite out of keeping with his senatorial dignity: he began to hum a popular song which was going the rounds of the Roman brothels.

He was humming it again when his litter was set down before the house of Metellus late that evening, but under the astonished gaze of his torch-bearer—who doubtless knew where the song was current—he composed himself and followed the path to the door.

Over the splashing of the little fountain in the atrium he heard an enraged yell in Metellus's parade-ground voice. "If that's someone to see me, tell him to come along with the rest of the *clientes* in the morning!"

"It is the senator Marcus Placidus, General," said the respectful nomenclator, and Metellus gave a grunt which the slave interpreted as permission to show the caller in.

The general was reclining on a couch with a jug of Falernian wine at his side. A pretty Greek slave was massaging his neck.

"It had better be important, Marcus," he said shortly. "I'm not in the best of tempers, you know. And you know why!"

"It is."

"All right. Make yourself comfortable. Pour the senator some of this filthy Falernian!" he added to the Greek girl, and she hastened to obey.

Marcus spilt a drop in ritual libation and swigged a healthy draught of the wine. Then he set the cup aside and produced something from the folds of his toga. On the open palm of his plump pink hand he showed it to Metellus. It was a rose.

The general came to an abrupt decision. "Get out," he told his slaves, and as they vanished soundlessly he added, "Well?"

"How would you like to be Emperor, Metellus?"

"I know you too well, or I should think you'd been chewing ivy, like a Bacchante!" the general said caustically. "Or have you changed along with everything else in Rome?"

"I assure you I'm perfectly serious. You were probably going to point out that Cinatus is firmly ensconced—which is true. It's also true that the court, and all Rome, are less turbulent than they've been in my lifetime. But Cinatus has made enemies apart from yourself. You know about my grounds for disliking him, to begin with."

"Something to do with a debt, wasn't it?" Metellus said, and gave a harsh laugh.

"A trifling matter," Marcus told him. "A question of a few tens of thousands. But it was the principle of the thing. He gave judgment against me, and I had to resort to most undignified methods to recover what I was owed. If I hadn't needed it so badly—"

"You're being strangely candid."

"I wish you to see how I would benefit from a change of Caesar. Others like me have been—shall we say, embarrassed by decisions on the part of Cinatus? A petty slight against someone in my position can rankle and ultimately fester. I suspect that those others whose cooperation I intend to enlist will agree chiefly because they imagine that once *we* have tumbled this immovable Caesar, it will be a matter of weeks before *they* topple his successor and install their own favorite. But I think they would find you hard to shift. Besides, you are popular with the plebs already. What more natural choice than our most successful general to assume the purple?"

"And how do you propose bringing this minor miracle to pass?"

Marcus told him.

At the end Metellus had a faraway look in his eyes. "Suppose, though, that Cinatus finds out from whom the suggestion originated? Will he not smell a rat?"

"Trust me for that, Metellus. I can arrange matters so subtly that the actual proposition will come from someone he relies on implicitly—who will himself believe he's making the suggestion in good faith."

"Ye-es," said Metellus doubtfully. He rose and began to pace the floor, head down, hands clasped behind his back. "But will Cinatus act on the proposal when it's made? Won't his accursed skepticism cause him to laugh the idea to scorn? Oh, Marcus, it will never succeed!"

"You're a man used to direct action," the senator said. "You're ill accustomed to the twists and turns of a court intrigue. I, however"—he gave a modest cough—"have some not inconsiderable skill in the latter field. I've already thought of the risk you mention. I'll forestall it by having Cinatus consent in order to be rid of those who keep plaguing him with concern about his health."

"We'll consult the auspices," Metellus said suddenly. "If they're favorable, I'm with you."

Marcus smiled like a contented cat. He had not expected so swift a victory.

First, he planted a rumor that the Emperor was a sick man. Since Cinatus was elderly, not to say old, people were ready to believe it. So often did he hear the whispered report from others, he soon almost credited it himself. Every time he saw Cinatus he studied him for signs of infirmity. However, the Emperor remained annoyingly hale.

So he planted his second seed. This was a single nebulous concept, whose pattern of growth he had chosen with extreme care. And, as the idea was relayed to more and yet more courtiers, it took exactly the form he had hoped for.

When it came finally to the ears of Cinatus himself it did so—as Metellus had been promised—from a close friend who honestly believed he was making a valuable suggestion.

"If it were only possible for Caesar to remain with us for another twenty years, we might see Rome even greater than she has been in the past."

"Faugh!" said Cinatus. "I'm fifty-four years old, and if I last another five under the strain of your pestering I'll have done well. Besides, who told you I wanted to put up with twenty more years of this job?" And, to drive home his point, he finished, "Anyhow, there's no way of making an old man young, so the notion is ridiculous."

"Is it?" his friend persisted. "There are stories of men who have chanced on potions to confer long life and good health. In Asia they tell of a king who discovered such a drug—a herb— but a serpent stole it from him before he could use it. And the Jews claim that their ancestors lived to an age comparable with that of the heroes—seven hundred years!"

"I'm not a Jew, and I'm rather glad," said Cinatus feelingly, for at that time those intransigent inhabitants of Palestine were once more in spirited revolt against their Roman rulers. "Are you suggesting I should become one?" he added with a glare. "If so, you can precede me. I'm told the process is rather painful!"

"Not at all, not at all," soothed the trusted friend, and then and there recounted the wholly fictitious news Marcus had so dexterously invented.

Cinatus did not yield at once. But after a month's importuning by more and more of his oldest friends, he gave in—as predicted—for the sake of peace and quiet.

"What did I tell you?" Marcus said smugly when he next called on Metellus. "Listen, I have the text of the proclamation here—it's to be made public tomorrow."

"How did you get hold of it?" the general demanded, and Marcus raised a reproving eyebrow.

"Do I inquire the secrets of your strategy? I think I may keep my own methods under the rose, then! But hear this. After the usual trifles about the graciousness of Caesar and how everyone wants him to reign a thousand years, it goes on:

" 'If any man bring to Rome medicine which after trial proves to bestow long life and good health he shall be richly rewarded, but if any man bring a medicine which is useless he shall be banished from the city and if any man bring a medicine which is harmful he shall be punished and if any man bring a poison his life shall be forfeit.' "

Apologetically re-folding the wax tablets he had been reading from, he added, "Three penalties for one hope of reward, as you notice. I'm sorry, but that was the only way we could get Cinatus to seal the proclamation."

"Hmm!" Metellus rubbed his chin. "Do men bet against such odds in this strange Cinatified Rome of ours? I mean, will there be any candidates at all?"

"Beyond a doubt. They may not love Cinatus as much as they say they do, but they'll come—to puff some cult or other, or for the hope of gain, or for notoriety . . . And anyway I've arranged a steady supply of quacks to keep the interest of the plebs whipped up."

Metellus gave a reluctant smile. "Yes, I've noticed the city is full of sorcerers and favor-seeking acolytes of the mystery cults. Some of them even have the gall to come howling at *my* door.

Well, let's assume a man turns up and produces some noxious drench: what then?"

"Why, then we try their potions on some slaves, do we not? For instance, you're aware that Cinatus has a trusted body-slave, a Greek called Polyphemus for his one eye?"

"I've seen him," Metellus granted.

"In your name I've offered him his manumission if he helps us. He's made good use of his position at court, and has a small private fortune. But Cinatus won't release him—says he depends on him too much. It's the worst mistake he's committed.

"Now, this Polyphemus thinks he can outwit me. Of course I have no intention of letting him go free with such a secret, and he suspects this, but he wants his liberty so much he's willing to gamble on the chance of blackmailing me afterward." Marcus sat back with a pleased expression.

"What secret are you talking about?"

"Why—! See: when *our* sorcerer, *our* doctor, comes to offer his potion to the Emperor, it will be something no more harmful than water."

"Not so harmless, that," grunted Metellus, thinking of the stinking stagnant liquid he had often encountered in the field. "But go on."

"Well, it's a detail we can settle. Make it a tasteless powder to be administered in wine, if you prefer." Marcus dismissed the point with an airy wave. "But I've arranged for Polyphemus, over the next few weeks, to feign occasional illness, severe enough to make Cinatus worry about losing him. When the medicine has been tested on some slaves and proved at worst innocuous, he's then going to volunteer to be the last experimental subject and will promptly make a miraculous recovery.

"It will then be the task of this same one-eyed Greek to give the potion to Cinatus. He'd trust no one else to administer it. And what he gives the Emperor will be—ah—stronger than water."

"I see. You're devious, Marcus, but clever, I concede! So we shall have to find culprits: the pretend doctor, and while we're about it, why not the one-eyed slave? Yes, neat and tidy like a good plan of battle!" In an access of uncharacteristic enthusiasm

Metellus almost clapped his hands, but cancelled the impulse on realizing it would bring slaves into the room. Then his mood changed.

"We'd better move swiftly, though! For if I mistake not, people are beginning to forget the tribute my campaigns brought to Rome."

"We shall be swift enough," smiled Marcus, and stowed in the bosom of his toga the tablets on which was inscribed the proclamation even now being carried to the four corners of the world.

Long, long before the sages of Egypt and the Druid mystics of Europe heard the news and began their preparations, the word came to Apodorius the Nubian as he shivered over a wood fire in a stinking little inn beside the Tiber. He was awaiting a ship that would bear him back to Africa.

Already he had travelled very far. He had sat at the feet of philosophers in Athens retailing the wisdom of their ancestors like parrots; he had bowed in the temples of Alexandria and the sacred groves of Asia; he had been initiated into mystery cults from Persia to the Pillars of Hercules; he had acquired very much knowledge. In fact, as he disputed anew with priests and adepts in every place he visited, he had begun to suspect that few men anywhere had studied so widely and absorbed so much.

And the suspicion had given him a certain courage.

The fact that a whim of Caesar had saved him an agonized death in the arena counted little with him. He was not as attached to his mortal frame as he had been when he was a youth. He cared more that he had sensed in the elderly Cinatus a quality unique among the many rulers he had seen: hard-headed common sense.

Apodorius, though Romans had almost cost him his life, was not blind to the benefits Roman mastery had brought to the world. He had been in many countries enjoying more peace and greater prosperity than ever under governments of their own. But should Caesar be weak, his deputies corrupt, the Empire could—did—bring misery.

The world needed the Empire. The Empire needed a good Caesar. Apodorius made up his mind.

Publius Cinnus Metellus *Augustus*—Caesar himself, latest of the wearers of the imperial purple—yawned. If he had been able to find a way around the right of all citizens to appeal in person to the Emperor, he would have done so. He hated dealing with petty squabbles, disputes over money, pretended claims against judges he had himself appointed... Unfortunately it was unavoidable. People who had enough funds to bribe their way past the various subordinates with whom he had surrounded himself, however, were also rich enough to be influential, and he had to continue going through the motions at least where they were concerned.

Marcus Placidus felt differently, of course. He enjoyed watching people scheme and weave devious plans, for the eventual pleasure of outwitting them. Metellus prevented his face from lapsing into a frown—just in time—as the senator himself entered the audience hall.

Too clever by half, the Emperor thought. *Something might have to be done about him...*

"Well?" he demanded. "I understood today's audience was at an end."

"I think," Marcus murmured, "you may be interested in one more of those who have been waiting at the door. Look, O Caesar!"

The doors opened again. Through them stepped a dark-skinned figure, very thin, old, ragged, yet bearing himself with a certain dignity. To his chest he clutched something reddish-brown—a pottery jar sealed with a lump of wax. He bowed vaguely in Metellus's direction; it was obvious that his sight was failing and an usher had to push him toward the throne.

Metellus's first impulse was to demand who had let this flea-ridden bag of bones into the hall. Then he checked. If Marcus had expressed interest in him, there must be a reason. He puzzled for a long moment, and at last said, "I see nothing significant about this scarecrow!"

"No? Think back, O Caesar," Marcus urged. "Think what that

jar he clutches may contain. Do you not recall a day of games following your triumph when—?"

"That Nubian? The one Cinatus pardoned—may the empty-headed fool drown in Styx! Why, of course!" Metellus snapped his fingers. "Ap . . . something. Apodorius!"

The Nubian, apparently more by guesswork than sight, for it was plain to Metellus now that his eyes were filmed with cataracts, halted facing him.

"Caesar remembers me?" he said with faint astonishment.

"Indeed we do," Metellus confirmed grimly. Watching, Marcus allowed a sly smile to creep across his face.

As though vaguely troubled by the sound of the Emperor's voice, Apodorius hesitated, lovingly stroking the earthenware pot he cradled in his skinny arms. Seeming to draw confidence from it, he spoke up.

"I come in answer to a proclamation of Caesar more than a year ago, which said that if a man brought medicine to Rome for the health of Caesar he would be rewarded. I want no reward. You gave me my life, and in return"—he thrust his jar forward convulsively—"I bring you *everlasting* life!"

There was a long slow silence, which soughed through the hall like an ice-cold wind.

It was broken by an undignified gurgle of laughter from Marcus. Metellus shut him up with a murderous glare and leaned forward.

"Why have you delayed so long, Apodorius?" he asked silkily.

"I beg Caesar's indulgence! It was often hard to come by the ingredients, so I had to search far and wide."

"And why, seeing you have this medicine, are you yourself old and sick, and nearly blind?"

"The ingredients were costly," said the old man apologetically. "I had little money. I could buy no more than would make one dose . . ." He tapped the pot. "And that dose is for Caesar, not for me."

Metellus slapped the arm of his throne. "Know, O stupid conjurer, that your kind is not welcome in Rome!"

"But—but there are no others of my kind, Caesar. None but I could have brewed this elixir!"

"If your eyes were unveiled," Metellus said, rising to his feet so that he towered over the Nubian, "you would realize that I am not Cinatus, who spared your worthless life in the arena, but Metellus, who ordered you into it! And sorcerers of your breed are unwelcome because one like you came to Rome offering an elixir which proved to be poison and from whose effects Cinatus —Augustus—died."

At each of the last three words Apodorius winced, as if under successive blows. Slowly, slowly, he lowered his cherished jar. He stood very still, a broken man.

"Guards!" barked Metellus. Two brawny soldiers closed on the Nubian. "Take that jar from him."

A fist moved swiftly and seized it.

"Break the seal and pour this charlatan's muck down his own throat!"

The order galvanized the old man. He stiffened, and babbled the beginnings of a plea. A broad palm shut his mouth for him.

"We notice you are less eager to drink your elixir than to have Caesar drink it," Marcus said dryly. "Go ahead, soldier!"

Forcing Apodorius's mouth open, the man spilt rather than poured a clear grayish liquid from the jar between the Nubian's bare gums. A quick jab in the stomach made him swallow convulsively, and again, and until the jar was empty.

"Let him go," Metellus directed, and Apodorius slumped to the floor in a faint.

"As I thought," Marcus murmured. "Oh, the subtlety of these philosophers!"

Metellus ignored him. He was too pleased with his own acumen to listen to self-praise from the stout senator. "Now take that bundle of skin and bones and dump it in the Tiber," he instructed the guards. "And let me hear no more of sorcerers."

"*Just* as I thought," Marcus said more loudly, and Metellus rounded on him.

"And what do you mean by that?" he demanded.

"Reflect, O Caesar! Is it truly possible that a man abiding

anywhere in the Empire should have failed to hear of your succession, or that having failed he should not have learned the facts on reaching Rome? No, doubtless this fellow thought that by pretending he was so blind he imagined he was offering his potion to Cinatus he could make you as gullible as his old benefactor and induce you to take his poison."

"Then why should he not have come sooner?" frowned Metellus.

The question troubled him for a few moments; moreover Marcus had no immediate answer. Then he dismissed it from his mind and called for wine, wishing he had conceived a more spectacular fate than mere drowning for this skillful would-be regicide.

Consciousness returned after what seemed like the passage of aeons to Apodorius. He was lying on a rough and hard support, a wooden bench, and was so astonished to find he had not been thrown in the river already that he sat up by pure reflex before he had taken in his surroundings. For the first time in many months he did not feel his usual twinge of rheumatism.

His eyes, too, were clearer. Though the light was bad, he could see he was in a stone-walled cell; its ceiling oozed green damp. A grille of metal bars cut him off from another, identical cell, where a man with one eye sat counting the fingers of his left hand.

Seeing the Nubian rise, however, he let the hand fall to his side and cautiously approached the bars. When he spoke, it was with a strong Greek accent.

"You're the last of the conjurers, aren't you? You're going to Father Tiber tonight, aren't you? Oh, yes! You've come back, and I knew you would, because I'm still here and I'm trapped the same as you."

He talked with a kind of explosive bitterness in which insanity rang dully like a counterfeit coin on a moneychanger's table.

"Marcus Placidus did for us both very nicely," the one-eyed man went on. "I thought I was cleverer than he was, but I was wrong, and he proved it to me. He proved it slowly, for a long, lo-ong, LO-O-ONG TIME!"

From a conversational level his voice rose to a screech. As though challenging Apodorius to doubt his words he thrust the stump of his right arm through the grille. It had no fingers left. The thumb was a mere blob of flesh and the skin from palm to elbow was seared with the marks of the torturer's iron.

"Who are you?" Apodorius said slowly.

"Polyphemus," said the Greek, and giggled. "Only I'm luckier than the real Polyphemus. Marcus didn't put my eye out with a hot stick, oh no! Marcus isn't as clever as Odysseus, but I'm not as clever as Marcus."

Abruptly he altered his tone again, and now cocked his head so that his one-sided gaze could study his new companion's face. "You came too late to poison Caesar, you know," he said. "I did it a long time ago. Marcus told me he'd manumit me for it, but he lied—he was clever! He proved it," he added inconsequentially, and thrust his left hand also through the grille so that he could count its fingers again, this time by touching them in turn to the blob marking the site of his other thumb.

Apodorius felt facts mesh together in his mind. Hoping against hope for a few minutes' clarity from the Greek's disordered brain, he spoke as things presented themselves to him.

"It was a plot by Marcus Placidus to poison Cinatus. You pretended to be a doctor and—no, that can't be right. You said you knew I'd be back . . . Ah. You were imprisoned here with the man who posed as a doctor and brought poison instead of medicine, who'd been put up to it by Marcus, and hence presumably by Metellus. You must have been one of Cinatus's slaves, promised your freedom if you substituted poison for the elixir."

"You know all that," Polyphemus said petulantly. "Why go on about it? You gave me the poison before you went to Caesar with water. Water! Even water can kill you, if you drink as much of it as there is in the Tiber!"

Footsteps sounded in an echoing corridor. Polyphemus moved away from the grille and listened intently. "I think they're coming to take you away," he said, unholy joy in his voice. "But you'll be back. Sooner or later you'll be back. You keep coming and going, but . . . I'm the proof, you know. The senator told me so. If ever he can't cope with Metellus, he said, he'll use me to prove it was a plot of Metellus's to poison Caesar. I hope he doesn't have to use me as proof, because they torture slaves before they make them talk, and I've been tortured. Did you know?"

He finished with a pathetic attempt at confidence, "But Marcus will be able to handle Metellus! Marcus is clever! Marcus is clever! Marcus is—"

"Shut your mouth, you!"

Apodorius turned, not too quickly, to see that the speaker was an officer of the guard who had halted beyond the grating set into the door of his cell. Bolts jarred back as the soldiers accompanying him heaved on their handles. The officer stepped inside.

"Awake, are you?" he grunted. "Hah! Can't have been very powerful poison, then. Still, no matter—it will please Caesar when I tell him you were conscious enough to enjoy the taste of the river." He gestured to the soldiers, and they moved purposefully forward. It would have been senseless to offer resistance; Apodorius let them do as they liked.

When his arms had been lashed behind his back and his legs so hobbled he could barely stumble along, he was jabbed into the corridor at the point of the officer's sword. The sound of Polyphemus counting—up to five, and then again up to five—died slowly in the distance.

"If it weren't ridiculous," the officer muttered, "I'd swear you were actually the better for that muck you swallowed. Not that it's going to make any difference now."

He swung open a door and they emerged on a stone ledge, under which the river ran chuckling. It was very dark, and the night breeze had a chill to it.

"*Vale*, brewer of elixirs," the officer said, and drove the point of his sword deep into Apodorius's left buttock. Yelling, he plunged into the water—and vanished.

The soldiers waited long enough to be sure he would not surface, and dispersed with no further thought of the matter. It was all in their day's work.

But deep in the swift-flowing Tiber Apodorius was hoarding his breath, conscious mainly of how glad he was they hadn't sewn him in a sack before they threw him in.

"At this hour?" said Marcus Placidus irritably. "Who?"

"He is a Nubian, senator," the slave explained, unaware of the effect he was about to have on Marcus's state of mind. "He is very wet and muddy, and if he had not sworn by all the gods that it was a matter of life and death I should have kicked him into the street. But he says I must tell you that his name is Apodorius."

"Wine," Marcus said faintly. "Help me to a couch. And quick —*get that man in here*!"

"I have come, Senator," said the unmistakable voice of Apodorius from the curtained doorway. Marcus's eyes bulbed in his fat face. He gasped and swayed, and the slave anxiously aided him to the nearest couch.

"I regret the state in which I call on you," the Nubian went on. "But Tiber is at the best of times an unclean river, and I had some trouble breaking free of my bonds."

"Come—come here," whispered Marcus. "Let me—No! You, slave! Touch this man and see if he is substantial!"

Astonished, the man obeyed. "He is warm flesh," he reported. "But slippery with mud, as you observe."

"No ghost . . . Praise be, praise be! What do you want with me?" Marcus wheezed.

"I have a grim kind of business with Caesar," Apodorius answered dryly. "But why should I approach him when it is known to all Rome and the Empire that the words are his and the thoughts are yours?"

Marcus could not help preening himself a little, and recovered some of his ordinary composure. "Slave!" he rapped. "Cleanse this man—he's my guest! Wipe him, give him a fair new toga, bring wine for him, and be quick!"

And he watched as his orders were put into effect, unashamedly goggling.

"I find it hard to accept that you're here," he said at last. "Still, I must do so or never again believe my senses. And such a trick as you must have employed to escape is one worth knowing. Speak!"

Refreshed, neatly clad, Apodorius gave a smile.

"Why, Senator, my elixir which you took for a lie was potent enough! Ask the guards who dropped me in the Tiber whether they did not see me sink with arms and legs bound!"

"I . . ." Marcus hesitated. "Granting that's true, why have you come to me?"

"To offer a bargain. A fair one, I think. You are in a position to give me what I most desire: revenge upon Metellus for what he did to me. Likewise I am able to give you what you want—what I already have against my will. I doubt you'll care much which Caesar wears the purple when you wield the power."

Marcus leaned forward with greed brilliant in his eyes.

"Destroy Metellus," Apodorius said, "and I will give you my elixir."

Marcus pulled at his lower lip. After a moment's reflection he said cannily, "Your elixir! How do I know it's not a sham? How do I know you weren't pretending to be old and blind, and sloughed the appearance of age as easily as you slipped your bonds in the river?"

Apodorius winced and rubbed a chafed ankle. "Do not term that 'easy,' Senator," he complained. "But I have proof for you. Setting aside the point that no hale man with any alternative open would have gone willingly to be torn apart by wolves—you remember?—I have taken so great a dose of my medicine that I am growing younger almost by the hour. See!" He opened his mouth and indicated his visibly toothless gums. "I feel an ache which may even portend . . ."

Marcus rubbed his finger along the shrivelled flesh and gaped in awe. Surely no conjurer's deception could make sharp new teeth grow in an ancient's jaw!

Even so, it was not until three days later when the first tooth was cut, gleaming and indisputable, that he sealed the bargain Apodorius had proposed. Then he was committed. In truth, what was it to him if Metellus went down to join the shades? An immortal man could become the power behind not one Caesar, but all Caesars!

Apodorius watched him grow drunk on the heady liquor of his dream.

He asked for what he wanted, and Marcus supplied it with no demur at the cost, which—as had already been said—was immense. The senator's desire for secrecy suited him; in a quiet room at the back of the house he worked with the strange mixture of substances bought for him, and weeks slipped by.

After two months, however, Marcus was at the limit of his patience, and Apodorius judged it unwise to make him wait any longer.

Accordingly he waited on him when he returned from the Senate, and to his fevered demand for news of progress gave a simple headshake of affirmation.

"Yes, I have prepared the elixir again. It goes quicker when one can buy from a bottomless purse instead of having to beg and even steal . . . What have you done to keep your side of the bargain?"

Marcus rolled his eyes to heaven and clasped his hands. He whispered, "I have arranged that next time Caesar goes to the circus a pillar below his box will be loosened. An elephant will be goaded into terror and caused to break the pillar down. If Metellus is not trampled to death, the care of such doctors as I have recommended to him can be counted on to help him join the shades."

"Good," said Apodorius. "Then come with me."

Marcus entered the room where the Nubian had been working, and stopped dead. Everything had been taken from it—all the pans, jars, braziers—all but a single small table on which rested a crock containing a grayish fluid. His eyes lit up as he recognized the color of the liquid that had been forced down Apodorius's throat.

He stretched out his hand toward it, and then checked himself. "No!" he croaked. "You first! Sip it before I do—and do no more than sip it, mind!"

"Have no fear," said Apodorius quietly. "I have made enough this time for more than a single dose." He picked up the crock and set it to his lips.

Marcus's eyes, alert for any hint of deception, followed his movements as he drank three slow mouthfuls of the stuff. Then he replaced the crock and rested his hand on the table to steady himself.

"You may feel a little giddy at first," he husked. "Remember, when I was forced to drink before Caesar I fell in a swoon. But you are not so old and weak as I was then."

His breathing grew easier and he straightened. Convinced there was no trickery, and impatient beyond endurance, the senator seized the crock and drained it in frantic gulps.

When he set it down, it was with a crash that shattered it and sent the shards flying across the floor. A burning began in his stomach. Dark veils crept across his vision as he sought to fix his eyes on the Nubian's face.

Through a rushing torrent of pain he heard Apodorius's voice, very cool, very detached.

"You are a dead man, Senator."

"What?" he whimpered. "What?"

"I have drunk the elixir—the real elixir. You have not. In that crock was the strongest poison I have ever found. I drank it, and I live. But you die."

Marcus Placidus clutched his belly as though he would squeeze the poison from it like water from a sponge. But blueness was already showing on his lips and around his fingernails. In a moment he could stand no longer, and crumpled to the floor. His eyes rolled; his chest barrelled out in a final despairing gasp of air. And he was dead.

"But that will make no difference to Metellus," Apodorius said to the corpse. "Not yet. Even if his doctors save him after the accident at the circus. I am sure, Senator, you were sufficiently skilled in flattery to let him imagine your decisions were his own. By himself—well, he is no Cinatus!"

And, his thoughts ran on, *his fall will probably bring the Empire down* . . . Another wave of murdered Caesars, and then barbarian invasions from the outskirts of the Empire—oh, the ultimate collapse of so mighty an edifice would take centuries, but it was now inevitable.

And afterward?

"We shall see," murmured Apodorius. And then corrected himself with wry amusement. "Or rather: I shall see!"

He dipped his finger in a drop of poison which remained in a fragment of the broken crock, and thought of the care he had taken to make its color exactly the same as that of the real elixir. He still felt queasy from the three mouthfuls he had swallowed. Enough of that poison would perhaps pierce his invulnerability.

Rising, he spoke to the air.

"Does it make you smile, Cinatus Augustus, there in the land of shades? You gave me my life, and I've avenged you. But Metellus outdid your gift! He gave me everlasting life, and because of that I have destroyed him. Do you understand, Cinatus? I think you do. I think if I had come to you, you would have turned me away.

"Perhaps, then, I would have been offended. But now I know why I brewed my elixir for an emperor, and not for me."

He stared down at the poison in the broken crock, and did not see it. He was contemplating the endless centuries ahead, and feeling himself grow cold.

"Next time I brew," he said, "which will I choose? This? Or a renewal of the other?"

The fat dead body of the senator did not answer him. Its mouth, though, was already curved in the sardonic corpse's leer known as the Hippocratic smile.

The Suicide of Man

Philosophically the most ambitious story in this collection, this is one of the few literary constructions I've ever seen that goes convincingly beyond life and death.

This is a story with a happy ending. The beginning, on the other hand . . .

Well, after all his care, all his precautions, there was absolutely no way he could not be dead.

And yet he wasn't. There were presence, consciousness, alarm, associated emotions. That which had been "I" for him was undestroyed.

He contrived an utterance, half a scream and half a desperate question. They answered, somehow.

What they told him was: "You are a ghost."

It was a place, no doubt about that. In fact it was a recognizable room, with a solid floor and solid walls and a solid ceiling that shed gentle light and even a piece of furniture which supported him in a relaxed posture. Also he was not alone. There were three with him, of whom one was definitely a man and two were indisputably women. But he was more concerned about himself. He looked down and discovered his familiar naked skin with scars from, at last count, eight unsuccessful operations. He identified the hands he had once been so proud of because they were deft and subtle. He knew his own limbs, his very body-hairs . . .

And was dazed and horrified and ultimately appalled.

Someone said, and he believed it was the woman who stood nearer of the two, "In your vocabulary we find no better referent for a person who is neither alive nor dead. You were Lodovico Zaras. You were a professor of experimental psychology. You fell victim to a form of cancer which disseminated rapidly. You decided in a year which you called by the figures one-nine-seven-eight that you would rather cease than continue to endure operations which could at best postpone your death but never cure the sickness. Is that what you recall?"

He replied, not quite understanding how he was able to speak at all, let alone do so in response to statements he knew not to be in English or Spanish or French or any other tongue he was acquainted with, "Yes, but how can I remember anything? I killed myself!"

Again the flat assertion: "You are a ghost."

At the moment of his death he had been sitting in a favorite chair, with the glass from which he had drunk his remedy for existence on a table at his side, a favorite recording of Bach's organ music ringing in his ears.

He was sitting (again?) now, on what was not except by remote derivation a commonplace chair. He could and did stand up, feeling no twinge of pain, none of that old stubborn heaviness in the limbs which cancer had weighed down. He felt ethereally light. Yet he did not perceive himself as immaterial; when he clapped his palms together there was a noise and the contact stung, and stare how he might he could not see through his hands.

"Ghost?" he repeated in bewilderment.

From somewhere the man who was in the room produced an object he could name although its form was strange. It consisted of a reflector surrounded by a frame; it was a mirror.

"Look for yourself," the man invited, and he did, and he failed to find what he was looking for. What he saw was the mirror.

Empty of his image.

Because of that he grew extremely frightened, but there was something worse to follow.

"Touch me," said the woman who had spoken before, and came to stand in front of him. For a long moment he hesitated, so disturbed by not seeing his reflection that he needed to register every sense-datum he could. The ceiling was white and luminous. The walls wore the rich, profound blue of a distant horizon. The floor was green and reminded him of spring grass. This before him was, yes, was a woman: taller than himself, slender, with an avian fineness of bone, not beautiful but so unusual—indeed so improbable—that if he had hurried along a street where she was walking the other way he would have checked and looked back, astonished at her having not enough black hair beginning too high on her forehead, ceasing too high on her nape, amazed at those over-long legs which endowed a child-size torso with the height of an adult, disturbed above all by the implication that while being very surely human she was also something . . . other.

Moreover she was naked, as he was.

Or was she?

There was something . . .

But it hurt his eyes, and he had to blink, and as his lids came down she repeated her command in a more urgent manner, holding up her thin right hand.

Diffident, he complied when the blink was over, and felt warm convincing flesh, perhaps a little sparse over the bones.

"I can touch you and I cannot see my own reflection," he said after a while. Giddying, the clash between the apparent reality of this alien woman and the plain incontestable nonreality of himself who could not make a mirror give back his portrait made him tremble and sway.

"But if I touch you . . ." the woman said, and reached out, and with a quick sidelong gesture like an ax-blow demonstrated how she could pass her own hand through his. Or—no! Where his hand seemed to be. He felt nothing, except the phantom of a chill, yet he witnessed and would have sworn on his life to the reality of her action.

Gasping, and realizing in the same moment that he could detect no rush of air into his lungs, he cried out, "I don't understand!" Still not knowing, either, how he could talk.

The man advanced, his face—which was too long, too skimpy, too much dominated by vast eyes—set in an expression of concern and regret.

"Lodovico Zaras, before we proceed with explanations, we must offer our deepest and most sincere apologies. It is to be hoped that a person such as yourself, a pioneer in your own day, an intellectual explorer as it were, may forgive the presumptuous interference we plead guilty to. I speak to you as what you were, not what you are, but I trust that the difference has not yet become unendurable. Inevitably the burden of that difference will grow greater as time passes, but we hope and predict that the series of shocks you are due for will be slow enough for you to make adjustments and ultimately grant us the forgiveness which we beg of you now. I am Horad. It is not a name as you would understand a name, but more of a title, which I think you would find meaningless. My companions, of whom the same ought to be said, can be addressed as Genua"—who had passed her hand through his—"and Orlalee."

Still in the grip of that impulse which had dictated his suicide, he nonetheless failed to prevent his mind from setting to work on the data offered. It had been his curse since childhood that he could not bear mental inactivity. The prospect of having to lie like a dummy for yet another year in a hospital bed, when he had hoped the latest operation might also be the last, had been what drove him to knock on the doors of death. There were drugs aplenty to cure pain; those which cured boredom were not recognized as part of the pharmacopoeia and most were illegal.

He said at length to Horad, "If I try and touch you . . ."

"Do so!" Horad held up his right arm. It felt much like Genua's, slim to the point of being scrawny. But . . .

There was something about these three which had already prevented him from thinking of them as merely naked, though none of them wore what he was accustomed to regarding as a garment.

In the case of Horad, it was far more striking than it was on Genua. It registered on his eyes as a zone where it was hard to focus; on his skin, as a vibration or a tingling; most, though, it impinged directly on his mind as a—a—

A state as much between *something* and *nothing* as he himself was between *alive* and *dead*.

On the women it might have passed for some form of protective garb; after all, who can predict what will happen in the vicinity of ghosts? But on Horad it could be—could be *detected* all around his head, across his shoulders, down his upper arms . . . To look at him any other way except straight in those excessive eyes was to be gravely disturbed by . . . *it*.

Lodovico swallowed: nothing, not even his own saliva. Yet it was as though he did. He remembered what he had formerly experienced as the act of swallowing, and this was much like it, and had his attention not been on the act it might have passed as well as the real thing.

Faintly he said, "What have you made of me, that you think I ought to call myself a ghost?"

The three exchanged pleased looks. Orlalee spoke up for the first time.

"We hope to be able to answer that question first of all. We need, however, to know how you perceive us before we can choose the proper terms to express our intended meaning. How do we seem to you?" And they struck poses for inspection.

He looked them over in detail as best he could, still finding it impossible to study certain areas of—no, that was inexact: *around*—Horad. He found all three alike in their fragility and near-hairlessness; on their respective pubes there was only down, not actual hair. Their feet, as he looked lower, he found to be high-arched, with the toes reduced to simple stubs, the nails to thin pale lines.

He pondered the implications, disregarding one sick notion which had briefly occurred to him: that he might be in Hell. There was no torment in his mind at the moment other than the sense of need-to-know-unsatisfied which had always been an integral part of his personality. On the contrary! He was in a dreamlike state of elation all of a sudden. In his mind, such total terror that it made him want to dissolve into eternal darkness balanced and teetered back and forth in competition with a sense of excitement he had not enjoyed since he was a boy, the excitement due to comprehending in the guts those abstract concepts which he knew his teachers were merely mouthing. He fancied for a moment he might do to these people what he had loved to do to his instructors, and surprise them. And abandoned the idea at once. On the other hand, conceivably he might please them.

Licking (or that was what it felt like) his lips (or what in this version of "I" now felt like lips), he said (or used whatever communication channel had been allotted him), "I think you must be people, but so much later than me that I don't suppose you can tell me what the date is."

For a very short time he was alone. The period elapsed was to brief by his standards, he might have dismissed it as an illusion but that on returning Horad said, "Excuse us, please. We were delighted by your response and wished to be-personal in conveying news of it."

The hyphenation of "be-personal" was audible (?) to Lodovico; this was a clearly identifiable proof that the language he was speaking (?) was none of his own time.

And in the same thought came awareness of the truth that he must no longer say "own"; he could, however, say "former."

Orlalee said, "We were particularly pleased that you have been able to express a significant truth. We are people, in part of the sense you would use the term. We are also much evolved past where you were. And if we were to try and give you a date, it might well be wrong by several thousand years."

"Revolutions of the planet," said Genua, "are not as important now as they were for you."

Lodovico experienced a biting-lower-lip sensation. He felt real to himself; these people were talking to him as though he were real; yet when they tried to touch him they could not do what he could, locate solid substance.

It was not simple, but it was also not impossible to resolve the conundrum.

"You must have a means," he said slowly, "of projecting an effigy, a counterpart, a simulacrum, of a personality for which you stumbled on sufficient data to make it seem real to *itself*, and yet which you can only half-perceive. Perhaps you are having to force yourselves to believe in me, while I have no trouble accepting that I am here and now although I wished never to exist again."

He clenched his fists.

"But being what you have made me, what am I—what can I do or be? Any world but mine must be illusion to me!"

"We could not ask permission in advance," said Orlalee, who was both fairer-haired and darker-skinned than Genua. It was impossible to determine whether she was either in respect of Horad owing to the vagueness he sort-of-wore. "This was because until we did it there was nothing of which permission might be obtained. Now there is. We will accordingly accept your instruction if you say: *desist!*"

They waited.

Eventually he said, looking past them at the blank blue walls, "First tell me what I can and cannot do. Do I—do I eat? Drink? Sleep, suffer, become intoxicated?"

Still they waited, until he forced out the last part of the multiplex question.

"I feel weak, only half-real. Have you resurrected me so that I must face death a second time?"

"You are a collective percept," Horad said. "As yet you are not strong because only we three perceive you. We hear you speak; it is not with sound. We see where you are, but it is not with light. We and you interact, but if we did not agree to perceive you there would be nothing."

"Yet I perceive myself!" Lodovico burst out. "I am aware!"

"That is because without your perception of yourself there

would be nothing for us to perceive. We did not choose that this be so; it turned out to be of the nature of the universe."

He wrestled with that for a while and eventually gave a feeble shake of the head.

"We may have some difficulty here," Orlalee said. "We are uncertain of the parameters you ascribed to a definition of 'consciousness' in your age. We have faint echoes of certain theories, but no indication of which if any you subscribed to. Permit us to question you on this subject and by stages our explanations will become more lucid."

"Ask away," Lodovico invited, folding his arms on his chest.

"When you killed yourself," Genua said, taking a step closer to him, "did you expect to re-awaken in a paradise or a place of torment?"

"I didn't expect to wake at all," was his prompt and emphatic answer. "Since boyhood I've been resigned to the fact that consciousness was a by-product of material existence. The fact that I seem to myself to be here, now, whenever and wherever the here-and-now may be, indicates that I must have been nearly right. You just told me that if I did not perceive myself you would have nothing to perceive, and moreover that I am a weak percept because no one apart from you three perceives me—Wait, I should re-phrase that. No one else *is perceiving* me."

"Could that"—from Horad—"have been expressed in the language of your time?"

"Yes!" the answer snapped back. "When I said it I wasn't aware of using a language I didn't grow up with."

Three smiles.

"Oh, we have chosen very well," Orlalee said. "Faced with the logical contradiction of being aware when he is-and-knows-he-must-be dead, he makes statements concerning not the self which cannot be present but the self which he's currently observing by being it. I judge that you, Lodovico, while surprised and startled at being imitated, are not angry."

"Angry?" He pondered, or imagined or suspected or believed or [a thousand possibilities] that he did. Eventually he said, "No, I don't think I have enough strength in the version of me which you three are perceiving to become angry. But in any case I would hope not to be. I would prefer to be fascinated by a unique chance, if it is unique, and even if it isn't I'd like to add something unforeseen and almost unimaginable to the total of my experience. It must be very long after my own epoch."

"But you have survived. In my time, for a while at least, we were afraid mankind might not. It follows that you must have cured the problems which worried us. I find I'm fascinated by the idea of seeing a far-distant future civilization, even though I may find many aspects of it incomprehensible. If I seem dull-witted, bear with me. Evolution must have taken place on the mental as well as the physical plane."

"Yes, that is true," Horad confirmed. "Still, the fact that we have been able to establish communication argues that there is continuity between humans of your age and of this. I have thought of a way of expressing how much time has elapsed since your original existence. We are approximately as distant from you as you were from the creatures who spoke in grunts, shaped animal-horns and branches into tools, but were still terrified of fire and ate their food uncooked. Yet there are few differences in form between you and me: somewhat less hair—for instance I judge you were capable of growing a beard although you did not do so, whereas I am not—and longer limbs and smaller torsos and marginally greater cranial capacity. We mature later, sexually speaking; we have lost the ability to metabolize certain essential compounds from their chemical precursors, or in other words we require two more vitamins than you did. And there are other petty differences. Nonetheless we are equipped to communicate with you, while you could not have conversed with your correspondingly remote ancestor."

"Because I'm not myself even though I imagine that I am. In fact I'm only your collective percept." The statement was hurtful to utter, but Lodovico felt obliged.

"True. Remember, though, you are as exact a percept as we, with millennia of knowledge and skill you're unaware of, have been able to contrive," said Genua. "In your day, if what data have endured may be relied on, reconstructions of extinct primitive organisms had been attempted by combining fossil relics with guidelines based on species still surviving that had changed little over aeons. Not much later, some of the great reptiles were actually bred again from modified cousins or descendants. You are the result of a corresponding technique applied to consciousness instead of physical shape."

"Why me?" Lodovico demanded.

"Chance brought us sufficient data to derive you. I regret to say"—this from Orlalee with a wry smile—"it is not because you became famous through the millennia!"

"No, I meant: why do it at all? Am I the first, or is this something you nowadays do routinely?"

"You are the very first," Horad said. "As for the underlying reason . . ." He shrugged; it was curious to see how the gesture had endured, and disturbing to see how differently the muscles moved on that bird-light body . . . and most disturbing of all *not* to see, because he couldn't bear to look, the matching movement of the whatever-it-wasn't that Horad "wore."

"So I am an experiment," said Lodovico.

"That is so."

"You plan to study me? Interrogate me?"

"Naturally."

"And"—with boldness that surprised him—"is there any bargain between us?"

"Yes, of course," Orlalee said. "Even before we commence studying you, we wish you to agree that the trouble you are being put to is justified. First, therefore, we must show you our world. If, after inspecting it, you decide you would prefer not to assist us, you may cease. Obviously we shall make another attempt, but we shall be resigned to the same outcome—and so on and on, if necessary for many generations."

"It is unbefitting," said Genua, "to run counter to another's will."

"All by itself that promise makes me like your world," said Lodovico. "Show it to me."

Struck by a sudden thought, he added, "By the way . . . is it still Earth?"

Visions of other solar systems blazed and faded in his mind in a fraction of a heartbeat.

"Yes," Horad said. "After all this time, it is still Earth."

But an Earth its inhabitants had learned to love, with all its ulcers healed. It still had mountains and oceans and rivers, valleys and forests and plains, blue sky and white clouds that sometimes darkened and uttered the ancient bark of thunder. Almost at once, however, he began to notice changes. There were trees he could not put a name to. Friendly fish of no species he recognized came ambling up beaches on stubby leg-*cum*-fin limbs, and often as he was passing a flowered vine it would reach out in his direction and breathe a gust of perfume over him, then fall back quivering as though with unheard private laughter.

Essentially, though, the planet remained as recognizable as its people, and in all respects bar one the latter delighted him. He found the children charming, while young parents behaved to their offspring with such a natural, unpremeditated blend of firmness and tenderness that they might have been animals uncomplicated by theory and dogma.

This much was a fulfilment of his fondest dreams.

But the older folk! They frightened him! They were all sort-of-clad, and what they "wore" was the finished version of the thing (?) that made Horad hard to look at.

Certain of these old ones, Lodovico could not even turn his head toward.

"It is because in your former existence, although you possessed the sense by which you now perceive them, there was nothing for you to use that sense on." This by way of explanation from Orlalee. It left him more confused than ever, and she tried to amplify her statement.

"You think you are seeing them," she offered. "This is not so. You are detecting them by their act in perceiving you."

"You mean I am a percept to them, as well? To—to a bunch of *garments*?" He understood well, now, why a mirror could not reflect him; this, though, was a fresh cause for dismay.

"That is not clothing. It is self. It is an example of the principle which you already know about: the one which imposes that you be conscious of self before we can perceive you."

Lodovico struggled gallantly after that concept.

"You mean you could not have perceived me unless I'd been a conscious being instead of a dead corpse."

"A dead corpse can be made easily from common substances."

He gave up. Seeing his bafflement, Genua—who was also with him, as usual—attempted another route.

"We have made calculations," she said. "In your time, persons died commonly after fewer than a hundred revolutions around the sun. We live much longer. When age begins to erode our memories, we arrange to have ourselves remembered by what appears to you to be a garment. It is a version of one's own personality that permits growth to begin all over again. Progress from one self to another may continue for thousands of years, though of course the first and final personalities would not recognize each other."

"These—these 'other-selves' are independent entities, then?"

"No, they are wholly dependent. They are reflections, they are objectified echoes, never more than copies of the persons to whom they belong. You, on the other hand . . ."

Abruptly the implications of that curtailed sentence came storming in on Lodovico's mind. The world grew dark for an instant. When he could see clearly again, he found Horad was there too.

"Yes," said Horad in a grave and sympathetic tone. "That is what you are: the first such reflection of a self which belongs to someone who was born and lived his life in what to us is the far-distant past."

For a while after that revelation, there had to be an interruption in his exploration of this new age. But he made a good recovery and was able to go on.

There were no more cities. When he asked his companions how many human beings there were now they surprised and indeed alarmed him: they paused long enough to count . . . And could not quite agree on whether it was more or less than thirty million.

People lived far apart, yet did not actually live anywhere. They were forever on the move, deciding that the mood they happened to be in deserved that climate, that season, that landscape, and acting on the conclusion.

Certainly they had homes. He was entertained at several and admired them extravagantly, for they were beautiful in ways that combined the supreme architectural achievement of literally hundreds of civilizations. He could not even try to keep track of all the cultures, long-vanished now, from which he was being shown relics. Occasionally he thought he recognized something as Egyptian or Assyrian or Greek; when he inquired, he was given names he had never heard, Uglardic or Canthorian or Benkilese . . .

Most agreeable of the survivals was the custom of celebrating by sharing food and drink, and beyond that scents and changes in the atmosphere which were sometimes more alarming than enjoyable, though all those around him seemed to know how to appreciate them. Feasts were held in his honor. He found he could taste, though he could draw no nourishment from, the miraculous dishes placed before him.

("You can eat, of course, since you are after your own fashion a person," Horad said. "But you need not. You are sustained by our awareness of you, and everyone you meet will make that existence stronger. We advise that you should eat if only because, perceiving that you do, we and everybody will find it easier to regard you as a real individual. If you enjoy the flavors, textures and scents, so much the better. We think of you as one who can." And he discovered the assumption was correct, though the logic behind it was still dreamlike, tantalizing, elusive.)

Art had lasted, but had spawned branches he could not see the purpose of. There was nothing for him in a communal ceremony which structured silence for a day and a night and a day, except boredom. Unable to become weary, he perforce witnessed the whole of it, and when the audience (?) roused and dispersed they were beaming with pleasure and showered compliments on the person who was part-host, part-administrator.

The going?

Belatedly he wondered about it, and realized that there was none. There was *being here*—interlude—*being there*, which automatically became *here* instead. He asked about it, and Genua said, "Again it is a talent which you possessed, but did not know of because in your time there was nothing to provoke its operation. I cannot explain it; no one could. You must feel it as it is happening. Then in a little while you will go alone, without the help of me or Orlalee or Horad. If I were to say to you, 'Contract in succession the following muscles, which I point out on this chart, in each alternate leg, and then relax them in this precise order, and then to keep your balance do this and that with the muscles in your torso, arms and shoulders . . .' Well, how many steps would you take in a day? Be patient. Soon enough you will have the principle in your bones."

He was secure enough now to essay a joke. He said, "What bones?"

Also there was the counterpart of work. This above all was as he had dreamed it might be, shorn of repetitive drudgery, free from commercial pressures: a series of acts undertaken at places where people came together for purposes of production, knowing always why they did what they did and informed about the benefits they were giving to others. He spent days and days watching fascinated as even very small children conjured useful objects (or at any rate objects he was told were regarded as useful, though he did not understand their function) from plants, from banks of clay, from roiling streams foul with sulphurous stench and dung-brown silt. He was running out of names, even of concepts; what adults did that they termed "working" was often as far beyond him as the other-selves he had mistaken for clothing.

Now the full force of his predicament hit him. He really was among people of a distant future age, and their thinking had changed even more than their bodily form. Hunting comparisons, he settled on the image of a convinced Christian from the Middle

Ages set down in a twentieth-century community where nobody was bothered by the notion of living on a moving ball of rock instead of at the fixed center of the universe, where it was not considered in the least blasphemous to tamper with natural forms but on the contrary it was regarded as sensible and useful to modify and improve wild plants and even animals, to revise what that medieval person would think of as the handiwork of the Almighty, sacrosanct. He was pleased to have reached that image, for it offered a useful peg on which to hang the more unpleasant of his frustrations. There were many. Each passing day (not that he or anyone else to his knowledge was counting them) added to his sense of impotence and isolation.

At first he had been delighted by the sheer novelty of his experience. Then by stages he had grown angry at not being able to grasp everything he was shown. Occasionally he had been shocked, especially when he learned that eroticism had endured and was now integrated into several art-forms, to the point where there were adults whose equivalent of a career consisted in instructing children, from babyhood up, about the amatory potential of their bodies.

He knew *a priori* that this was another medieval-visitor reaction, but it cost him much effort to reframe his thinking. He had been intellectually aware that even in his own age love-making had largely been separated from procreation, and it was logical enough that in the long run the division should become effectively total.

But there were private reasons why he had never partaken of whatever benefits this situation entailed. After leading a bachelor's life during his twenties and saying he was wedded to his work, he had been just about to marry when he was informed about his cancer. After which, of course, he had abandoned hope of any permanent involvement—wife, family . . . Too little time was left.

"Did you have regrets?" asked Orlalee.

They were on a hilltop overlooking a plain dotted with brilliant flowers, beyond which a stormcloud loomed blue as new-tempered steel. He could not remember how they came here.

He said, "Yes, I should have liked to bring up a child—one at least. But in another way, no. I made good use of what time I did have. I enjoyed myself, especially when I was finding out something new. In one respect I was unusually lucky. Ideas often came to me in dreams, and while most people's dream images turn out by light of day to be ridiculous, now and then mine proved to be sound, even important. Do you people still dream?"

"Of course."

"Why 'of course'?"

"It is in the nature of mankind to perceive unrealities as well as realities. You are a dream as much as you are a ghost, Lodovico. You are the fulfillment, the concretization, of one of the oldest dreams humanity has ever had."

"That being—?"

"The dream of the dead. The return of those who are no more. Those cut off before due time. Is it not there that one should seek the germ of the concept 'ghost'?"

"That makes sense," he conceded after a moment's thought.

And then, unexpectedly, she asked, "Lodovico, how do you like being a ghost?"

Without realizing how honest and unpremeditated his answer was going to be, he heard himself say, "Very well!"

"If the same occurred to me I think I would miss much. I should like to hear your reasons in the hope they will be accessible to me."

"First tell me this. When you put on the—other-self, is it the end of something for you? The conclusion of a stage of life, for example?"

"Oh, yes." There was something of sadness in her look. "It is exactly at the end of growth when we don them. To be full-grown is also to be dying; there is no boundary . . . Well?"

Lodovico pondered. At length he said, "Yes, I miss a lot, too. But much of what I miss is not to be regretted, like having a physical body that cancer could corrupt."

"It does not do so any more," Orlalee said. "But you do have a physical body."

"What?" The shock was wrenching. "But—!"

"Look."

She caught his arm in her thin but strong fingers, and clamped tight. After a moment she released him. Pale marks showed on his skin that took a minute or more to fade.

"I—" Lodovico put his hand to his forehead, giddily. "I . . .!"

"Yes, that is the word: I!" She was smiling, and suddenly she was not alone because Horad and Genua had joined them.

Horad said, "Congratulations, Lodovico. You are a reality to us. All those people now alive who have not personally met you have at any rate heard about you. Since you are present in the total awareness of the species, you exist."

"But—!" Inchoate arguments flared in his mind, on such grounds as conservation of energy. How could the mere process of perceiving someone convert that someone from an impalpable phantom into a solid living being?

"Now I can do something I wanted to do before which wasn't possible," Orlalee said, and put her arms around him and kissed him in a manner which was indescribably ancient, all bar the taste of her, which was new.

After which all three made love to him and proved him real.

There was a moment when he felt it would be amusing to say, "I am become a perversion incarnate."

But none of them got the point.

"Lodovico," Genua said later, "you have now seen our world. Do you approve?"

"Of those things which I understand in it, yes. Every ideal of my time seems to have come to pass. Between any person and any other there is peace. There is no jealousy, nor greed, because there is enough to satisfy everyone. Nobody lacks the chance to attempt, if not accomplish, his or her ambitions."

"Ah, there's the trouble," Horad said. "There are so many ambitions we can see no way to fulfill."

Startled, Lodovico said, "So many? What can they be?"

"Long ago, even as long ago as your original time, men dreamed of visiting other worlds and eventually the stars. Even to have explored the local planets would have been a great consolation. But we are here on Earth, are we not?"

"I had been wondering," said Lodovico slowly. "There must have been attempts."

"Indeed there were. People have circled the Sun more closely than Mercury does; they have dipped into the atmosphere of Jupiter, probed the frigid wastes of Pluto. But . . . Well, for every attempt there have been countless failures. Come with us."

They were at a crumbled mound surrounded by lapping waves.

"From here," Orlalee told him, "a decadent culture tried to launch a ship directly to the stars. The venture was insane. There was an explosion which sank half a continent."

They were at a creeper-covered clearing in the midst of a great forest of pines and birches, where a snow-capped mountain loured down on them.

"A long time ago," Genua said, "people here trapped a bit of sun-stuff in a magnetic holder. It was not strong enough. There was a vast fire which lasted less than an eyeblink, and that too ended."

They were in a desert where sand-scratched rags of metal whined in a constant wind.

"It is believed," murmured Horad, "that this is the only spot where men ever held converse with another intelligence. What was said, we shall never know. It was uttered in the form of radiation such as only a star can emit. Perhaps it was a star which answered us, focusing its signal on less space than my arms can span. That was recently. You see the desert; plants have not had time to claim it back."

The pattern grew in Lodovico's mind.

A person is fragile. Out where stars send messages to one another it takes a great deal to shield and protect a human body. Moreover the person who makes the voyage must spend so much

*time thinking about sheer survival, it is nearly a waste of time. So
long goes by; so little is discovered!*

"And what," he asked at last, "does this have to do with me?"

"Everything," they said. It was not Horad who spoke, or
Genua, or Orlalee; it was the combination.

"Why?"

"You are immortal."

"Impossible!"

"Oh, no. On the contrary." This was definitely Horad. Lodovico had grown to recognize and like his manner: a trifle dry,
often witty, always individual. "Perfectly possible. We intended it
to happen, and it worked out."

"How, though? How?"

"Because of the way you have been created. You are a compound percept: we have explained this already. Now, even to us
who were present when you first impinged on a present-time
consciousness, you are solid. You must eat and drink, or you
would die. You are in every respect bar one a person like any
other."

"The difference," Orlalee said, "is that we cannot conceive of
any means whereby you might be destroyed."

"But you just said I can die—" Lodovico began.

"By your choice. Your own choice. No other way," said Orlalee.

"Not the brutal gales of a gas-giant planet," Horad said so-
berly, "nor the furnace heart of a star can abolish what to us
constitutes Lodovico Zaras. For you *are not* Lodovico Zaras. You
are his incorruptible, indissoluble, inerasable image upon the
consciousness of all mankind."

"We can imagine you choosing to starve yourself to death
rather than perform the service we hope from you," said Genua.
"But the necessity will not of course arise. Were that to be your
decision, even now we could arrange that you cease to exist. But
we could not do it against your will."

"Service?" Lodovico repeated.

"Before we tell you what it is," Horad said, "we must emphasize that there is a good reason why you should say no. Now that we have made you real, you can feel pain."

"I was used to that in my original self," Lodovico said slowly. "Why should it be different, this time?"

"Because we want you to go where no one else can go, and come back and tell us what it's like."

He thought that over for a while, and said at last, not looking at them, "And this will hurt."

"Yes. As nearly as we can calculate, you will be hurt more than any other human being who ever lived. Worst of all, you will never have an escape route into death."

It was not until a long time afterward that he said yes.

They had been right about the pain. It was clear, it was a simple fact, that no human being had any right to stand by the bank of a river running liquid helium, on the side of Pluto currently turned away from the sun, and admire the way its flow competed with gravity. Yet . . . he did it.

Perhaps it was that for him pain no longer portended danger, inasmuch as he knew he would not die until humanity became extinct. The agony, at all events, was transformed, and little by little he became able to endure it.

It diminished, indeed, so rapidly, that even at the conclusion of his first expedition it paled into insignificance alongside the frustration he felt when he struggled to fulfill his part of the bargain. How to explain in words the sensation of cold so violent it was like a flame? How to describe the river's color, which lacking hue and brilliance and saturation was nonetheless seared into his memory like a scar?

Paradoxically, those who had sent him forth were well pleased. He had imagined failure, rejection; instead, when they had healed him they showered him with compliments and asked how soon he would be ready to leave again. (His going was by the route he had been taught since his resurrection. Any of the people who questioned him about what he had discovered could have taken it too, but for them it was useless when the destination

vas empty space or the surface of a hostile planet. He alone,
none other, could survive a visit to a place like that.)

Among those who came to congratulate and thank him, he
nearly did not recognize Horad because his other-self was more
triking now, more disturbing to the vision . . . even though Lodovico had grown to accept that its essence was his. Natural human
flesh clearly could not take the punishment he had consented to
endure. Therefore . . .

To Horad he put a question which went some short distance
toward relief of his frustration; from Horad he received an answer
which sustained him on the rest of his journey.

He said, "How is it that you people have drawn so much from
the little I was able to convey in words?"

And Horad explained, "It is long past your epoch, Lodovico.
For us, communication is not confined to speech. No more, to be
candid, was it for you; for the most part, it seems, you imagined
hat it was, but in practice what you took for misunderstandings
were very often the result of someone understanding another person 'only too well.'"

With a final dry coda: "That phrase has no equivalent in any
modern language, because in this tongue we are speaking there is
the facility to make quotation-marks."

All of which was a supreme achievement by an admirably
evolved modern mind, a condensation into a few sentences of
millennia-worth of reflection and analysis.

And because he understood this brief reply with such clarity
even though it belonged to a much later age than his own, Lodovico was able to convince himself that the people of today were
worth suffering for.

He went again. Again. Again.

They grew afraid. It had not been calculated that he should
become obsessed with his travels to unsurvivable environments.
Whenever they tried to tell him he had done enough, however, he
ranted and raved until they let him depart one more time.

By stages they became resigned. They had created him. He
was now himself. The creators had long ago lost control. It re-

mained to derive what data they could from having him to talk to, or simply be with. Mad, wild, primitive, berserk?

Unique.

But offering—still miraculously offering—reports that others could study and transform into comprehensible, and thus into fascinating, information.

It had been a long time, as the psychic evolution of the human species went, since there was anything their ancestors might have termed *news* . . .

They therefore tolerated it that he should learn: yes, they grow in Jupiter and Neptune and Uranus! Variously, from viciously to vicariously! (What does it mean? It means itself because no human ever before perceived it!)

As it became less than a marvel to him, for after all it was merely a not-Earth event and belonged to this universe, to this galaxy, this planetary system (shrinking by orders of magnitude with each review), he was able to describe his experiences in plainer terms.

In Uranus a creature ate him, fifty thousand miles long, and he survived. This among a million other recollections.

Naturally.

Neptune was the place where a sort-of-a-volcano was erupting icy lava at a yard per year and the nearby flora evolved to meet the threat and, as he watched, learned how to run at twice that speed. Again, among countless less communicable data.

As for Jupiter: there *something* greeted him, and told such a monstrous lie, he came home persuaded it must be true on some other axis of perception. But he did not at once insist that he should go back, preferring to postpone a second meeting with—whatever.

Whereas Saturn . . . He treasured that especially, not only for the methane-bergs and ammonia-bows and geysers, not even for the rings, but because whatever they were they were delicious and so proud of it and flattered to know their taste was being appreciated for the first time by a being from elsewhere. They had never realized that elsewhere was. It shattered their consciousness like the shell around an exploding chick (but there were neither chicks nor shells for them because they were distinctly *other* and had he not been immortal tasting them—and being able to accept they were delicious—would have done much more than simply kill him) #because of which there were potentially several trillion qualifications to any statement he was able to bring back and obviously it was futile to struggle with the# NATHELEES they went looking for other consumers. It was a hurriness. By the end of his visit none were left but there was no need to regret the extinction of their species because they provided a symbol intimating #how he knew he didn't know but he #knew# and—and the hell with it# *gone to find the stars whatever they may be in the hope-identical-with-conviction they also eat us well*.

Nobody back on Earth liked that report. It was overshadowing. First time and they got it right, for a ridiculous purpose!

"But in what sense were they delicious?" demanded practical Orlalee, whom he had grown very much to like.

"In the sense they couldn't help," returned Lodovico. "They had evolved toward that goal for a billion years."

"You being the collective percept of us all," Genua mused, "we imagined you would bring back information we could understand."

"Especially," Lodovico suggested with a *moue*, "because I belong to a less evolved age, and you comprehend my total consciousness."

"Perhaps," Horad said, "we'd have done better with a consciousness derived from our time."

"But you could not," Lodovico said. "You could not have recreated a personality as complex and modern as your own. I am at the lower limit of what you can derive from yourselves and externalize. Do not blame me, therefore, for my shortcomings; they are yours."

When they did not contest the statement, he added, "I am in luck. Being transported, as it were, to this time from another, far simpler age, I'm already primed with the assumption that there are many things I'm not equipped to grasp. Please stop thinking that because you could conjure me into existence you can do anything."

"Would it be fair to say"—this from Horad, in a pensive and leisurely tone—"that what consoles you for the horrors and agonies you go through is the impossiblity of digesting even our tiny corner of the universe within one conventional lifetime?"

With emphasis Lodovico said, "No!"

"What, then?" All three of them seemed taken aback.

"In my old life I was resigned to the belief that, just as no observer can know both the speed and the position of a particle, so no consciousness can comprehend the universe which is the frame of its existence. That is among the facts which have not changed over the millennia.

"What I failed to appreciate was how much more important it is to be-conscious than it is to comprehend. Possession of even a meager imagination permits the owner to envisage processes that are forbidden by the laws of nature. Therefore any consciousness automatically transcends its universe."

"You are sure of that in so short a time?" Horad breathed.

"I was led to believe," Lodovico said wryly, "that you were indifferent as to whether a time-span is long or short."

And he added, "May I now continue my explorations? Or do you have no further need of reports from me?"

"Indeed we do," said Orlalee. "We welcome them. They are and will remain unique."

"You mean you do not expect ever to go where I am going?"

Genua parried that question. She said, "Is there not a lot of the future still to come?"

The zone of the asteroids he found to be crowded with events, but almost all of them were of a similar kind: collisions. He had much time, while witnessing them, to ponder the implications of the conclusion he had voiced to Horad. It was no more than a matter of probability; however, given that this petty corner of the cosmos was typical of, if not the whole, then a very large volume of it, and given that he had met consciousness on several occasions already—what was more, versions of consciousness capable of recognizing him as an aware being even before he identified them—such data convinced him that consciousness must be of the essence of the universe.

It changed his own view of himself-as-he-now-was. Instead of that lingering resentment he still fought against when he set out, he was overtaken by a sense of gratitude so intense it was almost happiness. It might have been on any other conformation of awareness that the chance to be-first fell. It fell to him. Therefore . . .

(After his long spell in the asteroid belt, they asked whether he had grown bored on his quest, and he replied, "Bored? It would be impossible. A man who can grow old, fatigued, confused—he may feel boredom because it is senility in little. As you have made me, I am no longer vulnerable to it.")

The cratered plains of Mars—the wind-punished valleys of Venus—the bleak hot mask of Mercury . . . and at last, climactically, the Sun. He plunged from the corona to the core, and when he came back . . .

It took the longest time of all to heal him. Doing what he had done had strained the collective credulity of Earth, and he who had survived the crash of asteroids and the fall of methane avalanches was much less believed in than before.

And yet—and yet—it had been done . . . *He* knew, who had also doubted the possibility. Gradually the means came clear to other people, and with conviction healing followed. The mechanism? It was not and never had been mechanism, but only that-which-does-the-perceiving, liberated.

So the time arrived when those whom he now called his friends were able to visit him and talk.

"You have suffered," said one or perhaps all three of them. "Do you regard it as worthwhile?"

"Yes."

"Why?"

"Because what has been wrong with humanity since the beginning is not wrong with me. We have always had the imagination that belongs with immortality, but we have been trapped in destructible substance. It is small wonder that in ancient times there were so many religions that insisted on a life after death. Even our dreams rebelled against the idea of dissolution."

"But it has been considered by many of the cultures we know about that death is a boon."

"Is it so regarded now?" Lodovico countered. "Now that you've achieved so many of our old ambitions—peace, plenty, freedom from fear?"

They exchanged glances. Or, more nearly: a glance was exchanged among the three of them.

"We doubt it," Horad said at last.

"And you are right." He uttered the words with fervor. "It is what it was first believed to be, a burden we have labored under far too long. And how can you not credit this, you whose supreme achievement has been to create the other-selves, the reflections of your personae which make you halfway to immortal?"

"It is not that we disbelieve it," Horad said. And the other two seemed to join him in speaking. "It is that we did not until now realize how right we are. Before we evoked you, we had begun to wonder whether there might not be a proper time for a species to die, a time chosen by itself. Thanks to you, we have been satisfied on that score. We go to fix the date for the suicide of man."

He who had been crushed by clashing asteroids, who had been vaporized by the solar phoenix cycle and returned, was overwhelmed by the purport of that promise. When he recovered enough to formulate a counter-question, he found there was no listener to put it to. He was alone.

After he got over the need to rail and scream, very slowly the truth dawned on him.

His mode of thinking was ancient. Worse—it was primitive. At the heart of it lay an assumption he should have discarded long ago, only the idea had never previously occurred to him. It was by that assumption he had been misled.

He was used to taking for granted that he was *somebody*.

It was a measure of the success Horad and Genua and Orlalee

ad achieved that he should have gone on believing, or rather not
worrying about, this aspect of his nature until now. He must, he
realized, correspond in minute detail to the version of Lodovico
Zaras who, aeons ago, had discovered that he was due to die of
cancer and preferred to choose his own moment and his own way
to leave the world.

But he *was-not* that person.

He-now was not some body. He was some one.

And the distinction was indescribably important.

Ghosts!

"You arrived at understanding," they said when they returned.

"Yes, slow on the uptake though I was."

"There will be others." The problem was dismissed with
something like a casual wave. "For those who date back furthest,
it is not improbable that centuries will go by while they gradually
begin to perceive the universe as it is instead of in the manner
which their gross, half-evolved brains allowed them to accept.
But it is not of course the brain which matters, is it?"

Lodovico knew exactly what was meant. Now. And if he
could do it, so could others. He said, "Have you chosen the
date?"

"As nearly as we can. We have been at pains to calculate in
the sort of terms you used to apply. In less than half a million
years it will no longer matter what becomes of Earth. Let it freeze
or burn, let it wander the interstellar gulf or fall into the heart of
the sun. There will be no more men and women. We shall have
recalled and re-perceived every human being who ever existed,
free like you to go everywhere, experience everything, and survive to remember what happened. Thank you, Lodovico. You
gave us precisely what we dreamed of. There can be no greater
gift in time or space."

"But," he said, thinking of termination in his simple, primitive
fashion, "if there are to be no more humans . . ."

"It is for the best reason," they replied. "We created you to
help us determine whether our species has engendered as much
consciousness as is proper to it. The fact that you are as-you-are

is the evidence we wanted. The ambition of a rational, intelligent species is not as-much-as-possible, but *enough*."

"At Saturn I ran across a similar decision," Lodovico said. "I do not yet see what you mean. But in the certainty that I eventually shall, I am glad to abide by the conclusion of mankind."

"It is good," they said, and went about the necessary business.

So in ripe time it was done, and mankind died as a material species. But its hordes of ghosts were billions strong, and went to compare notes with strangers who had made the like discovery, to confirm or disprove what they had found out about the universe, and often enough learned they had been wrong.

Often enough to keep them curious and intrigued for at least the current cosmic cycle. Even immortality cannot shrink the gap between the galaxies.

Sic fiat.

The Vitanuls

There's a clever science-fiction, or science-fantasy, twist at the resolution of this story, but it's about far more than that.

It's about all those aliens out there. Five billion of them.

━━━ ━━━ ━━━ ━━━ ━━━

Before the soundproof, germproof double glass window of the delivery room, the matron of the maternity hospital came to a halt. "And there," she told the tall young American from the World Health Organization, "is our patron saint."

Barry Chance blinked at her. She was a brisk fortyish Kashmiri woman with an aura of efficiency, not at all the sort of person one would expect to make jokes about her life's work. And indeed there had been no trace of jocularity in her tone. But in this teeming subcontinent of India a stranger could never be sure how seriously anybody took anything. After all, the universe

267

was *maya*—illusory—according to the classical teaching.

He compromised. "I'm sorry," he lied. "I didn't catch that . . .?"

Out of the corner of his eye he studied the man the matron had indicated. He was elderly and balding; what little hair remained to him had whitened into a sort of halo around his heavily lined face. Most Indians, the American had noticed, tended to grow fat with age, but this man had become scrawny, like Gandhi. Surely, though, an ascetic appearance and a halo of hair weren't enough to establish a claim to sainthood?

"Our patron saint," the matron repeated, sublimely unaware of her visitor's bewilderment. "Dr. Ananda Kotiwala. You're very fortunate to see him at work. It's his last day here before he retires."

Struggling to make sense of her remarks, Chance stared un-ashamedly at the old man. He felt his rudeness was excused by the fact that this corridor adjoining the delivery room was a kind of public gallery. On every side there were relatives and friends of the expectant mothers, down to and including very small chil-dren, who had to stand on tiptoe to peer in through the window. There was no such thing as privacy in India unless you were rich. In any overcrowded underdeveloped country a minute fraction of the people enjoyed that luxury he'd taken for granted since child-hood.

The fact that toddlers could watch, fascinated, the arrival of their new brothers and sisters was accepted here as a part of growing up. Chance reminded himself sternly that he was a for-eigner, and—what was more—a doctor himself, trained at one of the few colleges that still administered the Hippocratic oath in full form to its graduates. He forced his personal preconceptions to the back of his mind and concentrated on unravelling the cu-rious comment the matron had made.

The scene before him offered no hints. All he could see was a typical Indian hospital delivery room, containing thirty-six mothers in labor, of whom two were suffering agonies and screaming—at least, to judge by their open mouths and contorted bodies; the soundproofing was extremely good.

He wondered briefly how the Indians really felt about their children entering the world under such circumstances. What it suggested to him was an assembly line, the mothers reduced to machines producing their quota of infants according to a pre-planned schedule. And all of it so dreadfully public!

Again, though, he was falling into the trap of thinking like a modern American, parochially. For untold generations most of mankind had been born publicly. Although it had been estimated that the world's present living population was just about equal in number to all the human beings there had ever been before the twenty-first century, the majority of Earth's people continued that ancient tradition, and made a birth a social event: in villages, an excuse for a grand celebration, or here in the city for a family outing to the hospital.

The modern attributes of the event were easily listed. The behavior of the mothers, for instance: one could tell at a glance which of them had enjoyed up-to-date prenatal instruction, for their eyes were closed and their faces bore expressions of deter-mination. They knew what miracle was going on in their bodies, and they intended to help it, not resist it. Good. Chance nodded approval. But there remained the women who were screaming, no doubt as much from terror as from actual pain . . .

He shifted his attention with an effort. After all, he was sup-posed to be conducting a study of the methods in use here.

The latest recommendations of the experts seemed to be being properly applied—you'd expect as much in a large city where most of the medical staff had had the benefit of training abroad. Some time soon he was committed to going out into the villages, and things would be different there, but he'd think about that when he had to.

The elderly doctor who had been called "our patron saint" was just completing the delivery of a boy. Gloved hand held up the latest recruit to the army of humanity, glistening. A slap—cor-rection: a beautifully restrained pat with the open palm, enough to provoke a squall and the first deep breath, not enough to ag-gravate the birth-trauma. And handed over to the waiting nurse to be laid on the little bench beside the bed, lower than the mother so that the last few precious ounces of maternal blood could seep down from the placenta before the cord was severed.

Excellent. All in accordance with the best modern practice. Except—why was the doctor having to explain so much so patiently to the awkward girl assisting him?

Chance's puzzlement was brief, then he realized. Of course. There weren't enough trained nurses in this country to allot one to every mother. So those girls standing neat and scared in their disposable plastic coveralls, their lank black hair bound in sterile plastic snoods, would be younger sisters or eldest daughters doing their best to help out.

Then the old man, with a final smile of reassurance, was leaving the worried girl and going to hold the hand of one of the women screaming.

Chance watched with approval as he soothed her, bringing about a complete relaxation within moments and—as far as could be guessed through the double barrier of soundproof glass and an incomprehensible language—instructing her how best to hasten the delivery. Yet there was nothing more here than he'd seen in a hundred hospitals.

He turned to the matron and asked directly, "Why do you call him 'patron saint'?"

"Dr. Kotiwala," the matron said, "is the most—now what would it be in English? Is there the word 'empathetic'?"

"From 'empathy'?" Chance frowned. "I don't know. But I get what you mean, anyway."

"Yes," the matron said. "Did you not see how he quieted the one who was screaming?"

Chance gave a slow nod. Yes, come to think of it, in a country like this, one could properly regard as a special gift the ability to break through the superstitious fright of a woman barely above peasant level and make her see what it had taken other women around her the full nine months of pregnancy and much skilled instruction to understand. Now there was only one woman with her mouth howling wide, and the doctor was soothing her in turn. The other he'd just spoken to was yielding to her contractions instead of fighting them.

"Dr. Kotiwala is wonderful," the matron went on. "Everybody loves him. I have known parents who consult astrologers not to determine the most fortunate birthday for their child but only to make sure it would be born during Dr. Kotiwala's shift in the delivery room."

Shift? Oh yes: they operated a three-shift day. Once more the image of the assembly line came to him. But it was far too advanced a concept to reconcile with the idea of applying to astrologers. What a crazy country! Chance repressed a shiver and admitted to himself that he'd be glad when he was allowed to return home.

For long moments after that he was silent, noticing something he hadn't previously spotted: how, when the labor pains permitted, the mothers opened their eyes and hopefully followed Dr. Kotiwala's progress around the room as though wanting to invite him to spend a minute or two at their bedside.

This time their hopes weren't fulfilled. There was a breech presentation at the far end, and it would take careful manipulation to reverse the baby. Plastic-clad, a beautiful dark girl of about fifteen bent to watch what the doctor was doing, putting out her right hand so that the tense anxious mother could clasp it for comfort.

By his own standards, Chance thought, there was nothing remarkable about Kotiwala. He was obviously competent, and his patients appeared to like him, but he was old and rather slow, and one could see how cautiously he moved now the end of his shift was near and he was tiring.

On the other hand, it was certainly admirable to find the human touch in a birth factory like this. He'd asked the matron, within minutes of his arrival, how long the average stay of a patient might be, and she'd said with a wry smile, "Oh, twenty-four hours for the easy ones, and perhaps thirty-six if there are complications."

Looking at Dr. Kotiwala one might have assumed there was all the time in the world.

From an American standpoint even that didn't constitute a claim to sanctity, but through Indian eyes doubtless things looked different. The matron had warned him that he'd come at a busy time, nine months after a big spring religious festival which people regarded as auspicious for increasing their families. The warning hadn't prepared him for the reality; the hospital was *packed*.

Yet it could have been worse. He shuddered a little. The back of the problem was broken, but there were still something like 180,000 new mouths to feed every day. At the peak of the population explosion there had been just under a quarter million per day; then the impact of modern education was felt, people even in Asia, Africa and Latin America began to recognize the need to plan only for the children they could afford to feed, clothe and support while at school, and the crisis diminished.

Nonetheless it would be years before the children of that tidal wave of births could become teachers, workers, doctors to cope with the tremendous pressure. Thinking along these lines brought him to a subject which had been engaging a lot of his attention recently, and he spoke aloud without intending to.

"People like him, in this of all jobs—that's who they ought to choose!"

"I beg your pardon?" the matron said with positively British formality. The Raj had left ineradicable traces on the intellectuals of this country.

"Nothing," Chance muttered.

"But did you not say someone ought to choose Dr. Kotiwala for something?"

Annoyed with himself, yet—once reminded of the dilemma shortly to be sprung on the world—unable to hold his tongue, Chance gave ground.

"You said it was Dr. Kotiwala's last day here, didn't you?"

"Why, yes. He retires tomorrow."

"You have someone lined up to replace him?"

The matron shook her head vigorously. "Oh, no! In the physical sense, yes, for another doctor will take his shifts, but men like Dr. Kotiwala are rare in any generation and in modern times most of all. We're dreadfully sorry to lose him."

"Has he—ah—passed the official retirement age?"

The matron smiled thinly. "In India we cannot afford the luxuries you Americans go in for, and that includes putting usable material—human or otherwise—on a scrap heap before it's worn out."

With his eyes on the elderly doctor, who had successfully reversed the breech presentation and moved on to attend the woman in the next bed, Chance said, "In other words, he's retiring of his own accord."

"Yes."

"Why? Has he lost interest in his work?"

The matron was clearly shocked. "Of course not! Though I'm not sure I can make his reasons clear to you . . ." She bit her lip. "Well, he is very old now, and he does fear that some day soon a child may die because he has let his attention wander. It would set him back many steps on the road to enlightenment if that happened."

Chance felt a surge of enlightenment himself. Believing he completely understood what the matron meant, he said under his breath, "In that case he damned well does deserve—"

And broke off, because strictly he ought not to be thinking about this subject, let alone talking about it.

"I'm sorry?" the matron said, and when Chance shook his head went on: "You see, when he was young Dr. Kotiwala was much influenced by the teachings of the Jains, to whom the taking of any life at all is repugnant. When his desire to cherish life led him to study as a doctor, he had to accept that some killing—of bacteria, for example—is inevitable to ensure human survival. But his kindliness remains founded upon religious principles, and it would be more than he could bear to think that his own arrogance in continuing to work when it was no longer safe had cost an innocent baby its chance to live a good and upright life."

"He can hardly actually be a Jain, then," Chance said, lacking any other comment for the moment. Privately he was thinking that if what the matron said was correct there were some old fossils back home, in medicine and in other fields, who could do with a transfusion of Kotiwala's humility instead of hanging on until they were dangerously senile.

"He's formally a Hindu, as are most of our people," the matron explained. "Though he tells me he has studied deeply in Buddhism too—which began, after all, as a Hindu heresy." She didn't sound greatly concerned. "But I'm afraid I still don't understand what you were referring to a moment ago," she added.

Chance thought of gigantic factories owned by DuPont, Bayer, Glaxo and heaven knew who else, laboring night and day with more expenditure of energy than a million mothers bringing forth commonplace human beings, and decided that the facts were going to be public knowledge soon enough for him to risk lifting a corner of the curtain of secrecy. It was depressing him to keep his mouth shut all the time.

He said, "Well, what I meant was that if I had any say in the matter people like him would get priority when it comes to—ah —the most advanced kinds of medical treatment. To preserve someone who is liked and admired seems better than saving someone who is mainly feared."

There was a pause.

"I think I follow you," the matron said at length. "I take it the anti-death pill is a success?"

Chance started. She gave another of her wry smiles.

"Oh, it's difficult for us to keep up with the literature when we work under such pressure, but there have been hints, haven't there? You in the rich countries like America and Russia have been trying for years to find a broad-spectrum specific against aging, and I think—knowing your countries by hearsay—that there must have been a long angry argument over who should benefit first."

Chance surrendered completely and gave a miserable nod. "Yes, there's a specific against senility. It isn't perfect, but pressure on the drug companies to put it into commercial production has grown so great that just before I left WHO Headquarters to come here I heard the contracts were being placed. A course of treatment will cost five or six thousand dollars and last for eight to ten years. I don't have to tell you what it'll mean. But if I had my way I'd pick someone like your Dr. Kotiwala to enjoy the results before all the stupid old men with power and wealth who are going to have their obsolete prejudices carried into the future by this breakthrough!"

He stopped short, alarmed at his own vehemence and hoping that none of the curious spectators surrounding them could speak English.

"Your attitude does you credit," the matron said. "But in one sense it's inexact to say Dr. Kotiwala is retiring. He might prefer to say he is changing his career. And if you offered to give him the anti-senility treatment I expect he would refuse."

"Why in the world—?"

"It is hard to make clear in English." The matron frowned. "You know perhaps what is a sunnyasi?"

Bewildered, Chance said, "One of those holy men I've seen around the place, wearing nothing but a loincloth and carrying a begging-bowl."

"And a staff, usually."

"A sort of fakir?"

"Not in the least. A sunnyasi is a man in the final stage of his life's work. He could have been anything previously—a businessman, commonly, or a civil servant, or a lawyer, or even a doctor."

"You mean your Dr. Kotiwala is going to throw away all his medical skills, all his experience, all the service he could still perform in this overcrowded country even if he did risk the life of a baby one of these days, and go out begging in a loincloth for the sake of his own salvation?"

"That is why we call him our patron saint," the matron said with an affectionate smile in Dr. Kotiwala's direction. "When he has gone from here and collected much virtue he will be a friend for us who remain behind."

Chance was appalled. A moment ago the matron had been saying that India could not afford to throw aside people with good work still before them; now here she was seeming to approve a plan that struck him as compounded of equal parts selfishness and superstition.

"Are you telling me he believes this nonsense about stacking up virtue for a future existence?"

The matron gave him a chill stare. "I think that is uncivil of you. The teaching of Hinduism is that the soul is born again, throughout an eternal cycle, until it achieves one-ness with the All. Can you not appreciate how a lifetime of work among the newly born makes all this real to us?"

"You believe it too?"

"That's irrelevant. But . . . I do witness miracles every time I admit a mother to this hospital. I witness how an animal act, a process with slimy, messy, *bloody* associations, brings about the growth of a reasoning being. I was born, and you, a squally helpless infant, and here we stand talking in abstract concepts. Maybe it is a mere function of chemical complexity. I don't know. I told you: I find it hard to keep up with the literature."

Chance stared through the window of the delivery room with a puzzled frown. He felt somehow disappointed—even cheated—after his near acceptance of Dr. Kotiwala on the matron's admiring terms. At last he muttered, "I guess maybe we'd better move on."

The sensation of which Dr. Kotiwala was chiefly aware was weariness. It went all through his body, to the marrow of his bones.

There was no hint of it in his outward behavior, no suggestion that he was mechanically going through the motions. The mothers who committed themselves and their offspring to his care would have detected any such failing with perceptions deeper than ordinary, and he would have known the truth himself and felt he was betraying their trust.

But he was unspeakably, incredibly tired.

More than sixty years had passed since he graduated from medical school. There had been no change in the way human beings were created. Oh, the trappings had altered as medicine made its successive impacts; he remembered the inarguable disasters caused by drugs like thalidomide, and the upside-down blessings of antibiotics, that swamped countries like his own with more mouths than it could possibly feed, and now he was working with techniques which meant that nine out of ten of the children born under his supervision were wished-for, loved by their parents instead of being a burden or condemned to the half-life of illegitimacy.

Sometimes things turned out well, and sometimes badly. In the course of his long and valuable career Dr. Kotiwala had come to place reliance on no other principle.

Tomorrow...

His mind threatened to wander away from what he was doing: bringing to independent life the latest of all those he had delivered. How many thousands of mothers had moaned on the bed before him? He dared not count. And how many more thousands of new lives had he helped to launch? Those he less-than-dared to count. Perhaps he'd introduced to life a thief, an ingrate, a murderer, a fratricide...

No matter. Tomorrow—indeed, today, for his shift was over and this baby he was now raising by the feet was the last he would ever deliver in a hospital, though if he were appealed to in some miserable village he would doubtless help...Tomorrow there would be an end to worldly attachments. He would commit himself to the life of the spirit, and—

He checked. The woman alongside the mother, her sister-in-law, very much disturbed by the things she had had to do like sterilizing her hands in disinfectant and stripping off her best sari in favor of a clammy plastic coverall, spoke a fearful question.

He hesitated over his answer. To the superficial glance nothing about the baby seemed amiss. It was a boy, physically whole, the usual flushed post-natal color, letting out an acceptable scream to greet the world. All was as it should be. And yet...

He cradled the baby on his left arm while deftly raising first one, then the other eyelid. Sixty years of practice had made him gentle. He stared deep into the vacant light eyes, contrasting almost frighteningly with the skin around.

Beyond them was—was...

But what could one say of a child as new as this? He sighed and gave it into the care of the sister-in-law, and the clock on the wall ticked away the last seconds of his last shift.

Nonetheless his mind remained on the indefinable impulse

which had compelled him to take a second look at the boy. When the doctor taking over from him arrived, Dr. Kotiwala concluded his summary briefing by saying, "And there's something odd about the boy just born in Bed Thirty-two. I can't put my finger on it. But if you get the chance, check him over, would you?"

"Will do," said the relief doctor, a fat young man from Benares with a shiny brown face and shiny soft hands.

The matter continued to irk Dr. Kotiwala even though he'd spoken about it. Changed, showered, ready to leave, he still lingered in the corridor to watch his colleague examining the baby as requested, making a thorough inspection from head to foot. He found nothing, and catching sight of Dr. Kotiwala as he turned away spread his hands and shrugged, his attitude implying, "Fuss about nothing if you ask me!"

Yet when I looked into those eyes, something behind them . . .

No, it was absurd. What could any adult hope to read in the eyes of a brand-new baby? Wasn't it a kind of arrogance that made him think his colleague was missing something of vital importance? In a dilemma, he considered the idea of going back into the delivery room and taking another look.

"Isn't that your patron saint standing there?" Chance muttered to the matron in a cynical tone.

"Why, so it is. How fortunate! Now you can make his acquaintance yourself, if you wish to."

"You've painted him in such glowing colors," Chance said dryly, "I feel I'd be wasting a chance if I didn't meet him before he forsakes the world."

The irony was lost on the matron. She bustled ahead with exclamations, but interrupted herself the moment she registered Kotiwala's glum expression.

"Doctor! Is something the matter?"

"I don't know," Kotiwala sighed. His English was good, but heavily accented in the singsong rhythm which the departed British had nicknamed "Bombay Welsh." "It is the child just born in Bed Thirty-two, a boy. I am *sure* something is wrong, but as for what it is I'm at a loss."

"In that case we must have him examined," the matron said briskly. Clearly she had implicit faith in Kotiwala's judgment.

"Dr. Banerji has checked him over and does not agree with me," Kotiwala countered.

In the matron's view Kotiwala was Kotiwala and Banerji was nobody; her expression said so louder than words. It struck Chance that here was his opportunity to find out whether the matron's admiration had any real basis.

"Look, rather than taking up more of Dr. Banerji's time—he has a lot to cope with in there—why don't you bring the child out and we'll take a look at him?"

"Dr. Chance, from WHO," the matron explained. Absently Dr. Kotiwala shook hands.

"Yes, that is a good idea. A second opinion, as they say. I'd welcome that."

It had been in the back of Chance's mind that his comparatively fresh training would enable him to apply some tests Kotiwala wasn't familiar with. In fact it was the other way around; the slow, thorough palping of the child's body and limbs, the delicate touching of the seven chakras, the traditional foci of the imaginary Yogic "vital force"—those were not in Chance's vocabulary of techniques. Of course, before the advent of modern instruments . . .

Anyway, valuable or not, such methods revealed nothing. Heart normal, blood-pressure average, all external appearances healthy, reflexes present and vigorous, fontanelle a trifle larger than normal but within normal range of variation . . .

After nearly three quarters of an hour, Chance was convinced the old man was doing this to make an impression, and consequently was losing his temper by degrees. He noticed that again and again Kotiwala rolled up the boy's eyelids and stared into the eyes as though he could read the brain behind them. On the latest repetition of the act he snapped, "Tell me, Doctor! What do you see in his eyes, hm?"

"What do *you* see?" Kotiwala countered, and motioned for Chance to look also.

"Nothing," Chance grunted a moment later. They'd checked the eyes, hadn't they, along with everything else? The iris displayed a regular infantile reflex, the retinal pattern was in no visible way abnormal.

"That's what I see also," Kotiwala said. "Nothing."

Oh, for pity's sake! Chance spun on his heel and went to dump his sterile examination-gloves in the bin beside the door. Over his shoulder he said, "Frankly I can't find anything wrong with the kid at all. What do you think could be the trouble? The soul of an earthworm turned up in his body by mistake, or something?"

Kotiwala could hardly have missed the scorn with which the words were uttered, but his reply was perfectly calm and civil.

"No, Dr. Chance, I think that hardly likely. After a great deal of contemplation I've come to the conclusion that the traditional ideas are inaccurate. The human condition is a human thing. It embraces the imbecile and the genius, but it does not overlap with any other species. Who could claim that the soul of a monkey, or a dog, is inferior to that which looks out of the dirty windows of a moron's eyes?"

"I certainly wouldn't," Chance said with sarcasm, and began to peel off his gown. Kotiwala sighed, and shrugged, and was silent.

Later...

The sunnyasi Ananda Bhagat wore nothing more than a loincloth, owned nothing in all the world bar the begging-bowl and staff he carried. Around him—for it was cold in the hill country this bleak December—the people of the village shivered in their cheap coarse clothes, spending as much time as they could huddled over their tiny fires. They burned woodchips, rarely charcoal, and even now a great deal of cow dung. The foreign experts had told them to use dung for fertilizer, but the warmth of a fire was closer to the present than the mystery of fixed nitrogen and next year's crops.

Ignoring the chill, ignoring the strong smoke of the fire as it wandered upward and filled the gloomy hut, Ananda Bhagat spoke soothingly to a fearful girl of about seventeen, at whose

breast a baby clung. He had looked into its eyes, and there he had
seen—nothing.

It was not the first such in this village; it was not the first
village where he had seen the same. He accepted that as a fact of
existence. With the abandonment of the name Kotiwala had gone
the preconceptions of a Doctor of Medicine, Trinity College
Dublin, who had obeyed the behests of intellectualism in the
sterile wards of a big city hospital. Throughout his eighty-six
years he had sensed a greater reality looming over him, and his
final decision had been to commit himself to it.

Now, as he gazed wonderingly into the empty face of the
child, he heard a noise. The young mother heard it also, and
cowered because it was loud and growing louder. So far had
Ananda Bhagat come from his former world that he had to make
a conscious effort before he identified it. A drone in the sky. A
helicopter, a rarity here; why should a helicopter come to any
particular one of India's seventy thousand villages?

The young mother whimpered. "Be still, my daughter," the
sunnyasi said. "I will go and see what this is about."

He let her hand fall with a final comforting pat and went out
of the misshapen doorway to stand on the cold windy street. The
village had only one street. Shading his eyes with his thin hand,
he peered upward into the sky.

Yes: a helicopter indeed, circling and glinting in the weak
winter sunlight. It was descending, but that was not owing to his
emergence into plain view. Before he recognised the sound of it,
it must already have been coming down.

He waited.

In a little while the people came chattering out of their homes,
wondering why the attention of the outer world in the form of this
curious humming machine should be turned on them. Seeing that
their marvellous visitor, the holy man, the sunnyasi—such as he
were rare these days, and to be cherished—was standing firm,
they drew courage from his example and likewise stood up
boldly.

The helicopter settled in a blast of whirling dust, a little away
from the beaten track called a street, and a man jumped down

from it: a tall fair-skinned foreigner. He looked the scene over slowly, spotted the sunnyasi and let out an exclamation. Calling something to his companions, he began to stride up the street. Two others came down to stand beside the machine and talk in low tones: a slender young woman in a sari of blue and green, and a man in flying overalls, the pilot.

Clutching her baby to her, the young mother also came out to see what was going on, her first child—a toddler—pursuing her on unsteady feet with a hand outstretched to catch at her if his balance failed him.

"Dr. Kotiwala!" the man from the helicopter cried.

"I was," the sunnyasi agreed in a rusty voice. The whole vocabulary of English had sloughed off his mind like a snake's overtight skin.

"For God's sake!" The man's voice was harsh. "We've had enough trouble finding you without your playing word games now we're here. Thirteen villages we've had to stop at on the way, picking up clues and being told you were here yesterday and moved on . . ."

He wiped his face with the back of his hand.

"My name's Barry Chance, in case you've forgotten me. We met at the hospital in—"

The sunnyasi interrupted. "I remember very well, thank you. But who am I, that you spend so much time and energy trying to trace me?"

"As far as we can tell, you're the first person ever to have recognized a Vitanul."

There was a silence. During it, Chance could almost see the sunnyasi's persona fading, that of Dr. Kotiwala replacing it. The change was reflected in the voice, which resumed its old "Bombay Welsh" rhythm on the next words.

"My Latin is negligible, for I only learned what was essential for medicine, but I take it that would be from *vita*, a life, and *nullus* . . . You mean: like this one here?" He gestured for the teenage mother beside him to advance a pace, and rested his hand lightly on her baby's back.

Chance looked the infant over and at length shrugged. "If you say so," he muttered. "She's only about two months old, isn't she? So without tests . . ."

His voice trailed briefly away.

"Yes, without tests!" he burst out abruptly. "That's the point! Do you know what became of the boy you said had something wrong with him, the very last one you delivered before you— you *retired?*" There was monstrous fierceness in his voice, but it was not directed at the old man he was talking to. It was simply an outward sign that he had been driven to the limit of his resources.

"I have seen many others since," Kotiwala answered. It was definitely not the sunnyasi speaking now, but the trained doctor with a lifetime's experience behind him. "I can therefore imagine. But tell me anyhow."

Chance gave him a look that reflected something close to awe. The inquisitive villagers gathered nearby recognized the expression, and deduced—though not even the best-educated among them could follow the rapid English words—that the stranger from the sky was affected by the aura of their holy man. They relaxed perceptibly.

"Well . . . Well, your friend the matron kept insisting that if you'd said there was something wrong with him there *must* be something wrong, although I'd said he was okay, Dr. Banerji had said he was okay. She went on and on about it until it was interfering with my work and delaying my departure. So I said to hell with it and had him taken to WHO in Delhi for the most complete battery of tests they could lay on. Can you guess what they found?"

Kotiwala rubbed his forehead wearily. "Total suppression of the alpha and theta rhythms?" he suggested.

"You did know!" The accusation in Chance's voice was enough to shatter the barrier of language and communicate to the listening villagers, some of whom stepped menacingly closer to the sunnyasi as though to defend him if they had to.

Kotiwala bestowed on them a reassuring smile. He said to Chance, "No, I didn't know. It just now came to me what you would find."

"Then how in heaven's name did you—?"

"How did I guess the boy wasn't normal? I can't explain that to you, Dr. Chance. It would take sixty years of work in maternity hospitals, watching scores of babies being born every day, to make you see what I saw."

Chance bit back a hot retort and let his shoulders droop. "I'll have to accept that. But the fact remains: you did realize, within minutes of the kid being born, even though he looked healthy and none of our tests has ever revealed any organic deformity, that his brain was—was empty and there was no *mind* in it! Christ, the job I had convincing them at WHO that you'd really done it, and the weeks of argument before they'd let me come back to India and try to track you down!"

"Your tests," Kotiwala said, as though the last sentence had not been spoken. "Many of them?"

Chance threw his hands in the air. "Doctor, where the hell have you been these past two years?"

"Walking barefoot from small village to small village," Kotiwala said, deliberately taking the question in literal form. "I haven't followed news from the world outside. This is the world for these people." He indicated the rough street, the mean shacks, the ploughed and planted fields, the blue mountains closing all of it in.

Chance took a deep breath. "So you don't know and don't really care. Let me fill you in. Only a matter of weeks after I first saw you, the news broke which led to my recall from India: reports of a sudden appalling rise in congenital imbecility. Normally a child begins to react in at least a sketch for a human pattern while it's still very young. Precocious kids smile quickly, and any kid is likely to distinguish movement and color, and reach out to grasp things, and—But I don't have to tell you!"

"Except these you have named Vitanuls?"

"Exactly!" Chance clenched his fists as though trying to seize something out of the air. "No life! None of the normal reactions! Absence of normal cerebral waves when you test them on the EEG, as though everything that makes a person human has been —has been left out!"

He levelled a challenging arm at Kotiwala's chest. "And you recognized the very first one of all! Tell me how!"

"Patience." Bowed by the weight of all his years, Kotiwala still held himself with immense dignity. "This increase in imbeciles—it struck you directly after I retired from the hospital?"

"No, of course not."

"Why 'of course'?"

"We were too tied up with . . . Oh, you've been out of touch, haven't you?" Chance spoke with bitter sarcasm. "A minor triumph of medicine was making all the headlines, and giving WHO enough headaches to be going on with. The anti-senility treatment had been made public a few days after I saw you, and everybody and his uncle was standing on line yelling for it."

"I see," Kotiwala said, and his aged shoulders finally hunched into a posture of despair.

"You see? What's that supposed to mean?"

"Forgive my interrupting. Continue, please."

Chance shivered, apparently as much at what he was remembering, as at the bite of the air. "We'd done our best, and postponed announcement of the treatment until enough was stockpiled to treat several million applicants, but of course that was as bad as breaking the news at the lab stage, because everybody's best friend seemed to have died last Friday and here were people screaming that we'd killed them by neglect, and—Hell, you get the picture. Whichever way we handled it, it came out wrong.

"And then shovelled on top of that mess came the new one. Congenital imbecility hits ten percent of births, twenty, thirty! What's going on? Everyone spins in little circles because just as we were congratulating ourselves on sorting out the row about the anti-senility treatment, here comes the most fantastic crisis in history and it's not going to break, it's going to get worse, and *worse* . . . Over the past two weeks the rate has topped eighty percent. Do you understand that, or are you so sunk in your superstitions it doesn't bother you any longer? Out of every ten children born last week, no matter in what country or continent, eight are *mindless animals!*"

"And you think the one we examined together was the very first?" Kotiwala disregarded the harshness of the younger man's words; his eyes were staring, unfocused, into the blue distance over the mountains.

"As far as we can work it out." Chance spread his hands. "At any rate, when we checked back we found the first kids of which this had been reported had been born on that particular day, and I happened to remember that the time of birth of the earliest we'd heard about was an hour or so before I met you."

"What happened on that day?"

"Nothing that could account for it. Every resource of the UN has been put to work; we've sifted the world's records to the very bottom, and not for that day only but for the time nine months earlier when the kids must have been conceived—only that doesn't fit either, because some of them were preemies as much as six weeks early, and they're the same, hollow, drained... If we weren't at the end of our tether, I'd never have done such a crazy thing as coming to look for you. Because after all I guess there isn't anything you can do to help, is there?"

The fire of rage which had burned in Chance when he arrived had turned to ashes now, and he seemed to have no more words. Kotiwala stood thinking for a minute or more, and the villagers, growing restless, chattered among themselves.

At last the ex-doctor said, "The anti-senility drug—it's a success?"

"Oh, yes. Thank God. If we didn't have some consolation in the midst of this mess I think we'd all go crazy. We've cut the death rate fantastically—I told you we had enough for millions of people in store before we published the news, and because we planned well we can hope to feed the surplus mouths, and..." He broke off. Kotiwala was staring at him strangely.

"Then," the old man declared, "I think I can tell you what happened on the day we met."

Dazed, Chance took half a pace forward. "Out with it, then! You're my last hope—you're *our* last hope."

"I can't offer hope, my friend." A sound like the echo of

doom's own knell colored the words. "But I can make what they call an educated guess. Did I not read once a calculation which showed that as many people are alive in this twenty-first century as have ever lived since the evolution of human beings?"

"Why, yes. I saw that myself, a long time back."

"Then I say that what happened on the day we met was this: the number of all the human beings there have ever been was exceeded for the very first time."

Chance shook his head in bewilderment. "I don't see! Or—or do I?"

"And it so turns out," Kotiwala continued, "that at the same time or very shortly afterward, you find, and make available the world over, a drug which cures old age. Dr. Chance, you will not accept this, because I remember you made a kind of joke about an earthworm, but I do. I say that you have made me understand what I saw when I looked into the eyes of that new-born child, what I see again when I look at this little girl here." He touched the arm of the young mother at his side, and she gave him a shy quick smile.

"Not the lack of a mind, as you have been saying. But the lack of a soul."

For a few seconds Chance imagined that he heard the hollow laughter of demons in the whisper of the winter wind. With a violent effort he rid himself of the delusion.

"No, that's absurd. You can't mean to maintain that we've run short of human souls, as though they were stored up in some cosmic warehouse and issued off the shelf every time a child is born! Oh, come now, Doctor—you're an educated man, and this is the rankest kind of superstitious rubbish!"

"As you say," Kotiwala agreed politely. "That is something I won't venture to dispute with you. But I owe you my thanks, anyhow. You've shown me what I must do."

"That's great," Chance said. "Just great. Here I come half across the world hoping that you'll tell me what to do, and instead . . . What? What must you do?" A final flicker of hope leapt up in his face.

"I must die," said the sunnyasi, and took his staff and his bowl, and without another word to anyone, even the young mother whom he had been comforting when Chance arrived, he set off with slow old-man's paces along the road that led to the tall blue mountains and the eternal ice, by whose aid it was lawful for him to set free his soul.

Winner of the Hugo Award and international acclaim...

JOHN BRUNNER